Double Dog Dare

The Dogfather · Book Seven

roxanne st. claire

Double Dog Dare
THE DOGFATHER BOOK SEVEN

978-0-9993621-3-6– ebook
978-0-9993621-4-3 – print

COVER ART: Keri Knutson (designer)
and Dawn C. Whitty (photographer)
INTERIOR FORMATTING: Author EMS

Critical Reviews of
Roxanne St. Claire Novels

"St. Claire, as always, brings a scorching tear-up-the-sheets romance combined with a great story: dealing with real issues starring memorable characters in vivid scenes."

— *Romantic Times Magazine*

"Non-stop action, sweet and sexy romance, lively characters, and a celebration of family and forgiveness."

— *Publishers Weekly*

"Plenty of heat, humor, and heart!"

— *USA Today's Happy Ever After blog*

"It's safe to say I will try any novel with St. Claire's name on it."

— *www.smartbitchestrashybooks.com*

"The writing was perfectly on point as always and the pace of the story was flawless. But be forewarned that you will laugh, cry, and sigh with happiness. I sure did."

— *www.harlequinjunkies.com*

"The Barefoot Bay series is an all-around knockout, soul-satisfying read. Roxanne St. Claire writes with warmth and heart and the community she's built at Barefoot Bay is one I want to visit again and again."

— *Mariah Stewart, New York Times bestselling author*

"This book stayed with me long after I put it down."

— *All About Romance*

Dear Reader:

Welcome back to the foothills of North Carolina, where the Dogfather, Daniel Kilcannon, is once again pulling some strings to help his six grown children find forever love. On these pages, you'll discover my favorite things in life and fiction: big families, great dogs, and lasting love. As always, a portion of the sales of this and all the books in the series is donated to Alaqua Animal Refuge (www.alaqua.org) in my home state of Florida. That's where these covers were shot by photographer Dawn Whitty (www.dawncwhitty.com) using *rescue* dogs from the shelter. (That's Jimmie and Darla on the cover of Double Dog Dare, both now in happy homes.) So you don't only buy a terrific book…you support a fantastic cause!

Special thanks to reader and veterinarian Linda Hankins, who helped with this book, as well as the many readers on the Dogfather Facebook group who shared dozens of stories about blind dogs they have known and loved. Of course, I owe so much to my content editor, Kristi Yanta, who has loved Darcy from day one; copy editor Joyce Lamb, who should be an honorary member of the Kilcannon family by now; plus proofreaders Marlene Engel and Chris Kridler; cover designer Keri Knutson; and the formatting geniuses at EMS. All professionals without equal on my publishing team!

Don't miss a single book in The Dogfather Series!

Available now
Sit…Stay…Beg (Book 1)
New Leash on Life (Book 2)
Leader of the Pack (Book 3)
Santa Paws is Coming to Town (Book 4 – a Holiday novella)
Bad to the Bone (Book 5)
Ruff Around the Edges (Book 6)
Double Dog Dare (Book 7)

Coming soon
Bark! The Herald Angels Sing – (Book 8 – a Holiday novella)
Old Dog New Tricks (Book 9)

Find information and buy links for all these books here:
http://www.roxannestclaire.com/dogfather-series

And yes, there will be more. For a complete list, buy links, and reading order of *all* my books, visit www.roxannestclaire.com. Be sure to sign up for my newsletter on my website to find out when the next book is released! And join the private Dogfather Facebook group for inside info on all the books and characters, sneak peeks, and a place to share the love of tails and tales!

www.facebook.com/groups/roxannestclairereaders/

xoxo
Rocki

Dedication

For Tommy and Odie, my newest neighbors and furry friends. And one massive shout-out and loving hug to their owner, Sandi Fitch Hutton, a reader who reached out to me years ago and is now my bestie down the street. This book is a testament to her patience, humor, and brainstorming skills!

Chapter One

There were no rules about getting engaged. Because, if there were, Josh Ranier would follow them and feel a lot more comfortable than he did this morning. But he was winging this, hoping it all went according to a loosely thought-out plan. Which was another thing that made Josh uncomfortable. Plans should be set in stone, and rules should be followed.

But there were no rules for love, right? The only thing he knew was that he wanted to spend the rest of his life with Savannah Mayfield and would probably get down on one knee sometime today, because he did know *that* was a rule of engagement.

Sliding his truck into a parking spot at Savannah's apartment complex, he turned off the ignition and reached into the glove compartment to grab the small velvet box he'd been carting around for a few days. Flipping it open, he angled the box so that the single, sparkling diamond caught the early morning sun and winked at him.

Yes, it was small and she might have been hoping for something a little more…grand. But Josh was a

Ranier, not a Bucking. He was building his own business, not living off his stepfather's fortune. And Savannah, a businesswoman in her own right, had supported his decision to break ties with the Bucking Properties empire and strike out on his own.

He closed the box with a noisy snap, knowing what the ring cost and, more important, what it meant. She wouldn't be disappointed, would she?

He stuffed away the nagging thought and cleared his throat to practice one more time.

"Savannah, for one amazing year, you've been the light of my life. Would you do me the honor of becoming Mrs. Joshua Ranier?"

Too cliché. Plus, she'd probably want to keep her own last name since she'd established herself as one of the top stylists and personal shoppers for the wealthiest women all over Lake Norman and as far south as Charlotte.

So, he had to do better than that.

"Savannah, would you make me the happiest man on earth and marry me?"

Too cheesy. Did he really have to say anything while down on one knee and holding a diamond? *Keep it simple, stupid.*

"I love you, Sav."

A smile pulled because he could already hear her response. *I hate when you call me Sav. It sounds like something you put on a wound.*

But in so many ways, that's what Savannah was for him. She seemed to fit into the Bucking family in a way he never did, but had a humble enough upbringing that she wasn't "entitled" like they were. She worked *with* them, as his mother's stylist, not *for* them, and seemed comfortable around the überwealthy. Not Josh, though. He'd been dragged kicking and screaming into the Lifestyles of the Crazy Rich when his widowed mother married a multimillionaire twenty years ago.

From that day on, Josh had been saddled with a stepfather who could never replace Josh's real father—quite possibly one of the greatest men who'd ever lived—and two stepsiblings who were not his favorite people. Especially one, a stepbrother who would never be anything but a pompous, insecure jerk whose life motto seemed to be Make Josh Miserable.

Josh had survived life in the Bucking family by keeping his nose clean, following the rules, and planning his escape. He spent his twenties learning the property building and management business from the ground up, unlike his stepbrother, who wouldn't dirty his hands by picking up a hammer.

Gideon would be handed the Bucking Properties reins anyway, and Josh had made the extremely unpopular decision to leave the company and start his own property renovation business. Could he have made that decision without Savannah? Probably, but she made the transition easier.

He loved her for that and knew that it was time to make this relationship official.

Today. This morning. At sunrise on her thirtieth birthday.

He'd actually wanted to do this at midnight last night because he didn't want Savannah to spend one minute of her thirties without her whole heart and soul committed to him. But she'd had to work some big philanthropic ball with three clients demanding her time all evening and into the wee hours. You'd think once the women were dressed, made-up, and bejeweled, the stylist who did all the work would be able to leave. But no, she actually had to go to the event and be on call until three in the morning in case of a wardrobe or jewelry emergency.

He was so over these people. So anxious to escape this upscale, high-end Lake Norman life that she lived and get to a small town where he could step out of the Bucking shadow. His own home on the Catawba River about a half hour from here was still too close to the family and business for his taste.

He climbed out of the truck and peered at the apartment complex, not surprised to see the drapes still drawn in her unit. Could he propose to her in bed?

The thought made him smile. That might be against the rules, but it sure would be fitting considering how much time they spent there. Not that he was complaining, only lucky as hell. Didn't every couple spend most of their time together horizontal? That was normal and healthy, and he hoped it never changed.

Crossing the parking lot, he used the resident's code to get into the building, then nodded when he saw the familiar and friendly face of the doorman behind the desk. But Terry did a double take at the sight of him.

"Mornin', T-man," Josh said with a huge grin. "Beautiful day, isn't it?"

The older man's ruddy complexion deepened. "It is, Mr. Ranier. Going to see Miss Mayfield?"

He put his finger over his lips. "Shhh. Don't call me up. I'm surprising her."

Terry frowned. "I don't know, Mr. Ranier. That's against our policy."

Josh angled his head in acknowledgment. "I understand that, Terry. But today..." He took a deep breath. "I'm breaking some rules." He pulled the box out of his pocket, held it up with one hand, and hit the elevator button with the other. "And I'm getting engaged."

"But, Mr. Ranier—"

Terry's warnings were drowned out by the swish of the doors closing. Slipping the ring box back into his pocket and pressing the button for the fourth floor, Josh caught his reflection in the mirrored wall.

He stabbed his fingers into thick brown hair, pulling it back to see some worry lines etched between his brows and lines in the creases of his eyes from hours in the sun working construction. He looked every one of his thirty-two years, a man ready to settle down with the perfect woman and start a life and a family of his own. Not Buckings, but Raniers.

That's what he wanted. That was all he'd ever wanted—a family of his own. A son or daughter he could take fishing like his father had taken him. A wife he could count on in good times and bad. A family who had each other's back, and not so they could aim the knife into it.

Stepping out of the elevator, he went to one of the two doors on the floor, took another steadying breath, and tried to decide if he should knock, ring, or use his key. Savannah was a hard sleeper, and she probably had the chain lock on anyway. Either way, Stella would bark noisily any second.

He put his finger on the electronic bell, but the

5

door yanked open before he pressed, halting when the three-inch security chain pulled taut. So, Terry had warned her. Okay, that made him a good security guard.

Through the crack, he could see Savannah's brown eyes were smudged by makeup, which was weird because she religiously washed her face before bed. Her hair was wild, too, and the remnants of red lipstick stained the skin around her mouth. Or was that a rash?

Instantly, Stella, the dog he'd given Savannah on their six-month anniversary, trotted to the door and wormed her way closer, but only barked once at Josh instead of her usual fifty bark greeting. Then she backed into the hall and pressed against the wall, which was also weird.

As weird as the look on Savannah's face as she dragged her hand through her hair. "You said morning, not dawn."

"Rough night with the mannequins?" He used her nickname for her clients, hoping for a smile.

But he didn't get one. Instead, she gave her head a gentle shake as if any more than that would really hurt.

"Are you hungover?" After a night of work? Because that would be odd.

"Mmmm." It seemed like that was all she could manage.

Okay, sometimes she had a few cocktails after her clients released her from duties. He added the slightest amount of pressure to the door. "How 'bout I get a cold cloth and some Advil?" He dipped a little closer, getting a whiff of a familiar, feminine scent. "And a gentle morning massage?"

But she pressed back, still not opening the door to let him in. "You have to come back later, and I'll..." She glanced in the general vicinity of her bedroom. "I need to sleep it off."

He inched into the space, trying to reach his hand in to graze her chin. "I can sleep it off with you."

"No." Her eyes flickered in something that looked like fear, making him instantly withdraw his hand. "No, you can't. You...*no*."

"You okay?" Because he didn't understand this response at all. "Are you sick? Clients give you a hard time last night?" Sometimes these rich prima donnas could be brutal to staff, even someone as vital to their egos as the stylist.

She brushed some dark hair off her face, giving him a chance to see her complexion was a little blotchy, and her chin was chafed, and there was a...

He stared at the slight purplish mark on her neck, and something began to burn in his gut. Low, hot, ugly. The burn of...betrayal.

"It was a crazy night."

No shit. He dug for composure, sanity, and whatever it took not to push that door open and demand to know just how *crazy* the night had been.

"Then we better talk," he ground out.

She shook her head. "I can't. I'm...not alone."

The words slammed, like someone took a solid-steel I-beam and shoved it right through his chest. "You're...what?"

Did she say *not alone*? He inched back and dropped his gaze lower. She wore nothing but a baggy, faded T-shirt that skimmed her bare thighs.

She was naked under that shirt. Naked and *not alone*.

"Savannah." Her name came out as a strangled choke of dismay.

She swallowed, hard and loud. "You better go, Josh."

"Are you freaking kidding me?" He managed not to raise his voice, but jammed the words through clenched teeth, his anger coming off in waves strong enough to make poor little Stella, who was still backed up against the wall, take a step forward, turn in a circle, and whimper.

"Josh, you really need to go."

"You *cheated* on me?" His voice cracked. Or maybe that was his heart shattering like she'd thrown a brick through glass.

She didn't answer, but looked down to the ground, so all he could see of her eyes were the backs of her lids and the eyeliner that she used to camouflage false eyelashes, which she only wore when she wanted to look flat-out gorgeous.

The lashes were gone. The hickey was visible. And that redness around her lips?

Was that a…*beard burn*?

With each realization, he stepped back, reeling like he'd been shot. Not that a bullet could hurt any more than this. "How could you?"

"I just…" She breathed out, working for calm, which was actually pretty funny when he thought about it. *She* needed to be calm? "I'm going to tell you everything. Let me…" She glanced behind herself again.

"Get rid of him?" he suggested.

"Deal with it."

Deal with it? What the ever-lovin' hell did that even mean? "How about you deal with *me*?"

Closing her eyes, she shook her head again. "You need to leave now. I'm sorry, but—"

Behind her, the bedroom door opened. "Hey, Sav. Where'd you go?"

The man's voice bellowed from the hall, loud, insistent, and…familiar.

"Go away," she insisted to Josh, pushing the door closed. "Let me handle this."

Bile rose up in Josh's throat, and it wasn't because the son of a bitch called her *Sav*. It was… "Gideon?"

Any color remaining in her face drained away. Just then, a shadow appeared behind her. Not very big, not very ominous, but still a shadow that Josh had stood in for the better part of twenty years.

"Gideon?" he repeated in utter shock.

From the floor, Stella let out a low, distrustful groan, circled again, and dropped to the floor as if in pain. *I feel you, kid.*

Of all the men in this town, this state, this country or, hell, the world, no one could be a worse betrayal than his arrogant asshole of a stepbrother.

Through the small opening, Josh could see Gid lift his sculpted jaw, showing exactly whose whiskers had chafed Savannah's face. He narrowed green eyes with a condescending look meant to put Josh in his place. And of course, he put his hands on his hips like he was standing there in one of his six-thousand-dollar suits and not his underwear, because Gideon Bucking was cocky in every situation.

Josh might have four inches and thirty pounds of

muscle on this clown, but he had nothing in the attitude department. Gideon was the king of that.

"You should leave, Josh." Gideon's voice sounded far away, like Josh was underwater and drowning.

He sucked in a steadying breath, getting a lungful of that familiar, feminine scent. The smell of sex, emanating from both of them. Fisting his hands, he leaned in. "And you should die, dickhead."

"Josh!" Savannah fought to keep the door from opening all the way to him, a scolding look in her eyes. "There's no reason to act like a caveman about this. I'm a grown woman. I know what I did."

"You *cheated* on me."

She held his gaze and blinked. "It's not what you think."

He actually let out a dry laugh.

"I mean…" She threw a pleading look over her shoulder, then finally opened the door wider. "Tell him, Gid," she demanded.

But Gideon shook his head. "I don't have time for this shit, Sav." He turned and headed down the hall, walking away like the chickenshit slime he was. "Close up shop with him and get back to bed."

Josh felt his nostrils flare.

"Gid, you promised we'd tell him." Her voice rose, but Gideon disappeared around the corner into her bedroom.

"We just did." He slammed the door like a parting shot.

Slowly, she turned back to Josh, gathering up her thick hair and pulling it through her hand in a nervous gesture he recognized as well as any of his own. "I guess I'm sorry isn't going to cut it," she said quietly.

"Why would you do this?" He still couldn't wrap his head around the fact that she'd sleep with anyone else, let alone Gideon. Now. Last night. While he was practicing proposals.

How could he be so blind?

"We've been seeing each other for a few weeks," she said. "I was going to tell you today."

And he was going to *propose*.

"We started talking a lot at the hospital fundraiser your parents hosted last month," she said, leaning against the doorjamb.

He hadn't gone to that party because he stayed late to finish a job, happy to have a good reason not to wear a tux and go to some stupid fundraiser at Bucking*sham* Palace, as he thought of his mother and stepfather's mansion. But he'd encouraged Savannah to go. She loved his family, and they loved her. Literally, it would seem.

"It was so fast, Josh. I didn't even know what happened."

Gideon happened. The man who resented everything about Josh, who'd hated him since the day Malcolm married Mom, and who constantly lorded the Bucking name, money, and status over him, as if Josh gave a flying fig about any of that.

How could Josh not see this coming? Gideon was a reckless, thoughtless, selfish prick who broke rules and used people and took whatever he wanted with no regard for anyone's feelings. What made Josh think that he wouldn't go after a prize like Savannah?

And *get* her.

How was that possible? She loved Josh. Or had said she did. Many times. Many, many times. Yes, it had frequently been said when she was flat on her back and writhing in pleasure, but—

"I guess if I didn't do something drastic, we'd never break up."

He stared at her. "If you wanted to break up, why not tell me?"

"I didn't know I wanted to," she admitted in a thick voice. "But the closer we get to…you know…the more scared I get."

You know. "Marriage." It wasn't a question.

She bit her lip, barely nodding. "I can't see it with you, Josh. And I know that's what you want."

"So you had sex with Gideon?"

"Josh, please." She heaved a sigh. "Things change. People change." She hung her head. "You want to leave your family, and I don't."

"My family?" No, they weren't his family, damn it. They were a *step*family. And she wanted them more than she wanted him. With Gideon, she got that—with no pesky "step" in the way. "What do you mean?"

"I mean I like them. I love Brea like she's my own sister. And your mom and dad—"

"He's *not* my dad."

Her eyes shuttered as if she'd known that was coming because she'd heard him say it a thousand times. "He's not a bad guy. He loves your mom. And you won't give them a chance…" She glanced over her shoulder. "But Gideon is—"

"You're picking him—*them*—over me." That's what she was doing, without a doubt.

"You're the one who always says you marry a family, not a person."

"Because of what my mother did to me, Savannah. And whoever talked about marriage?" Even as he uttered the words, the weight of the ring in his pocket dragged him down. And the look on her face told him this proposal wasn't going to be a surprise. Had she expected it today? This morning? Did she plan...*this*?

"Josh, what we have is...*physical*. You know that."

Apparently, he'd foolishly mixed up *physical* and *real*.

"It can't last once that wears off," she added. "I mean, it's good. It's great, but you have so much hate in you."

"Hate?"

"You hate the Buckings."

He gave a dry laugh. "I think it's the other way around, Savannah. And if you need proof of that, go take a look at who is in your bed."

"I know how you feel about Gid," she said. "But he's..."

"Priggish? Condescending? Self-centered? Or a *Bucking by blood*?"

She flinched, almost imperceptibly, but he saw it. He knew which of Gideon's list of spectacular qualifications were important to her. She said money didn't matter, but he knew Savannah had grown up dirt-poor. He knew that money meant freedom and security to her. He knew his stepsister was her closest friend, and Savannah belonged in that damn mansion more than he ever would.

"Look, Josh, I want to stay friends so that we can see each other at family events and have things be comfortable if I'm with Gid."

With Gid? What the holy hell did that even mean?

What did it even matter? Everything was gone. The hope of a life with her, the dreams of a future, the possibility of a family. She didn't want that, not with him.

She wanted Gideon. Fine. They deserved each other. "Don't worry about family events, Savannah. I'm leaving for Bitter Bark today. I'm done with this town, this family, their business, and you."

She looked relieved. "Josh, you know I'd never be happy there. It's a cute town, and that building you bought has potential, but I'd never get enough clients in a sleepy little place like that. There's no real money there, just a lot of dogs and farms and people who never dress up."

"Exactly." It sounded like heaven to him.

As if the mention of dogs lured her closer, Stella moved slowly around Savannah's legs, and Josh noticed she was trembling a bit. Without thinking, he bent down to comfort the little dog.

"Hey, kid." He ruffled the crested rooster tail on her head, suddenly realizing how much he'd miss this spunky little creature.

But Stella didn't look so spunky right then. She actually looked scared, her eyes darting from side to side, but not even looking at Josh like she was too ashamed of her owner's behavior to make eye contact.

"Josh, I'm sorry." Savannah's apology sounded genuine, he'd give her that. "I wish this didn't happen this way."

"I wish it didn't happen at all." None of it. Not one minute with Savannah was worth this.

Silent, he coaxed Stella closer, giving her head a scratch. She nuzzled his hand and finally looked up at him. Actually, past him, like she saw a ghost in the hall behind him. In fact, she stared so intently, he turned to look over his shoulder, wondering if Terry had followed him up there.

He hadn't, so maybe that was Stella's way of telling him it was time to go. With a sigh, he scooped her up and stood, holding her close to rub his thumb under her chin, making her head roll back because she liked that so much. "Gonna miss you, kid."

"She'll miss you, too." Savannah reached for her. "She's been acting weird."

"Seems to be going around," he muttered, tightening his grip when he felt her belly quiver like it did when thunder rolled in the distance. Stella always knew when a storm was brewing.

He didn't relinquish the dog, but held her tighter, memorizing the feel of her. He hadn't had a dog since Roscoe, when he was a little boy. His father had found that old black mutt at a rest stop where he'd parked his rig once, but Roscoe died not long after Pops did. Suddenly, an ancient pain welled up and threatened to strangle him.

Silently, he gave Stella a kiss on her head and handed her to Savannah. "Happy birthday, Sav. Hope all your dreams come true." With that, he turned and went back to the elevator, grateful that the doors swished open right away when he touched the button. As they closed, he heard Stella bark one more time.

Stepping into the lobby, Josh met the gaze of Terry the doorman, who looked a little worried, confused, and sympathetic.

"You doin' okay, Mr. Ranier?" he asked.

He reached into his pocket and pulled out the box,

wanting nothing in the whole world as much as a way to get rid of it. "I'll survive." He flipped the box to the man, who caught it with one hand. "Give that to someone you love," he said. "Or hawk it and buy yourself something nice."

The other man's jaw dropped. "You might change your mind, Mr. Ranier," he said. "You might find someone else." He didn't have to add *someone faithful*, but Josh could see the unspoken words in the man's eyes.

"I will not change my mind," Josh assured him. "I will not find someone else." He took a few steps closer to make his point. "You be my witness, Terry. I will never fall in love, trust a woman, or spend more than one night with anyone. You got that?"

Terry lifted the box. "I can hold on to it for you in case you change your mind."

"Don't. I won't change my mind. Sell it. Swear to me you'll sell it."

Terry scowled at him. "I can't—"

"You can and you will. Don't sit on that thing, and don't wait for me to come back for it, because that's not happening. You'll get decent money. Take your wife on a nice trip. Nothing could make me happier." He started to turn, but stopped. "But make me one promise."

"Anything."

"Don't ever cheat on her, lie to her, or break her heart."

"I never have and I never will," Terry assured him, extending his hand for a shake. "I give you my word."

Josh took it and shook. "And I give you mine. Never again. Never, ever again."

Terry's eyes glinted. "You might change your mind."

But Josh knew that would never happen. With a nod goodbye, he headed to his truck, and by the time he got there, he was pretty sure his heart was safely in deep freeze, where it would stay until the day it stopped beating.

Chapter Two

When Gramma Finnie came out of the kitchen with a birthday cake ablaze with thirty candles, Darcy Kilcannon knew her moment had arrived. At least, it would, once the singing, cheering, and cake eating was over and she could get her father alone.

All around, the massive family she loved more than life itself hooted and hollered, teased and clapped and, oh yeah, sang. Loud. Bad. Like a bunch of tipsy Irishmen and women, which was exactly what most of them were, unless you counted the spouses, who were Irish by association, or children, who were too young to drink.

"Look at that cake, Gramma," Darcy cooed, touched that her grandmother had worked so hard on this one. The frosting and candles were pink, of course, which made perfect sense for a girl who chose that color over all others. Except…there were thirty candles, so she wasn't a *girl*. And maybe this was the year a nice, refined *blue* could be the new pink.

The final off-key note faded away. The candles flickered and threatened to drip wax on the flowers.

More than a dozen Kilcannons and five Mahoneys stared at Darcy, most of them egging her on to make a wish.

Like she was five.

Of course, she couldn't let her siblings and cousins down by actually *growing up.* Not their little sister, the youngest of six, the perennial baby of the clan. She sighed and pulled back her long hair as she leaned over the cake, looking up to catch her father dabbing at a tear he was certain no one had noticed.

Because he missed Mom? Or because the last thing he wanted was Darcy to be thirty years old? But she was. And it was time to make her declaration of independence. Today. Sometime in the next half hour, in fact.

Very slowly, she straightened, still holding Dad's gaze. "Christian?" she asked, reaching out a hand to her young nephew. "Would you do the honors of blowing the candles out for me?"

"But it's your birthday, Aunt Darcy."

"I'll make the wish, you make the air."

His gap-toothed grin widened, and he scurried closer. "Okay!" He sucked in a noisy breath and held it. Darcy looked across the table at her father, who returned her gaze with nothing but love in crystal-blue eyes that were so much like her own. They shared more than that gene, too. They both loved this family unconditionally and unabashedly and would set themselves on fire so the rest of the clan could stay warm.

Darcy had been burning for four years, and it was time to step away.

Please understand, Dad. Please.

Christian sent a wind gust over the candles, missing only two, which her cousin Declan snuffed with his bare fingers. Christian looked up at him, in awe of the trick.

"Only firefighters can do that," Declan said quickly. "And you need to be a captain, like me."

"Cake for everyone!" Christian announced when the clapping ended.

There was always cake for everyone, most often during this weekly Sunday dinner gathering at Waterford Farm. With six Kilcannon kids, all but one now attached to a significant other, plus three in the next generation, and four Mahoney cousins, then throw in Dad, Gramma, and Aunt Colleen, and there were a lot of birthday celebrations, sometimes two in one week.

Mom had made sure there was cake for every single one of those occasions, and that tradition blessedly hadn't died with her. But Darcy had been both dreading and anticipating this one, and not because the cake was for her.

She was telling Dad her plans today, and the only person at the table who knew that was her cousin Ella, who sat directly across from her, silently communicating full sentences because Ella and Darcy had a secret look language that they'd perfected since they were toddlers.

Today, Ella's raised brow and knowing gaze said: *You have to do this, Darce.*

She replied with a nod so imperceptible, no one at the table would ever have seen it.

As the chatter, volley of jokes, and almost constant sound of laughter rose and fell, Darcy grew quiet, waiting for her chance to corner Dad for a private conversation. This wasn't an announcement she wanted to make in front of the whole family...not until she had the blessing of their patriarch. Once she had that, everyone else would rally behind her.

"Did you hear Cilla Forsythe is retiring?" Dad asked.

Darcy froze in the act of stabbing the yellow cake with her fork, not even trusting herself to glance at Ella. Of course, *they* knew the travel agent who had the storefront next to Ella's was retiring. And they knew what was to become of that space. But no one else did...yet.

"She is?" The question came in unison from at least five people around the table.

Dad rose and studied Fiona in her infant carrier a few feet away on the floor where Jag sat like the baby's personal German shepherd bodyguard. "Did she cry? I thought I heard her cry. I better get her."

Every person around the table chuckled at Daniel Kilcannon's unabashed obsession with his new granddaughter, but Darcy knew her baby niece might have created the opportunity she needed.

"Fiona's fine, Dad," Liam said, shooting a knowing smile at Andi, his wife.

"Wait, wait. Back to Cilla." Molly, Darcy's older sister, seemed particularly flabbergasted by this news, shaking her head full of auburn waves. "Where is she going?"

"Not sure what her plans are," Dad said, in between tiny clucking sounds at the baby. "She said she's getting out of the travel business because everyone thinks they can find their own deals on the Internet now."

"But is she leaving Bitter Bark?" Molly persisted.

She wasn't, Darcy knew. But she was leaving nine hundred square feet of prime retail space in the middle of town and someone else was taking over.

"Didn't ask." Dad bent over Fiona. "Oh, she *is* awake. Hello, precious. Of course Grandpa will hold you." Without asking for permission, he reached down to cradle the infant and lift her, making half of them laugh and the other half roll their eyes. But Darcy prayed that he took the baby somewhere quiet and alone.

"Any excuse." Andi shook her head, smiling.

"Donchya worry, lass," Gramma Finnie assured her. "You canna spoil a wee one. Not one barely two months old."

"If Cilla Forsythe leaves town..." Molly said, looking at her brothers in dismay.

"Then you lose big-time," Shane, the second oldest in the family, whispered to her.

"Shut up, Shane." Garrett jabbed his brother in the ribs, throwing a look at Dad, who positioned the tiny baby in his arms and walked toward the center hall, murmuring words of affection to the little bundle.

The second he was out of earshot, Liam, the oldest and usually quietest, leaned forward, making them all pause to listen for whatever pearl of wisdom he'd impart. "If Dad finds out that we're actually placing bets on who he'll date, we're all dead."

Only some of them laughed.

"He won't," Molly mouthed back, turning to Shane. "Anyway, Cilla was a better bet than Marie Boswell. Good heavens, Shane. She's *older* than Dad."

"But she loves dogs more than life," he shot back. "He needs that."

"I'm still pulling for Linda May," Andi joined in. "My office is right above her bakery, and I'm telling you, I'd see him in there four times a week before I went on maternity leave. And I happen to know she'd be happy to give him her croissant recipe *anytime*."

That got a few laughs, and groans.

"My money's on Bella Peterson," Garrett said. "Who better to lure the Dogfather than a cat lady?"

At her end of the table, Gramma Finnie huffed out a noisy breath and adjusted her bifocals to scan the table with wise blue eyes. "If any of you lassies or lads think there's another woman in my son's future other than the wee one in his arms, you'll be sorely mistaken." Her Irish brogue thickened as she dipped her head to continue. "'Death leaves a heartache no one can heal, and love leaves a memory no one can steal.'"

"You're so right, Gramma Finnie." Pru, Molly's teenage daughter, and Gramma's closest companion, nodded heartily. "It's only been four years since Grannie Annie passed, and you all need to stop trying to fix him up."

"Anyway, he's not done with us," Shane said, pointing at Darcy. "Tick tock, li'l sis."

The clock was ticking all right, but not for *that*. "Sometimes it's like no one in this family thinks about anything but *love*. There are other ways to find happiness, you know."

"Name one," Garrett cracked, making the many newlyweds or nearlyweds lift their glasses in a toast of solidarity and agreement.

Darcy rolled her eyes so hard it was a wonder she didn't injure herself. "A person can be entirely happy on their own, you guys. A woman isn't incomplete without a man. A human isn't unfinished without a partner. Not every creature mates for life, I'll have you know."

Every person at the table stilled as she ended her little speech, making for a long, awkward beat. Probably because at least ten of them wildly disagreed with her, and anything that even had a whiff of an argument was forbidden at Sunday dinners.

Darcy felt some heat on her cheeks, so she picked up the dregs of a Bloody Mary she'd been nursing all day and knocked it back, then set it on the table. "Now, if you'll excuse the birthday girl, I have some business to discuss with Dad."

"Business?" At least two of her brothers choked softly on the word.

And that, right there, was the problem. The "business" of running the largest canine rescue and training facility was their job, and Molly's, as the head vet. Darcy was "just the groomer," and that, among other things, was about to change.

"You'll be ready when your time comes, lass," Gramma mused, watching her closely and probably thinking Darcy's thoughts were all about love. She couldn't be more wrong. The last thing a woman champing at the bit for financial, emotional, and psychological freedom wanted was a man who'd take it all away.

"What I'm ready for is a life of, for, and on my own," she said carefully. "And if you'll excuse me, I'm going to talk to Dad to get that started."

"You go, girl," Ella said with a raised glass.

Around the table, they all looked like they knew exactly what was going on with Darcy—that their flighty little sister was about to take off for parts unknown again. They couldn't be more wrong.

Darcy snapped her fingers twice, and a flash of white fuzz shot out from under the table. "Look sharp, Kookie." Darcy reached down to straighten her baby girl's bow. "We are on a mission."

"A mission for what?" Shane asked.

"To do what everyone does on a birthday," she said. "Grow up."

Without waiting one more second, Darcy headed toward the formal living room, a space rarely used by the big family except at Christmas, when it became Holiday Central. But lately, it had become one of Dad's favorite places to have quiet time with the new baby.

Tapping on the doorjamb of the arched entry, she asked, "Can I talk to you, Dad?"

"Come on in, sweetheart. I was telling Fiona about her Grannie Annie." He looked up from the chair next to the fireplace, a sadness in his eyes that made Darcy want to run back into that dining room and tell all her siblings to lay off the dating game and get out of Dad's business. The man was still in mourning, no matter how wonderfully he held it together.

She leaned over the baby in his arms, reaching down to stroke Fiona's tiny, dark-tufted head. "She looks like Liam with all that dark hair."

"She looks like every one of you," Dad replied. "Even you and Aidan had dark hair at first."

Darcy smiled and perched on the edge of the sofa,

and immediately Kookie flew up and curled into a ball next to her, almost as if she sensed how much her mistress needed a wingman right now.

"Dad, can I talk to you about something serious?"

His raised-brow response was no surprise. Darcy didn't do serious. Her role was the "fun" child who flitted about continents and made everyone laugh.

"Talk to me about anything," Dad said, splitting his attention between the baby in his arms and Darcy as she settled onto the couch. "But if you want me to go out with Bella Peterson, Linda May Dunlap, Marie Boswell, or Cilla Forsythe, don't waste your time."

She drew back. "You know about that?"

He chuckled and addressed his response to the baby, who had fallen back to sleep in his arms. "They think I'm deaf, dumb, and blind to their shenanigans."

Darcy gave a quick laugh. "You should talk, *Dogfather*. You're the king matchmaker around here. You think I don't know why you sent me on that errand to your accountant's office last week?"

"You think I was trying to set you up with Eugene McMasters? He's fifty-five and happily married."

"No, I think you knew full well that Mr. McMaster's somewhat attractive and recent-Yale-graduate son would be in the office."

His innocent look was almost believable. Almost. "Oh, honey, that Jeremy's a nice kid, but you…him…" He shook his head. "Not a chance."

Right. "And that new mechanic who recently opened up in town that you thought was the only guy who could work on my hybrid car?"

"You thought…that guy…" He chuckled. "I guess I do have a well-deserved reputation, but it never occurred to me he could be anything but someone to check that engine light."

"Well, good, because he's not my type."

"Now you know how I feel when they fling Cilla and Marie and Linda May at me."

"Apparently, misery loves company."

His smile faded. "Your brothers and sister are not miserable," he corrected. "I've never seen any of them this happy."

"And they think I'm next."

"You're just a kid."

And that was the heart of this problem. "A kid who turned thirty."

"Yeah. But to me, you're a kid. And the last one, to boot. Why?" He suddenly looked a little horrified. "Are you asking me to find you someone?"

"God, no," she exclaimed. "I can do my own work." She narrowed her eyes to add, "I'm a grown woman."

Dad regarded her with a steady gaze, with maybe a little fear darkening his eyes as he waited for more. "I'm painfully aware of that," he admitted softly.

"And I'd like to start my own business."

He blinked at her. "You would?"

"In fact, I've already applied for a business license at town hall."

"You...have? What about the grooming work you do here?"

She nodded, expecting that pushback. "You know as well as I do that trimming and clipping the dogs on-site isn't a big moneymaker. I can do more, but not here. Not at Waterford when the clients' dogs come before my own."

"This business isn't just about money," he interjected. "You know we started it to honor your mother's legacy and love of fostering dogs and to give everyone in the family a role."

"And mine's grooming, which I love, but I'd like to break out and do it on my own."

He let out a slow exhale that sounded nothing but sad. "You're leaving." It wasn't a question.

"Not Bitter Bark," she answered quickly. "I'm renting Cilla Forsythe's space in town and turning it into a grooming salon. I'm thinking about calling it The Dog Spaw." She added a smile. "Get it? Spa with a w?"

But he didn't smile back. "So, this is a done deal?"

She swallowed. "I signed the lease last week, but I can't open until I do some minor construction in there. But think about it, Dad. That space is next door to Bone Appetit," she said, referring to Ella and Aunt Colleen's recently opened canine treat and supply shop. "Thanks to Chloe turning Bitter Bark into the dog-friendliest town in North Carolina, I'd be successful in no time."

He considered that, and she knew he couldn't argue. "Can you afford the construction?"

Barely. Especially since this was only half her plan. "You might have noticed I haven't taken a trip for over a year. I've been saving."

"Because if you need an investment, we can work something out."

She smiled, expecting that, too. "Thanks. I'm okay for now, but it will be a stretch because…" She took a deep inhale, ready to drop bomb number two. "I also want to move out into my own place."

His gaze barely flickered, but it was enough to see the words hit hard. "Don't tell me you've signed a lease for that, too."

"No," she said on a laugh. "One lease at a time, but I would like to start looking."

His sizable shoulders dropped, and he looked down at the sleeping baby for the first time since they'd started talking "Well. This *is* a big day for you."

She tamped down the urge to do whatever she could to ease his disappointment. That was how she'd ended up living at home for the four years since Mom died.

"I want to live on my own, Dad."

He moved the baby a bit, shifting her with the ease of a man who'd handled, well, six of them. "Of course you do, but…"

"Please." She reached out and put her hand on his arm. "I can't be your baby forever. You have Fiona now, and Christian. It's only a matter of time until the rest of your matchmaking efforts pay off in oodles of grandchildren. I'm ready to move out and move on."

For a long time, he said nothing, but then sighed slowly. "You're ready, but I'm…" He didn't have to finish the sentence. She knew he wasn't ready.

"Dad, I moved back to Waterford Farm after Mom died because I didn't want you and Gramma Finnie to be alone without her. It made sense at the time because Molly and Pru needed their own house, and the boys certainly weren't going to live here. I was twenty-six, and it was fine. But it's not fine anymore."

"You come and go as you please, Darcy. No one is watching you, if it's freedom you need. And with the money you save, you get to do the one thing you love most—travel."

She sighed, seeking the words to make him understand and not hurt him. If it were Mom sitting in that seat, she wouldn't have to search for words. They'd spoken in a secret, silent language exactly like she did today with Ella. She and Annie Kilcannon had been connected in a way that was different than any other kid in the family, which made sense, since Darcy was the youngest.

But Mom had never *babied* her. She'd never treated Darcy like she was incapable of anything, and that sense of independence that Mom had fostered seemed to be melting as fast as those birthday candles. She had to get it back.

"Dad, the reason I love to travel isn't just for the thrill of adventure, you know."

"It's to get away from us?" he guessed.

"No." Not *exactly*. "You know I love this family and this house and Waterford Farm more than anything, anywhere. But when I leave, I can make my own decisions and live my life without all my older siblings who know so much more than I do. I can make my own mistakes without my father and grandmother offering guidance." At his look, she squeezed his hand. "I love that guidance," she assured him. "And I don't want it to stop, ever. I just…" She sighed. "I have to grow up, Dad. I need to be living and working on my own."

He searched her face, taking it all in. "That's what your mother wanted."

She almost fell back on her chair with relief that he did get it. "Yes, it was. We had many talks about it. She wanted me, and Molly, to grow up as strong, independent women."

"You are," he insisted.

"I can be," she corrected.

For a long time, he didn't say a word, but his wheels were spinning, she knew. No doubt it was about the business as much as the living situation.

"I can keep grooming at Waterford two days a week indefinitely," she said, already willing to work seven days a week if she had to. "Molly is in town part of the time at the other vet office, and it would be the same for me. I'll train some groomers so someone is always here, and I'll be on site whenever you need me. But, Dad, I have to be the woman Mom wanted me to be. And I don't think that was living upstairs at thirty or turning down the chance to start my own business."

"Oh, Darcy, you already are the woman she wanted you to be." He leaned forward, forgetting the baby as he focused on her. "Your heart is so good and your joy is so constant. You're the brightest light in this family, and you always will be. When you're not here, it's like someone switched off the power supply in this house."

She melted on a sigh. "Thanks, but I need to supply the power to my own life now."

"I know that...but..." He shook his head, words failing.

"What is it?"

"Once you leave, little Darcy, it's all over," he whispered. "Yes, I have this granddaughter and our great business, but the last Kilcannon leaving the nest is...hard."

She felt her eyes well. "Dad, I'm sorry—"

"No, I'm sorry to be a sentimental old man."

"It's not over," she assured him. "We all work here. There's a Kilcannon kid, spouse, or offspring in this beautiful old house seven days a week and twice on Sundays—literally, for a weekly dinner we'd all die before we missed."

He chuckled at that, and the sound made the baby stir, pulling his attention back to her. He stroked her little cheek, quiet for a long time.

Finally, his gaze slid to the wall covered with family portraits and pictures, settling on the young woman in a 1970s version of the same wedding dress Andi had worn to marry Liam. "I think your mother would love this new life plan of yours and support it."

"Yes, she would. But do you?" She wanted his blessing. That didn't make her a baby—it made her a Kilcannon.

"Yes," he said simply. "And I'll help you any way I can. In fact, if you need a construction guy, I have the perfect—"

"Dad." She glared at him.

"What?"

"I was born thirty years ago, not yesterday," she chided. "Do not set me up with anyone. Ever. The very last thing I want infringing on my independence is a man."

"I wasn't…" He shook his head, giving up the argument. "But as far as living in town? I want you somewhere safe, and you can't tell me that's wrong."

"Bitter Bark is safe, Dad."

"Still…" He repositioned Fiona to safely hand her off. "Hold her for a second. I have an idea."

Darcy took the tiny bundle, making Kookie sit straight up and stare with unabashed jealousy. "Don't worry, Kooks. You're still my baby, but this is my niece."

Fiona's long lashes fluttered, and a whimper escaped her little rosebud mouth. "Oh, sweet thing. I love you," Darcy cooed. After a second of staring at her, she looked up and found her father looking at her the same way she was looking at the baby.

"What?" she asked on a laugh.

"Are you sure you want to live alone, Darcy? Couldn't you and Ella get a place together?"

"Ella's signed a year-long lease on her house, and I need to be alone. How will I ever grow up if I don't stand on my own two feet, personally and professionally?"

"There's a big difference between independence and loneliness."

"I'm not going to be lonely," she said. "I didn't say I wouldn't date a guy, just not one that you picked out for me."

He snorted softly, looking down at the phone he'd pulled out, skimming the screen with his index finger. "Oh, here it is. A beautiful, renovated brownstone in Ambrose Acres."

Darcy's eyes widened at the mention of the tony section south of Bushrod Square. "Ambrose Acres might be out of my price range."

"Maybe not. The owner came in to present to the Gentrification Committee the other day, and he needs to have another tenant within thirty days to qualify for a permit to renovate the next unit. If the right person comes along who can move in immediately, then you can probably negotiate a very reasonable rent."

"A brownstone would be cool," Darcy said,

standing up and rocking the baby a little with excitement at the idea. "And I love all those Victorians in that section, with the courtyards in the back and fabulous curved windows."

"Good man, too. Worked by the rules, which you can't say for every contractor. He'd want a solid referral." He tapped the phone screen, texting.

"Pretty sure you could give me that referral, right?" she asked. "I've been a model tenant in this house."

He looked up from his phone, no humor in his eyes. Just the opposite, in fact. "I've loved every minute you've lived here, sweetheart. From the day we brought you home from the hospital and decided you were the prettiest of them all." His voice grew thick with emotion. "It'll be tough to let you leave."

Holding Fiona carefully, she leaned down to kiss his head. "I'll always be your little girl. But please let me be my own woman."

"I'll do my best." He stood slowly and, without a word, took the baby from her arms. "And I just texted Michelle Monroe, the real estate agent handling the deal."

She inched back, a little wowed by Dad's speed on this one. "You have Michelle Monroe's phone number? Really. 'Cause she's attractive *and* single."

Dad dipped his head and gave her a look. "You know how much you don't want me to set you up with anyone? Multiply that by thirty-six."

"Thirty-six?"

"The number of years I enjoyed with the one and only woman of my dreams," he explained. "She's gone, and there is no room, time, or interest for others."

"Got it," she said. "But there's no room, time, or interest for me, either. So can we both back off?"

"Darcy." He put his right hand in the air. "I swear I haven't set you up."

"Yet," she finished.

He chuckled and nudged her toward the living room. "Come on. Let's go tell the family your news."

Chapter Three

No pets allowed.

"*What?*" Darcy did a double take at the tiny gold-plated sign under the address of what was about to be her new home. Had she seen that when Michelle took her through the apartment? There had been no mention of a pet clause. Was it on the contract?

She let out a little moan of despair, loud enough to make Kookie look up from the tiny patch of grass she was sniffing. Kookie's big brown eyes and sweet face folded Darcy's heart in half, as they had since the day Mom rescued this dog and gave her to Darcy to heal a broken heart.

Darcy could barely remember what the guy responsible for that heartbreak looked like now, but she owed him. That breakup brought her Kookie, a white and mushroom Shih Tzu who was apparently named after some 1950s TV show character famous for having long hair. A cotton ball on steroids, Shane called her.

But…*no pets allowed.*

Sorry, but Darcy would pack up, go home, and surrender all her independence before she'd consider living without her baby girl. Just thinking about it made Darcy bend over and swoop up ten pounds of spice and spunk into her arms, giving a squeeze.

"We'll find a way around that little roadblock," Darcy whispered, pressing a kiss on the soft little fur she kept long and coiffed and usually in a tiny bow. Kookie squirmed and stuck her head into the opening of Darcy's handbag, hunting for treats she knew were always packed into the side pocket along with lipstick and breath mints. "Oh, of course," Darcy cooed. "I'll hide you in my purse while we sneak in. After that? Well, we'll figure something out."

All she wanted to do tonight was see the place again, give Kooks a chance to sniff around, and measure the bedroom so she could decide which dresser to pack onto Shane's truck tomorrow. Anyway, Dad knew the landlord. And he'd said the guy was reasonable or...something?

She honestly hadn't heard many details after "brownstone in Ambrose Acres," which was a dreamy section of Bitter Bark. And the sunny one-bedroom apartment she came to see with the real estate agent the next day had delivered on every level.

The second-floor unit was roomy, cheery, and both the eat-in kitchen and spacious bedroom had narrow balconies that overlooked an enclosed courtyard in the back. The apartment had been renovated in neutral tones with a washed-gray wood floor, and Darcy had instantly seen how she could decorate to her super-feminine taste, with generous pops of color. Not pink. Well, not *entirely* pink.

But no one had said a word about pets. Although the landlord hadn't been here when Darcy toured the unit, wouldn't the agent have been informed?

Darcy had stood right out here on the front steps listening to Michelle's side of the conversation when she'd called him that day. Both downstairs units were occupied, but the other, much larger apartment on the second floor was about to undergo a gut job, meaning the person who took the one bedroom up there would have to put up with construction noise and dirt. That must have been the reason it was still available and helped Michelle negotiate a sweet rent with a promise that Darcy could move in immediately.

Everything was perfect except...*No pets allowed.*

She threw the sign a dirty look. No one could stop her from bringing Kookie, who went everywhere with her, made no noise or trouble, and could be hidden as easily as a pair of gloves. Still, she glanced around, her gaze settling on one of the two units on the first floor, fairly certain Michelle had said the landlord lived in one of them.

Hopefully, the man was nice and not some surly old fart who hated dogs. Just in case, Darcy tucked Kookie deeper into her oversized bag and stroked her head. "No barking, baby girl."

She gave one last whimper, knowing full well what "no barking" meant, because Kookie was Obedient with a capital O and understood English as well as everyone around her. Better, in some cases.

As Darcy used the key code to open the wrought-iron-gate entrance, she was already working out a plan. First of all, until the other apartment was renovated next door, she'd be the only tenant on the second floor.

She rarely went anywhere, including work, without Kookie, who fit into almost any bag, which could be how she'd sneak the dog out to the grass morning and night. If she had to go somewhere without Kookie, Darcy would leave her at Waterford Farm, so the dog would never be home alone barking. And she was too small for the person downstairs to hear her footsteps.

"Easy-peasy, little squeezy," she whispered, opening the shiny black door into a main hall with marble floors, black inlay, and a twinkling crystal chandelier. She tiptoed past the doors to the two apartments downstairs, then darted toward a gorgeous turn-of-the-century curved stairway that led up to her unit.

God, she loved this place. "And it's all mine!" In the bag, Kookie squirmed a little at unfamiliar scents. "Okay, mine and yours," she corrected as she practically flew up the stairs.

At the top, she reached Unit 4 and flipped through her key ring to find the one she'd picked up at the real estate office that morning. As she turned the latch and inched the door open, she blinked at the unexpected light inside.

Many lights, as a matter of fact. Like, every overhead in the place flooded the whole unit in what looked like daylight. She stepped inside and peered into the entryway, getting a glimpse into the living room.

Had someone been here? Left on the lights? Was that why it was so hot in here?

Walking with trepidation, she made her way to the door to the bedroom, seeing a stepladder and…the lower half of a man visible from a square hole in the ceiling, booted feet on a ladder step.

Just as she gasped softly in shock, something white came falling to the floor, hitting hard and cracking.

"Son of a bitch, it's drywall." The deep voice came from inside what she guessed was an air conditioning duct.

Stunned, she reeled back, momentarily forgetting the dog under her arm as she tried to imagine why a man would be hanging out of the ceiling at nine at night. Fixing the AC, she supposed, peering at the shape of him to try to guess what she was dealing with and decide if she should run or stay.

A handyman or construction worker, she supposed, but as the tenant, she had every right to be here. Assuming she was safe. She inched back to the door, mentally planning an escape route if she needed one.

"How the hell did this happen?" Another chunk of drywall hit the floor.

Darcy stared at the jean-clad backside not ten feet from her. His waist was narrow, his thighs strong, his legs the length of a man who probably stood well over six feet.

She stared at the masculine form in front of her, her breath and the grip on her bag tightening with each slow second of her thorough inspection. Under her arm, Kookie growled softly in protest.

"Is someone there?" The man's work boots moved, finding balance on the ladder as Darcy stayed frozen in place, unsure of what to do. "Is someone down there?"

Kookie barked once at the deep, masculine voice.

"Is that a *dog*?"

Darcy cleared her throat and coughed hard enough to sound like, well, a bark. "I'm the new tenant." *With the dog who's not allowed.*

She coughed again, trying to match Kookie's pitch.

"Oh. Oh, really?" Suddenly, he moved effortlessly down each step, revealing a bare torso, broad shoulders, and so many ripped, cut, tanned, and sweaty muscles that Darcy didn't know where to look. Except away. She could not look away. "I wasn't expecting you tonight."

He wasn't expecting...oh crap! This was *the landlord*?

Kookie barked again.

So Darcy coughed louder and seized a handful of treats, stuffing them deeper into the bag to buy time and quiet.

He dropped to the floor, turned, and for a split second, they both stood in what felt like stunned silence.

Oh God. This was her landlord? This hot, hunky human built for a joyride was her *landlord*? She had to muster more self-control to keep her gaze on his face and not the stunning bare chest that was right about at eye level. "I thought you were..." An old, bald, grouchy, dog-hating *landlord*. Not...a Greek god with a disarming face, scruffy whiskers, and soft lips that were *not* relaxing into a smile of welcome.

And don't even think about that body...although it might be a while before Darcy thought about anything else.

"What are you doing here?" At least his gruff voice matched the image of the crotchety old man she'd been dreading. The rest of him was...not gruff. Not crotchety. And so not old. Not a day over thirty-five, she guessed.

"Uh, I live here?" she managed to say, still fighting the urge to let her gaze drop over him again.

"Not yet, you don't."

Was he serious? "I will in about three hours when the clock strikes twelve. Just call me Cinderella. Who are you? And if you say Prince Charming, you might have my heart forever."

He didn't smile. "I'm the building owner, and our contract states that the tenant will not move in until midnight on the agreed-upon date, though I was not expecting you until tomorrow morning."

Oh, *that's* what Dad had told her. This was the guy who followed the rules. Just her luck. Especially when one of the rules was "no pets."

Rather than shake his hand and introduce herself, which she would do under any other circumstances, she turned in an attempt to hide her bag and the contraband inside. "I came to measure for furniture," she said quickly. "But I don't need to do that tonight."

He narrowed dark eyes to intense, distrusting slits, making thick lashes come together as he openly appraised her, his gaze landing on her purse.

Instantly, she coughed again. Hard, three times in a row, tapping her throat. "Oh, that dust."

"Exactly why you shouldn't be here yet."

Okay, she had to flip the switch on this conversation and fast. She pointed to the two chunks of drywall on the floor. "Will that be gone by tomorrow?" she demanded.

"Yes. That's why I'm working tonight."

"What's wrong? Is something wrong? Maybe I shouldn't take the apartment if something's wrong," she added, purposely putting him on the defensive.

It worked. His expression instantly changed from accusation to assurance. "Oh God, no. You..." He took a slow breath, as if trying to find the right words, the move making his chest rise and fall and distract her completely. It wasn't just the impressive size of it, but the sheen of sweat and the dusting of hair in the middle, all of it leading down to a thick, dark line under a sexy bellybutton peeking out from his jeans. "You're, I mean, it's *fine*," he finished.

So are you.

"Doesn't look fine," Darcy shot back. Although, actually, it did. So fine her neck prickled and legs wobbled and there might be some toes curling in her sneakers. "And it's really hot in here."

"It's the AC," he added, sounding a little defeated as he turned and grabbed a red rag from the ladder. "The duct was blocked." He lifted his arms to slide the rag—which was actually a paint-spattered T-shirt— over his head, giving her a split second to say goodbye to that spectacular chest.

His head popped through the top. "I found the problem, though. I promise the air will be coming through the duct and I'll have this all cleaned up before tomorrow. Which is why you can't be here tonight. It's not safe, Miss Kilcannon."

For some reason, the fact that he knew her name threw her a little, despite the fact that he, of course, must have seen it on her signed lease. But she didn't know his, and he sure as heck wasn't offering it along with a handshake and hello. So he was hot *and* cold.

"I can send you the room measurements by email if you like," he said. "You did put your email on the contract, right?"

Did she? She certainly hadn't read the thing closely enough, or she'd know about his stupid no-pets rule. The question was, should she try to get him to change his mind, or sneak Kookie in and out of here and risk eviction?

"I think so," she said. "But it's okay. I can see the size of the room now. I know which dresser to bring."

He snapped the ladder closed and slipped it under his thick bicep like the metal contraption weighed a few ounces. "Goodbye, then."

She stayed where she was for a moment, vaguely aware that even Kookie, the world's best dog, was getting restless. But Darcy wasn't one to back down from anything. "I'm sorry, did I say something to offend you? I mean, other than showing up a hundred and twenty minutes early?"

He didn't answer, swallowing a little, but continued to stare as if her very existence offended him. And he didn't even know about the dog.

"I don't want you to be disappointed in your new apartment," he finally said. "I've worked really hard on two of the four units, and I need a good tenant to be able to finish the overhaul of the whole building."

Then why had he looked at her like she was anything but a good tenant, but his worst possible nightmare? "I will be," she assured him.

"Yeah, that's what the real estate agent said." He nodded, surreptitiously checking her out and maybe not for her tenant qualifications. Perspiration tickled her back. "She said you were from a good local family and your dad…" His voice trailed off.

"What about him?" she asked.

"Just that he's well-known. Good connections. Solid citizen."

Why did her father's qualifications matter? A pinch of resentment grew, but then it got extinguished as fast as her next breath.

Oh, Dad. Seriously? Was this…oh, of course it was. Look at the man in front of her. Dad had already met him and… "I could kill him sometimes," she muttered.

"Excuse me?"

"My dad. He's being the Dogfather again."

"The what?"

"It's a nickname. Like the Godfather, pulling strings to get what he wants, only no marinara sauce or guns."

He almost smiled, making her realize it was the very first time even the hint of a smile lifted his lips. The near miss made him really cute. Cut*er*. Of course Dad would know she'd be attracted to him. Of course he couldn't resist a setup. He probably had this in mind the minute she mentioned wanting an apartment and he'd met this "good man" who "played by the rules."

"Sounds like an interesting guy," he said. "I'll have to remember that if I ever meet him."

"You already met him. At the Gentrification Committee meeting. Tall guy, silver hair, a semiretired veterinarian?"

"Oh, the dog guy. Of course I remember him. We had a brief conversation."

"Let me guess." Darcy cocked her head and imagined the dialogue. "He wanted to know how old you are, if you have any vices, and whether you're single."

"No." His frown gave way to a quick laugh. "Wait, actually he did ask me if I was married. Wanted to get a handle on my stability."

"No, on your *availability*, not stability." A whole new wave of frustration rolled over her. "I love him," she said. "I really do. But the man literally thinks he's a human dating app."

Confusion made his eyes even darker and more intense. "I'm sorry. You lost me."

She dropped her head back with a soft grunt as it all became clear. "He seriously wants me to think it was totally random that I landed in this apartment with you as my landlord. Someone needs to teach him a lesson."

"You want to teach your father a lesson? Definitely not following this."

She put a hand on her hip, the need to hide Kookie forgotten with this new travesty. "My father thinks I'm going to marry you."

"*Excuse me?*"

Did he have to be *quite* that aghast at the prospect? "He firmly believes he has this magic touch, and to be fair, he's five for six in my family."

She could have sworn his tanned skin paled. "That's…insane."

"Right? Someone has to prove him dead wrong, or he'll be setting up every single person in Bitter Bark."

"You have nothing to worry about, Miss Kilcannon," he said. "I have no interest in marrying anyone, ever. His plans are doomed."

She tried to ignore a wee thud of disappointment. Not that she wanted to marry him, or anyone, but did he have to be *so* certain?

She shook her head. "He'll never stop. If it's not the accountant's son, it's the car guy. If it's not the new EMT, it's the hot landlord."

He gave another one of those half smiles that made her whole body remember she was a human female with wildly functioning hormones. "So, you should pick your own boyfriend and your dad will back off."

"If only it was that easy."

He hoisted the ladder a little higher and nodded for her to step to the side. "You're at zero risk of an arranged marriage with me. I'm single for life, and nothing will ever change that. Nothing and no one."

For some reason she hated and didn't understand, that vehemence in his voice sent a little zing of a challenge through her. "Wow. Dropped a few bitter pills, did we?"

"Nope. I'm just smart."

Or scared to death. "Well, don't tell my dad you're anti-marriage, because he'll start another full-court press, and I don't feel like living my life not knowing who'll be my next surprise blind date."

"Your secret's safe." He inched by her, and the ladder brushed her bag. She tried to turn before Kookie responded, but it was too late. A white furry head with a pink bow shot straight up, making the man freeze and hiss in a surprised breath. "Oh, you have more than one secret."

Busted. "Say hi to Kookie Kilcannon, my beloved pupper and partner in crime."

He blinked at Kookie, and graced them both with one more smile. Then his gaze shifted to Darcy. "She's cute, but I have a strict no-pets policy."

"You should have told my father that. Then he'd

know we don't have a chance, because I'd have no interest in someone who doesn't like dogs."

"I like dogs," he said quickly. "And that's why they can't be in the building."

She tipped her head. "Man, you *are* terrified of attachment."

He flinched a bit at the comment, which she suspected hit too close to home. "This is a construction zone. The unit next door is being demolished down to the studs and rebuilt, and I know you are aware of that. An animal that gets into a hard-hat area is a liability to itself and the workers, so, sorry, this is policy."

Kookie would never be out of her sight. "Well, it's a dumb policy."

"It was in the contract."

"Must have been very fine print."

"Not at all. It's stated clearly under special terms and conditions, provision three, line six. Until such time that there is no construction taking place, tenant may not house uncaged animals."

"Uncaged animals?" She snorted. "I thought you were referring to lions and tigers."

"Snakes and gerbils are fine, assuming they're in a cage."

"But adorable creatures with big eyes and pretty hair who want nothing but affection are not?"

He lifted a brow. "I let you in, didn't I?" When her jaw dropped, he used his free hand to slide it back in place. "Really sorry, but if something happened to it, the liability could put me out of business."

"*She*, not *it*." She narrowed her eyes at him to make her point. "This dog is a being with a heart and soul. Which might be more than I can say about you."

That didn't faze him as he walked to the door. "Like I said, I'm sorry, but those are the rules."

"I don't like rules."

"Shocker," he murmured as he opened the door and stepped outside, leaving her fuming as the door closed behind him.

"You know what else is a shocker, Hot Landlord? Kookie isn't going anywhere. She'll live here come hell, high water, or all your stupid rules."

Kookie barked once, in complete agreement.

Chapter Four

Darcy spotted Ella Mahoney sipping a white wine at the bar as soon as she walked into Bushrod's a few minutes later. But she wasn't alone, of course. Darcy and Ella had learned right around the time they'd turned sixteen or seventeen that having so many older brothers meant having bodyguards. But at least her now-married or nearly-married four brothers had backed off a bit.

Not so the Mahoney men. Somehow, they always knew if Ella and Darcy were meeting for drinks, and one or more managed to show up and "join" them. That had obviously happened tonight, since Ella was flanked by two muscular, handsome men who looked like they could kill anyone who came close to their baby sister.

"Hey, Mahoney crew," she called as she crossed the scarred wooden floor and navigated a few crowded tables of the locals' favorite watering hole, Kookie leading the way on her leash. Like almost all of Bitter Bark's businesses, Bushrod's was not only dog friendly, but welcoming, with at least three other dogs in the bar right at that moment.

Braden, the youngest of Ella's three older brothers, slid off his barstool to give Darcy a hug and offer her the seat.

Both he and Connor wore navy blue Bitter Bark Fire Department shirts and khaki pants, probably fresh off duty at the station where they worked with their oldest brother, Declan, who'd recently made captain.

She hugged Connor, too, sharing a knowing smile with Ella over his sizable shoulder.

"God forbid we get girl time alone," Ella said dryly, running a hand through her short, spiky dark hair and somehow making it look even more adorable and tousled.

"We finished a shift and wanted a beer," Connor said.

Ella rolled her eyes. "You should be dead on your feet after a shift and trust your sister and cousin to have a glass of wine without needing supervision."

Braden gave her a look that said the very notion was insane. "You give yourself too much credit. I don't see a line of guys trying to buy you drinks, Smella."

"'Cause the firefighters would hose them down." She waved him off, unaffected by the nickname her brothers had hung on her since she was a child. With her pixie haircut, giant brown eyes, and a wide showstopper of a smile, she could have been called Stink Bomb—and probably was by those three—and it wouldn't have put a dent in Ella Mahoney's self-confidence.

Even though Darcy was younger than Ella by a few months, she was the more careful of the two, not nearly as impetuous as her cousin. Ella did things—

like start her own business—while Darcy only thought about doing them for a year.

But all that was about to change.

"Champagne, Darcy?" Connor asked. "We hear you're celebrating."

She slid onto the barstool. "I'll have the bad white wine that Ella's having. I'm only almost celebrating."

Braden leaned closer to talk over the bar noise as Connor flagged down the bartender. "But Ella told us that you found a place in Ambrose Acres. Pretty ritzy, I'd say."

"I did, but I had a run-in with the landlord." She snapped her fingers at Kookie and pointed under the bar, where she wanted the dog to sit. Instantly, Kookie obeyed, like the angel she was.

The angel who wasn't welcome in her new apartment.

"What's the problem?" Braden asked.

"I wish it was *just* that the owner has a no-pets policy, but it's worse than that."

Ella gasped. "You can't live without Kookie."

"I won't. I'll hide her if I have to, but no, that's not what I'm upset about."

They all looked at her expectantly as Connor handed her a glass of wine.

"It's a setup."

"What do you mean?" Ella asked.

"I mean, this apartment is one big blind date arranged by my father." She took a healthy gulp of wine as they reacted with an expected howl of hilarity. "Laugh all you want, but the man drives me to drink."

"Uncle Daniel?" Connor asked. "The guy's a saint."

"A saint who thinks he knows everything about

romance and is some kind of Fiddler on the Roof with a magical touch and a mission to marry off every kid he has." She looked skyward. "I can't imagine why he'd think I'd like..." She stopped and pictured the hot landlord. "Yeah, I can."

"Oh." Ella inched forward, always in tune with Darcy's subtext. "How's your dad's taste?"

"Impeccable," Darcy deadpanned. "Because of course Daniel Kilcannon wouldn't want to water down the gene pool."

Connor and Braden laughed at that, but Ella put her hand on Darcy's arm. "Details, please. Hair that kisses the collar and begs to be touched? Eyes that draw you in, hold you forever, and refuse to let go? A body that makes a grown woman cry?"

Darcy cracked up over her cousin's penchant for drama in everything, but Braden choked and Connor gave his little sister a playful jab of his elbow. "And you call men sexist."

She waved him off. "Stay home if you don't want to know the soft underbelly of what we say about the less fortunate gender. Hit me, Darce."

She sighed and easily conjured a memory of the man. She probably could have said, *All of the above*, and been done with it, but she didn't want to admit Dad's choice was *that* dead-on.

"Chestnut hair, dark eyes, and his body is..." *Sublime. Ridiculous. Delicious.* "You know, a body."

"What does that mean?" Braden asked.

"So good she can't possibly put it into words," Ella supplied, making Darcy lift her glass and tap her cousin's, thanking God they were so utterly in tune with each other.

"You know what else I can't put into words?" she asked. "How ticked off I am that my dad won't let me live my own life." She took another deep drink. "How is a person ever supposed to achieve independence when her father thinks he's Cupid?"

"Uncle Daniel is not anything but one of the greatest guys who ever lived," Braden shot back.

"Hear, hear." Connor lifted his glass. "You're not going to get any of his nieces or nephews to talk smack about our favorite uncle."

Darcy smiled at them both, loving their loyalty. Their mother had been widowed much longer than Darcy's dad had been. The Mahoney kids had grown up without a father, and she knew that their uncle Daniel had relished the role he'd played in helping Aunt Colleen raise such amazing people.

"Then get back to the smoke-fest landlord and why this 'setup' is a problem for you?" Ella said. "Because so far I'm thinking I should put my name on Uncle Daniel's list for when he runs out of kids and wants to start hottie hookups for single cousins."

"He doesn't hook anyone up," Darcy replied. "He gets them engaged, married, and sometimes with child." She gave her cousin a warning look. "I don't want any of that. Not yet. Not now." After a lifetime of being cared for by everyone, she might not want it ever. "Plus, why wouldn't he simply say, 'Hey, you might like the landlord,' instead of subterfuge and manipulation?"

Ella shrugged. "Probably because he knew you'd say no to the apartment and the guy."

"Exactly."

"He's not manipulating," Connor said. "He wants

his kids happy, is all. And most of them are."

"*All* of them would be," Darcy shot back, "if the youngest could be given a chance to breathe without assistance."

"So tell Uncle Daniel he's barking up the wrong tree," Braden said, adding a grin. "See what I did there? 'Cause he's the Dogfather? And a vet?"

Ella and Darcy both rolled their eyes, but the bad joke made Connor reach over their heads and give his brother a high five in solidarity.

"If I do that, he'll start the clock ticking on the next guy," Darcy said. "He's not going to stop, no matter what he says or promises."

"You need to use reverse psychology on him," Ella suggested.

"Tell him I'm dying to get married and he'll freak out and let me be?" she guessed. He *was* having trouble with her moving out.

"Tell him he nailed it. Tell him you're totally into the landlord and the feeling is mutual and please leave you alone for a while so you can get this thing off the ground." Ella crossed her arms and gave a smug smile. "Problem solved."

"Until he finds out we can't stand each other."

"Maybe that won't happen," Braden suggested. "Maybe you'll like each other."

"And then he'll have done it again and my life will be over because some guy who lives and dies by the rules gets control over me." She squeezed her eyes and grunted in frustration, making Kookie rise up and lick her toe to make sure everything was okay. "How could he even dream I'd be attracted to a man who has a no-pets policy in his apartment building?"

"Does he hate dogs?" Ella asked. "Because, whoa, major deal killer."

"He says he likes them, but the unit next to mine is undergoing a complete renovation, and he said he can't risk having a dog near a hard-hat area. It's a *liability*." She drew the word out, mocking his seriousness. Which was kind of hot, too, if she had to admit it. Which she wouldn't, especially not to Ella, who'd drill down until she figured out that Darcy was fried by the very sight of the guy. "As if I'd be so reckless as to let my dog in a construction area. She goes everywhere I do—to work and play."

"Then maybe Ella's got a good idea," Connor said. "Tell Uncle Daniel you're into the guy, and he'll back off."

"But what if they meet? Mr. Rule Follower isn't going to lie. I'm sure he thinks his face would fall off."

"Which would be a shame," Ella added.

"You have no idea." They shared a laugh and tapped glasses again. "But it was a good thought, and we have much to celebrate, Cuz. I'm moving into the place tomorrow. *With* Kookie, so Smoke-Fest Landlord can cry me a river."

"You need help?" Connor asked. "Braden and I are both off shift."

"Thanks, Con. Pretty sure every Kilcannon in town has announced that they'll be helping me." Which she loved them for and certainly didn't want to move in without help, but it wasn't like anyone gave her a chance to figure that out on her own. They merely all announced they'd be there with trucks and Jeeps and doughnuts.

Because…Kilcannons.

"So, what about the grooming business?" Braden asked.

"Is this studio going to be the color of candy like the one at Waterford?" Connor teased. "'Cause I get a toothache walking in that place."

She laughed. "Actually, I'm thinking about something very contemporary, maybe cool blue or gray. It's going to be a salon, not a studio. Full service, with reception, holding areas, bathing and drying, styling and finishing, and a workflow."

"Oh, I found a picture on Pinterest," Ella said, pulling out her phone. "It has the perfect little bathing area. Look."

The conversation easily shifted to the space that Darcy had leased and how they could build it out for dog grooming, taking her mind off the encounter with the landlord.

Mostly. But even as she talked, laughed, and finished her glass of wine, Darcy's thoughts slipped back to that apartment and the man with intense eyes, a sexy mouth, and that impossibly strong chest.

But it wasn't the eyes, mouth, or chest that had made Dad select this one for Darcy. No, she saw something else in this man, something that went deeper than looks. Probably the same thing Dad saw.

And that's what really scared the hell out of her.

She was crazy.

Crazy gorgeous, crazy smart-mouthed, and crazy trouble.

Which was why he'd been so cold the night before. And why Josh looked out his living room window the next morning and swore he would not, under any circumstances, go out and help Darcy Kilcannon move in, no matter how unchivalrous that might be.

The universe was testing his resolve, and he wouldn't lose this fight.

It had been a month. And three days. But nothing had changed since that morning he'd found Savannah in a T-shirt fresh out of bed with Gid. Yeah, the sharp pain had dulled to a numb ache in his chest. The metallic taste of hot anger and raw betrayal every time he swallowed had all but disappeared. And he was sleeping again, waking up bathed in sweat and loneliness, but he solved that with a cold shower and a renewed sense that he would never again make himself vulnerable.

Then a woman so insanely attractive he could barely speak when he laid eyes on her landed in his building as a tenant. If Darcy had been right in her musings about her father, then the man couldn't have picked a worse prospect for his daughter.

But he needn't have worried about doing the decent thing and helping a single woman move furniture, he realized as he sipped his coffee and studied the little caravan that had pulled up outside his living room window. Fact was, it looked like the cast of *The Waltons* had shown up to help their little sister move into her new apartment, arriving in two pickup trucks, an ugly yellow Jeep, and a twenty-year-old refurbished Plymouth Voyager.

Each vehicle was driven by a different jacked-up guy, all accompanied by attractive women, plus a little boy who was regularly reduced to fits of giggles. Oh, and there was a teenage girl and an old lady with their heads huddled over a tablet computer.

He let his gaze scan the group, seeing a definite family resemblance among many of them. Most of the men shared a strong jaw and similar bone structure. One of the women, though she had wavy auburn hair, had that same enchanting smile he'd seen a few times in his brief exchange with Darcy the night before. A sister, he guessed.

So these must be the Kilcannons and the significant others Darcy claimed were a result of her father's matchmaking. He glanced around for the tall, commanding figure of the man he'd met at the town meeting, but Dr. K, as everyone called him, hadn't come for the moving party.

And then Darcy pulled up last in a bright red hybrid with all the windows and a sunroof open, classic rock reverberating loudly enough for him to make out Robert Plant's voice.

She whipped into a spot behind a truck and in front of the van, then popped out of the car like a sex kitten exploding from a cake. Blond, bright, beautiful, and somehow more alive than most of the people on earth.

Through the open window, he could hear her laugh, a sound that seemed to reach into his chest and readjust everything that was supposed to be frozen in place by the ice that had formed around his heart.

Oh, no. She wasn't melting that with all her warmth and wit. Not happening.

The family gathered around Darcy like she was the sun at the center of their galaxy, laughing, hugging, planning their attack on Josh's building. She lifted the little boy in her arms, whispered in his ear, then pointed to the second floor, making the child kick with glee over whatever she'd promised.

Josh never imagined he'd be so jealous of a second grader.

One of the men said something that cracked them all up, but Darcy set the boy down so she could elbow that guy in the ribs, shaking her head with sassy defiance that made her long ponytail swing like a pendulum. Then she strode to one of the trucks and whipped off a blanket to reveal a sofa the color of cotton candy.

Good God, was there anything subtle about her? No, nothing. Not a single thing about his new tenant could be ignored. Not her waves of corn-silk hair or eyes the color of his favorite cobalt vortex marble that he'd treasured as a kid. Certainly not the lean, shapely figure that moved with grace and attitude and…sex.

He tried to swallow and remember that swearing off women meant swearing off *everything.* Unless…no. Not with her. Not with her name on the lease for his apartment. Not with a face he could look at for days. Months, maybe. That would blow the rules to smithereens.

He watched the men and women buzz about like uninvited ants at a picnic table, industrious, organized, and having way too much fun. Their banter, laughter, and incessant teasing drifted in like someone else's music he didn't recognize or like. Did any family really act that way? Because the one he came from sure didn't.

For one thing, the Buckings would never move themselves. They had staff for a job like that, paid professionals who preceded them from the mansion on the lake in Cornelius to the summer place in the Hamptons and the Christmas place in Aspen. Of course, no Bucking would holler a joke over a truck bed, high-five when a lamp got tossed—and caught—from one man to the next, or even think about driving a Jeep.

He turned away and went back into the formal dining room to work on the renovation plans spread out over the table. He had to have these to the subs by—

"Where do you want Kookie's bed, Darce?"

He straightened from the plans as the question floated in from outside. Kookie? The *dog*? She was bringing a bed for a dog that wasn't living there?

Damn it. Did she think he was an idiot?

Setting down his pencil, he walked to the window in time to see one of the men hoist a cradle out of a truck. What the hell? Her dog slept in a crib?

Darcy came darting around the Jeep, carrying a box. "Would you be quiet, Shane? I don't want the landlord to know she's here."

Too late, sweetheart.

"The landlord Dad thinks you're going to marry?" The man lifted the cradle over his head, showing off an impressive physique as he shook his shoulders and started singing "Another One Bites the Dust."

An emotion Josh couldn't identify rocked through him. Was that...envy? Because this moron was singing in the street?

Another guy swooped by, carrying a chandelier. He was tall, dark, and wearing a shirt with the face of a German shepherd and the words *Ears Up, System Armed* on the front. "Don't listen to Shane, little sister."

"Always good advice." This from the Jeep driver, who carried a massive wardrobe box and wore a fedora or cowboy hat. *Something* that had seen better days. "And I really like that you're back in the game to get Dad a date."

Wait. Didn't she say her dad was the matchmaker? Not the other way around? He shook his head. Why did he even care about this crew? Still, he lingered to listen to the exchange.

"Oh, I'm in," Darcy said. "After trying to thrust me on some tool-toting, dog-hating, rule-obsessed Neanderthal? Dad's going *down*."

Neanderthal? And he told her he didn't hate dogs. What the hell?

"Give Dad a break, you guys." The auburn-haired woman, flanked by a man with tattoos all over his arms and the teenager dragging a rolling suitcase, cut into the conversation. "He can't help himself now that Darcy is the last Kilcannon standing."

That brought on a volley of inside jokes he'd never translate or laugh about.

For a long moment, Josh stood in the window, transported back in time, feeling the old sting of being an outsider looking into a family he didn't fit into at all. Then the group dispersed with boxes and belongings, laughter, chatter, and one gaudy chandelier that she really shouldn't be allowed to hang, but something told him Darcy Kilcannon was a force of nature who would do whatever she wanted and he'd be the one blown away.

She stood alone for one moment, hands on her hips, head tilted back, staring up at the building with the same smile he'd seen enough times to already have it memorized. A few stray strands of blond hair lifted with the summer breeze, and he could practically hear her sweet sigh of satisfaction.

A familiar, unwanted ache deepened in his gut. Okay. That was a little lower than his gut.

But how could he *not* respond to her?

Easily. By following his own rules. Flings only. One-night stands. Hookups. Whatever they called meaningless sex that didn't lead to a heart that felt like a nine-pound hammer had whacked it. He hadn't attempted anything like casual sex yet, but he wasn't about to start with her.

There was nothing *casual* about Darcy Kilcannon, and he'd do well to remember that.

All of a sudden, Darcy let out a little squeal that might be annoying on another woman but sounded like a song on her lips, pointing down the street. "What an adorable pupper! Is that a Chinese crested? I love that dog!" She crouched down as a little white dog came trotting closer, on a leash, but turning in circles. No, not any little white dog. That was…

"Stella." Josh barely breathed the name, letting his gaze shift to the other end of the leash.

A few white lights popped in his head. The sour taste returned, his frozen heart burned, and his fists formed with the urge to punch a wall as he stared in shock.

What the hell was *she* doing here?

Chapter Five

"Hello, little love." Darcy leaned over to get closer to the fluffy little doggo, surprised when it continued trotting right by her.

"Sorry." The owner, an attractive brunette who looked to be about Darcy's age, tugged gently on the leash. "She's blind."

"Oh, I'm sorry to hear that." At the sound of Darcy's voice, the dog stepped back, growled, and turned toward a bed of flowers for a quick, nervous pee. "Diabetes?" Darcy asked.

The other woman shook her head. "No, she was fine, and then, wham. It happened a few weeks ago. She started bumping into things and acting really strange, then I had her at a client's house, and she walked right to the stairs and fell down."

"Oh no!" Darcy put her hands in front of her mouth and moaned in sympathy.

"She was fine, but shaken up. So was I. The vet said it happens and she's blind for life now."

"She has SARDS?" Darcy asked. The acronym was for a blindness that was fairly common in dogs, especially females this size.

"Yes, that's it," the woman said with a nod. "Sudden…"

"Acquired Retinal Degeneration Syndrome," Darcy finished. At the woman's surprised look, she said, "I'm a dog groomer. Dad and sister are vets. Brothers all train."

She smiled. "Then you understand that Stella's really struggling."

"Stella." Darcy eyed the little doll, who kept turning in circles and growling at nothing. "Don't tell me. You're a fan of the Marlon Brando movie?"

"Nope. Stella McCartney designs."

Darcy smiled, glancing at the woman's impeccable outfit and deciding that made sense. But the snazzy outfit couldn't hide the sadness in her eyes.

"I bet you're struggling, too," Darcy said, inching closer to the dog and reaching in her pocket, certain she'd stuffed a treat or two in there for Kookie. "Can she have a treat?"

"Oh, sure. Come on, Stella. Treat!"

The dog turned at the word, her head moving back and forth as she navigated her way to the treats she smelled in Darcy's hand.

"Aww, she's a sweet little nug." Once she ate the treats, Darcy slowly petted her head, careful not to scare her. "Blind dogs need special training," Darcy told her. "You should bring her to Waterford Farm. We have—"

"Savannah."

Both women turned at the man's voice, but the dog barked at the sound of it.

"Hello, Josh."

Darcy inched back, looking from one to the other. So Hot Landlord had a name—Josh—and, from the way Stella was barking at the sound of his voice, at least one fan.

His gaze was straight-up ice as he looked at the woman, but after a second, it dropped to the dog and melted. "Hey, kid. I've missed you." He crouched for a second, petting the dog, who sat on the sidewalk, tongue out, face up, begging for more like any female would in front of him.

After a moment, he stood slowly, and all the ice came back. "What are you doing here, Savannah?" He asked the question in the same tone one might use on a mortal enemy or possibly the devil incarnate. *Ouch.*

"I thought you'd like to see…Stella." The woman, Savannah, had plenty of hesitation in her response, Darcy noticed, and crossed her arms in a way that said she was no more comfortable with this than he was.

So this was private drama, and Darcy wanted out.

"Well, I better get back to moving in," Darcy said quickly. "You want these?" She held the treats out to the woman, anxious to get out of the way of whatever confrontation was going down.

"Thank you." She took them. "Where did you say this dog should go?"

She glanced at Josh, who stopped glaring long enough to pet the dog. "Waterford Farm," Darcy said. "It's an excellent canine training center about fifteen minutes out of town. Like I said, we can treat—"

"What's wrong with her?" Josh interjected. "Why is she acting so strange?"

"Stella's gone blind, Josh," the woman said.

"What?" His eyes flashed with anger that instantly shifted to something deeper and more personal. "When did that happen? How?"

The other woman glanced at Darcy, then at him with a plea in her eyes. "Um, Josh, can we talk?"

Darcy got the message, backing up with one hand raised. "Let me know if you need the number for Waterford," she said quickly. "Good luck, Stella." She gave the dog a quick rub on the head, but that made her scoot back and cower in fear.

"Stella," Josh whispered. "You poor baby."

Okay, so that big old chest wasn't hollow. Good to know. She hustled toward the apartment building entrance.

"Is she moving in with you?" The woman's question came right as Darcy disappeared inside, but the door hadn't closed.

Darcy couldn't help it. She had to listen. She had to know how vehemently he denied that possibility.

For a long moment, he didn't respond, making Darcy wonder if he was shaking his head and giving the other woman a look like she was insane.

"Yeah," he said. "She's moving in right now."

Darcy froze. Did he...was he trying to imply that...

"Oh, Josh. I'm glad you found someone," the woman cooed. "And so fast."

Very slowly, without making a sound, Darcy let the door close. So Hot Landlord had used her as a revenge girlfriend. Normally, it would tick her off to no end. But this time? Well, that ought to buy her at least a month of having Kookie live here with no repercussions.

With a hoot, she charged up to her new apartment, feeling oddly victorious and excited.

"She's really blind?" Josh's question came out as a croak, but the news hit hard and he couldn't hide it. "How is that possible? She was fine when I…when you…before."

"I figured out she was blind a few weeks ago. Your, um, girlfriend knew exactly what caused it."

"Girlfriend?" He looked up from the dog, frowning, then suddenly realized that she'd misunderstood him and when she said he'd found someone, he thought she meant a tenant. "No, she's renting one of the units," he explained. "How did she go blind, Savannah?"

"She got something called SARDS, they say."

"Is that why you're here? You wanted to tell me in person?" Because if she thought for one minute he'd take her back because of this, she was out of her mind.

"No." She shook her head, studying Stella as she turned in a circle, walked into a small wrought-iron rail, and backed away with a sudden bark of fear, making Josh's heart twist for her. "I came to ask you a huge favor, Josh. So, can we talk?" Once more, she glanced at the apartment building.

"Let's take a walk," he said, not wanting to settle in for a long conversation. The sooner Savannah left, the better. He watched Stella walk right up to a light post, tap her nose, and work her way around it, the whole process breaking his heart.

She'd been a lively, spirited, trusting little dog

afraid of nothing but thunder. But not now. "How did this happen to her?"

Savannah gave Stella's leash a gentle tug. "I don't know." There was real pain in her voice. "Maybe God was punishing me." Pain and guilt.

"I don't think it works quite like that," he said. "Was it sudden? She's awfully young for some kind of senior-dog thing, right? They told me at the shelter she was under five years old." He remembered the day he'd gone to an animal refuge to find a rescue for a six-month anniversary present. The high-strung dog hadn't been able to find an owner, but she'd calmed down around Josh, enough that he picked her for Savannah, who'd loved her.

But then, he thought she'd loved him, too.

"It's not an age thing. It just happens. And it's awful," Savannah said. "She's scared of everyone and everything. Doesn't even trust people she knows. She hides under tables and chairs and has to be coaxed out with treats, and when she's out, she pees on the floor and won't stop shaking."

"What does her vet say to do?"

She shrugged. "Live with it."

She was quiet for a long time, letting Stella set a slow and careful pace as they walked along the street.

"So, Gideon and I are taking a trip and will be gone for a while. We're going completely off the grid, just the two of us, no phones, no Internet, no family."

He waited for the sucker punch of pain, but felt nothing except a little relief. "That's nice," he said.

"Mmm." The response was noncommittal and a little strange.

"You sound less than enthused," he noted.

"There's a problem."

With Gideon, there always was.

She pointed at Stella. "We can't take her."

He threw her a look, but waited to hear the rest, even though he already sensed where this was going. And not to "a kennel."

"He's pretty upset about her being blind."

"Upset that she's blind or upset that she's a more difficult dog?" A rhetorical question, though, since he knew Gideon "I'll Take the Easy Way" Bucking well enough to know the answer.

She didn't reply, but he heard her swallow. "She's complicating an already complicated situation."

A situation of *Savannah's* making. He didn't say a word, though.

"So, will you?" she asked.

"Will I what?"

"Take her while I'm gone? I absolutely cannot bear to leave her in a kennel or with a stranger. No one can handle her because she's so...erratic."

She wanted him to take Stella while she went on vacation with his stepbrother? Ire shot up his spine. "Why don't you ask Brea?" he said, knowing his stepsister had watched the dog on more than one occasion for Savannah.

She shook her head. "Brea and I aren't..." She huffed out a breath. "We're not really as close these days."

Surprise, surprise. His stepsister must have taken his side when she found out what Savannah had done. He'd have to thank her next time he saw her. Which could be a long time, because he had zero plans to go back to the Land of Buckings anytime soon.

"Josh, remember when you gave Stella to me? You said if I ever needed backup..."

"We were dating," he said. "I'm sorry, Savannah, but I work on a construction site all day, and you can't leave her alone all day. I can see that in five minutes with her."

"But you're in your own building, right? You could check on her every hour or so." At his look, she tipped her head to acknowledge how difficult that would be. "And your girlfriend is a dog person who knows all about training."

"She's *not* my girlfriend."

She gave a knowing smile. "She's really pretty, and she's a dog groomer."

She was? How did Savannah find that out in two minutes and he had no idea what Darcy did for a living? Because he'd sworn off women. "That's not a solution," he said simply.

She stopped walking and turned to him. "Please, Josh. I know you love Stella like I do. She's not stable enough to be anywhere else but with you."

And, truth be told, he didn't want her anywhere else but with him. "It could be dangerous. It's a construction zone upstairs." And he'd already told one tenant there were no pets allowed because of it.

"Oh, she can't climb stairs. And she loves you. Look at her, Josh." She gestured toward Stella who, when they stopped, came right to Josh and started sniffing his sneaker.

Just then, another dog came trotting by on a leash, looking straight ahead, not even aware of them. But as they got closer, Stella danced backward, her gaze darting helplessly from one side to the other as she growled and spun in circles and then barked violently in warning to the other dog.

"And she hates the smell of another dog, which is why I can't even think about boarding her," she added, as if that was going to help her case. "I mean, no one wants her."

"I do," he said softly. It was a mistake, a challenge he didn't need, a rule he had to bend. But for Stella? He'd bend the rules until they broke in two.

As if she read his mind, Stella got her teeth into his shoelace and started to whip her head from side to side, untying his shoe. Savannah smiled as if she knew she was victorious, until her phone buzzed and she pulled it out, cringing when she looked at the screen.

"Don't tell me. Gid's ready to leave and you need to run."

She looked up at him, something in her eyes he never remembered seeing before. Fear? Worry? Something…not good.

"Savannah, is everything okay?"

"Here's my car," she said, pointing to her SUV parked on the street. "Let me give you her stuff."

He couldn't help noticing that she'd skirted the question, but he didn't push it. Instead, he nodded and took the leash while Stella licked his calf so thoroughly, he wished he'd worn jeans instead of shorts.

"Thank you," Savannah breathed, touching the car door to unlock it. "Now, listen to me, Josh. She has to have her stuff near her at all times. It's her comfort." She reached into the car and pulled out a cushy, fuzzy dog bed. "She has to sleep in this bed every night and usually all day. It's very important for her happiness. Keep it with her all the time. Even if you go somewhere, she has to have the bed, okay? Otherwise, she'll get her days and nights mixed up, and believe me, you don't want that if you value sleep."

He took the pillowy bundle, looking down to see some toys, treats, a blanket, and a few cans of dog food. "Got it. When are you coming back?"

"I'm...not entirely sure how long I'll be gone."

"A week?" he suggested. He could handle a week. He might be able to handle two.

She bit her lip, brows drawing together, with a look of uncertainty on her face. "Maybe a month or so?"

His eyes popped.

"She doesn't need much but food and love," she said quickly. "And maybe you can get her trained so that when I get back she won't be so hard to deal with. You can ask your pretty new tenant to help."

Oh, that would be a fun conversation to have after he'd told her his stance on pets. "I'll figure something out," he said, watching Stella circle again.

Savannah searched his face, her eyes full of that unreadable emotion again. It had to be guilt, but it seemed to go deeper than that. "I know I screwed up, Josh. I know I did a stupid thing giving you up, but I need to do this. It's the right thing to do."

Take a vacation with his stepbrother? In whose world was that the "right" thing to do? He shook his head, unwilling to discuss it anymore. "Okay," he said. "Have a good trip."

"Thank you, Josh. You're a doll. Always were the sweetest guy." She blew him a kiss and yanked the driver's side door open. In less than five seconds, she revved the SUV and took off, leaving him staring at the North Carolina plate as it got smaller.

And then he felt something warm and wet dribble down his sock and into his shoe. Looking down, he and Stella were both standing in a pool of pee. She looked up, terrified, then nuzzled his sneaker in shame.

"It's all right, kid," he said, tugging the leash and nearly dropping the bed and all its contents. "You're a poor blind fool who's been thrown overboard for Gideon Bucking. Trust me, I know exactly how that feels."

Chapter Six

D arcy woke at the sound of a bark coming from outside, pulling her from a dream. She'd lived with and around dogs for most of her life, so a dog wouldn't usually wake her, but this one sounded...strange.

She rolled over to check Kookie, who was curled up in one corner of the antique cradle that had rocked two generations of Kilcannons next to their parents' bed. Of course, her brothers had teased her mercilessly about the dog bed, but even in the teasing, there had been love and a little sentimentality. Hell, if Kookie didn't sleep in it, she thought Andi and Liam would have wanted to claim the cradle for baby Fiona, but it was so old it no longer met modern safety standards.

Who could blame them? Their mother had retired the cradle after six kids, turning it into a toy for Darcy's many dolls. When Darcy had moved back home after Mom died and stored some stuff in the attic, Kookie had discovered it, jumped in, and fallen sound asleep. She'd slept in it ever since, in a corner in Darcy's room.

Outside, the dog barked again, a little louder, followed by a whine. And it definitely came from the courtyard. Throwing off the comforter, Darcy sat up, and of course, Kookie did, too, the moonlight streaming in to show her little hairy head lifted in curiosity.

Climbing out of bed, Darcy headed to the French doors and opened one side, stepping on to the small balcony that faced the courtyard. Now she could really hear another stream of barks, some shuffling, then a man's voice that was too low to make out what he was saying, but Darcy could detect a note of desperation in the murmured words. What the heck was going on down there?

She squinted into the moonlit area, scanning the shadows and small path that ran the perimeter and crossed in the middle.

A man stepped out from behind a bush, making Darcy suck in a soft breath. Well, if it wasn't her *boyfriend* the hot landlord in nothing but sleep pants.

"Stella!" he called in a hushed whisper.

She bit her lip, almost laughing. The dog might be named after a clothing designer and not a character in *A Streetcar Named Desire*, but the man sounded like a bad Marlon Brando impersonator.

She heard a bark from the shadows and bushes in the far corner. Was that the blind dog she'd met today? So the ex must have left her dog with him…in the House of Rules.

"Oh, irony. How I love thee."

In the scant moonlight, she could make out his stance, hands on hips, head turning from side to side as he tried to find the dog.

"Stella, *please*. I can't see you either." Even from two stories above him, Darcy could hear some heartbreaking ache and frustration. Peering into the darkness for a few minutes, she finally spied the dog, using the advantage of height and the light of the moon on her white fur.

The moon that was also like a spotlight on Hot Landlord's shirtless jaw-dropper of a body. Man, God must have been in a good mood the day he made that one.

He moved with the kind of masculine grace that always caught Darcy's attention, easy and solid and comfortable with all those muscles. His dark hair looked tousled from the million times he must have run his fingers through it, making Darcy's hands itch for a chance to do the same thing.

When he stopped, turned his back to her, and put his hands on narrow hips and huffed out yet another noisy breath, she stepped to the wrought-iron railing and leaned over to see it all. Yes, that was one very sculpted, sexy stunner of a man who not only didn't want dogs in the building, but currently had responsibility for one he couldn't even handle.

Kookie padded around the cradle, whimpered, and let out her own little bark at the disruption of her precious sleep.

"Shhh." Darcy waved over her back.

"Stella, please come out." True despair floated up to her balcony, taking Darcy's attention from the man to the dog, who really might need help.

Stella let out a soft wail, furrowing under some bushes. That sound reached Kookie, who stood straight in alert mode and started to bark, loud and hard. If there was one thing Kookie couldn't take, it was an unhappy dog.

And neither could Darcy.

She let out a soft whistle, making him turn and look up. "She's over there. To your right, about twenty feet."

She saw those big shoulders drop a bit—probably because Mr. No Pets Allowed was breaking his own rules—then he nodded thanks and took off after the dog. She watched from her vantage point, saw him get closer, then a flash of white when Stella got spooked by something and darted to the other side of the courtyard.

He let out another sigh and looked up at her and even from this distance, she saw concern for the dog in his eyes. "Hey. Rapunzel."

"I prefer Juliet."

"Did you see where she went?"

She didn't hesitate for even a second. "Hang on," she called down to him. *And you better be prepared to bargain.*

She closed the door and headed to Kookie's cradle to comfort her. "There's a poor little blind dog down there who needs my help."

Kookie barked as if to say "Then move it."

Darcy gave her quick pet. "And a big handsome sexy landlord who's about to put a little addendum to the renter contract."

Kookie shuddered and sighed, as if she understood and approved of that, then tucked into a ball to go back to sleep.

Slipping into flip-flops, Darcy grabbed a handful of treats from a jar on the counter and headed out, taking the steps to the back door that led to the courtyard.

Once outside, the night air cooled her skin, making her aware that she wore little more than a thin tank top and cotton PJ pants. Oh well. It was more than he wore. And surely it would help her at the negotiating table.

It took Josh a moment to catch his breath after Darcy disappeared, and it wasn't because he'd been running after the dog. She left him freaking breathless, that's why. Up there on that balcony, she was like an angel, an apparition, a goddess in the sky hovering above him with her sweet voice and halo of hair and…

Shit. He had to get a grip. She was a woman, and his tenant. And no doubt she'd extort a pound of flesh from him for this favor.

Not that he'd mind one single pound of her flesh.

He shook off the thought, forced himself to focus, and walked to the doorway where she would come out from the back stairs. He could still hear Stella whining, a sound that cracked his heart wide open. But every time he'd get close to the sound, she'd scurry under bushes and out of sight.

He'd finally had her settled down in that bed Savannah left, but then Stella had gotten up and started trotting around the apartment, bumping into every piece of furniture until she made her way to the door. Without bothering to find her leash, he ran her out here, set her down, and wham, she bolted.

The back door opened with a noisy creak that he made a mental note to fix. Then Darcy stepped into the moonlight, and all mental notes evaporated. How did she roll out of bed and look like that, all soft and sweet and sexy?

She raised a cupped hand. "I have the magic."

No kidding. "Treats?" he guessed.

"And the view from above." She hesitated a second as she reached him, her gaze dropping over him, searing him with a slow, interested appraisal. Then she notched her head to the left. "She's back there, and if you let me go alone and quietly, I'll get her for you."

He nodded, and she breezed by him, leaving a wake of something that smelled like spring flowers and fresh-cut limes and heaven. Helpless, he followed.

She tiptoed to the far edge of the courtyard where the landscaping was thick and low. Without saying a word, she tossed a treat in the air, letting it land on the path, and a few seconds later, he heard the tap of tiny paws.

Crouching down, she opened her hand and beckoned Stella, whispering her name very softly. Josh stayed back but had a full view as Darcy sat on the ground, one hand out and one skinny strap of a tank top slipping over her shoulder.

Oh boy.

Finally, Stella came into view, moving with uncertainty and distrust. That poor kid, Josh thought, finally focusing on something other than Darcy.

"Here you go," Darcy coaxed without moving from her spot. "You can do it. You can have another."

Finally, Stella was right in front of her, eating the

treat from the ground. Instantly, she sat down and looked straight ahead for more.

"Oh, someone taught you to sit for treats."

Josh had taught her, and it had been easy because when he first adopted the dog for Savannah, she was spunky and smart and fearless. Now, she didn't trust anyone or anything.

Except this woman with the treats.

"Good girl." Darcy lifted her hand, making sure the dog could smell the cookies. "Here you go, baby love. All for you."

She got up and came closer, giving a soft mewing sound from her throat that could have been fear or distrust or utter relief to have been found.

"I won't hurt you, honey. You can trust me. I have goodies that you want. Sweet goodies. Delicious treats."

Oh, she sure did. Josh managed a slow breath at the invitation, issued to a dog but hitting him right in the libido.

Darcy's words must have been enough for Stella to relax, because she finally came all the way to the treats, letting Darcy carefully and tenderly lift her onto her lap. There, Stella settled down to accept this woman's slow, loving strokes and tender kisses.

Holy crap, how did a creature get that lucky?

"Nice work, dog whisperer," he said, standing above her and looking down.

She dropped her head back and gazed up at him, as beautiful upside down as right side up, with the added benefit of unwittingly offering him a peek down the tank top. Everything in him short-circuited, so he instantly walked around her and dropped to the stone path to sit across from her.

"I come from a long line of dog folk," she said, still petting Stella. "Not much experience with blind ones, though."

"Could have fooled me." He reached out and patted Stella's head. "Hey, kid. You okay?"

The dog nuzzled deeper into the nest of the warm woman, avoiding his touch.

"She's shaking a little," Darcy said, as if that explained why the dog would shun him for a stranger. "And maybe she's more comfortable with females, having been raised by one."

He huffed a breath. "She used to be my pal," he said. "And I've only been gone for a month and four days."

Darcy's brow shot up with interest. "Still counting the days, are we?"

He let out a guilty laugh. "It was a tough breakup, and leaving this little thing…" He leaned closer and managed to pet her paw. "Was a little harder than I expected it to be."

"So you're dog-sitting for an ex who tore up your heart." That made her smile. "That's a point in the Nice Guy column."

"Or the Big Idiot column," he replied. "I'm keeping her dog for a month while Savannah goes on vacation with her new boyfriend, who happens to be my stepbrother."

She inched back, making a face. "Dude. That's a helluva sob story. Almost makes me like you."

"Don't go overboard."

She laughed softly and nestled Stella closer, leaning over to whisper, "Think he'll make a deal with me, Stell?"

"Oh, I already know what you want, Miss Kilcannon."

"No, you don't, Hot Landlord."

That made him laugh. And instantly wonder *what* she wanted and how—or *if*—he could possibly say no. "You want to keep your dog," he guessed. "Who is currently asleep in a cradle up there on Juliet's balcony. Am I right?"

"Not *on* the balcony," she corrected. "That would be a *liability*." She dragged out the word, mocking him with the sweetest twinkle in her eyes.

Oh, yeah. This assist was going to cost. And he might like it a lot.

But then she squished up her face. "And how'd you know about the cradle?"

"I saw it being moved in on the shoulders of who I'm presuming is one of many brothers."

"Four. All moving me into the Dog-Free Zone. Or...what *was* the Dog-Free Zone because you can't enforce your precious rules on me and break them yourself."

He huffed out a sigh of resignation. "Yes, you can keep your dog if she doesn't go near the construction. Kookie, is it? I mean, she," he corrected quickly.

Darcy pointed to him. "There's hope for you yet."

"I really do like dogs," he said, surprised at how important it was for her to believe him.

"Ever have one of your own?"

"One. Roscoe." He gave a humorless smile. "He left me far too soon." Along with others in this life.

"Aww. Well, you have decent instincts, but don't take out a blind dog out without a leash."

"Lesson learned. I'm still getting used to her being

blind." He let his gaze slide down to Stella, who looked as happy and content as she had since arriving earlier that day. "You seem to have quite a touch."

She stroked the white fur, silently confirming that. "There are some really specific things you can do from a training and home setup standpoint for blind dogs," she said. "I don't know if you heard me tell your ex, but my family owns a canine training and rescue facility a few miles out of town. We could help you."

A rush of relief rolled over him. "That'd be great."

They both were quiet for a beat, the only sound was Stella's low-grade snore. Thank God, she was relaxed.

"But I want more than Kookie in my new apartment," she finally said.

He swallowed as she looked at him, her blue gaze steady and warm and direct. Good God, please let her say she wanted him. "You have more dogs?" he guessed.

"I have a different...need."

Okay, here we go. There was no way he'd turn this down. Heat rolled through him from the bottom up, making him lean a little closer. "You do."

She nodded slowly. "I need something from you."

A trickle of sweat meandered down his back as tension and desire and everything that made him a man tightened and hardened and threatened to choke him. He looked down at Stella, curled on her thighs, her back pressing against small but feminine breasts, her tail resting on the silky skin of Darcy's arm.

Right at that moment, he'd kill to be that dog. "What do you need?" His voice came out gruff through a thick throat.

"Be my boyfriend."

"*What?*"

She laughed at his outraged response. "Only if my father asks."

He shook his head, stunned at the request. "I can't do that. I don't even know you," he said.

"Well, it's not for *real*. I need you, if you run into my dad for any reason, to give him the impression I'm, you know, off the market. Maybe be seen with me out in public so the rumor mill whispers something in his ear."

She wanted a fake boyfriend? "Why?"

"So he'll stop trying to turn my life into an episode of *The Bachelorette*."

"Why don't you tell him to stop?"

"And tell the sun not to shine while I'm at it." She rolled her eyes dramatically. "You don't know this man. He's relentless. And he already said he'd back off, or I thought he did. But as soon as I met you, I knew what he was up to. Going for match number six in the Kilcannon family."

"Maybe if he's that good at it, you'll like one of these guys he's setting you up with," he suggested. "Then you'd have a real boyfriend." The idea hit a little harder than it should.

"I don't want a *real* boyfriend," she replied. "I've finally moved out on my own, and I'm starting my own dog grooming business in town. The last thing I need is a boyfriend. I need a deflection. Could you do that for me?"

For a long time, he scanned her face, zeroed in on her mouth, and felt his whole body gear up for a trip down heartbreak lane. Then Stella snuggled tighter against Darcy and lapped her tongue over the rise of the breast he'd been admiring and all bets were off.

No, he wouldn't. Not ever again. He'd never put himself in that position again, and any amount of time with her would be…dangerous. This was not a woman he could resist, and she wasn't one who'd ever be a one-night stand.

That was all he was allowed under current Joshua Ranier Rules, and unfortunately, that part wasn't on her little bargaining table.

"I can't," he managed to say, knowing it would have been easier to eat nails.

"Do you have another girlfriend hiding in the woodwork?" she challenged.

"I don't have or want a girlfriend," he said, vehemently enough that she drew back an inch.

"Savannah really did a number on you, didn't she?"

"Yes, and the number was zero, which is the amount of times I will ever let myself get deeply involved with a woman again." Casually, physically, and horizontally? Yes. But not with a woman like Darcy. Once would never be enough.

"I'm not asking to get *deep*," she insisted. "On the contrary, it's my complete desire *not* to settle down that makes my father act like this. If he thinks I'm even toying with the idea, he'll cool off completely. At the right time, we'll 'break up' for his benefit as easily and painlessly as we got together."

He studied her for a long time, trying to imagine spending any amount of time with this woman and not wanting more. "No," he said. "I have one rule—"

"You have fifty rules."

"—and that is no lying, ever. And that would be a mess of lies. So, sorry, the answer is no."

"Really." She angled her head and added a playful frown of confusion. "No lying, huh?"

"Never, ever. I despise liars."

"But I heard you lie."

"No, you didn't."

"What would you call it when you told your ex I was moving in with you?"

Oh, man. "It just came out that way. I didn't…" He scowled at her. "You were eavesdropping?"

"Don't tell me, that's rule number two."

"But you *listened*?"

"But you *lied*?"

He shuddered out a breath. "She got the wrong impression, which I immediately corrected."

"Then let my dad get the wrong impression, and don't correct it…" She inched forward. "And I'll help you with the dog." Still holding Stella, she extended her hand. "Deal?"

He stared at her fingers and inched back, already feeling himself being reeled in by this impossible, adorable, irresistible woman. And when she was done with him, she'd toss him back in the water and look for the next catch. "The answer is no."

Her whole face fell in disappointment, doing something stupid to his heart…like make it long for that smile to come back.

She let out a sigh and stood so gracefully that she didn't even wake up the dog. "Okay, then. Bye."

Bye? "But will you help me with her?"

"Sure, but don't expect me to cover for you when Stella's owner comes back and wonders why only one pillow on your bed has a dent in it."

His gut squeezed at the thought of her in his bed, denting pillows and mattresses and *each other*. "I don't expect anything," he said, also getting up. "And neither does she."

She looked up at him, a good eight inches shorter than he was in bare feet. "And I get to keep Kookie even after you've given this dog back."

He nodded. "Just don't let her near the construction site, okay?"

"Of course not." She handed her furry bundle to him, making Stella squirm as she was transferred to a harder chest and thicker arms. "I'll pick her up in the morning and take her to work with me," she said. "I'm at my family's canine center all day tomorrow, and she'll be fine. In the evening, we can go over some simple rules for having her in your home. You'll like that, right? More rules."

"I love rules." Like the one he was clinging to right now: *never, ever again.*

"Great." She tipped her head to the side and gave him that crazy-cute smile. "I'd kiss you to seal the deal, but I'm sure there's a no-kissing rule, right?"

Wrong. "Right."

"Smart."

Really? Because right then it felt really stupid to him.

Chapter Seven

The sight of Gramma Finnie rocking on the porch, laptop open, gnarled fingers flying, gave Darcy a kick of joy. Not only because her grandmother was probably one of the few successful octogenarian bloggers on the Internet, but also because Gramma had had a blind dog once and Darcy needed some advice.

The ride over here from home had been sheer hell. Stella snarled, snapped, and growled at Kookie, rejecting any attention from her, terrified to let any person or any dog close to her. But Kookie, used to being loved by everyone, wouldn't let her be. Darcy had ended up putting Stella in a crate in the back of her car, making the poor baby whine all the way over, and Kookie barked until Darcy wanted to cry.

All of Darcy's brothers and the trainers were with dogs and clients, and Darcy had only twenty minutes until her first grooming appointment. But that would be long enough to get some input from Gramma Finnie, and maybe some help keeping an eye on her. Kookie shot toward the training pen and kennels as soon as Darcy opened the door, as if to show that whining pooch in the back just how well she was liked by others.

Darcy reached into the crate and cradled little Stella, whispering soothing words as she headed to the porch.

"And who is this wee darlin'?" Gramma asked, setting her laptop to the side to pin her gaze on Darcy and the new arrival.

"My latest project," she said, carrying the dog closer. "Her name is Stella, and she's completely blind."

"Oh, a Chinese crested!" Gramma was up in a flash, so remarkably spry for a woman deep into her eighties, coming close to greet the dog. "Are you grooming her today?" she asked as she slid her hands into the soft fur.

"I'm watching her to help out my landlord, who's been asked to keep her for a month, but oh my heavens, she can't stand Kookie." She rubbed the dog's fur some more and found that spot under her chin she seemed to like to have scratched. "I'm telling you, it was hate at first sight."

"Hate?" Dad's voice made her turn to see him stepping out on the patio, a look of concern on his face. "You hate the man who owns your building?"

Darcy snorted a laugh. Of course that would panic the Dogfather. Well, Rule-Obsessed Ranier might not go along with her plan, but that wouldn't stop her from steering Dad in the other direction. "I wouldn't call it hate," she said with a sly smile.

But she wasn't sure he'd heard her, because his attention was fully on the dog now, frowning as if Stella was the only thing this veterinarian cared about. "She's blind?" he asked.

"SARDS," Darcy confirmed.

"How old?" he asked, taking the dog's head in his hand with the strong and gentle touch that animals—and his kids, for that matter—always responded to.

"Uh, I'm not sure. She belongs to Josh's girlfriend—"

"He has a girlfriend?"

"*Ex*-girlfriend," she corrected quickly. "He's got Stella for a month and is utterly clueless about how to manage a blind dog. Which worked in my favor because he has a no-pets rule, so now I can keep Kookie. Did you know that, Dad, when you set me up…to live there?"

"I most certainly did not." His focus was torn between the conversation and the blind dog, but the dog won. "You look like an otherwise healthy little girl."

"Except she hates Kookie and she's scared of every sound, movement, and breath. I don't know more than rudimentary things about training a blind dog, but wasn't Laddie blind, Gramma?"

"Aye, he was," she confirmed. "Of all the setters we've had in this family, I had such a weakness for that one."

"Speaking of, where's Rusty?" Darcy asked. "If he comes tromping out here to sniff a new dog, Stella will lose her mind."

"Let me see this sweet Stella," Dad said gently, easing the dog from Darcy's arms. "Rusty's asleep in my office, so we're safe for now. Let's take a look at you, little one."

Everything else was momentarily forgotten as Dad settled the dog in his arms with the same tenderness

Darcy saw when he held baby Fiona. "Do you know if she has any other diseases or issues? Kidney problems?"

"No idea."

"How long has she been blind?" Dad was in full vet mode now.

"I think the owner said a few weeks. I'd have to confirm."

"Oh, that's good. Less than a month is very good."

Darcy felt a frown pull. "Why?"

"I want to see if she's a candidate for reversal." He stroked the pup's cheek again. "She might be just the dog we're looking for."

Darcy inched back. "Reversal of the blindness? Is that even possible? I thought SARDS was permanent."

He gave a look that said he wasn't so sure of that. "It has been, for the past ten years or so since it was first diagnosed, but veterinary ophthalmologists have been working, with some success, on an experimental treatment. Judith Walker, who teaches at Vestal Valley College, and I were talking about this when we had dinner last week."

"You had dinner with a lass?" Gramma inquired with way too much interest.

"She's a professor of veterinary medicine," he said, throwing her a look. "And she asked if Molly or I had seen any good candidates for a study they're doing on a new procedure to cure this very disease. They're approaching the final approval stage and need one more round of perfect candidates." He held Stella a little higher, scrutinizing her eyes. "Which you might be, pretty girl."

"Dad." Darcy clasped her hands. "How awesome if you could give this dog back her sight!"

"Well, there are a lot of research study hoops to jump through, first, but we'd have to do them fast before Judy gets another patient lined up."

"Judy, is it?" Gramma Finnie asked with a sly smile.

Dad narrowed his eyes at his mother. "Et tu, Brute?"

"I'm a wee bit surprised, is all. You never mentioned having dinner with a Judy Walker."

"Because he's sixty and doesn't need us clearing his dates," Darcy said.

"It wasn't a date, it was a…a *professional encounter*, and if you want this dog in the running for the treatment, we need to get the owner's approval for certain injections and quickly. The dogs in the program have to have acquired SARDS recently. Thirty days, forty-five tops."

"Well, Josh said she was normal when he last saw her, which was a month ago." A month and four days, but that seemed excessive to add.

"Where is this ex-girlfriend of Josh's?" He added a look. "You did say *ex*, right?"

"Most definitely an ex. All he said is she was traveling for a month, but I'm sure he can reach her and get approval. Of course, he'll want to know the risks and process. And so do I. Is it a dangerous procedure?"

"Not at all, and they've had some success in the past, but Judy needs to find three more candidates before she can go ahead with the experimental treatments and have them qualify for final approval. So Josh should meet her as soon as possible, because time is of the essence. I'd love to give this dog her sight back, Darcy."

A thrill rippled through her at the possibility. "That would be amazing, Dad."

"Great. Why don't the four of us have dinner and she can explain everything about the surgery?"

The four of them have dinner? "Like a double date?" Darcy asked on a smile. "Or would this be a 'professional encounter'?"

Even Gramma snickered at that, but Dad managed a totally straight face as he pointed to Stella. "It's about the dog, Darce."

"Got it."

Still, she didn't mind the idea at all, and from the look of satisfaction on his face, neither did Dad.

"Hello? Knock, knock? Anybody up here?"

Josh turned off the noisy heat gun he had aimed at the linoleum floor, cocking his head at the woman's voice he'd heard over the buzzing noise.

"Hello? I'm coming in, ready or not."

Not. He was never ready for her. Not last night in the dark courtyard. Not this morning, when she'd shown up all glowing and glorious in a baby-blue T-shirt that matched her eyes and hugged her body. And not now when he was trying hard to work and not think about Darcy Kilcannon.

But he'd thought of little else that day.

"Don't bring a dog in here," he called out, looking at the materials and sharp tools spread around the kitchen floor.

"No dogs, just me and some really exciting news." She appeared in the framed kitchen doorway, tucking her hands into the front pockets of her jeans. "Whoa, what are you doing?" she asked.

"Testing the linoleum seams to figure out the best way to lift it."

She glanced around, making a face at the yellow metal cabinets and chipped Formica counters. "Did my apartment look like this before you renovated it?"

"Worse, actually."

"And you did it yourself?"

"Mostly." Setting down the heat gun, he pushed the goggles over his head and grabbed a rag to wipe his hands. "How's Stella?"

"She's fine. Great, as a matter of fact, or could be." She gingerly stepped over some tools and leaned against the counter, regarding him like she had a secret she could barely contain. "How would you like to restore her vision?"

"Is that possible?" He'd read a few articles on SARDS after Savannah left Stella with him, and nothing he'd seen said it could be cured.

"We're not sure, but my dad thinks she might be a candidate for a specialized, experimental treatment to cure SARDS that is in the final stages of approval in a study. He's friends with the head of veterinary ophthalmology at Vestal Valley College right here in Bitter Bark, and she's looking for canine candidates."

Still wiping his hands, he processed this incredible news. "What do we need to do?"

As the words slipped out, he realized they'd just become a *we*, something he'd sworn wouldn't happen.

But these were extenuating circumstances. He'd be a *we* if Stella could see.

"We need to get her health history, all of her records, and, of course, her owner's approval," Darcy said. "They need to know how old she is and as close to a specific date as possible for when she started losing her sight. Didn't Savannah say Stella only had this a few weeks?"

"That's when she noticed it." He frowned, thinking back to that morning and the way Stella had circled and stared past him. "You know, she could have been going blind before that. She was weird the last time I saw her."

"It matters a lot," she told him. "The longer she's had the disease, the less chance of a cure."

"I'll try and find out, but I don't know…"

"Swallow your pride and call Savannah," she said. "Do it for the dog."

"It's not about pride, Darcy." He blew out a breath, remembering their last conversation. "She's off the grid. Went on some adventure vacation."

"But she didn't go without a cell phone," Darcy replied. "Anyone with a brain—and a blind dog—has to be reachable. What about if there was an emergency? Who would leave her dog in someone else's hands and not be sure you have a way to reach her?"

He replayed the conversation in his head. "She was in a hurry, and all she told me about was the bed Stella likes."

"She didn't leave a medical release, by any chance? It's common when dogsitting for a long period."

"No, and I was too stunned by the turn of events to think of it at the time," he admitted. "My mother or stepfather might know how to reach Gideon, so we could get to her that way."

"What about her family? Mother or sister or someone?"

He shook his head. Savannah had cut ties with her family years ago. She'd left the double-wide where she'd grown up and never looked back. "Maybe her clients can reach her," he said. "She's a stylist and personal shopper for a lot of my mother's friends."

"Worth a try to help that little darling," Darcy said. "She really doesn't play well with others."

"I thought I heard some barking when you were getting into your car."

"She's so scared of other dogs," she told him. "And people. And walls. And grass. And—"

"I get the idea," he said. "All the more reason to do whatever is necessary to help her."

"She's getting some help today," she told him, glancing around again. "My brothers are the best in the dog training business, and I handed her over when I left." She pointed at a kitchen cabinet. "If my place was this ugly, you do really good work."

"Thanks. What will they do to help her?"

"They'll start her slow with our friendliest, most tolerant dogs. She might not be a pack dog by the end of the day, but I'm hoping she can tolerate the smell and sound of another dog. I need her to get along with Kookie, at least. So you actually added that balcony?"

"The balconies were there, but needed reinforcement and new railings. Then I knocked out the window and made it floor-to-ceiling. Same with the bedroom, like yours. The balconies were there, but only for decoration. Now you can use them. Where's Kookie? I thought you never went anywhere without her."

"She was pretty happy to be back home, so I let her hang with my grandmother while I had a break and zipped over here. I wanted to tell you this news in person." She reached out and put a hand on his arm. "Josh, we have to make this happen. We have to help Stella get her sight back."

He glanced down at her fingers clutching him and sending electrical charges up his arm. Or maybe that was the fact that she'd finally used his name and not some inane nickname.

"A chance like this won't come along often," she continued. "We have to find Savannah."

"I'll try calling." He suddenly found it incredibly weird that not only didn't he know where his ex was, right that minute he was having a hard time remembering what she looked like.

"And our next step is to meet with my father and Dr. Walker, the vet ophtha handling this. Dad wants to set up a dinner with the four of us to tell you everything about the procedure."

He let out a breath, studying her. "Darcy."

"What? Please don't tell me that's against some rule, because it's not a da—"

"No." He stopped her with one finger on her lips.

Her eyes widened, and she inched away from his touch. "It's not a date," she insisted. "You don't have to worry."

"That's not what I was going to say." He searched her face, looking into her eyes—falling into them, honestly—trying to figure out the last time he'd ever met anyone like her. Never. "I don't know how to thank you."

"Oh, that." She gave a quick shrug. "Dogs are life to us, and this is what we do."

"But you just swooped in and..." Gave him the first glimmer of hope he'd felt in a month. "I'm really grateful."

"How grateful?" Her brows rose in a question, making him let out a nervous laugh. What did she want? Another lie? Another deal? Something better?

"Very grateful." He hesitated and then had to ask, "Why?"

Once again, she looked around the half-demolished kitchen. "Are you grateful enough to help me transform a real estate office into a grooming salon?"

A mix of relief and disappointment rolled through him. "Of course. It's the least I could do for what you're offering my dog."

"*Your* dog?" She gave him a playful poke in the arm. "Watch it, big guy. Potential attachment with heartache possibilities if you're not careful."

As much as he didn't want to, he laughed. Because there was truth in all humor. And there certainly was potential attachment with heartache possibilities dead ahead.

Chapter Eight

Dad arranged the dinner meeting for that very night. A fact, Darcy figured out quickly, that made its way all around Waterford Farm by midafternoon. First, Shane came into the grooming studio to bring Stella in for a rest after training and peppered Darcy with so-not-subtle questions. Oh, sure, he had a report on Stella's progress—slow—but mostly he was interested in the dinner...and Dad's friend.

Liam was a little more open in his questioning, but after Darcy assured him this was strictly business, he spent the rest of his brief visit talking about Fiona. And yawning, since he got up with Andi every time the baby cried, so they were both sleep-deprived.

Garrett came in a few minutes later, bringing along a brand-new rescue named Boomer, a springer spaniel with a thick brown coat and white chest. Except the chest was currently as brown as the coat.

"Boo hit some mud down by the creek," Garrett told her with a laugh. "Needs a Special Darcy Bath, fast."

"Dip him and whip him...into shape?" she teased, already making room for him on her table. "I can do him right now before my next appointment."

"Oh, great, Darce," her brother said, hoisting up the dog. "I've got a family coming in late this afternoon to consider adoption, so make him gorgeous."

"He is gorgeous." She gave his head a scratch and got close to his face, gazing into sad green eyes. "Don't worry, Boomer. You're going to save someone real soon, I promise."

Garrett smiled and headed toward the back, looking like every man did in here—out of place in her glittery, sparkly, pink grooming studio. "Oh, I didn't know anyone was back here," he said as he came upon the comfy crate where Stella slept.

At the sound of his voice, the dog got up and barked, backing away, then turning in a circle.

"That's our Stella, blind and beautiful and terrified of the world."

"Oh, this is the dog Shane was working with before. I was giving a class with a new group of trainees, so I missed her arrival." Garrett opened the crate very slowly, easing closer to let Stella get a sniff.

"Then you haven't heard the latest family gossip," she said with a tease in her voice.

"That Dad's seeing Dr. Walker?" He kept his voice soft and modulated, knowing Stella's hearing would be hypersensitive because of the blindness. "And you're tagging along with the landlord that Dad thinks you should marry?"

"Or maybe you *have* heard the latest family gossip."

"Bits and pieces," he admitted.

She clipped Boomer into the bath harness. "I'm hoping that this new project will take Dad's mind off fixing me up for a while."

"He won't." Garrett laughed. "The man has issues."

"Huge."

"Well, maybe he'll be so into Judy Walker that he forgets you." He added a sly grin. "Jessie's put her money on Judy for the betting pool, so of course I have a vested interest."

Darcy rolled her eyes. "If Dad finds out there's an actual pool, he won't be happy."

"Only 'cause he's not in it." Garrett managed to get Stella to calm down, reaching into the crate to pet her with a magical touch all the Kilcannon men had in spades with dogs.

"I'm hoping he gets mad enough to see that all this matchmaking should stop for any of the single people in the family."

"That would be you, him, and Gramma."

"If you don't count the Mahoneys and the next generation."

He laughed easily. "Oh, yeah, his grandkids. He has four now. By the time he's Gramma Finnie's age, it could be a full-time job."

She frowned as she brushed some knots out of Boomer's coat before turning on the spray. "Four? Pru, Christian, and Fiona make…" Her voice faded as she looked over the dog's head to meet her brother's horrified expression.

"Whoops," he said. "Wasn't supposed to mention that yet."

"Garrett!"

"Darcy!" he echoed, laughing as he slid Stella back

into her crate, knowing that he was about to get smooshed in a sisterly hug.

"Oh my God!" She abandoned the dog on the table and rushed to her brother. "Jessie's pregnant?"

"Shhh." He hugged her back, adding a squeeze. "It's a secret until Sunday. She wanted to tell everyone at the same time, at dinner. I blew it, probably because I can't think about anything else."

"This is so wonderful. Jessie Curtis used to practically live here, and now you guys are having a baby." She pressed her hands to her face. "I'm so happy for you."

"Why are you so happy for him? Jessie's the one having the baby." Molly's voice came from the hall, making Darcy slap her hand over her own mouth as she realized she'd let out Garrett's secret. "Sorry," she muttered.

"Don't be," Molly answered for him, coming into the studio. "Do you forget that Jessie was my best friend before she was yours, Garrett?"

"Of course not."

"Congrats, my darling brother." She slipped one arm around Darcy and one around Garrett. "I had lunch with your wife today, and she blew it. And I don't mean the secret, I mean lunch. Barely made it to the bathroom."

"She got sick?" Garrett drew back, concern all over his handsome face. "Why didn't she call me?"

"Because you were teaching a class, and she gets sick every single day because she's..." She leaned in close and whispered, "Pregnant!"

Garrett laughed as Darcy and Molly gave each other congratulatory hugs for being aunts again.

"Between this and the blind dog, I'd say you're in the clear for a while with Dad," Garrett said to Darcy.

"Except Gramma told me there's a double date tonight," Molly added. "She's now officially betting on 'Dr. Judy.'"

Darcy dropped her head back with a grunt. "This family is cray."

Garrett backed away. "Couldn't agree more, so please, you two, at least let Dad be surprised on Sunday. Jessie wants us to tell the whole family together."

"Promise," Molly said.

"Cross my heart," Darcy agreed. "Now, go and make sure the kennels are sparkling so you can impress Boomer's adoptive family. I'll make him handsome."

He gave each of them a quick kiss on the cheek and started out, then stopped and turned. "My kid's really lucky being born into this family, isn't he?"

"She," they replied in perfect unison, making him laugh.

"And yes," Darcy added.

After he left, Darcy and Molly shared another happy embrace.

"More babies!" Darcy cooed with glee. "Think you and Trace could squeeze out one more?"

Molly laughed, her hazel eyes dancing. "Well, we do have to get married first, and that's not until December."

"Oh please. Pru's two months shy of fourteen. You sure didn't get married first that time."

Molly let out a sigh. "You know, God had other plans."

"Which worked out perfectly." But it hadn't been easy. When Trace showed up after being in prison for almost fourteen years only to find out Molly had had a baby, there were some dicey days. Molly had shared many of the details with Darcy.

"So, can I see Stella?" Molly asked after giving Boomer some love. "I've had quite a few SARDS patients, so I'm interested to see the lucky girl who'll get the treatment."

"Who *might* get the treatment," Darcy corrected. "If Hot Landlord can track down his wayward missing ex-girlfriend."

Molly snorted at the nickname. "How hot?"

"Ask Dad. He's the one who set me up with him."

"Oh, Dad," Molly said on a laugh, but then her expression grew serious as she reached the cage and Stella let out a terrified bark and growl. "But, wait. You mean this guy is watching someone's dog and might not be able to reach her?"

"It's a long story."

"As if that ever stopped us."

"Truth, Sister. Hold that dog for a few minutes and I'll tell you everything."

While Molly calmed Stella down with a rest in the rocker and Boomer submitted to a bath, Darcy relayed the entire story, omitting nothing, not even their cousin's suggestion that they fool Dad to get him to back off.

"Can I just say that really sounds like an Ella Mahoney Dumb Idea?" Molly rolled her eyes. "One I'm sure you rushed to implement."

"Oh yes. And failed completely. He wanted no part of this scheme."

"Good for him." Her sister rocked the dog, slow and steady, the way she probably had held Pru all those years ago when Molly was a young, single mother. "It shows integrity and a strict moral compass for a man to refuse to lie."

"It also shows he's not the least bit interested in me," Darcy mumbled, a little surprised that she dug that feeling out, but then, Molly always got her to be completely honest.

"And how do you feel about that?"

"I couldn't care less." As she lathered Boomer's fur into a froth, she looked over his head at Molly, who smiled like she could read Darcy's mind. Which, of course, she could.

"Okay, I suppose if I tried *really* hard, I could care a little less," Darcy admitted.

Molly's grin grew.

"Well, you should see him, Molls. He's big and strong and so stinking good-looking. He has these incredible brown eyes, and he's got to be six-two, and did I mention he's big?"

"You're not usually taken by a guy's looks," Molly mused.

"I don't usually get handed looks like these," she quipped. "Plus, he really adores Stella, and he's funny and sweet, but man, he got burned in his last relationship." She angled her head and remembered shreds of conversations. "Not to mention he's a rule follower and I'm a free spirit. It can't possibly work."

"I guess it depends on what 'it' is that you want to work."

"I don't want anything," Darcy replied, grabbing the sprayer to rinse Boomer. "Nothing at all."

106

Molly chuckled. "Then why are you whipping that hose around and gnawing on your lip and wallowing in denial?"

"Molly!" She turned off the water to give her sister all her attention. "I'm not in denial. I don't want anything. I mean, not anything serious. Not anything like my lunatic matchmaking father wants."

"I thank him every day for being a lunatic matchmaker," Molly said on a sigh. "If he hadn't urged Trace to come here and have me do surgery on Meatball…"

"You'd be free and single."

"Who wants that?"

Darcy stared at her.

"Oh, Darce. You'll get through this phase."

Irritation spiked up her back, making her straighten. "It's not a *phase*, Molly. It's a lifestyle. It's a choice. It's called not depending on a man for happiness, or anyone, at least not while I figure out who I am and what I can do on my own."

For a long time, her sister rocked and looked at her, while Darcy hosed off Boomer with maybe a little more enthusiasm than was necessary.

"I understand," Molly finally said. "I don't know what 'freedom' is like, either, since I had a child before I started my second year of college."

Darcy conceded that with a shrug.

"But I fully understand you wanting to move out and start your own business."

"That's not what we're talking about," Darcy said. "This is about a man."

"This is about fear. And control."

"And here I thought you were a vet, not a shrink."

Molly stood slowly, careful not to scare the pupper she held. "You know what, Darcy? Having a man in your life doesn't mean you give up control or freedom. In some ways, you have so much more."

Her poor deluded madly-in-love sister. "Mmmm."

Molly laughed. "What's that supposed to mean?"

"It means I want to figure this all out for myself, okay?"

"Fair enough. If you ever have any questions or want to talk, I know I'm not Mom, but I'm always here for you."

The offer touched her, surprising her with a sudden burn behind her eyelids and making Darcy press a warm towel against Boomer with the same ferocity she wanted to hug her sister.

"Don't sell yourself short, Molls. Mom would be so proud of your ability to give advice and rock a dog and make me laugh and cry all in one ten-minute visit. You're cut from the same beautiful cloth she was."

Molly's eyes filled at the compliment, and she somehow managed to wrap Darcy, Boomer, and Stella in her arms. "She sure did leave big shoes for us to fill."

"But you've done it, Molly. Pru's amazing, and you're running two vet offices, and now you're marrying a great guy."

"And now you're going to strike out on your own, live alone, and start your own business."

"I know." Darcy sighed, giving in to a wave of grief that was so rare these days, but still came, unexpected and strong. "I wish I had her here to encourage me. To root me on. To listen to me and understand, because while you're every bit as good at it, I'd still love to hear from her, too."

"I know you and Mom had a very special relationship, Darcy. And she is rooting you on and encouraging you. She is."

"Wish I could hear her, you know? I wish I could hear her voice again."

"She'd tell you to follow your heart."

"Would she tell me to follow any other parts? 'Cause this guy makes me feel…" She blew out a quick breath. "Have I mentioned that Hot Landlord is hot?"

Molly laughed. "Yeah. A few times."

"What would Mom say about that?"

"She'd tell you to be very careful, because she had six kids and I got pregnant from a one-night stand. Hot Landlord might be hot, but Kilcannon women are fertile."

Darcy gasped, horrified. "I'm not…I won't…I'm smarter than that and older than you were, and I could never…" She couldn't finish, the thought was so awful.

"Hey, you asked what Mom would say, and that's what she'd say."

At the sound of Garrett's footsteps in the hall, they ended the conversation right there. But Darcy filed it as one more reason to keep her heart—and other parts—away from Hot Landlord.

Josh hung up the phone after leaving another voice mail for Savannah when he heard a soft tap on his front door.

"Special delivery," Darcy called out. "One very happy little pooch."

But that wasn't the special delivery that made him

take a steadying breath as he rose to answer her siren call.

He needed half an hour to focus after spending five minutes with her. And another hour to stop inhaling the garden of fragrance she left behind. And two more hours to forget the sound of her laugh or the warm touch of her fingertips. Add some time to shake off the occasional strand of long blond hair he found, and bam, there she was again and he had to start all over.

He opened the door slowly, not at all sure what to expect from either female on the other side.

Pink. There was lots and lots of pink. Darcy in a soft pink dress with skinny straps and silky bare shoulders. She held up a wire crate with pink fur and a pillow making a soft throne for Stella, who perched on the cushion wrapped in a pink…thing.

"What is she wearing?"

"An anxiety jacket," Darcy said as she carefully handed over the crate and followed him back in. "We discovered how much and how tightly this dog needs to be held. An anxiety jacket works wonders. See how calm she is?"

"Incredible." He slowly set the crate on the coffee table, but Darcy put her hand on his arm to stop him. And there was that warm touch he'd need two hours to forget.

"In a corner. Under a table. Best of all, under a desk."

Really? "She's blind, Darcy."

"But she can still sense that she's on the ground and surrounded by walls or security. It's the only way to let her spend this evening in the crate."

"Savannah said she had to be on that bed to be

happy." He gestured toward the beige dog bed in the corner.

"We can put the dog bed in the crate, but she's really happy now. I wouldn't mess with success since we have to go out for a few hours." She glanced up and down his body with none of the usual warmth he'd noticed when she'd checked him out before. "Ricardo's is a nice restaurant, by the way."

He plucked at his filthy T-shirt. "I'll shower and change."

"We need to leave in ten minutes."

"It'll take me five. You can wait right here." He could have sworn a little color deepened her cheeks.

"Okay, I'll hang with Stella. But hurry, because my father cannot abide lateness. Move it, hot stuff. Go get...clean."

"I'll be fast," he promised. And he would be. He wasn't about to take a twenty-minute shower thinking about Darcy Kilcannon...calling him hot stuff.

He succeeded, stayed focused, got dressed, and came out to the living room to find Darcy on the floor, pink skirt spread around her and all his sofa cushions in a big square. "Did you build a fort?"

"She loves it," she said, carefully maneuvering the top pillow to get it right. "The pillows muffle the sound, so she knows she's all safe and secure." Turning to him, her eyes glinted in appreciation. "Oh. Wow. You clean up nice." She turned away quickly, her attention on the dog again. "She's made great progress today, which means we can really work on convincing Dr. Walker that Stella is a great candidate for the procedure."

"I haven't reached Savannah yet. The phone isn't

even ringing, but going straight to voice mail, which makes me wonder if she even has it turned on." He walked over to her and bent down to peer into the pillow fort. "Hey there, kid. Did you learn how to share the sandbox at school today?"

Darcy looked up at him, blinding him with an upside-down smile that made him feel like he was at the top of a roller coaster staring down a free fall.

"She stole a lot of hearts at Waterford," she told him. "Mostly two-legged ones, though. She's struggling with other dogs and really uncomfortable in a strange place. That's why it's fine to leave her crated tonight, but we shouldn't stay out too late."

"Where's Kookie?" he asked.

She raised her brows. "Home. Upstairs. You know, where she lives, breaking all the landlord's rules."

He smiled back at her, reaching to help her up. "We have a deal." No surprise, her hand felt small and sweet and right in his. He tried to cover his reaction by looking at the pillows, tapping the top one to confirm how secure it was over Stella's crate. "And anyone who makes Stella a pillow fort with such an eye toward solid construction has my undying professional respect."

"Thank you. I couldn't fit her favorite bed in there, but I put it close so she can smell it." She was suddenly close to his face and…tall.

"You grew."

"Heels." She extended a leg to show off a pair of shoes that someone designed with the sole purpose of making men lose their literal minds. "Whoa. Those are…wow. I didn't notice them before." Which made him the blinder one in this room.

"I had them on when I came in."

"I guess I was distracted by the dog." Hours. It would take many hours to forget those shoes. "Is it even legal to wear those things?"

"Please don't tell me you have rules against heels. How could they not be legal?"

"Because they look deadly…to walk in," he added.

"I do just fine." She strutted a few steps to demonstrate, twirling to make her skirt flare and show off long, sexy legs. "See? Not deadly."

"You're not the one who's going to die," he murmured.

She laughed and leaned her shoulder into his. "Careful. You might convince my dad to stop the setups, and you don't want to tell a lie."

He picked up the remote and turned on the TV. "I'm starting to forget what's real and what's a lie."

"What are you doing?"

"She used to like *Wheel of Fortune* and *Jeopardy.*" He coded in the channel. "Less lonely with Pat Sajak and Alex Trebek."

"Sweet." Darcy smiled at him, nothing but warm affection in her eyes. "But isn't it against the rules to leave the TV on while you're gone?"

He took her arm and led her to the door, squeezing a little bit in response. "Clearly, I break rules where Stella is concerned."

"Good to know."

As he pulled the door closed, he took one last look at the fort, seeing the dog curled in the corner of the crate. "Wish me luck, kid."

Because, with this woman, he needed it.

Chapter Nine

Darcy forgot to eat, which was ridiculous considering she was at one of her favorite restaurants in town. But there were so many distractions that kept her from chowing down on Ricardo's incredible chicken Parm. The whole reason for the dinner—restoring Stella's sight—was enough to keep Darcy's fork in suspended animation as the two seasoned vets at the table explained the arcane details of immunoglobulin injections.

And there was the little bit of chemistry between those two doctors that had Darcy itching for a private moment to text Garrett and tell him Jessie might be on to something with Dr. Judy Walker in the betting pool.

But the real distraction was next to her, inches away on her side of the sizable booth, his thigh occasionally brushing hers, his shoulders so broad and close she could practically rest her head on one, and his intelligent, caring questions showing him to be far from the dog hater she'd once mistook him for.

"How did your research into SARDS start?" Josh asked Judy after their dinners were served.

"For the past decade or so, there's been no hope for

these dogs who were suddenly going blind with no apparent reason." Judy took a sip of wine and smoothed back a lock of dark hair, pinning an intense gaze on Josh and Darcy as she answered. "Then the treatment was developed for humans with immune-mediated retinopathy, and some vets started the research of applying it to a similar disorder with dogs."

"So you're not the only one doing this?" Darcy asked.

"A few other university departments are working on it, and everyone wants to be the first to get it through government approvals," she replied. "It would be a huge coup for the Vestal Valley veterinary program."

"Which is one of the best in the country," Dad added with pride. "I graduated from there, and so did Molly," he told Josh.

Judy gave him a warm smile. Very warm. "You are some of our finest alumni."

"And you're absolutely certain the only downside is that the dog doesn't regain sight?" Josh asked them both. "No chance of any illness or long-term damage or side effects?"

"I give you my word this is safe," she said, adding a smile to the man at her right. "Daniel's been watching me test this new injection mix for well over a year now, and we do have quite a few success stories."

Well over a year? Darcy filed that one away to share with the rest of the Kilcannons.

"But it's not approved by the vet associations and government yet?" Josh asked.

"Some of these immunoglobulin injections are approved for use, but the one we're developing should work much faster. The right candidate could have vision back in three weeks, but only if the patient has been blind for less than forty-five days. And, of course, meets health requirements, especially no diabetes or kidney disorders."

"You still don't know exactly when she went blind?" Dad asked.

Josh shook his head. "Is it gradual?" he asked.

Both doctors shook their heads. "It comes on fast," Judy said. "A week, sometimes two, and the owners rarely notice because dogs are smart and can navigate their familiar environment."

"Did she gain weight or show increased thirst?" Dad asked.

Josh shrugged. "Not noticeably, but she isn't my dog. I wasn't with her every day. The last time I saw her, it had either started or she was already fully blind. I can tell you that she was not herself, already acting scared and staring past me. That was a little over a month ago."

"How little?" Judy asked.

"I'd say thirty-five days."

There was *that* benefit of counting breakup days, Darcy mused, sipping her wine.

Judy bit her lip and looked at Dad. "We have not one second more than ten days if she's going to get the treatment. Maybe less."

Josh glanced at Darcy, surprise and hope in his eyes instead of the pain she'd expect from a man still dressing wounds inflicted on the battlefield of love. "We should do it without her approval," he whispered as Judy and Dad discussed something about the treatment.

"Pretty big rule to bend, Josh."

"Stella deserves this chance."

An all-new tsunami of attraction threatened to drown her. "I agree," she whispered.

"Well, there's one of my favorite customers." Ricardo Mancini broke the moment. He was dressed as always in his chef's jacket and totally unnecessary toque blanche, approaching the table with his infectious laugh and outstretched, always-moving Italian hands. "Hello, Dr. K."

Dad started to stand to greet him, but Ricardo waved him back down and put a hand on Judy's back. "And so nice to see you here again, Dr. Walker."

Because Dad brought her there? Curiosity burned while introductions and greetings were exchanged all around, but then Josh leaned over to get closer to Darcy's ear while the other three talked about some menu changes.

"Is there anyone who doesn't know your dad?" he whispered, sending chills down her back. "He's like the mayor of Bitter Bark."

She slyly pointed to a table across the restaurant. "No, that's the mayor of Bitter Bark, Blanche Wilkins. She's my sister-in-law's aunt. Welcome to Small Town America." She put a hand on his arm to quietly ask, "Do you think you can give the go-ahead without Savannah's approval?"

He studied her, thinking. "I want to, but I don't know if it's the right thing to do."

"Ask my dad," she said without thinking. "He's the king of doing the right thing. He'll give you good advice."

"I will," he promised. "He's obviously a very knowledgeable vet and a caring man."

"I'll have tiramisu sent for the table," Ricardo promised. "I remember you both liked it so much last time."

Last time? So they *were* dating.

Taking another sip of water, Darcy studied Dr. Walker, who had jumped right back into the conversation about Stella. She was, what? Forty-five or fifty at the most? Smart, personable, very attractive, and...not Mom.

How did Dad do this setup thing with such ease? she wondered. Didn't he feel that proprietary sense of—

"Right, Darcy?" Josh asked, yanking her from her thoughts.

She looked up at him, blank.

"I mean, there's a possibility I won't be able to reach her until too much time has passed," he added. "Do I have the right or option to make the choice for her?"

"It's a little complicated," Dr. Walker answered. "To participate in a test procedure like this, the owner has to sign a waiver that's witnessed by at least one person. That document essentially spells out everything that we will do, how we will treat any complications, and waives legal action should anything happen to the patient."

"So, I can't sign on her behalf, even though she left the dog with me while she's gone?" He directed that question to Dad, who didn't answer right away but was clearly considering the idea.

"I suppose you technically do have 'custody,' since Stella is in your care," he said.

"I'd bring her in for emergency care if something happened to her," Josh said.

"But this isn't an emergency," Dad replied.

"She's *blind*." Darcy and Josh said the words at exactly the same time, in the same tone, making the other two smile.

"Why don't you exhaust every resource first?" her father asked. "Talk to her closest family members and friends and maybe those of the person she's traveling with. She isn't alone, right?"

Josh flinched so imperceptibly that most people wouldn't notice. But then, most people weren't staring at his face, memorizing the angles of his jaw and the shape of his lips and the way his long lashes met when he narrowed his eyes in thought. Only Darcy was.

"No, she isn't," Josh answered simply. Of course, Dad had no way of knowing *who* Josh's ex-girlfriend was traveling with or how close to home it hit.

"Can you contact her traveling companion's family?" Dad asked.

He blew out a breath. "I can, but I'd like to do it in person, and then, if someone can reach her, get the document to her immediately by fax or scanning. Would that work?"

Dr. Walker nodded. "We can accept that, but we also have to have Stella's vet records."

Josh's face fell in disappointment. "I don't even know the name of her vet."

"When you reach her owner, she can tell you, and the vet office can email the records on Monday," Dad said.

Of course her father thought this should all be simple, but only Darcy knew the complicated family dynamics and the betrayal Josh had to muscle through. But something told her he'd do that for Stella.

He nodded slowly, thinking. "There's someone who lives in her apartment building who recommended the vet. She might know. I'll probably have to go there," he added. "It's not far, near Lake Norman, north of Charlotte."

"If you go, I'll take care of Stella," Darcy said.

He turned to her. "I was hoping you'd go with me."

She froze, blinked, and willed her heart not to beat so hard it was visible to all the eyes on her at that moment.

"Then *I'll* take care of Stella," Dad said without missing a beat or, Darcy noticed, waiting for her to actually respond. "In fact, we can get some of the preliminary tests out of the way."

Judy leaned forward. "Yes, she needs an optical coherence tomography scan, and I think we could do that this weekend without permission," she said. "It's one hundred percent noninvasive, merely a simple scan that will give us some critical information about her retinas."

Josh was still looking at Darcy, waiting for an answer, holding her gaze with one she couldn't begin to interpret. Was he asking because he needed moral support? To help her with the Dad problem? Or because…he wanted her with him?

Didn't matter. She already knew the answer.

"I'll go," she said. "I don't have appointments this weekend. I was going to work on trying to figure out how to turn a real estate office into a dog grooming shop."

"We've got that covered," he assured her. "I'll go there with you next week, and we can figure out what it will take."

Darcy didn't dare look at her father. Surely she'd see the smug smile of victory, or maybe a question of how this arrangement fit into her burning need for independence. It fit well, she rationalized, since his assistance meant she didn't have to beg Kilcannons for help.

"That sounds great," she said. "And tomorrow, we can bring Stella and Kookie over to Waterford in the morning and drive down to Charlotte and see whoever we need to see."

"*We* can." He put his hand on hers and added the slightest amount of pressure, enough to make her struggle with her next breath. "Thanks."

"No problem." Well, yes, it was a problem. Those delicious lips were a problem. That strong hand was a problem. Those shoulders and that smile and the fact that Darcy wanted to kiss him so much she almost did it right there in front of Dad were all big, fat problems.

And this *we* business could be a problem, too.

But Ricardo arrived with a plate of tiramisu oozing with cream and covered in shaved chocolate, changing the tenor and tone of the table, moving things into the happy, easy laughter that came with the anticipation of something sweet and wonderful.

But, no surprise, Darcy couldn't eat a thing.

Chapter Ten

After saying good night, Josh and Darcy headed out of Ricardo's and paused as they stepped onto the brick-paved street outside.

"I'd suggest we walk through Bushrod Square instead of Ubering back to the building, but..." He pointed at the shoes he hadn't forgotten about all night. "I better get us a ride."

"Are you kidding? These babies are like slippers, and it's a perfect summer night in Bitter Bark." She gestured toward the green space that took up at least a square mile in the heart of town. Inside the stone walls of the square, dozens of hundred-year-old oaks and pines twinkled with white lights, and plenty of late evening walkers strolled with dogs. "I love this place at night."

"You love your town, don't you?" he observed. "I mean, for a person who seems to like travel so much, you have quite the heart for home, too."

"Oh, I do. In fact, that's one of the best parts of traveling—the joy of coming home. Also, I love the start of a trip, too. So much potential. And the thrill of new discoveries and adventures." She tipped her head in gratitude. "So thanks for the opportunity to have another."

Was that what his invitation was to her? For him, it was an impulsive idea that he couldn't resist. "Happy to help."

"So," she said, inching a little closer as they passed a small group of tourists and their dogs, "what do you really think? A thing or not? Dating? In love? Or just friends?"

He replied with a surprise blink. "Should I know that now?"

"Oh, come on, HL. I know I can count on you for the unvarnished truth. What is the nature of this new romance? Maybe I'm seeing things that aren't there, though, but I need to know what to tell my family. Is it just sex or the real deal?"

"Your..." He damn near tripped off the sidewalk. "Okay, well, I thought it made sense for the two of us to go because there's strength in numbers, and you know so much about animals. Plus, you like to travel, and...and...what?"

She bit her lip, and her eyes danced with an unreleased laugh. "I meant my father and Judy. Not anyone else at that table."

"Oh." He chuckled at the mistake. "Sorry."

"I mean, if you want to take a pass at that, knock yourself out. Sex or the real deal?"

Oh man. Slowing his step, he let his gaze slide over her, pausing at every sweet thing along the trip, and there were many. Could it be sex *and* the real deal? No. Hadn't he learned that the hard way? "Let's go back to your dad and his date."

She elbowed him. "Chicken."

Like you wouldn't believe. "Not that my opinion matters, and I've met your father a total of two times, but I picked up a nice vibe."

"A nice vibe? What does that mean?"

He laughed at the way she posed the question and the sheer fun of hanging out with her. "It means they're friends with…"

"Benefits?"

"Mutual interests," he supplied.

"Ahh. Do you think they've kissed?"

"Not yet."

"Really?" They crossed the street and headed to the square, and her ought-to-be-illegal heels tapped on the stone with a perfect rhythm that matched his heart just being this close to her. "How can you tell?"

"Do you spend a ton of time thinking about your dad kissing women? 'Cause, you know, it's a little weird."

"It's my family's new obsession," she told him. "Now that so many Kilcannons are all sewn up and off the market, they all want to get back at him for the matchmaking. In a good way, of course."

"But I thought you were morally opposed to setting people up and blind dates and giving nudges instead of letting nature take its course."

"For *me* I am. And I guess I am for my dad, too, since he doesn't want it. But the truth is, he's such an incredible guy and still so young and has so much love to give. He's mourned a long time, and deeply, but…"

She certainly hadn't talked much about her mother, but he'd picked up bits and pieces and surmised she'd died unexpectedly and within the last few years. "You think he's through his grief?" he asked. "It can take a while."

"He'll never be through it completely. They were the happiest couple and a team like you've never met." She studied him for a moment, empathy in her eyes. "You sound like you know a little bit about losing someone."

He was quiet for a moment, thinking of his story. "I was eight when my father died. My parents were a good couple, too, at least in my memory and from what my mother said."

"Was he sick?"

"Not a day in his life." At her curious look, he dredged up the words he'd shared many times and never stopped hating. "He was a semitruck driver and was killed in an accident on the highway."

"Oh, I'm sorry for you."

"Yeah, it was bad. I…" He struggled to find the right words, wanting her to know what Pops meant to him, but not wanting to get sappy and emotional or bring down the night. He settled for the simple truth. "He was the greatest guy I ever knew."

"Oh." She slid her arm through his, pulling him closer. "I know that feeling. I know that loss. Felt it every day for four years. It's…devastating."

Her sympathy, and the shared experience, touched him, more than he'd expected it to. Not that he wanted to compare, but he'd never talked about his father with Savannah. She'd invariably launched into a tirade about her dad, a gutter drunk, and the mother she never spoke to. She didn't understand what an awesome parent could mean to a person, but Darcy did.

"How long until your mom remarried?" she asked.

"Four years." He added a smile. "Could be the magic number."

But she was focused on him, and again, that attention and concern hit a chord that hummed deep inside. "How'd she meet the new man?"

"She got a job as the administrative assistant to the president and owner of Bucking Properties. Have you heard of it?"

"Of course. Real estate development and sales?"

"Well, Malcolm Bucking liked his assistant. A lot. They're celebrating their twentieth anniversary this month."

"Oh, wow." She slowed her step, letting that sink in. "So...your mom went from being married to a semitruck driver to a...gazillionaire?"

He laughed. "Yup. And consider it my cautionary tale for your family."

"How so? I mean, if they've been married for twenty years, I assume they're happy."

"I guess they are, but you should know that a wife for your father could change everything. You willing to take that chance?"

"I doubt he'd marry," she said.

"You never know."

She was quiet for a moment as a pack of rowdy kids, probably from the local college, came toward them, laughing and taking up most of the path that meandered through the square.

He took her hand and led them around the group, careful to keep her on pavement with those spiky heels.

"So that's what happened to you," she said. "Your mother brought you into a family you didn't like?"

"Yeah, that's my excuse," he said with a smile. "And to be honest, 'didn't like' is an understatement."

"I know you have an evil stepbrother. Only one?"

"And a stepsister who isn't truly evil, but is fully capable of stabbing a back if given a knife and a cause."

She lifted the hand still holding his to brush some hair off her face, giving him the unexpected thrill of stroking her hair with her and accidentally grazing her smooth cheek with his knuckles. The tiny move was enough to heighten every sense in him.

"And your stepfather? Also evil?"

He took a moment to conjure up Malcolm Bucking and think about how to describe him to Darcy. "He manipulates people to get things to go his way. Is that evil?"

"Hey, my dad is trying to marry off the free world and we think it's cute."

"At least he's not out chasing his next hundred million."

"No. His next grandchild. How does this man treat your mother?"

"Like a queen," he said without hesitation. "But that has changed her. A lot. She was living in a little brick house in a middle-class suburb of Charlotte, stretching every dollar and wham! We move into an estate with staff and silver and drivers and...Gideon."

"The evil stepbrother who resents your arrival and hates your mother and makes you miserable?"

He stopped dead in his tracks. "Yes. Am I that much of a cliché?"

"Well, I saw *Cinderella*. Er, *Cinderfella*. And I know your version ends with a pretty rough betrayal."

His heart suddenly felt heavy and warm, as if it was melting right in his chest. It felt good to talk to someone like her. No, not *like* her. Just *her*. "Yes. Very rough." He punctuated the word by squeezing her hand.

She was quiet for a few more steps. "Well, I appreciate the warning about my father," she finally said.

"You know, lightning could strike twice for your dad." And he hoped it would for her family, but he couldn't help but be skeptical. "You need to remember this mysterious perfect woman will come with kids and exes and baggage of all sorts, so you better be ready for that, because it changes everything and everyone."

They reached the massive tree in the middle of the square, next to a life-sized statue of a soldier. He'd walked by it many times cutting through the large square from his building to the town hall, but never bothered to read the plaque. "Captain Thaddeus Ambrose Bushrod," he said. "Well, that explains a lot of the names around Bitter Bark."

"Which is named after that tree," she said, pointing to the giant. "Except, it's a hickory, not a bitter bark, and for a while, we were *Better* Bark, thanks to one of my sisters-in-law."

"I've heard about that," he said. "The tourism specialist who opened the town to dogs and changed the name for a year."

"That's the one. My dad was trying to get Liam to that meeting because Andi was there, but Shane had already met Chloe and jumped in."

He dropped his head back and laughed.

"I'm telling you, it's insane. The person who should be scared is the one coming into my family." She looked up at him, her eyes shining so much he wondered if that was her natural brightness or the reflection of the lights in the tree. Didn't matter. He could look at her all night.

Holy crap, this was not supposed to happen. He was not supposed to be inches from a woman, his heart thumping, his blood pumping, his brain short-circuiting and forgetting every rule he ever made.

"Josh," she said softly. "I lied to you."

And that is why.

"My feet really hurt."

Or...that. "Want me to carry you?"

She trilled out a laugh. "Sitting for a few minutes will probably do the trick. I'd walk barefoot in the grass, but, you know, there are a lot of dogs around here."

"C'mon, there's a bench." He walked her to it, knowing he should get her home and end this nondate before he broke all his rules and really started liking her.

Oh, too late for that.

She dropped onto the bench with a noisy sigh and instantly lifted her feet, even before he sat. "Just take them off. Please. It'll feel so good."

He stood in front of her, shaking his head as he reached down to her ankles.

"What?" she asked. "You're smug because you called it when you saw these shoes."

"I'm not smug. I'm..."

"What?"

"I don't think you *try* to be that seductive, do you?"

She raised a brow and lifted her ankle another inch so he could glide the strap off. "I am not seductive."

"I'll be the judge of that." He held the shoe for a minute, lifting it toward the soft light to really appreciate how glittery and high and strappy and feminine it was. Just holding her damn shoe turned him on. "Definitely not regulation footwear."

She shrugged. "Guess it depends on the game." She raised her foot higher, enough that he could get a peek at a shapely calf and toned thigh. "I honestly am not trying to be seductive. I mean, who even says that anymore?"

"The poor schmuck being seduced."

"Poor schmuck?" She pulled her bare feet out of his hands and let them drop to the ground with a thud. "That's not what I'd call you."

"It's no worse than Hot Landlord or Cinderfella." He smiled at her, setting both shoes at the end of the bench and sitting down next to her.

"But why poor schmuck when it comes to…seduction?" she asked as they got close enough to touch.

"You just said it—the story ends in betrayal."

She sat back, eyeing him. "Will you tell me what happened, or is it too personal?"

"You already know. My former girlfriend cheated with my stepbrother. How much more personal can it get?"

She ran a finger over his knuckles, annihilating his concentration. "How'd you find out?"

He stared straight ahead. "I went to her apartment at sunrise to propose on her thirtieth birthday, and he was there, in bed with her."

She sucked in a noisy breath. "Her thirtieth…with your…oh man. That *blows*."

"Yeah."

"Holy hell."

"Yeah."

"That's so wretched."

"Yeah."

"No wonder you hate women."

"Ye—I don't hate women," he corrected. "But my ability to trust a woman has been permanently damaged."

After a second, she fell back on the bench. "Wow. Proposing on her birthday. You must have really loved her."

He snorted. "I know what you're thinking," he said. "How could I be that blind?"

"They say love is blind."

"And stupid," he added on a mirthless laugh. "She changed, Darcy. She changed like…" He snapped his fingers. "That."

"What changed her?"

"*Who*. And his name is Gideon Bucking."

"He can't be that great. I mean you…well…" She raised her brows. "You're a snack, honey. Ain't gonna lie."

He laughed softly, the sassy compliment hitting its mark and making him take her hand and bring it to his lips, but then he remembered his rules and silently set her hand back on her lap. "Thanks, but she found a different snack more to her liking."

"Maybe she didn't like the idea of getting engaged. I turned thirty last week, and if some guy popped the question, I'd have popped *him*."

"First of all, I wasn't *some guy*," he told her. "We'd been dating for a year."

"Okay, well, I didn't mean some guy, but anyone is scary if you're not ready."

"Fair enough. And I guess she wasn't, because she knew I'd forgive almost anything but that. I've given it a lot of thought, and I think she wanted to break up but didn't know how or why. This was an easy way out for her, and it was a surefire relationship ender."

They sat quietly for a moment, then he curled her fingers deeper into his, remembering something she'd just said. "You turned thirty last week? Happy birthday."

"Thanks."

"Did you get anything good?"

"My independence."

"By moving out?" he guessed.

"And starting my own business. It was my thirtieth-birthday present to myself. The thing I wanted most in the world—a chance to prove to myself and my family that I'm not the baby anymore, that I can stand on my own two feet, and that I can be a successful, adult woman with no help from brother, sister, father, or man."

"Hear me roar," he teased.

She narrowed her eyes. "Don't make me. My roar is a thing to be feared."

He laughed. "I don't doubt that. But you did take help moving in."

"Because I pity them," she said with a playful wave of her hand. "They'd have all rolled up in balls and cried if I hadn't let them."

"And you're taking help on Stella from your dad."

"Of course, for Stella. Even you're willing to break a few rules for that dog."

He couldn't argue with that.

"That makes us people who love dogs and want to help a blind one see again," she said. "That's not dependence. That's intelligence."

"You're right. You're…" Smart and beautiful and witty and good-hearted and…and… "Great, Darcy. You're a great girl. Er, woman. A strong, independent woman." At her raised eyebrows, he added, "You're also a hot tenant."

She laughed at that, leaning into him. "Is that why you gave my father the impression you really like me? I thought you were helping the cause."

"No." If only it were that simple. "I *do* like you."

Her eyes flickered, but he couldn't decide if that was interest or fear or a combination of both.

"And since I do," he continued, "I'm happy to be your cover or whatever you need to get him off your case. It's not a lie."

She nodded slowly, watching him with an intense blue gaze. "Okay, good."

He dipped his head to look deeper into those eyes. "You don't sound like it's good."

She took a slow breath, letting it out before she spoke. "I like you, and I'd like to…"

He swallowed and waited for her to finish, hoping for one thing, dreading something else.

"You look like you're in more pain than my feet," she said softly. "I'm sorry."

"I know I need to trust someone again, Darcy. A woman, a friend."

"I can be both those. One without trying, the other

133

with a slew of people who will vouch that I'm a damn good friend when you need one." She put her hand on his cheek and pressed gently. "And you, Cinderfella, need one."

He smiled. "I kind of like Hot Landlord."

"So do I." She inched closer, the scent and warmth killing him, making him ache for that kiss. "But I'm getting the impression that's a problem."

He put his hand over hers, loving the sensation of having her skin pressed against his. "Only for me."

"Well, you're half of the equation."

He held her gaze, the need for a kiss so strong, he couldn't possibly ignore it. "Darcy…"

"Don't worry," she said. "I'm not a threat to take down your Woman Walls."

"My *Woman Walls*? Why does that sound like something I should see a doctor about?"

"A shrink, maybe."

He knew exactly what she meant, and she *was* a threat to those walls. A big threat.

"Listen." She sidled a little closer to make her point. "I don't want anything or anyone in my life that can take away that independence I recently gifted myself. And I firmly believe that serious relationships do exactly that. I'm not serious; ask anyone who knows me. So let's do something else, and neither one of us has to worry."

"Something else?" That could go so many ways…some of them very, very nice. "What are you suggesting, Miss Kilcannon?"

She held his gaze long enough to stir his blood and make him hope that something else would be exactly what he needed. Tonight. Now.

"We can be friends," she finally said.

"Friends with…" *Oh God, please say benefits.*

"Dogs," she finished. "Friends with dogs, especially one that's in desperate need of our help."

"Friends with dogs," he repeated. "That's a new one on me."

She stood slowly, pulling him up with her. "Me, too. But let's try it. Friends with dogs. That can work for us, can't it?"

He looked down at her, much farther down now that her heels were off, reaching to brush a lock of blond hair back from her face, threading the silken strands through his fingers. "What exactly are the guidelines and restrictions for friends with dogs?"

"You want rules."

"Have you met me?"

She laughed a little, letting her cheek press his palm. "Okay, let's see. The dogs come first. Both of them. Kookie and Stella. Their needs come before ours."

He nodded. "Of course. The dogs I never wanted in my building are now a higher priority than anything."

She grinned in victory. "Absolutely. And second, we're in the Stella thing one hundred percent together. Finding Savannah, doing whatever we need to do in order for Stella to be part of the study, and tending to her during the procedures. Whatever it takes, we're a team."

"I love that," he admitted. "I feel like I'm getting the better end of that, because you know so much about dogs and have the vets in the family."

"It's okay, because I want to be involved. I'm committed to that little darling now."

"Awesome." But what about them? "Anything else?"

"Before and during the treatments, or even if she doesn't qualify, Stella gets trained to be around other dogs, and we are going to get her to be friends with Kookie. It might take work and patience, but I'm down if you are."

"Fine. Friends with dogs means our dogs are friends, too. This keeps getting better." But still not good enough. He stroked her cheek lightly, looking into her eyes, already aching to break rules and barriers and kiss her right here under the white lights of Bushrod Square. "Are there any other parameters? Like, for us? Rules about...kissing?"

"Kissing," she whispered, and just the word on her lips made his body respond.

"Yeah," he said, his voice husky, and he inched closer to her. "That."

She drew in a slow breath, her eyes darker and deeper as they focused on his. "I could kiss."

"Oh, I bet you can."

She bit her lip. "But I can't make any promises about...stopping."

Her honesty rocked him, and the look on her face slayed him, and the way his body responded to her wet lower lip, he knew he couldn't stop, either.

"We'd have to stop," he whispered. "Otherwise..."

"We wouldn't be friends. We'd be lovers with dogs. Big difference."

Lovers. His skin felt fiery at the idea, his muscles taut, his blood thrumming hard out of his brain and headed for trouble.

"You really don't want that," she said, searching his face.

"Oh, I really do."

She exhaled softly, dropping her gaze over his face, settling on his mouth, then looking back into his eyes. He could tell she struggled with the next breath and felt her pulse pound under his thumb as he stroked her jaw.

"Darcy," he whispered. "If I get into bed with you, I'm a dead man."

"Not sure it'll be quite that good, but thanks."

He didn't laugh. "I won't stop at once. I can't be satisfied with casual. I won't want to walk away."

Her expressions shifted slightly, going from tantalizing to tense. "I don't want that."

"Neither do I," he said. "I swore that I'd never put myself in that situation again."

"So...you're going full-on celibate?"

"I'm going full-on meaningless. When I'm with someone, I don't want to..."

"Risk anything," she finished for him.

"Exactly."

She touched his face with her fingertips, grazing his cheek and jaw and lower lip. "You're as scared as Stella."

He couldn't deny that. "And I was as blind, too."

"So maybe there's a cure for you, too." She tipped her chin up, a little closer, a hairbreadth away, offering a kiss, comfort, and, possibly, that cure.

If only he could trust that's all she offered. If only he wasn't still black and blue from the last time. "I can't," he whispered.

"And I shouldn't," she replied.

For a long moment, they held each other's gaze, both of them battling the couldn'ts and shouldn'ts they'd stacked around their hearts.

Darcy eased back first, scooping up her shoes. "I know of one little girl who's home alone in a pillow fort right now, and *Wheel of Fortune* is long over."

He swallowed his desire and tamped down the tension gripping his body. "Let's go," he said. "Let's go be friends with dogs."

She grimaced as she pulled on her shoes. "And rules."

"And walls."

"And doubts."

"And fears."

But not so many that they couldn't hold hands on the way back to the dogs that mattered most.

Chapter Eleven

"You lied." Josh's accusation was barely audible over the cacophony of Stella's whining, Kookie's frantic barking, and the breeze blowing through the open windows of Josh's black Ford F-150.

"About what?" Darcy asked, trying, and failing, to calm Kookie on her lap. But every time Stella cried, Kookie barked and tried to scramble off Darcy's lap to get to the other dog.

"You called your family's place a 'canine facility.'"

"That's what Waterford Farm is," she said as they drove past the white fence that lined the western border of the property. "And it's been home to the Kilcannon family for sixty-some years."

"I was picturing an animal shelter." He gestured to the rolling hills and glimpses of the buildings in the distance.

"Oh, well, yeah. It's more of a refuge," she said. "In so many ways."

"This place is huge."

"'A hundred acres of happy,'" she said, quoting a line she'd often used in Instagram posts about

Waterford Farm. "We run the largest canine training and rescue facility in the state. It's all right here on the land that Gramma Finnie and Grandpa Seamus bought in the 1950s when they moved from Ireland to Bitter Bark, North Carolina." She didn't bother to hide the pride in her voice.

"What brought them here?"

"Oh, no," she teased. "That's Gramma Finnie's story to tell and your test to pass."

"Test?"

"If she likes you, you get the long version. And trust me, when an Irish storyteller wants to give you the long version, you better pour a drink and settle in."

"And if she doesn't like me?"

"You'll know it. No Irish proverbs stitched on pillows for you. But you can read her blog."

He threw her an understandably confused look. "Her blog?"

She merely gestured toward the gate and the WF logo made more festive by some playful paw prints Pru and her father, Trace, had painted recently. "Welcome to Waterford Farm, my friend."

Inside those gates, they followed the long, winding drive at about five miles per hour since Josh was taking in the scenery as much as the road, which was nothing but tall trees, rolling hills, and deep-green grass.

Darcy inhaled deeply, sucking down the glorious smells of woods and earth and home.

"Let me get this straight." Josh looked from one side to the other, then settled his gaze on her. "You *voluntarily* left this place?"

"It was time," she said simply. "And I'm here practically every day and twice on Sundays, literally."

He whipped around at the sight of a pond with ducks paddling about. "Can you fish out there?"

"Sure, and on a bigger lake we have on the property." And a smaller one at the north quadrant on a piece of land her father had given her, since Waterford was technically divided into seven sections, each owned by a different Kilcannon. Only Liam had built on his, but some day, they all might.

"Wow. Has it always been a canine training facility?" he asked.

"No, the business of Waterford Farm started about four years ago, right after my mom died. Before that, we had some kennels because she was an obsessive dog adopter and foster parent. But it wasn't until she died and we were all..." She couldn't even think of a word to describe the darkness of losing a mother in the prime of her life to a heart attack. "Well, we weren't good. Especially my dad, who will be the first to tell you Annie Kilcannon was his whole life. Anyway, the day after her funeral, my dad had this wild idea that we would all move back to Bitter Bark and help him realize Mom's lifelong dream. And we did, every one of us except Aidan, who was in the Army at the time. But he's here now."

"So you had moved out?" he asked.

"Yeah." Darcy stroked Kookie's head as the dog finally quieted, her mind drifting back to the early days that, in some ways, seemed like a lifetime ago. But in others, those miserable moments were as clear as yesterday. "I was in Seattle with a few of my siblings working at my brother's dot-com business.

Garrett founded PetPic and sold it to FriendGroup, and we all worked there, except for Molly, who has a daughter, Pru. Molly's a vet with my dad."

He shook his head with a chuckle. "I'll never get them all straight."

"They all fall into place pretty easily," she promised. "Everyone has a distinct personality and style, from two-month-old baby Fiona to octogenarian Gramma Finnie."

He considered that and the surroundings some more. "And you all run this business harmoniously?"

"Of course."

"I noticed an awful lot of digs and insults flying when you were moving in."

"Not insults, but teasing. We kid a lot, yes, and we don't let each other get away with much, but at the base of everything is the love that my parents had for each other and us." She added an apologetic smile. "Sorry for the Hallmark commercial, but that's who the Kilcannons are."

He let out a soft whistle. "Not how the Bucking family works," he said. "Bulletproof vests are required at every board meeting. Even my ninety-four-year-old stepgrandmother fires shots, that's if she can remember when we *have* board meetings."

"Well, we don't have board meetings," she said. "But we do have dinner together every Wednesday night and Sunday after church. All the decisions about running a business are made over Gramma Finnie's bread pudding, and the only shots are Irish whiskey."

"And what exactly does a 'canine training and rescue facility' do?" he asked.

"What *don't* we do is a better question. For one thing, we teach people who want to be professional dog trainers and prepare them to start their own businesses. They come and stay here for whole semesters and learn all the tricks of good training and how to run a small business. Shane, my second-oldest brother, is in charge of that."

"And the rescue business?"

"That's the really fun part. We rescue and place dogs all over the country now that my brother Aidan has a plane to help Garrett get the dogs to forever homes. And fairly recently, we added a program to train service dogs, which is mostly done by my soon-to-be brother-in-law, Trace. And my oldest brother, Liam, heads our work with K-9s and law enforcement, and he also trains *Schutzhunds*, which are special guard dogs for high-end security clients."

He laughed. "Oh, is that all?"

"No, actually, it's not. My sister has a thriving vet business with four full-time vet techs helping out. Oh, and I believe I mentioned the blogging Gramma." She pushed her hair back with mock smugness. "I come from a long line of superstars."

"And the youngest of the family does all the grooming, which I imagine is a lot."

She shrugged. "It's a small contribution to the big picture, but it's taught me my trade and kept me close to the family."

"But you're ready to strike out on your own?"

"I can do both," she assured him. "Work here and in town."

"I have no doubt you will do that with style and success."

His faith in her, which she could tell was genuine, made her want to reach over and take his hand, but…she wasn't sure if the friends-with-dogs rules allowed any displays of affection. And that was going to be a problem if she spent too much time with him, because all she wanted to do was break rules and display affection.

He pointed at Garrett's Jeep, parked along the side of the drive. "That's quite the color yellow."

"The color of a forever home. Garrett takes that and wears his 'doggone hat' whenever he takes a rescue to his or her new family."

He gave her a quizzical look. "He wore it to move you into the apartment."

"It was a family joke," she told him with a roll of her eyes.

"Insiders only?"

"My brothers think it's hilarious that Dad is up to his matchmaking tricks with me," she explained. "So Garrett was making 'forever home' jokes." She flicked her fingers to tell him not to worry. "Just ignore them. And my dad if he starts, you know, trying to set wedding dates."

His eyes widened a little.

"Kidding." Kind of.

"Well, I told you if you want him to back off because he thinks we're, you know, a *thing*, we can."

"We *are* a thing." She poked his shoulder, hitting that wonderfully solid muscle and maybe the shell he so protectively kept around his broken heart. "We're friends with dogs, remember? If that's not 'a thing,' then I don't know what is."

He smiled. "Is it enough of a thing to keep your dad from lining up every unmarried guy in Bitter Bark like an all-you-can-eat buffet?"

The image cracked her up, but she nodded. "It might be."

"Good."

She studied him for a minute. "Good, because that's what I want, or good, because you want to help me, or good, because..." *You don't want me to date anyone else.* She swallowed that thought and waited for his answer, surprised at how tight her throat was and how much it mattered. It shouldn't matter. It had no right mattering. She'd known him for a couple of days.

But ever since last night, after sitting barefoot on that bench next to him, Josh Ranier had started mattering way more than he should.

"It's just good," he said, turning the last corner where the big yellow house with green shutters and tall chimneys and a wide wraparound porch came into view.

He stared at it as he pulled the truck to the side of the driveway. "That right there? That's one of the prettiest places I've ever seen."

She sighed at the change of subject, shifting her attention to the rambling, sunny farmhouse that represented the heart and soul of Waterford Farm.

"My grandparents built the original house when my dad was a baby," she told him. "It's been added to a lot, over the years, especially by my mother. After he and my mom got married, they lived here and raised us all here. In fact, that was my room right up there..." She pointed to a second-floor window.

"Nice."

"But now I have my Juliet balcony."

"Rapunzel," he teased, looking left to the training pen at the center of the facility. There, Shane stood with his hands on his hips, and Liam was circling with a new German shepherd he was training. Garrett was with them, too, listening and laughing about whatever Shane was spouting off. "Looks like my brothers are taking training breaks. Let's take Stella over and talk to them."

From behind the wheel, he regarded the three men carefully.

"They're not like your wicked stepbrother," she assured him, sensing hesitation. "They're friendly and nice and, in the case of Liam, love dogs much more than people."

"Which one of them worked with Stella yesterday? Shane, right?"

"Yes, and he's a true dog whisperer, though they are all amazing with animals. Shane gets into a dog's head the most, though. Liam is super consistent, like you would expect from a guy who trained dogs in the Marines. And Garrett loves them into submission. Aidan has only been back a few months, and he's really found his calling with the air transport business. Oh, he and Beck, his fiancée, have already adopted two of their own dogs, and rumor has it they're looking into fostering some more since they're buying a house and getting married next year."

"He's only been back a few months and he's engaged? Did he know her before?"

She made a face, almost not sure she should answer.

"The Dogfather," he said, figuring it out.

"It's a little freaky," she agreed. "But don't worry. We're on to him." She hurried to unlatch her seat belt before the conversation got awkward. "Come on, meet my family. You'll love them."

He sighed as he got out of the truck. "That's what I'm afraid of," he muttered under his breath.

Afraid of? Darcy stilled in the process of climbing out, ready to ask for an explanation of that, but he was already standing next to the truck, and something told her she wasn't supposed to hear the throwaway comment anyway.

What was he afraid of? Liking her brothers? Or that her father was about to make match number six? Hadn't she been clear enough in telling him that wasn't what she wanted?

"Any of them specialize in blind dogs?" he asked.

"That one." She pointed at her grandmother, who was coming down the steps of the porch, carrying a tray with tall glasses of water and lemonade. She was headed toward the living quarters, probably to help Crystal, the housekeeper, set up a midmorning snack for the trainees.

"Don't tell me. Gramma Finnie the storytelling blogger?"

Still holding Kookie, she opened the passenger side door of the cab to get some of Stella's things, leaning down to catch his gaze across the bench seat where he unlatched the crate. "She's also one of the coolest people you'll ever meet."

His hand rested on Stella's cage, but he studied Darcy carefully. "Unwanted advice?"

"You need some, or you're going to dole it out?" she asked.

"Dole." All humor had disappeared from his face. "Trust me on this, Darcy. You do not want to mess with this family dynamic."

"Mess with…" She angled her head, confused. "Do you mean by fixing up my dad?" she guessed.

"Or anything that would upset an apple cart so perfect it actually hurts." His gaze shifted away as if he didn't want to elaborate, but she read his expression anyway. Something about all this actually hurt him.

Darcy turned from him to set Kookie on the ground and set her toward Gramma Finnie. "Go tell her, Kooks. Tell her how upset you are with this new dog."

Barking in full agreement, Kookie took off across the grass, long hair flying as she zipped by Shane, who was on his way over to greet them.

"Hope you brought that pretty girl back for me," her brother called easily as he approached. "She's smart as a whip and tons of fun."

"I did," Josh replied, then winked at Darcy as he reached into the crate. "And Stella, too."

Of course, every already-fired-up hormone in her body responded to that wink and compliment. Oh, how she wished they were doing anything today other than trekking across the state to dredge up memories of the woman who hurt him so bad, he wouldn't even kiss her.

Some rules really were made to be broken.

Darcy was right about one thing—every Kilcannon he met had a distinct personality. It didn't take Josh long to tell them apart and appreciate each of the individuals who made up this extraordinary clan.

It came as no surprise that every one of them seemed to care deeply about Stella's blindness and knew all about the study at Vestal Valley College already. They welcomed Josh and his dog with an ease and warmth that could have felt fake, except that everything at this place was so real. Even her precious grandmother and friendly older sister joined them in the training pen, each of them taking turns trying to coax Stella closer for some tender petting, all the while making small talk and jokes with Josh.

He could have hung out in that sundrenched pen with these people for hours, laughing at the dogs everywhere, but Stella hit her wall after a bit. She curled into a ball, barking and snarling at any dog or person when she realized they were close.

"Did we remember her jacket?" Josh asked Darcy.

She snapped her fingers. "Good call. It's in the truck." As he started to go, she touched his arm. "I'll get it. Stella needs to be taken into the vet office."

"I'll take Josh over there." Liam, the tallest, darkest, and most serious of the bunch, gestured toward one of the clapboard buildings.

Josh easily picked up Stella, since she recognized his voice and scent, and walked with Liam toward one of the clapboard-covered outbuildings.

"She made some progress yesterday with Shane," Liam told him. "But she is freaked out by loud noises and other dogs more than anything. How'd she do at home last night?"

"Slept through the night," Josh said, not adding that he, on the other hand, had flipped around, sweaty and lonely and thinking about that kiss he should have enjoyed. And more. If he had, he might not have been sweaty and lonely. Well, sweaty.

"Sleeping through the night? Sounds like heaven," Liam added on a wry laugh. "I have a two-month-old daughter, and man, can that girl wail at three a.m."

Josh smiled, looking at the other man who was about his same height and build, but looked to be a few years older. "Congratulations," he said. "How do you like being a new dad?"

Liam's grin made the corners of his eyes crinkle. "It does not suck," he admitted. "Even with the three a.m. wakeup call. But I'm married to an angel."

"That helps," Josh said.

"Yeah, I thank my dad every day for his little romantic shenanigans."

"I've heard he's pretty good at those," Josh said as they ascended a few stairs next to the hand-carved wooden sign that read Kilcannon Veterinarian.

"He's five for six," Liam said, sliding a sly look at Josh.

Just then, Darcy came back to them, talking to the brother closest to her in age, the shaggy-haired former helicopter pilot, Aidan.

"What were you two talking about?" she asked.

Josh waited, giving Liam a chance to answer first.

"I'm wondering if you'll make it back for Sunday dinner tomorrow," he said easily.

Darcy looked at Josh with raised brows of hope. "Maybe."

"Well, make it by two and you're in for a treat," Aidan told them.

Weren't their Sunday dinners their 'non-board

meetings'? "Important business being discussed?" Josh asked.

Aidan snorted. "Monkey business."

"What?" Darcy asked, obviously intrigued.

"Beck's aunt and uncle are dropping Ruff over for a visit," he said.

Darcy frowned, clearly not getting the significance of that. "Okay, and Ruff will be up to his usual wildness? Is that what you mean by monkey business?"

"Nope. Aunt Sarah is bringing a friend and..." Aidan lifted his brows. "She handles show dogs. I think she could be the one."

"The one?" Liam practically gagged. "Anyone involved in show dogs is going to tick Dad off."

"Total waste of time, anyway," Darcy added. "Dad was mighty cozy with Judy Walker last night, and I'm sure they've been out before, based on things Ricardo said."

"Ricardo stretches the truth as wide as his pizza dough," Aidan quipped. "Wait till Dad meets Una."

"Una?" Darcy screwed up her face. "Doesn't sound Irish, big bro."

"It sounds like—"

"Shhh!" Darcy cut off Liam's comment with a sharp look past him and a finger to her lips. "He just came out of the house."

Liam backed off with a nod of gratitude for the save.

"Good luck today, you two," Aidan said to Darcy and Josh. "Hope to see you back here with good news tomorrow."

The men left a few seconds before Dr. Kilcannon approached with a smile and handshake for Josh, a hug for his daughter, a head rub for Stella, and the paperwork they needed to have signed by Savannah.

Poor guy. Did he have any idea what his kids were up to? Didn't matter. Josh was certain Dr. K had faced worse hijinks with his clan and managed them well.

"Let me have that little patient," he said, carefully taking Stella from Josh. "We're going to run very simple, very safe tests, then let her sleep the day away."

"Oh no, we forgot her bed," Darcy exclaimed.

Dr. K shook his head. "Not to worry, Darce. We have plenty of dog beds."

"But she has to sleep in that one, or she'll be up all night," she said.

Her father looked unfazed. "She'll sleep in Gramma's room and think she died and went to Irish heaven."

She laughed easily. "Thanks, Dad." She reached up to kiss him on the cheek and give another to Stella. "You be a good, sweet girl. Play nice with the other dogs. Especially Kookie."

"Go on," Dr. K said with a nudge. "The sooner you get this waiver signed, the sooner we can get Stella lined up for the procedure."

"Thank you, sir." Josh extended his hand for another shake. "I really appreciate everything you're doing."

"My pleasure." The older man held his gaze for a moment and added another squeeze to their joined hands. "Good luck, son."

For a quick second, Josh was transported to the last time someone had called him that, a little surprised by the impact of the word. He was still thinking about it as he and Darcy returned to the truck.

"So, you've met most of the family," Darcy said as she pulled on her seat belt. "Are they crazy? Scary? Are you able to tell them apart now? What do you think?"

"I think…" He turned to her to tell her the truth. "You should count your blessings, Darcy."

"I do," she assured him. "Are you a little jealous of my good fortune?"

"Not a little," he told her. "A lot. And by the end of today, you'll understand why."

Chapter Twelve

About three hours later, they reached the vibrant Lake Norman waterfront town of Cornelius. It didn't take Darcy long to sense old and new wealth oozing from every manicured side street and preciously decorated storefront. But when Josh drove through large private gates and along a drive that made Waterford's entrance look like a sidewalk, she nearly choked on the smell of money.

"Holy...wow." She dipped down to see the whole white-washed castle complete with turrets, round windows, and professional gardens, almost unable to take it all in. "And you thought Waterford Farm was nice."

"Waterford goes beyond nice," Josh said, echoing the many, many wonderful observations he'd made about her family and home during the drive. The Kilcannons had clearly made a great impression on him. They'd talked for the whole trip about dogs and life and what she wanted to do with the grooming business and which properties he'd like to buy in Bitter Bark, but with every subject change, he'd get back to her incredible family.

"Bucking Manor is a statement," he said. "Waterford Farm is a...state of mind."

She chuckled at that, especially considering he'd been there a half hour. Wait until he whiled away a Sunday afternoon in Nirvana. "Fair warning, when I tell Gramma Finnie you called Waterford Farm a 'state of mind,' I guarantee you she'll use that in a blog post."

"It's all hers," he said.

"But what *is* the statement Bucking Manor is making?" she asked. "Other than, 'There be cash in them walls.'" Of course, Darcy had expected opulence—Bucking Properties was a well-known builder with real estate offices in every major city and huge developments all over the country. The Bucking logo was practically synonymous with a For Sale sign, and the company was considered one of North Carolina's biggest business stars. But, still. She hadn't been expecting mega-money like this, if only because Josh seemed so down-to-earth.

"That's the statement," he said. "Brace to be impressed. I mean, if vast amounts of money impress you." As he rounded a behemoth fountain in the center of a thirty-foot-wide driveway that could probably valet-park twenty cars, he gave her a slow smile.

No, money didn't do a thing for her. But that smile made her a little weak in the knees.

"My guess is money isn't a big motivator for you," he surmised.

"I'm a dog groomer, Josh, with modest ambitions. And..." She looked down at her equally modest outfit. "I honestly didn't think about my impression on them. I thought we were on an errand to get a phone number and the name of a vet. Should I wait in the car? Use the servants' entrance? Shop before we stop in?"

He laughed. "Nope. Just relax."

"If you're going to try and tell me that the people who live here aren't going to judge my less-than-pristine white jeans and Waterford Farm T-shirt, I won't believe you. I honestly thought the cute little paw logo would bring dog sympathy for our cause."

He gave her a funny look she couldn't interpret.

"What?"

After a second, he closed his hand over hers, giving it a squeeze. "You know, I think I forgot women like you even existed. Maybe I never knew it."

She took one second to let the little thrill of the compliment make its way through her and settle somewhere in the vicinity of her heart. And the longer he looked at her like that, the lower that thrill dropped. Shouldn't all that sexy tension slow down a little after three hours in the car? If anything, it had gotten worse.

"Women like me?" she asked. "Women who wear dirty sneakers to fancy houses?" She tried for a joke, but her throat was tight. Like every other part of her body around him.

"Women who defy conventions."

"Oh, the unconventionals? Yeah, we're right here, under your nose."

He leaned a little closer. "Good place for you to be." For a second, she thought he'd close the space and kiss her. And she wasn't going to mind that a bit. But he didn't, easing back to say, "We shouldn't be too long, so don't worry. In and out. Five minutes to ask my mom if she has a way to contact them, five more to talk to Gideon's staff and butler—"

Darcy drew back. "Wait, what? He has a butler here? Why?"

"He lives here," he said. "So does Brea, but I called her and left a voice mail she hasn't responded to."

"How old is Gideon?"

"Thirty-three. Now *you* can judge a thirty-three-year-old who lives at home."

"You're telling this to a thirty-year-old who moved away from home a week ago."

"But you did move," he said. "Gideon will die here, because he fully expects this place to be his one day, along with everything in it. Plus, he only has one direction in life: the easy way." He opened the door and climbed out and was around the truck to open Darcy's side before she even had her seat belt off. "Come on. Let's get this over with."

She put her hand on his arm. "If you hate it so much here, why didn't you simply call your mother and talk to her?"

"I tried. Her secretary told me she preferred to talk in person."

Darcy's jaw loosened. "Seriously?"

"I told you, money changed her. And if she can think of any way to get me here, she will."

Just then, a massive front door opened and an older man in a bright yellow golf shirt and sharp white trousers stepped out.

"Well, look what the truck dragged in," he called down the stone stairs.

Josh, with his back to the house, didn't turn, but

closed his eyes. "Damn. I was hoping he'd be out of town."

"Malcolm?" she guessed on a whisper.

"The one and only."

"When they called from the gate, I nearly had a heart attack." Even Darcy could hear the accusation in the man's voice from twenty feet away. "You shouldn't surprise us like this."

"They didn't know you were coming?" Darcy asked under her breath.

"The secretary did." He cleared his throat and called, "Good to see you, too, Mal." Then he looked into Darcy's eyes and whispered, "I'm glad you're here."

She reached out and touched his face to show some support and solidarity. "They're people, Josh. They're *family*."

"Easy for you to say, Miss *Kilcannon*." He placed enough emphasis on the name for her to know exactly what he meant. Her family was dreamy. His was…

"Does this mean you're ready to come back and be a Bucking now?" Josh's stepfather came down the steps as he posed the question, cutting a tall and imposing figure.

"Not a Bucking, Mal," Josh said. "Still a Ranier."

The older man laughed, showing deep crinkles around his eyes and well-tanned skin. "You can run, but you can't hide, Joshua." There was enough of an edge in the cliché that Darcy suspected the words straddled the fine line between a tease and a threat.

Next to her, Josh stiffened but covered it by introducing them to each other.

"A pleasure to meet you, Mr. Bucking." Darcy held out her hand for a solid, brief shake.

"Call me Mal," he insisted. "And lucky for you, Joshua, your mother is just back from the club with me. Let's get out of this heat and wait for her inside."

The whole encounter felt forced and formal, making Darcy wonder what it would be like to be so dang uncomfortable when coming home that you had to wonder if a secretary had told your parents you were on the way. And had she ever, in her life, come and gone through the front door? That's what kitchen doors were for—to open without knocking, to find love inside, and to feel secure.

This house was built with the sole intention of making everyone feel *in*secure.

And mind-boggled. Inside, marble gleamed, ceilings soared, gold leaf adorned, and priceless art hung over furniture that looked like it should have velvet ropes around it.

An older woman in a simple gray dress ushered them into a sitting room and offered drinks, moving like a robot meant to blend in with the surroundings. As soon as she left, Malcolm did, too, on the pretense of getting Josh's mother—as if a staff person couldn't do that.

Alone in a museum of a front room, Josh turned to her with a wry smile. "Welcome to Buckings*ham* Palace."

She smiled at the wordplay, but couldn't argue that this sure didn't feel like a home. "The real Buckingham Palace can't be much more grand."

He rolled his eyes and then gestured to a grouping of chairs and sofas, one whiter than the next. "Relax."

As if anyone could in this place. She pointed both index fingers at her jeans. "I still have Kookie on me, and something tells me there are no dogs in this house."

"In the stables with the horses. And some beasts guarding the perimeter of the grounds."

Before she could tell him she watched those beasts be trained by her brother on a daily basis, she heard the click of high heels on the marble. "Joshua? Is that you?"

"Right here, Mom."

A slender blond woman breezed in with outstretched arms, a mile-wide smile, and a whiff of lemon-scented perfume that instantly made the room lighter. "What a treat," she exclaimed, giving and getting a genuinely warm hug.

Malcolm came right in behind her, practically on her heels. "And this is Darcy," he said. "Joshua's friend. Darcy, meet my beautiful wife, Christine."

"Darcy!" She turned and her brown eyes widened, the name on her lips sounding like she'd waited a lifetime to make this acquaintance. "I'm so delighted to meet you, dear."

Darcy took the hand she offered, drinking in the woman with the same awe she'd felt when approaching the house. There was so much—beauty, style, grace, and a hand so soft, Darcy wondered if it had ever done anything but be slathered in expensive creams.

"Please sit down, both of you." Christine ushered them to the snow-white settee, seemingly without a care about who sat on the furniture or what they wore. "Has Elaine been here?" she asked Malcolm as they sat.

"She's bringing drinks," Malcolm assured her, placing a hand on her knee. "I figured you'd like iced tea with lime, not lemon."

She smiled at him, dark eyes glinting with love. There was really no other way to describe it. It was as real as the crinkles around her eyes and the giant diamonds on her fingers. "Thank you, sweetheart. Now, Joshua, I hope you brought pictures of your new project. I cannot wait to see what you've done with that beautiful brownstone. Have you finished that smaller upstairs apartment yet?"

"I have." He glanced at Darcy, a smile reaching eyes that were precisely the same shade of espresso as his mother's. "Darcy is renting it."

"Oh, how lovely," Christine said. "I know Joshua was worried about getting a tenant with the upstairs construction."

So they weren't estranged, Darcy mused. She knew what was going on in his life. "It's a beautiful apartment," Darcy said. "The renovations were done to perfection, and we're very happy there."

"We?" Christine asked, looking from one to the other with unabashed interest.

"My dog, Kookie, and me," Darcy explained.

Malcolm let out a deep sigh. "Of course the reno is perfection," he said. "Joshua is gifted. He could turn a fishing shack into a resort. In fact, I've seen him do it."

For some reason, the compliment really surprised her. With all Josh had said or implied, she'd expected ice from these two, but Mal's praise was genuine. "I wanted my stepson to head a national remodeling program for Bucking Properties," he continued, talking to Darcy. "With his talent, we could be the premier house-flipping company in the country, which would launch a whole new business for us."

"Really?" Darcy looked at him. "You don't want to do that?"

"Oh, no," Malcolm answered for him. "It would mean working for Gideon. And Joshua would have none of that."

"That wasn't it at all." Josh looked directly at the other man with a cool gaze. "And you know that, Mal."

Immediately, Christine put her hand on her husband's leg. "I bet these two are hungry as well as parched," she said. "Can you please get Elaine to make some finger sandwiches? Oh, and cookies. As a matter of fact, why don't you ask her to set up an early lunch on the patio? I know they're stretched to the limit down there in the kitchen getting ready for tonight, but they can handle it."

"We can't stay, Mom," Josh said. "We just have a quick question."

"You can't stay for the party tonight?" Genuine disappointment came through in the question. "Why, I assumed that's why you're here."

"Party?" Josh's whole body tightened so completely, Darcy could feel it a foot away. "No, we can't stay for any party."

"Joshua! It's our twentieth anniversary party. Surely you got the invitation."

"I did, but I totally—"

But Malcolm was already up. "You'll stay, or you'll break your mother's heart." He dropped a kiss on her head. "And I'll go talk to Elaine and make sure your suite is ready, Joshua."

"No, we can't—"

But Malcolm was gone and Josh was left staring at his mother, who shifted her gaze to Darcy. "I'll tell my stylist your size and have something for you to wear, dear. And Mal's right." She turned to Josh, her expression softening. "Honey, you break my heart when you fight with the man I love more than life itself."

Josh closed his eyes like the comment hit its target. "We're not here for a social visit, Mom, or to hear about why I don't want to work for a man that doesn't share my ethics or my last name."

Christine flinched slightly and gave an apologetic look to Darcy before turning back to Josh. "What do you need? Money? I'll arrange for—"

"Mom. I do not need money. I need Savannah."

"Oh." Her shoulders sank as she glanced at Darcy again. "I thought... Oh well. Sorry, but she isn't my stylist anymore, for obvious reasons."

At least his mother didn't support the stepbrother-hopping Savannah had done, Darcy thought. Point in her favor for firing her.

"I need to reach her," Josh said. "I want her signature on a piece of paper, ink or electronic."

"Whatever for?"

He glanced at Darcy, the slightest warning in his eyes, but not so slight that Christine might not have seen it. But the other woman didn't react if she had.

"She isn't answering my messages or texts," Josh said, pointedly not responding to his mother's question. "So, can you reach Gideon?"

She frowned. "I think so, but the time difference would mean it's the middle of the night in Singapore."

So they were in Singapore. Darcy checked out Josh's reaction to that, but there was none. "I don't care what time it is where they are. I need to talk to Savannah and email her something today. Now."

But his mother looked even more confused. "I can call him, but…" She angled her head and furrowed her brow. "What would make you think Savannah is with him on Bucking business?"

"Because he's not on Bucking business, he's…" Josh's voice trailed off. "When did he leave?"

"A few days ago, on the Bucking jet. Yes, he's on Bucking business, talking to a distributor. In fact, Mal was supposed to go, but a new board member called a meeting, so Gideon left New York and went on to Singapore in his stead. Why?"

"But Savannah is with him?"

She looked stunned at the suggestion. "Josh, Savannah is persona non grata around here after what she did."

"What *she* did?" He choked on the words.

"Oh, she did it, all right." His mother looked from side to side, as if some of the staff could be lurking about, and inched closer.

Darcy sat perfectly still, looking from one to the other, trying to figure out how much his mother knew about Savannah's cheating and if that was why she was on the outs. Josh didn't say a word, either, watching her.

"Savannah Mayfield is a liar and a thief," Christine said quietly. "And you, Joshua, dodged a bullet when you broke up with her."

"I know I did, and she is a liar, but I don't think she's a thief."

Christina's eyes flew open. "Her work as a stylist was merely a way to access the finer things that belonged to others, take them, then claim they'd been 'lost.' Malcolm's mother has been losing jewelry ever since Savannah started visiting her and 'offering' her assistance free of charge." French-tipped nails dug at the air when she made air quotes. "Brea and I have contacted everyone who'd hired her to warn them away, and she'll never work anywhere in or around Charlotte or Lake Norman again. And to think I introduced her to you and all those clients."

"Have you reported this to the police?" Josh asked.

Her jaw loosened as if the suggestion appalled her. "Certainly not. Bucking Properties does not need that kind of media coverage. No, we handled it the way we handle things."

"By cutting out her livelihood and ruining her life."

Christine drew back, horrified. "Are you defending her? I thought you told me you two were completely finished. Now I haven't known why, but I suspect you discovered her true colors."

"Yes, I did, but I honestly never thought she was stealing anything."

She huffed. "Well, she was. And, frankly, I never thought she was right for you, and I think it's fair to say my gut instinct was correct. Would you argue with that?"

"No. But I still need to talk to her, even by phone. I get voice mail when I call."

Christine lifted a narrow shoulder. "I can't help you."

"You have no way to reach her?" He had the slightest note of desperation in his voice, which Darcy knew was for Stella, but Christine's look of disapproval meant she interpreted the question differently.

"Absolutely not." She gave a delicate sigh. "And I'm certain we'll never hear from her again."

Josh shook his head. "Then I have to talk to Gideon. Maybe he knows where she is."

She looked confounded. "Why on earth would Gideon know where she is?"

So Mom was entirely clueless about what caused the breakup, Darcy mused. Maybe the problem with this family was straight-up communication. No one told anyone *anything*.

"Brea?" he asked.

"You can talk to Brea tonight." Malcolm breezed back in, the timing making Darcy wonder if he'd been standing outside the sitting room waiting for the perfect moment to make an entrance. "At the party that you will be attending."

"No, we won't be." Josh stood and reached for Darcy's hand. "We've got some business in town, then we're leaving."

"But didn't you say you wanted Savannah's signature on something?" Christine asked.

"I do, but—"

"William Mitchell will be here," she said.

"Your attorney?" Josh asked.

"And the attorney we had Savannah use when she needed to sign some confidentiality agreements, not that she kept them. However, in the process, she gave him power of attorney in a far more sweeping way than she realized. Perhaps he can sign what you need in her place."

Josh gave Darcy a dubious look. "Might be a stretch

from non-disclosure to full POA, but it's worth a try." He tugged her to her feet. "I know where his office is."

"It's Saturday," Christine reminded him.

"Then I'll figure it out." He moved like a racehorse itching to get out of the gate. He really did hate this place.

"Let's try calling him in my office," Malcolm said, stepping between Josh and Darcy to put a hand on his stepson's shoulder. "We'll be right back, ladies."

Josh hesitated a moment, then nodded, obviously smart enough for Stella's sake to take help no matter where it came from. When they left, Christine stood and reached out to take Darcy's hands. "Please accept my deepest apologies for airing such ghastly dirty laundry in front of you, Darcy."

She managed a shrug and a smile. "I'm the youngest of six. Our closets are full of skeletons and dirty laundry." Although nothing quite on this scale.

"You're kind. And beautiful inside and out. Seeing you with Joshua gives me hope that he can recover from the unhealthy relationship he was mired in with Savannah."

Unhealthy because *she banged his stepbrother*. And Darcy wasn't *with* Josh. Should she clear that up right now? But then, Josh hadn't. Who could tell? There was so much damn subterfuge in this house.

But she couldn't walk out without trying one more time to find out if Christine Bucking knew an easier, faster way to get that paper signed. A lawyer could take until Monday, and who knew if that would even work or if the man would agree to use the power of attorney for a dog's medical situation? She had to push this.

"Mrs. Bucking, we really need Savannah's signature," she said, adding pressure to the other woman's hands. "It's important to…" Why hadn't he told them about Stella? She exhaled and decided he must have his reasons and she didn't want to step on them. "To both of us," she finished.

Christine's smile slid wider. "I was hoping that's what this was about. Whatever…*thing*…Savannah signed—a prenup or relationship agreement or whatever they're calling them—it can be undone, especially in light of her recent behavior."

"Especially," Darcy said dryly.

"Even if your relationship started before theirs ended."

No. That's where Darcy drew the line on bad communications. "Mrs. Bucking, I met your son days ago. We are not—"

She pulled Darcy closer, desperation turning her eyes nearly black. "Please. Please come to our party tonight, and I promise we'll help you right then and there. Our attorney does whatever we say." She added a laugh. "Which is nice."

Darcy tried to ease her hands away, knowing Josh would refuse. "I can't—"

"Do this mother a favor, dear." She inched closer and gripped tighter. "I long for one thing and one thing only, and that is that my children—*all* of them—would be close and loving to each other and to my husband. Joshua's coming home for this party is a major step in that direction. Help him see how much we love him, please? Help him get that chip off his shoulder that he's been carrying around for twenty years."

Was that even possible with all the resentment Josh

harbored? And Gideon's betrayal? Darcy searched her face, trying to determine if this plea was real and if she could help heal any of the wounds.

"He simply can't accept that I truly love Mal," Christine continued. "You marry a family, you know, not a person."

"I've heard him say so." And man, this family was a doozy. But could there be hope for it? Something in her wanted so much to help Josh unload some of that hate-filled baggage.

"Help me, Darcy. Help him see that Mal and I are forever. And help him where Gideon is concerned. He'll be a happier, healthier man, and..." She lifted her brows and added a very knowing look. "Much better prepared for matrimony himself."

Matrimony. Apparently she missed the *we just met* part. "We're friends, Mrs. Bucking." With dogs. Dogs they weren't even allowed to mention.

Christine laughed. "I'd be blind and deaf if I believed that. Now, come back here in the late afternoon, enjoy a siesta in your suite, and I'll send up a selection of gowns and one of Joshua's tuxedos. The opening cocktail party is on the veranda at eight, then dinner and dancing until the wee hours. Such fun!"

Except, by the wee hours, Josh will have imploded.

"We'll see," Darcy said. "We still have a lot to do today." Like get Savannah's signature and find the name of the—wait a second! "Mrs. Bucking, do you happen to know the name of the vet Savannah used for her dog, Stella?"

She paled, and her face dropped to the dog paw logo on Darcy's T-shirt. "I don't, but whoever he was, I hope you seek another."

"Why?"

"Because if it weren't for him, that dog would still be alive."

"Excuse me?"

"And if you ask me, and I know you didn't, but if you did, I'd tell you that Savannah's problems were probably caused by the medical bills for that dog. With Joshua breaking off from the company and turning down all family money, he couldn't help her with astronomical vet fees."

"For her eyes?" she asked.

"I have no idea what was wrong with that dog, but if it wasn't one thing, it was another. I hated when she'd bring it to fittings." She shook her head. "It's in a better place."

Yeah, *it* was. Waterford Farm. But what the holy heck was going on? Was Savannah a pathological liar, or was this whole family made of crazy?

"Bill's unreachable," Malcolm announced, coming into the room. "But his wife said she'll see us tonight."

"Where's Josh?" Darcy asked.

"Probably in his truck. Kid can never get out of this house fast enough." He sounded sad enough that Darcy felt compelled to smile and give them both warm handshakes, thanking them for their time.

As they said goodbye and she walked out, Darcy spotted Josh behind the wheel, staring straight ahead, anguish on every feature.

Her heart hurt for him. She'd never left home feeling that way.

Chapter Thirteen

Josh stayed silent as they pulled out of the circular drive, letting his heart rate return to normal before he even attempted to answer the many questions Darcy would have.

"I don't know where to begin," he finally said as he pulled out on the main road and headed south toward Savannah's apartment.

"Oh, I guess you can start with why your parents don't know Savannah cheated on you with Gideon."

"Let's get one thing straight," he said, swallowing hard. "They aren't 'my parents,' and I don't like the term."

"Semantics, dude, and you know it. Why don't they know? Why won't you tell them about the dog? Oh, and did you know that your mother thinks Stella is dead?"

He whipped around. "What?"

"Oh yeah." She leaned back and propped her sneakers on the dash. "Do you mind? I feel the need to settle in for a nice big post-mortem from my first meeting with the Addams family."

He laughed, something he couldn't ever remember doing this close to that house. "Told you."

"Oh, no," she said. "You didn't even begin to tell me."

He glanced at her, warmed by her very presence after leaving the hell house. "I wanted you to go in with no preconceptions, so I didn't color your thinking."

"Okay, my observations? One, your mom and dad—sorry—stepfather, but please let me use shorthand, because there's so much to say."

"Fine." He ached to reach over and take her hand, longing to hold it while they talked about his family, but she had her hands steepled under her chin, tapping her fingers, organizing her thoughts.

"First of all, Christine and Mal love each other. That's as plain as the nose on my face."

He took a quick look at that nose, enjoying the way it tilted up a tiny bit and was peppered with freckles. "I don't argue that point. They genuinely care for each other. Enough that they could rationalize the collateral damage of their union and wear blinders where Gideon is concerned."

"Their union is a marriage," she fired back. "And it's real. And good. Your mom deserves it, because I think she's got a good heart, and she genuinely loves you."

He exhaled, turned onto the interstate, and considered that. "All true. No argument."

"But none of you actually communicate, have you noticed? You talk around stuff, you let assumptions rule the day, and no one is honest. That's why the family is broken."

"Maybe."

She snorted her response to his maybe. "And what's with Savannah and Gideon?"

"They're together, I'd bet money on it. If he's in Singapore on business, she went with him, in the jet, no doubt."

"Even though he knows she's been accused of stealing things from clients? Why would he want her?"

"She was mine," he said simply. "And that makes her infinitely attractive to Gideon."

"Then why haven't you told your mother she cheated on you with him?"

"Because I'm not twelve, and she didn't take my side then, either." He heard the bitterness in his voice and tried to tamp it down. "I've been the recipient of Gid's resentment and jealousy for twenty years, and one thing I've learned is I will not be believed because he is a Bucking and I am a Ranier."

"Your mother doesn't defend you? Her kid doesn't come first?" Her voice rose with disbelief and a lifetime of being raised in a "normal" paradigm.

"Malcolm comes first, and for him, his son and daughter come first."

"Ah, yes," she said. "Cinderfella."

"Not funny anymore," he shot back.

"Why are you mad at me?" she asked.

"Because you're taking the wrong side."

"I'm not taking any side." She whipped her feet down and leaned forward to make her point. "Except the dog's. Remember? The dogs come first. Why did Savannah tell your mother Stella is dead? I didn't ask because I thought you might have a legitimate reason for not mentioning Stella other than—"

173

"They don't need to know."

"That is not legitimate, Josh. Why wouldn't you tell them why we're doing this, or the truth about Gideon and Savannah? Maybe they'd help you."

"I don't share things with them," he said. "Experience tells me that anything they know about me can be ammunition used against me at a later date. Unwittingly, maybe, but still. Information is ammunition, and I won't give them any."

"Except they need to know Savannah is lying about Stella being dead."

"To what end? They already think she's a thief. Why add pathological liar?"

"And cheater," Darcy interjected.

"Maybe she is all those things, but…" He blew out a breath and ran his hand through his hair, pulling a little with frustration and anger at the world. And himself. "Two months ago, I would have fought to the death to defend her from these accusations."

"You fought a little today," she murmured.

He gave her a sideways look. "I was about to propose to her, Darcy. I loved her. Accepting all this about her makes me feel and look like the idiot I am."

"You're not an idiot," she said softly. "Love is blind, remember?"

"And so is Stella." He finally got hold of her hand. "And we have to do everything we can to give her a fighting chance."

"Yes," she agreed, tenderly stroking his knuckles with the same touch she'd use to calm Stella or Kookie. "So what do we do next?"

He felt himself fall into her soft voice and gentle question, the weight of the visit already lifting. "I'm going to try and find out who her vet is, and if he or she is open on Saturday. Getting the dog's records shouldn't take a freaking court order. I know her neighbor who has a dog and recommended the vet. Hopefully, she's home today, because I don't have her phone number."

Darcy nodded, still holding his hand. "What if Savannah isn't with Gideon? What if she's in trouble, missing in action, and telling people Stella is dead because she isn't ever planning to come back here to live? Maybe she's setting up shop far away from these allegations and a close-knit community who blackballed her."

Or maybe she's getting boned by a Bucking.

"And maybe she isn't ever going to come back for Stella," Darcy continued. "And that would make Stella—"

"Mine." He tapped the brakes and steered into the exit lane for Savannah's apartment.

"Right. If she never comes back, you qualify as her owner now, right? I mean, dog ownership isn't legal, it's just that my dad wants to do the right thing, because that's pretty much his motto in life."

He smiled. "My dad, too. So, do you think Dr. Walker would accept that argument and let me sign the papers if we tell her we have reason to believe Savannah won't ever be back?"

"Even better, what if that attorney signs a paper saying he 'gives' the dog to you?" Darcy suggested.

He frowned. "I don't know about that."

"Think of it as bending the rules, not breaking them, Josh."

He played the scenario through in his head, starting with… "That means going to that party tonight."

"How bad can it be?"

He grunted, but she threaded her fingers through his and leaned over. "I'll be your date."

Stopping at a light, he threw her a look, hoping he didn't give away how much he liked that idea.

"For Stella," she added. "We'd be doing it for our sweet Stella."

He held her gaze for a few seconds, until the light changed and he turned into the apartment complex he hadn't visited for more than a month. He waited for a wave of hurt to hit, but none came. All he felt was happy to have Darcy next to him.

"Let's see how this goes. We need the name of the vet. And who knows? Maybe Savannah's really hiding out in her apartment, and then we can get her signature, hit the road, and make your family's Sunday night dinner."

"You really want to go to that, don't you?"

"A helluva lot more than a black-tie party that celebrates the anniversary of the unhappiest day of my life."

"Yeah, I see your point. Well, maybe we can do both, then spend all of next week comparing families."

"Trust me, you'll win that comparison."

Josh was quiet as they headed to the double glass doors that led into the lobby of the high-end building, and Darcy couldn't really blame him. It couldn't be easy learning that Savannah was not only a cheater, but a liar and a thief.

They stepped inside after Josh entered a code, and

he immediately broke into a wide smile at the older man behind a security desk. "Man, am I glad to see you, T-man," he said.

"Mr. Ranier." A soft flush of color rose, and narrow shoulders dropped. "Oh Lord. Janet was right. I shouldn't have sold it."

Josh frowned, looking uncertain.

"But I can get you the cash," the guard, whose name badge read Terrance Phillips, said. "By Monday when the bank opens? Janet wouldn't let me spend a dime of that money. She said you might want to give it to some…" He paused and looked at Darcy. "Other lady."

He gave the guy a ring? The one he'd intended to give Savannah? Darcy tried to process that as Josh went closer to the desk and extended a hand. "A deal is a deal. I don't want the ring or the money."

The other man looked visibly relieved as he shook Josh's hand. "You're a good man, Mr. Ranier." He glanced at Darcy. "And…"

"Terry, this is my friend Darcy. We were hoping to talk to Savannah."

"She's not here," he said. "Haven't seen hide nor hair of Ms. Mayfield for a few days, and last I did, she said I should save up her mail and packages for a long time and tell anyone looking for her that she is not in the country."

He glanced at Darcy, who shrugged, not at all surprised at this news. "Plan B?" she suggested.

"Any chance you could call Emily Goodwell in 6F?" he asked Terry. "I need to ask her a question."

But he was already shaking his head, and more disappointment kicked at Darcy. "Ms. Goodwell's gone home to see her parents in Connecticut this weekend, and I don't have her cell number, sir."

What could they do now? Give up? Call every vet in town? Cut a deal with the lawyer? She already sensed Josh didn't like that idea, since he'd apparently never met a rule he couldn't follow.

"Terry." He leaned over the desk. "I have a key. What are the chances you'd let me go into Savannah's apartment?"

Unless it was for Stella…then rules could be damned. A zing of attraction ricocheted through Darcy for that.

Terry lifted his brow. "Mr. Ranier. You know I can't do that."

"You can come with us, Terry. I'm trying to find the name of her vet. I'm watching her dog while she's gone."

His whole expression dropped. "That sweet dog who went blind?" he said, genuine sadness in his voice.

At least she hadn't told *this* guy that Stella was dead.

"Which is why I need to get into her apartment."

Terry shook his head. "Mr. Ranier, I know I took that ring and I'm grateful for the gift, but I can't let you go into the apartment. It's our policy, and my job would be on the line."

Josh's shoulders sank a little, but Darcy stepped forward, sensing Terry had a soft spot she was about to exploit the hell out of. "We want to help Stella regain her sight," she said. "My father is a vet, and he can get her into a special research program, so she could see again."

Terry stared at her, the first crack in his armor

visible by the expression of sympathy and hope. "Really?"

Darcy reached into her bag and pulled out her phone, tapping to get the last picture. "See? Here she is this morning at my family's canine facility. We can help her, Terry. But we need to know the name of her current vet so we can get her medical records. That's all we want, honestly."

Terry looked at the picture, then up to Darcy and Josh. "I've never seen a dog change so much. She used to run to me for treats, then, suddenly—"

"It's curable," Josh said, holding the other man's gaze. "Please help us."

"Help Stella," Darcy added.

The man let out the longest, most pained sigh, then reached under the desk. "God, I love dogs."

Darcy and Josh shared a look as Terry brought out a small Guard Will Return Momentarily sign and then gestured them to the elevator.

On the way there, Josh took her hand, brought it to his lips, and kissed her knuckles. She could read his expression, too. Something like, *What's a little invasion of privacy if it's for the dog?*

She didn't know what thrilled her more—his lips on her knuckles or the fact that they'd silently communicated, a feat only possible with Ella and, long ago, her mother. But it had happened, and she couldn't deny that it made her feel…things.

She tamped those things down in the elevator, and then Terry led the way into a wide, carpeted hallway with soft lighting and expensive finishes. The building wasn't Darcy's style, that was for sure, but she could understand the appeal.

The security guard discreetly stepped aside and let Josh use a key to open the door to the first unit they reached. Inside, Darcy blinked into a dimly lit living room, taking in all that she saw. A dozen different descriptions bounced in her brain, but not one of them was *neat*. Spacious. Gloomy. Trendy. Feminine.

But also cluttered, disorganized, messy, and crowded.

"Whoa." Josh stood stone-still in the middle of the room, and something told Darcy he was thinking the same thing. "What happened here?"

The coffee table was covered in drawers from the kitchen, each emptied of cooking utensils and silverware that were grouped in distinct piles. A floor-to-ceiling bookshelf had been almost completely emptied, with stacks of books on the floor and knickknacks piled on top of one another. Glancing into the kitchen, she could see that the contents of most of the cabinets were spread out on the counters—wine glasses, plates, pots, and pans.

It was a mess, but almost a systematic mess.

"Maybe she started packing to move out," Darcy suggested.

But Josh shook his head. "This kind of chaos would make her crazy," he said. "She'd never leave it this way."

He turned and headed down the hall, and Darcy followed, but slowed when he continued toward the double doors of a master bedroom. She didn't want to go in there, in that room where he surely had memories. It would feel invasive.

Instead, she gestured toward another, smaller room, set up as an office. "Can I?" she asked Terry.

"Maybe she has the vet records in there."

He nodded and went with her as she stepped inside to find more of the same organized chaos. It was like every item had been taken out of its place and laid out on open surfaces.

She stepped to a large white desk, noticing that all the cubbies in the hutch above it were empty, but the desktop was filled with papers, pens, files, notebooks, even empty picture frames.

Savannah was planning to pack and move, Darcy decided. Taking inventory of her life, perhaps. Darcy had just done that with her things at home—laid out all the clothes and belongings to decide what to pack.

"Is Mr. Ranier okay?" Terry's question pulled her from her thoughts, making her turn.

"I think so," she said. "You want to check on him?"

"I mean since he broke up with Ms. Mayfield."

She exhaled, not entirely sure how to answer that. "I only recently met him," she said. "I don't know how different he is. She hurt him, that's for sure."

He nodded. "Damn shame, since he's a nice guy."

"Was she…nice?" Because based on what she'd heard so far, Darcy was starting to doubt Josh's ability to judge character.

"Very," he said. "Always kind. But…"

Darcy waited, silent.

"I hear things."

"I bet you do."

"These are small towns around the lake," he said. "People talk. I think she's in some trouble."

"Trouble, as in someone is trying to harm her, or has already? Or trouble, as in she's mismanaged her finances and needs a bankruptcy lawyer? Because I don't need to know about the latter."

"It's...that," he said. "About her money and her clients."

She shook her head and turned, uncomfortable gossiping with the guard about the accusations against Savannah. It was bad enough they were poking around the woman's apartment.

She scanned the desk, a single bookshelf, and glanced at a daybed along the wall, when the word *Stella* written neatly on a manila file folder tab caught her eye. "Oh, look!" Loath to touch anything she shouldn't in another person's home, Darcy pointed. "Can we open that?"

Terry angled his head, giving silent consent.

Josh walked in as she lifted the file and opened it, reading the first piece of paper. "It's a receipt from her vet!" she exclaimed, turning it to show him. "Name and phone number. Bingo!"

"Fantastic." He came next to her to look closer.

"You can't take it," Terry said.

"Pictures?" Darcy asked.

Terry grunted softly, but his eyes shuttered closed. "I'll stand in the living room."

They didn't even bother to read the papers, but snapped a photo of each page, then Josh closed the file and returned it to the pile with a deep sigh.

"You okay?" she asked.

He shook his head. "It's like I didn't even know her."

She gave his arm a sympathetic squeeze before they stepped back into the hall to find Terry.

"That's all we need," Josh said, putting a hand on the guard's shoulder. "I'll bring Stella here to see you when she's cured."

Terry nodded. "Let me give you my cell phone so you can keep me updated."

A few minutes later, they headed back downstairs, and while the two men exchanged numbers, Darcy clicked through the pictures on her phone to make sure they had all the information they needed to reach the vet, but the files were so thorough, she realized they wouldn't have to.

One of the papers noted the date that Stella had been diagnosed with SARDS. Darcy did some quick math. Five and a half weeks ago.

They had very few days to get Stella into this program. By the end of the coming week, it would be too late.

That knowledge assuaged all her guilt for plowing into another woman's apartment and taking pictures of things on her desk. If Stella's sight could be saved, it would be worth it.

Chapter Fourteen

I f he hadn't needed Savannah's lawyer's help in getting permission to treat Stella, Josh and Darcy would have been halfway back to Bitter Bark by now. Sadly, they weren't.

Going to his parents' anniversary party was the last thing on earth Josh wanted to do. The very last. Dressed in a monkey suit of a tux he hadn't worn since the last shindig he was forced to attend, he paced the sitting room connected to his bedroom while he waited for Darcy.

Mom had put her in a room down the hall, while he'd taken his old suite, a suggestion he kind of wished he hadn't so gallantly made so Darcy would feel comfortable.

Then she walked in.

And he could file that gallant suggestion under Stupid Josh Moves.

He stared at her for five solid seconds, not trusting his voice or his brain to deliver the right words, because there were none.

"Do you think I should thank Savannah?" she asked.

He blinked at her. He should thank Savannah—for leaving and leading him to the woman in front of him. Darcy shone with a light that came from inside, and when she took a step, sparks seemed to fly from her whole being. Okay, there were a lot of sparkles on that deep-blue gown, but…

"Thank her for what?" His voice came out huskier than intended.

"The gowns. Your mother said they were left here a while ago, so I'm guessing that was courtesy of your ex, her stylist." She held her arms out and twirled, blinding him with all the blue light and silver sparks.

No, not blinding him. He'd been blind before, but the woman in front of him was vivid and beautiful. He could see everything about her, from her heart for doing the right thing, to a sly playfulness he hadn't even realized he wanted so much in a woman.

"She must be good at her job." She waved her hands down the length of the dress, which was little more than a strapless column that clung to every curve he so badly wanted to touch. "I couldn't decide which one I loved more, but I picked this."

"It's…you…I'm…" He laughed.

"Cute," she finished for him, coming closer to reach up and tug the edges of his bow tie. "Good look for you, Hot Landlord."

He smiled down at her. "Are you going to call me that tonight?"

"Secretly. And what are you going to call me?"

"Other than beautiful?"

A soft flush rose to her cheeks, and her shimmery lids shuttered to acknowledge the compliment. "I meant, what's my title? Your friend? Your tenant?

185

Your partner in crime? People will assume…other things."

"I don't care what these people assume," he said. "I hope we're not there long enough to worry about it. I want to corner that lawyer, get this paper I drafted and printed signed—" he tapped his jacket pocket "—and leave."

"And miss dinner and dancing?"

He searched her face, wondering if the little blend of disappointment and anticipation was real. But he knew the answer. Everything about Darcy Kilcannon was real. "I bet you like to dance."

"As much as I like to breathe. And dinner's always good, too."

He relented with a tip of his head. "We can stay if you're having fun."

"What if you're not?"

"I won't."

She narrowed her eyes at him. "You know what my dad would say? 'Not with that attitude, you won't.'"

He laughed. "Mine would have said that, too." He let his gaze slip down. "Okay, maybe I will have a little fun."

That made her smile, which was like flipping an electrical switch. "It's not against the rules to have a little fun at a party, Josh, no matter where it is or what they're celebrating. If you start to slip into a family funk, just tell me you like my shoes and then kiss me."

"Excuse me?"

"You heard me. It's like a secret code. I have those with Ella all the time for when we're out and need each other's help."

He frowned. "You like her shoes and kiss?"

Poking his shoulder. "We have an escape. A code word or line, which means 'get me out of this situation, fast.' You say 'nice shoes,' and then we'll kiss." She punctuated that by sticking out her foot to show off another pair of insanely high shoes better suited for a stripper than a dog groomer.

"Oh. Nice shoes. Very nice shoes."

She gave a low, sexy laugh while he let his gaze take another slow trip down her body, from the blood-pumping shoes, over long legs and the outlines of taut thighs, along narrow hips and a slender waist, pausing at the rise of her breasts, the achingly sweet cleavage, sliding over her collarbones, up her throat, and settling on a mouth he wanted to kiss more than he'd wanted anything, ever.

"Don't forget the save," she teased. "A kiss."

He forced himself to wait, savoring the anticipation of that first kiss.

"You want to, don't you?" she teased.

"Want? You are the queen of the understatement."

She inched ever so slightly forward. "I double-dog dare you, Hot Landlord."

Leaning closer, he placed his hand under her chin and lifted her face. "I'm pretty sure that means you have to go first."

She rose on her tiptoes, slid her arms around his neck, and leaned into him. "Let's do it together," she murmured. "Because we're a team, remember?"

He laughed softly, closing the space between their lips and sipping his first taste of her mouth. It was warm, sweet, and as delicious as he'd known it would be. He could feel her whole body soften against his and hear the softest whimper escape her throat.

Heat and need clawed at his lower half, making him embrace her tighter, so there was nothing but beating hearts and clothes between them.

"Uh, am I interrupting something?"

He froze, released his hold, and swore he hated this family more than anything in the world.

Brea Bucking stood in the doorway with one hand on her hip, swathed in pure white from head to toe, her black hair coasting over shoulders toned by a private trainer. Without waiting for an invitation, his stepsister strode into the room, pinned her ebony gaze on Darcy, and nodded slowly.

"Definite upgrade, sweet brother of mine."

Unfazed by the interruption, Darcy let her lips curl up and extended her hand, but Brea brushed it aside and put both arms around her to squeeze. "Oh, no. I'm a hugger. Welcome. Darcy, is it? Christine said you were a knockout, and she wasn't kidding."

"Darcy, let me introduce my stepsister, Brea Bucking, who has zero filter and an infinite amount of opinions."

Brea laughed, a quick and easy laugh that Josh knew could morph into a dagger-sharp insult without a second's notice. "I speak the truth, that's all." She pointed her finger at him. "And I heard you are on the hunt to have Savannah sign something. Don't tell me she robbed you blind, too, Josh."

Worse, he thought. Much worse. "No, she..." He caught Darcy's look and understood it as clearly as if she'd spoken out loud. *Tell the truth. It's family. Communicate.* Except...

He replied with an infinitesimal nod. "I'm watching

her dog, who is very much alive, despite what she told you and my mother."

Brea's jaw dropped wide open. "*What?*"

"She's staying with Josh," Darcy added, the light in her eyes telling him that his honesty pleased her. Which only made him want to offer more of it.

"And Darcy's father is a vet who's hooked us up with a researcher at a local college who is doing experimental research to restore blindness in cases like Stella's. That's why I need Savannah's signature."

Brea almost couldn't lift that jaw yet. "Savannah gave the dog to you?"

She sounded surprised enough that he wondered if Savannah had confided the truth to Brea about the breakup. "Only while she's gone with…"

"She's not with Gideon," Brea said when he didn't finish. "Christine told me you made that insane leap of logic."

So Savannah hadn't confided. Well, Josh wasn't going to be that honest with her, despite what Darcy thought.

"And we can help Stella see again," Darcy insisted, almost as if she sensed that Brea wasn't excited enough about that. Probably because Brea didn't like dogs, if he remembered correctly. Refused to have one in the house, and being the spoiled baby of the family, she got what she wanted.

Brea nodded slowly, as if still she couldn't quite process the fact that Josh had Stella. "I'm so… Oh my God. That's…yes. Wonderful. But why did she lie about everything?" Her voice rose, and she caught herself. "I'm sorry. I get emotional about Savannah.

She was my friend, too," she explained to Darcy. "She was like a sister to me, but she was using us. *All* of us." She underscored that with a sharp look at Josh.

"Do you have any way to reach her?" Darcy asked. "Another number? A working email address? I can't believe she'd go off on an extended vacation and leave her dog with someone and no way to reach her and no medical waiver in case something happened to Stella."

Brea's brows shot up. "She probably thinks we'll sic the police on her, so, no, I don't have any way of reaching her. And, honestly, she doesn't care about that dog." She closed her eyes and shook her head. "I'm sorry. I'm being petty. Savannah was my friend, but she struggled with some issues. We all have something to hide, right?"

Darcy looked right at her. "I don't," she said.

Brea's smile was a little sly. "Oh, I bet if I gave you enough champagne and dug deep enough, I'd find something." She draped an arm around Darcy's shoulders. "Can I try?"

Darcy laughed. "All you want." She and Brea shared a long look and a smile, and Josh could practically hear them connecting in that way women did. Over dresses, men, life, and wine.

The three of them headed down the hall while Josh tried to shake off the feeling that the walls of Buckin*gsham* were already closing in on him.

Josh rarely let go of Darcy's hand. If he did, it was only to touch her back or waist or skim his fingers over her shoulder, sending chills over her skin despite the summer heat on the veranda.

The sexy contact enhanced an already magical cocktail hour, livened up with a glass of the most expensive champagne Darcy had ever tasted at one of the poshest parties she'd ever attended.

A dressed-to-the-nines crowd of well over a hundred people gathered on a massive patio bathed in the golden streaks of light as the sun set over Lake Norman. Waiters weaved among guests offering drinks and hors d'oeuvres, while a small jazz band played from an alcove that looked like it was built for the sole purpose of housing live music.

The truth was, Darcy didn't even want to think about leaving early. Not that she longed to live in this galaxy glittering with diamonds and dropped names and designer everything. But it was a little like traveling to an exotic locale—an experience she'd never had and wanted to enjoy. Josh surprised her, too, working the crowd and introducing Darcy to friends, distant relatives from Malcolm's extended family, lakeside neighbors, and oodles of Bucking Properties executives and their spouses.

They didn't take a break until it seemed he'd introduced her to twenty people, but when they did stop for another glass of champagne, she spotted someone she hadn't yet met—a man whose face was familiar to her.

"Actor? Newscaster?" She studied the handsome fortysomething man, trying to place the familiar angles of his strong features and slightly roguish long hair with a bit of salt strewn through the pepper. "That's somebody, right?"

"Clay Slater, the NASCAR driver, and his wife, Lisa," Josh told her. "And I actually like that guy a lot."

"Oh, of course. My brothers are racing fans. He drove the car with the logo of the Kincaid Toy clown on the side, right?"

"That's him. He and Lisa live on Lake Norman, too. Want to meet him?"

"Yes! Is it gauche to ask for an autograph?"

"Completely, but if anyone could carry it off, it would be you." He tugged her closer. "I don't know how you fit in in this place, but you do."

"I like people and new adventures, that's how. Come on. Let's meet a celebrity."

They headed over to the couple, who might have been in a room full of people but held each other's gaze like there was no one else on earth but the two of them. The man lowered his head, whispered in his wife's ear, and she tipped her head back to laugh like they'd shared the sweetest, most secret joke.

Something deep inside Darcy stirred, a little awe, a little envy. She'd spotted that kind of intimacy around her brothers and sister and their new loves so frequently in the past year, and she remembered it from her own parents. Was she denying herself that kind of joy by clinging so steadfastly to independence?

After greeting Josh with a friendly man-hug, Clay Slater shook Darcy's hand and introduced Lisa, a beautiful blonde with warm blue eyes.

"Shouldn't you be on a racetrack somewhere in the middle of summer?" Josh asked Clay.

"I'm taking this year off with an eye to retirement

now that our son Keith is ready to take over the racing reins." He nodded to someone behind Clay. "In fact, he's right over there, schmoozing potential sponsors."

Darcy turned to see a tall, handsome young man who looked like he was in his mid-twenties chatting easily with Malcolm and Christine Bucking.

"Good heavens," Darcy said, looking at Lisa. "You don't look old enough to have a son his age."

"Keith's nineteen going on thirty," she said. "He's always been mature for his age, probably because I was single until he was nine, so he became a young man early. We also have a sixteen-year-old who keeps us busy."

"In the best possible way," Clay added, then angled his head. "Love those kids."

"Aww." Lisa slipped her hand through her husband's arm. "In the ten years we've been married, Clay's been the most amazing dad to my boys."

"It's been easy," Clay said. "Especially considering I married you before we ever had a date."

Darcy gave them a confused frown. "How did that happen?"

They both cracked up, shaking their heads. "It's kind of a funny story," Lisa said. "He hired me to be his wife, and a year later, we made it official."

"He *hired* you?" Darcy asked, not hiding her disbelief. "That's a new one."

"It was what we in racing call the Silly Season," Clay said on a laugh. "And it sure was." He turned to his wife and kissed her cheek. "Best hire I ever made."

"I was the one who lucked out," Lisa told them. "I was a single mom, struggling to pay the rent with the world's worst boss hitting on me, and in walks my own personal Santa Claus." She tightened her grip, leaning closer.

"Right into the arms of Lisa the Opinionated Waitress," Clay said, his eyes gleaming with affection when he looked at her.

"Your story sounds wonderful," Darcy said, then whispered to Josh, "My dad would love that one."

"It's been an extraordinary eleven years together," Lisa agreed, but her gaze moved past them. "And by the way Malcolm is shaking Keith's hand, it looks like Thunder Racing just got a new sponsor."

"That's my boy," Clay said with a little fist pump. "Let's go congratulate him, hon. Great to see you, Josh. And good to meet you, Darcy."

When they left, Josh turned to her. "No autograph?"

"Better. I got all the insider scoop I needed from that conversation," she said. "When I throw that personal tidbit around while my brothers are watching a race, I'll win the day."

"He's a good guy who never let the money and fame go to his head." He glanced around the room. "Can't say that about most of these people."

"Is it really that bad?"

He looked down at her, his eyes dark, deep, and focused on her so intently, it made her dizzy. "I feel the need to talk about your shoes."

She laughed, getting a shiver of chills at the thought of another kiss, even here in front of all these people. "Anytime."

He got a millimeter closer, then instantly straightened. "There he is."

For a moment, she thought he meant Gideon, and

she turned to brace for the evil stepbrother, half wondering if she'd like him as much as she liked Brea. But something told her the bald man walking side-by-side with Christine Bucking was much too old to be Gideon.

"The lawyer?" she guessed.

"Yes." His voice was taut, and Darcy peered up at him.

"You worried that this is breaking a rule? Maybe even a law?"

He didn't answer, but he didn't have to.

"Josh, you heard Brea. Savannah doesn't care about Stella, and even if that's wrong, and she does, then she surely wants her to be able to see. You already went into her apartment and—"

He put his finger on her lips. "I know. You're right. It's for Stella. Let's do this."

Christine and William Mitchell approached them, and after a flurry of introductions, Christine easily guided them all to a quiet study off the massive patio. "You men can chat in here privately," she said. "I'll take Darcy with me to refill our champagnes."

With a quick look and silent agreement, Darcy left Josh and the attorney and headed back to the party with Christine.

"Joshua is so happy," his mother whispered as she guided Darcy toward the crowd. "I can't remember ever seeing him look at a woman like he looks at you."

She wasn't quite sure how to respond to that, but couldn't help smiling. "He's...special." Yeah, maybe she was the queen of the understatement tonight.

"It's rare to see him happy here," she admitted.

"He's never forgiven me for taking him away from Charlotte and the memories of his father."

The surprisingly personal confession touched Darcy, making her lean closer to the other woman. "I lost my mother a few years ago," she confided. "It's very hard to adjust to that change, no matter your age."

Christine's expression softened. "I've spent twenty years torn between two men," she said. "I love Malcolm and I love Joshua who, by the way, is the spitting image of his handsome father."

Darcy tucked that little tidbit away, very happy to have an idea what Josh's father looked like. "He often says that remarriages aren't between two people, but two families."

"He's right," she said. "But I do think some blend better than others."

"There you are." Brea floated up to join them, her dark eyes dancing as if she had a secret. "What are you two gossiping about?" She put an arm around each of them. "How deliriously happy our Joshua seems to be?"

Our Joshua. How would he feel if he heard that?

"That's exactly what I was telling Darcy," Christine said, beaming at her. "And seeing him like that is all I've ever wanted."

"So don't be a stranger," Brea said to Darcy. "Come back again. How about next weekend? We can go out on the boat and shopping. I'm a world-class shopper, you know."

Darcy laughed, a familiar warmth rolling over her. This was family. Josh had one, and they weren't that bad, at least not on the surface. No, she hadn't met

Gideon and people were different behind closed doors, but—

A man's hand slid around her waist and pulled her back against his front, and instantly she recognized the feel and scent that was becoming more and more familiar.

"I got what we need," he whispered.

Slowly, she turned and looked up at him. "You did? How?"

"He has Savannah's power of attorney, although I'm not sure she realized she gave it to him for anything except Bucking-related business. Still, he was able to sign the paper on her behalf and we're good to go." He glanced around quickly. "Now, if you'd like."

She didn't hesitate. "Actually, I'd like to stay, Josh. I'm having a blast."

He searched her face, considering the request, and then responded with a smile. "Then we will." He gave her a hug, and over his shoulder she caught the looks of complete satisfaction on his mother's and stepsister's faces.

This man was loved—he just didn't know it.

Chapter Fifteen

They stayed until the last dance. Until almost every guest had left. Long after Josh's mother and Malcolm retired and the music changed to something younger and louder and more upbeat. Well later than Josh had ever dreamed he'd stay at a party in this house.

But he'd never had so much *fun* at a party here. He wrapped his arm around Darcy and finally walked up the wide curved stairs and down a long hall to the western wing where their rooms were.

She was much shorter again, her sexy shoes dangling from her fingers, long ago discarded for comfort on the dance floor. She'd had a few glasses of champagne, though he hadn't finished one. Didn't need a drop around her.

"You're down the hall a bit," he said when she slowed near his door.

"Mmm." She rested her head on his shoulder. "Am I? Feels like I'm right here where I should be."

He tucked her into his side, planting a kiss on her head, inhaling the sweet scent of her hair and a perfume he'd been dizzy on all night.

She smiled up at him. "I know what you're doing."

"Taking you to your room and making sure you're safe and sound?"

"*Not* taking me into your room so I can see how teenage you lived."

He laughed. "My mother's had decorators in there three times since I moved out. Any shreds of teenage me are long gone, or rotting in a storage center somewhere."

"My, aren't we a sentimentalist?" She looked up at him with a tease, but her eyes were as clear as the subtle accusation. Maybe she wasn't so tipsy, just genuinely happy.

"I can be, about certain things."

"Like?"

He thought for a minute. "A vortex marble collection. A wood-handled MegaCast fishing rod. A 1967 Pontiac GTO toy car the color of that dress you're wearing. And a dog named Roscoe."

She angled her head, confusion in her eyes. "Things you had as a little kid?" she guessed. "Things that..."

"That didn't make the move to Buck100*sham*."

"Oh." She brushed her knuckles along his jaw. "Home things. I get that."

He nodded, realizing that he'd never shared a single one of those missing pieces of his life with Savannah. And realizing, too, that merely having this conversation was a gross breach of every one of his rules and restrictions not to get close to a woman again.

But right then, with nothing but a door between them and his bed, he wanted every rule to disappear until morning.

"You get everything." He pulled her closer, trying to satisfy himself with the sexy shape of her against his body and the insanely good smell of her hair when he kissed her head.

"Mmm." She tipped her head back. "Hold me like that a little longer, Hot Landlord, and we'll both get everything."

He lowered his head and met her lips, each kiss still incredibly new and shockingly sweet. They'd kissed on the dance floor a few times and once by the bar. And one more time out on the veranda looking at the full moon.

But this kiss was different. This was one step away from *everything*.

She arched her back, her breasts pressed against his chest, angling her head to offer the tender skin of her jaw and throat. He kissed it all, dragging his lips over the smooth flesh, and running his hands up and down the hollows of her back.

"Josh..." She whispered his name into their kiss. "I don't want to stand out here making out and get caught by your stepsister or mother or one of the butlers."

He reached behind him and twisted the doorknob. "Are you sure?"

She backed away an inch, her pupils black with the same arousal that whipped through him. "Not sure of anything," she admitted. "But...I like you."

He searched her face, not sure what to say other than the obvious, which, by the way he was holding her, should be pretty damn obvious.

"And I want you," she whispered, enough of an invitation in her voice for him to know she meant business.

And so did he. He nestled her into him, taking another long, wet, hot kiss. Their tongues danced and curled, while each breath grew shorter and more difficult to take. She flattened her hands over his chest, sliding down the tuxedo shirt, flicking at buttons, and—

"Get a room, kids."

Brea. He gritted his teeth and relaxed his grip, realizing they'd both been so caught up they hadn't heard her coming down the hall.

"There's one right behind you," she added as she breezed by, changed into jeans and a T-shirt, with a weekender-sized tote bag over her shoulder. "No one will do a bed check, if that's what you're worried about."

He glared at her. "Good night, Brea."

She disappeared down the steps, leaving a trail of laughter behind her.

Darcy exhaled a breath he suspected she'd been holding for a few seconds longer than normal.

"Would you like to come inside?" he asked.

She searched his face, thinking. "Yes, but…that's not what you want, is it?"

Yes…and no. "I want you to come in my room. In my bed. In my arms all night."

The color in her cheeks deepened. "Then…we should…" She notched her head to the door.

"Go home." The words—the truthful words—were out before he could stop himself.

"Excuse me?"

"Not here, Darcy. I don't want to sleep with you for the first time in this house."

She didn't say anything, but held his gaze, waiting for more, which she deserved.

"I want it to be somewhere…" Perfect. "Else," he finished. "Without the layer of this place hanging over me like ashes."

She laughed a little. "It's really not that bad here," she said. "And your family, at least the people I met, have your best interests at heart."

So they'd fooled her, too. "I have a house about an hour from here."

She lifted her brows, surprised. "You do?"

"I built it. I'd love to show it to you, but the truth is, tonight, I'd rather go back to Bitter Bark and make your family's Sunday dinner."

Her jaw loosened. "Wow, you *have* been sprinkled with Kilcannon fairy dust."

"One Kilcannon in particular."

She smiled. "But not enough fairy dust for you to open that door behind you and make me a happy woman."

But would he be a happy man? "I'm not supposed to be falling for you, Darcy. I don't want to get emotionally involved. And this doesn't feel like friends with dogs. But…" He tilted her chin up toward him. "I *am* falling for you. I'm already emotionally involved. And whatever we call this, I'm not going to start it in this house."

She nodded slowly, stroking his shoulders as she thought about that. "And whatever we start is going to change everything."

"Everything," he agreed.

"Is that smart?"

"I don't know," he answered honestly. "But God knows I've done dumber things."

She laughed softly and eased away. "I'll sleep in my own room."

He grunted a little. "Speaking of dumb things."

"No, Josh, you're right. It's dangerous. It's too soon. It's…"

All we both want.

But she managed to extricate herself from his arms, wiggle her fingers. "If we leave now, we can be home by dawn, get a little sleep, and be at Waterford before the first Bloody Mary is poured."

He snagged her for one more kiss. "Now. Are you sure?"

"Nope," she said. "I'm confused, achy, and ready to throw caution to the wind."

He tunneled his fingers into her hair to gently rub her head. "Not yet," he said, knowing it was the right decision. "Let's go home to Waterford."

She backed up and narrowed her eyes. "Not to put too fine a point on it, but it's not technically my home. Or yours."

"It was just a figure of speech."

But the look on her face said she wasn't sure. And neither was he.

Chapter Sixteen

"**O**h, lassie. I'm so glad you're home." Gramma Finnie swooped into the kitchen moments after Darcy and Josh walked into the house at Waterford Farm the next day. She wore her church clothes, because Darcy had carefully timed their arrival for when the family who'd attended this morning showed up after the service.

"So am I," Darcy said and surprised herself by how much she meant it.

They'd pulled into the Ambrose Acres parking area at sunrise and separated for a few hours of sleep and showers. Darcy was still a little beat from the middle of the night drive home, when she and Josh had talked non-stop from Cornelius to Bitter Bark. But the moment they drove up to Waterford, Darcy knew the loss of sleep was worth it. And one look at Josh told her he completely agreed.

She'd prepared him well for what to expect at a Kilcannon Sunday dinner that got rolling in the early afternoon once those who'd gone to church arrived. There would be pitchers of Bloody Marys or shots of

Jameson's, legions of Kilcannons, and possibly some Mahoney cousins, plus many dogs and mediocre food because Dad cooked on Crystal's day off. Oh, and killer dessert, because Gramma handled that.

Mostly, there'd be a lot of laughter and teasing and late afternoon dog walks, four-wheeler rides, or, if it rained, a highly competitive Mario Kart tournament.

With each description, he looked almost as excited as Christian, Andi and Liam's little boy, who somehow always won that racing tournament, most likely because one of his uncles secretly let him.

As they'd walked up to the house, Darcy had taken a moment to appreciate how good Josh looked, even without sleep. He wore a soft maroon T-shirt with the sleeves pushed up, showing off strong forearms with a dusting of dark hair, and crisp khaki pants. A whole different look from his tux, but every bit as easy on the eyes. Maybe better.

But Gramma Finnie didn't even take a moment to notice him.

"I need to show you something," she said, tugging at Darcy's hand after they hugged. "Quick, lass."

"Okay, but Josh and I want to see Stella and Kookie. Where are they?" She'd totally expected Kookie to come flying at them the minute her Darcy Radar went off. But the only dog in sight was Rusty. The setter was curled in the corner of the kitchen, waiting for his master to arrive.

"Exactly. Come with me." Gramma gestured to Josh. "You, too, lad. Quickly, though."

Curious, they followed her up the main stairs, around a corner, and to the back stairs that led up to the third-floor apartment where Gramma lived. Darcy watched her navigate the stairs with ease, feeling a burst of love for the little old lady who loved to tell stories and write blogs.

Glancing over her shoulder, Darcy winked at Josh, who gave her a secret, sexy smile. And another message: *Your house beats my house by a long shot.*

Oh yes. She'd found another person to silently communicate with. She didn't know whether to cheer or run. Not that Josh seemed like the type to step all over her hard-won independence, but still. The way she'd felt in his arms last night? Scary. Wonderful, but scary.

Cool heads had prevailed, but that kind of resistance wasn't going to last long with this insane chemistry.

"I checked on them a minute ago," Gramma whispered as they got to the top of the steps and reached her sitting room. She barely paused as her low-heeled shoes, worn only on Sundays, tapped on the hardwood and crossed the braided rug. "So I bet they're still in the same position." She ushered them toward her bedroom without glancing at the desk in the corner with a closed laptop and the graphic on the wall above it that said, *Life is short, blog unconditionally.*

But Josh did. Darcy caught him drinking in the cottagelike feel of Gramma's private apartment with the juxtaposition of her modern habits, giving Darcy another jolt of pride.

"Look." Very carefully and silently, Gramma Finnie opened the bedroom door and waved them both to peek in.

Darcy sucked in a soft gasp at the sight of Kookie perched on one of Gramma's many pillows, staring at the cradle that Darcy and Josh had brought over with the dogs. And in that cradle, Stella was curled up in a corner, snoring softly, utterly content.

"She loves it in there," Gramma whispered. "Kookie let her sleep there last night."

"The ultimate sacrifice," Darcy muttered, turning to Josh. "Kookie wouldn't share that cradle with a stuffed animal, let alone a live one."

"A live one who despises her," he added in the same hushed tone.

"I swear Kookie guarded her all night," Gramma said.

"Oh." Darcy pressed her fingers to her lips to contain her response, but it was loud enough for Stella's ears to perk and the little white dog to lift her head. Kookie stood and took a few steps closer to the cradle, barking once.

"What are they talking about?" Josh asked on a laugh.

"Dog speak," Darcy said, stepping into the room, unable to keep her hands off her sweet pupper for one more second. "Kookie, you are such a good girl taking care of Stella."

She gave in to the joy of seeing Darcy, scampering across the bed to jump into the arms of her mistress with her feathery tail whipping from side to side. "Good girl," Darcy repeated, lifting her chin to accept the slathering of kisses Kookie bestowed.

In the cradle, Stella was up now, growling low at the voices with a low-grade frustration as clear as if she was saying, *I can't see you!*

As though he understood that, Josh was next to her in a flash, picking her up and petting her head. "It's okay, kid. I'm here. Shhh. You're at Waterford Farm, and it doesn't get any better than that."

He placed a kiss on her head, his big, masculine hand adding reassuring strokes that totally calmed her down.

But not Darcy. Oh, no. She was anything but calm. No, her chest swelled with a wave of emotion that crashed over her when she looked at his silhouette against the sunshine pouring in through lace curtains. He was tender and sweet but big and sexy, and all she wanted to do was...heal Stella and heal him.

"She's shaking," he told them, gripping Stella's little body closer to his chest.

Who wouldn't be in his arms?

"She needs her jacket," he added.

"It's right here." Gramma Finnie snagged the pink anxiety wrap off the dresser. "She doesn't seem to need it in the cradle," she said, handing it to him.

Josh set Stella on the bed and turned the jacket one way, then the other, trying to figure out how to put it on. "Can't believe she slept in that cradle," he said. "She supposedly wouldn't sleep anywhere but her bed. Does this go..." He glanced up at Darcy, who handed him Kookie.

"Here, I know how to do it."

They switched dog for jacket, and she easily slipped the Velcro straps around Stella's neck, but Kookie barked as she watched.

"Don't be jealous," Darcy warned her. "I get to love other dogs."

Kookie barked again, then added a low growl, making Darcy look up as she tightened the jacket under Stella's quivering belly.

"She's not jealous," Gramma said. "She's protecting Stella. Once Stella let her close, everything changed. Kookie licked her and nuzzled her and stands guard when anyone comes close."

"That is so sweet," Darcy exclaimed. "How did this happen?"

Gramma Finnie came closer and tugged at the sleeves of her summer-yellow cardigan. "I may have sung a wee Irish blessing over them."

"And Shane trained them together, I'm guessing," Darcy added, earning a frown from her grandmother.

"They were lovely with me," Gramma continued. "And, in fact, inspired me to write my blog about friendship."

"Aww." Darcy put an around her grandmother's narrow shoulders. "Did you whip out the good ships and wood ships?"

"Of course." Gramma's blue eyes twinkled as she looked at Josh, no doubt hoping for a new audience. "'There are good ships and wood ships and ships that sail the sea.'"

"But the best ships are friendships and may they always be," he finished, and Gramma Finnie actually gasped out loud.

"My mother's mother was Irish," he explained.

"Oh…my." For a moment, Darcy thought Gramma was going to kiss him. *Get in line, toots.*

"Not first generation or anything," he added. "But enough."

"One drop of Irish blood is enough," Gramma practically cooed. "'Tis time we celebrate with your first shot of Kilcannon Jameson's."

"Do you think Stella would come down for Sunday

dinner?" Darcy asked Gramma. "Otherwise, I think I've lost Kookie to her."

"I'll leave my doors open so she can come and go." Gramma patted both dogs, then smiled up at Josh. "I hope you brought us good news for her, lad."

"We did."

Darcy's heart did a little dip. *We.* Did he have to say that? He could have said, *I did*, but…she was the one who'd said they were in the Stella thing together.

"I have a signature from Stella's owner's lawyer, who has the power of attorney to approve the study and procedures," he said.

"Wonderful!" Gramma Finnie clapped her hands. "Then we have much to toast today. Garrett has an announcement he can barely keep secret. Baby Fiona slept through the night for the first time. Stella is going to be our miracle dog. And there's another Irishman at the table."

"And rumor has it Beck's aunt has a friend coming to drop Ruff off…and be considered as an entrant for the Daniel Dating Competition," Darcy added.

"They're running late and will be here after dinner," Gramma replied without so much as blinking an eye.

Darcy laughed and looked up at Josh. "Welcome to Sunday dinner at Waterford. Only slightly different from Buckingsham Palace."

He let out a wistful sigh. "Slightly."

"And that is how Waterford Farm came to be." The sweet old lady leaned close to finish the saga.

"Hashtag Kilcannon history." Then Gramma Finnie stood and left the oversized farm table, where the two of them had been seated while all the others somehow disappeared into the kitchen, family room, and outside.

Just then, two delicate but surprisingly strong hands landed on Josh's shoulders, and the familiar floral scent of a beautiful young woman replaced the powdery scent of a grandmother.

"Congratulations," Darcy whispered in his ear. "You got the long version."

He looked up at her, never tired of how pretty she was upside down. And right side up. And from behind, in profile, and in his imagination. "She likes me."

"I believe we zoomed past 'like' when you dropped the 'I've got Irish blood' bomb."

He smiled.

"Or maybe it was when you checked on Stella five times during dinner."

"Three," he corrected. "And she was quiet up there."

"But you sealed the deal when you announced that was the best bread pudding you'd ever had. Nice work, laddie." She delivered the last line in a sweet brogue that imitated her grandmother's and did something *insane* to his heart.

He couldn't help it. He reached up with two hands, clasped her head in his palms, and brought her closer for an upside-down kiss. It was short, sweet, and better than the bread pudding, which really was the best he'd ever had.

She took a second to open her eyes, as if the kiss had the same effect on her, then slowly sat down in the empty seat next to him. "So, how was your first Kilcannon Sunday dinner?"

The first of many, he hoped. He flinched a little at the thought, which was so not in keeping with his rule of "no attachments with women, ever." Could that rule be bent…and not break him?

"Your whole family is spectacular."

"Whole? Shane didn't drive you crazy?"

"He's funny. A little cocky, but I like him. Plus, he's given me so many tips for Stella."

"And Liam doesn't intimidate you?" she asked.

"A man who turns to blubbering mush when he holds his baby? Nothing intimidating about that." That made her laugh, but he continued. "Garrett's a great guy, too, and so excited to be the next father in the family. Aidan's anecdotes from Afghanistan are so fascinating, but I love how he and Beck are helping her uncle recover from his stroke and rebuild the pizza parlor. And man, you'd never guess Trace's story if he didn't tell you."

"You sure are a good listener," she said.

"There are so many great people to listen to."

She chuckled, tapping his nose. "You're smitten by Kilcannons."

"Every one," he whispered, tapping hers right back. "Even the little ones. Pru's a hoot, and Christian already challenged me to a game of Mario Kart, which I will let him win," he added.

"You catch on fast, HL."

"The only thing bad about today is how this group makes me realize how sucky mine is."

That again. "Are you sure you're not being too hard on them? I know you don't like them, and I don't know the whole history, but Brea is fun, and your mom is rooting for you, and your stepfather seemed genuinely disappointed that you're not working in his company."

"But you didn't meet Beelzebub."

She laughed. "Well, every family has one black sheep."

"Not this one."

"Yeah, well." Of course she didn't bother to argue against the perfection of her clan.

"And they hardly pestered your dad about dating," he added. "Although Shane isn't exactly subtle when it comes to the subject, is he?"

"Any subject," she agreed. "But there were too many other headlines today for that. And speaking of my dad, he's out in the pen with some dogs and asked if we wanted to give Stella a chance to socialize. That is, assuming we can get past Guard Dog Kookie, who's watching the cradle."

"Let's give it a shot."

As they stood and headed toward the stairs, Darcy whispered, "I also think Dad wants to talk to you privately."

"Really? Now should I be intimidated?"

She shook her head. "But remember he has an agenda."

"To set you up and marry you off?"

She sighed. "Let's not dignify that, but he was watching us pretty closely at dinner, so don't freak out if he starts asking you about your intentions." She looked up at him. "Because I know one thing about you, and that is that you won't lie."

"Nope, but what should I say?"

Slowing halfway up the wide stairway, she shrugged. "The truth, I guess, about your intentions. Other than to take my rent checks and fix any problems in the apartment."

He was quiet as they reached the top and turned the corner, imagining the conversation with the father of the woman he very much wanted to sleep with.

"My intentions are…" He gave in to a slight laugh. "I'm not sure you or he would want me to be *that* honest."

She smiled, her deep-blue eyes glinting with humor and maybe a little anticipation. "Then throw him off course with something else you intend to do with me. For me," she corrected.

"Help you build out the grooming salon?"

"That'll work." As they slipped into the stairwell that led to the third floor, she slowed and gave him a spectacularly sexy look. "But you can tell *me* the truth about your intentions."

"Okay." Why fight it one more minute? He wrapped his arms around her and nestled her into him. "I intend to kiss you."

"Mmm." She closed her eyes and tilted her head up to him. "Yes, please."

Like every other kiss they'd shared, she tasted as sweet as the pudding and as smooth as the whiskey. And far too good to be something he'd take and leave.

The thought weighed on him after they collected the dogs and headed across the wide lawn to the training pen, where Dr. K was with Rusty and two other dogs.

"Oh boy, no brothers around," he murmured to Darcy.

"A bunch of them went out riding four-wheelers, and Liam took Andi and the baby home so Fiona can nap. Aidan and Beck are walking their new dogs. Why? Are you that worried?"

"Darcy, I'm a Southern boy, born and raised. I know what it means when a young woman's father calls in her...her...friend for a talking-to."

"Just remind him we're friends *with dogs*. That'll satisfy my dad."

But would it satisfy her...or him?

As soon as Darcy opened the gate, Kookie started to take off toward the other dogs, then stopped and turned around, trotting back to Stella, who was on a leash that Josh held. Kookie went right up to Stella's face, licked her on one side of the cheek, then the other.

"It's like she's telling Stella where she is and that she's safe," Josh said, astounded again at the two of them. "I can't believe what happened to these two while we were gone."

Darcy looked up at him. "It's like they really like each other now."

"Funny how that happened so fast." To dogs *and* humans.

Her father came closer, with Rusty right on his heels, and two other dogs who looked like hounds of some sort trotting along on the other side.

"Is that Tommy and Odie?" Darcy asked. "I haven't seen these two boys in ages." Darcy dropped down to a knee to pet one and rub the other, who flipped like a pancake and offered up his belly for affection.

"Marie Boswell dropped them off last evening for a week's boarding," her father said. "I knew they'd be perfect for Stella. They're so good with other dogs."

Darcy settled on the ground, and the two dogs vied for her lap. While she cuddled them, she looked over at Kookie, who stayed steadfastly next to Stella.

"Whoa. She usually hates when I love another dog," Darcy said. "Look at her, Dad. She's attached to Stella."

Dr. K bent down on one knee, reaching a careful hand and murmuring some soft words to Stella, warning her he was going to touch her but Kookie barked at him.

"I'm not going to hurt your friend, Kookie," he said. "I'm going to introduce her to two of your favorite dogs. Bring them over, Darce."

She scooted the dogs forward while Rusty headed off to another part of the pen. "You'll love these two, Josh. This is Tommy, he's a purebred beagle, and Odie is a bagle." At his look, she explained, "A basset mixed with a beagle."

The two portly boys trotted over on short legs with wagging tails as they approached the other two dogs. Kookie blocked them, offering her face for a sniff and refusing to let them near Stella.

"I don't think she's going to let Stella socialize," Dr. K said. "Darcy, why don't you take her in the kennel and distract her while Josh and I work with these guys?"

Darcy looked up with a flick of her eyebrows to send a silent message to Josh, something they'd started to do with surprising frequency. This one was either *I warned you* or *I can stay if you want*. But he gave his head a quick shake to let her know he was fine.

Whatever "the Dogfather" was going to ask or say, Josh was confident he could handle it.

"Sure thing," Darcy said, moving fast to stand and scoop up Kookie before the dog realized what was happening. She gave a quick bark of displeasure, but Darcy snagged a treat from the bag hanging on the fence and set off. "Have fun, you guys."

Was it his imagination, or had she skedaddled a little too fast?

"All right, then, Odie, Tommy. Be nice to Stella," Dr. K instructed, keeping a hand on Stella's head while the other two dogs came closer. "I'm letting her know she's safe," he told Josh. "But also giving them room to introduce themselves and sniff each other."

"It's quite the dance these dogs do," Josh said.

Dr. K chuckled. "They're fascinating creatures, don't you think?"

Stella backed up a few steps, then gave in to the attention from the other dogs.

"Like I told Darcy, I haven't had a dog of my own since I was a kid," Josh said. "I've always wanted one, but I'm gone all day at work, almost always at construction sites, so it didn't seem good for a dog."

"The right dog finds you, I always say." He carefully took his hand off Stella's head and stood, both of them watching her closely for any signs of discomfort or fear. "Kind of like the right person to love, don't you think?"

Whoa. That didn't take long. Josh fought a smile, not because of the speed of the question, but thinking about telling Darcy about it later. "I suppose," he said.

The older man looked up, his blue gaze clear and steady, and maybe one shade lighter than Darcy's. "Was it difficult for you?" he asked.

"Finding the right person? I haven't." *And never plan to.* But that didn't seem like a response that would go over well.

He laughed softly. "I meant going back to where you lived before, hunting down your ex, facing the past?"

Josh exhaled and considered all the possible answers, but knew the truth. "For the most part, it was very easy with Darcy along. Fun, actually," he added, thinking of the night before.

"That's her gift," Dr. K replied. "She's like light in a human form."

"Yes. That's *exactly* what she is."

The older man looked amused, making Josh wonder if maybe his response was a little too enthusiastic.

"So, it's worked out well with her as a tenant?"

Was that a joke? *Well?* They'd nearly fallen into bed together last night, and every kiss was hotter than the one before. How should he answer that?

"It hasn't been very long," he finally said. "And Stella's blindness threw us into a tailspin. But, yes, I think Darcy will be a great tenant."

Dr. K nodded, quiet for a moment as they watched the three dogs interact. Stella was doing really well. Not exactly rolling around and playing with the other two, but not backing off in fear, either.

Dr. K put his hands in the pockets of his trousers and looked at the kennels where Darcy had disappeared. "She thinks I arranged this, doesn't she?

That you two would meet and hit it off? I mean, I'm not blind—no offense, Stella," he joked.

Josh laughed, knowing it sounded a little nervous. "We have hit it off," he admitted. "And, yes, she does think you've done some of your world-class matchmaking."

"The irony is that I didn't," he said. "Certainly not intentionally, because I don't..." He hesitated, thinking for a moment. "I don't relish the thought of losing her."

Josh had no idea what to say, so he stayed quiet, waiting for more.

"I haven't even nudged her toward anyone because..." He blew out a half sigh, half laugh. "I'm not ready to let go of her."

"She is your youngest," Josh said. "And very special."

The compliment made her father smile. "*Very* special."

Yep, this was a good old *if you lay a hand on my daughter* talk that he'd like to say he didn't need, but he had laid a few hands on her last night, and every minute that passed made him want to lay everything on her. He stayed silent.

And Dr. K looked at him. Oh man.

"Um, sir, if you want me to back off, of course I can..." He let his voice trail off as the other man looked sharply at him. "But I'd rather not," he finished.

"You're very recently out of a serious relationship."

Josh nodded, answering with the utmost care. "With no intention of getting into another."

That made Dr. K laugh. "My mother would say

you don't always get what you pray for, and that's the real blessing."

"I think the Rolling Stones said the same thing, only with, you know, guitars."

Another laugh, the sound of it taking Josh's tension down a notch.

"So what is it that you want?" Dr. K asked.

And the tension went ratcheting back up again. "I want to help Stella regain her sight," he answered without hesitation, because it was not a lie.

"With Darcy?"

"She and I are both invested in Stella." Just then, Stella turned from one of the dogs and made her way to Josh, finding his shoe and taking a few sniffs of something familiar. Without thinking, he crouched down to pet her. "I care for Darcy a lot, sir. And I think it's mutual."

"Well, that's…"

Josh looked up when he didn't finish, catching a look of dismay that he didn't think he was supposed to see.

"That's great," Dr. K finished. "I'm pleased that…" He chuckled at himself as he struggled with the words. "Actually, I'm kicking myself."

"Because you didn't set us up?"

"Oh, if only it were that simple. No, I'm kicking myself because she's…the last one. Sometimes I think I saved the best for last."

Josh straightened to his full height. "They're all pretty great, but I might agree with you."

He put his hand on Josh's shoulder, giving him a friendly, fatherly pat, then looking him right in the eyes. "Don't hurt her."

"I won't." But could he keep that promise? He wasn't ever going to be vulnerable again. He'd never trust anyone, no matter how sweet or bright or warm or perfect. He wouldn't ever let down his guard, but he was going to sleep with her. It was only a matter of when, where, and how frequently.

"And don't tell her about this conversation."

That was another impossible promise to keep. "To be honest, sir, I think she'd be relieved to know you didn't pull strings. She rebels against that, you know."

"Oh, I know. But I kind of like having her think I did it, especially if I get one more W on the scoreboard."

A W on the scoreboard?

"It really helps my reputation as the Dogfather," he admitted.

Josh smiled at him, ready for the internal response that would deny he was even that close to winning at his matchmaking again. Because that would mean...

But nothing like that denial rose up in Josh. Another emotion did. Along with an old memory and a familiar longing that stretched inside his chest.

Pops.

What was it about this man that reminded him of his own father? They couldn't have been more different. One had been a working-class, hardscrabble, roughhewn man of simple needs and basic pleasures. The other held domain over a hundred acres, six amazing offspring, and exuded a raw and real power that demanded respect.

But they both had soft hearts for their kids, deep love for their wives, and a straightforward code of ethics that guided them through life.

God, he missed that. He missed Pops. So much, in that moment, it choked him up.

"Kookie was not happy being away from her little charge."

Darcy's voice made him turn toward the kennels as she came out, walking with her brother Aidan and his fiancée, Beck, and at least three other dogs of various sizes and shapes.

A few feet ahead of them, Kookie tore over the grass to get back to Stella and Darcy followed. Both woman and dog moved with spirit and joy, one barking, one laughing, both tugging at him in ways he swore he couldn't be tugged. As Kookie came closer, he scooped her up the same way he wanted to snag and hold and love on Darcy.

And she kicked and thrashed and wagged her tail furiously, rejecting the love when she wanted something else. Also like Darcy.

He lowered Kookie to the ground, and she practically dove at Stella, licking and pawing her little friend.

Josh bent down to pet them both. In a second, Kookie climbed back into his arms and Stella jumped up on his leg to snuggle closer, but his attention was immediately stolen by Darcy.

"Look at that sight," she teased. "A man and two females who adore him."

And look at that sight, he thought. A woman with a smile as blinding as the sun behind her, her blond hair swaying, her body moving with grace and ease, her whole being drawing him closer and closer to the very place he swore he'd never be. Vulnerable. Open. Willing to go through it all again.

Dr. K pulled his phone out of his pocket, and for a second, Josh thought he was going to take a picture of Josh, a portrait of a helpless man, almost on his knees, covered in dogs and internal torture. But Dr. K merely read a text, and his face broke into a wide smile.

"Darcy, Josh. I think congratulations are in order for you."

Darcy almost tripped as she reached them. "*What* did you two talk about?"

Her father turned the phone so she could see the screen. "Judy said the Vestal Valley veterinarian department has accepted Stella for admittance into the SARDS study, with the first treatment scheduled for tomorrow morning."

"Really?" Josh set Kookie and Stella on the ground and was up instantly, looking at the phone.

"Woo-hoo!" Darcy exclaimed, throwing her arms around him. "We did it!"

As he hugged and twirled her with unabashed joy, he glanced over her head and caught her father watching them embrace, a profound look of sadness in his eyes for a veterinarian who should be very happy right now.

Darcy might never believe her father didn't set them up, but Josh believed him. Right there was a man who wasn't ready to hand over his last child to anyone.

"Oh, look." Darcy pointed over his shoulder, making them turn toward the drive, where a late-model sedan was rolling in with one big brown boxer's head sticking out of the backseat window.

"Ruff!" Aidan and Beck exclaimed the word in perfect unison, both of them starting to rush forward to greet the newcomers and the dog that Josh had learned at dinner had brought them together, but now was a therapy dog for Beck's uncle.

Beck got ahead, but only because Aidan slowed his step when he reached his father. "Come on over, Dad. Aunt Sarah's friend from Boston is here. Her name's Una Duval, and she's a professional dog handler."

The older man had to work to keep from rolling his eyes.

"I know," Aidan said. "You're not the biggest fan of dog shows, but she's had one win at Westminster. You'll like her. C'mon."

Dr. K managed a nod as he put his hand on his youngest son's sizable shoulder and gave him a nudge. "You greet the guests, and I'll be over in a minute."

When Aidan left, he turned to Darcy. "When is it going to stop?" he asked on an amused sigh.

"When you get beaten at your own game, Dad."

He looked from Darcy to Josh and shook his head slowly. "You know, I think I have been."

Neither one of them said a word as Dr. K finished the conversation with one last rub of Stella's head. "Excuse me, little one. I need to go meet Una, yet another woman I swear I'm *not* going to fall in love with."

As he left, Josh turned to Darcy and held her gaze, trying to repeat the same promise in his head. He failed.

Chapter Seventeen

"All right, kid. This is it. Big day for you." Josh reached over the console of his truck to take Stella out of Darcy's arms. "I'm sorry you had to leave your pal Kookie."

Darcy handed her over with one last kiss on her head. "Not as sorry as Kookie. I've never heard her actually cry like that when I closed the apartment door." She still wished she could have taken Kookie to Waterford Farm before they left for Vestal Valley College, but there hadn't been time. "I should have expected it, though. They were glued together all night. I never dreamed Kookie would actually share the cradle with another dog, but when I woke up, they were spooning."

"As soon as Stella's settled and we say goodbye to her, we'll go back and get Kookie," Josh assured her. "I need to pop into the job site anyway to check on the crew that's doing bathroom demo, then..." He blew out a breath. "I honestly don't think I can work until we have her back."

Darcy laughed. "I feel the same way. I'm so nervous for her, Josh."

He met her gaze over Stella's head, his chocolate eyes shifting from concern to something softer. "I'm so glad we're in this together."

"Friends with dogs," she teased, reaching over to tap his chin. "Blind dogs that need to see. Let's go."

He nodded, but didn't move for a moment. "What are you doing today?"

"Fretting until we're able to pick her up, but that could be much later this afternoon." They'd already been warned that the vet team wanted to do the measurements and make sure Stella didn't have any negative response to the immunoglobulin shot.

"Let's stay together."

Her heart flipped, more because of the way he said it—low and certain and warm—than the idea that he wanted to spend another day with her. "I don't have appointments, but I was going to go to the new space and start planning the salon," she said.

"Without me?" He sounded genuinely hurt.

She opened her mouth, ready to pounce on that. Of course she could go alone. It was her space and her plan and her new life. But it would be so much better with him. *Damn it.*

"I figured you were working," she said, trying to keep any emotion out of the response.

"Let's go draw up plans, and I'll make a schedule for the build-out." He inched back, searching her face. "You do want me to help, right?"

"Of course. I'd be a fool not to."

"But you're worried."

"That's one way of putting it. Terrified would be another."

He nodded. "Because it goes beyond friends with dogs, infringes on your independence, tests your resolve, and makes you feel like you're giving up control to yet another man who might not be your brother or father, but still threatens what you want."

She actually laughed because he was so utterly correct. "Did you sneak in and read my diary?" she joked.

"You keep one?"

"No, but if I did, that might have been last night's entry."

He reached around Stella and cupped her cheek, his hand rough and callused, making desire snake its way through her. She ached for him. Right here, on a Monday morning, in a parking lot at Vestal Valley College, with a blind dog shaking between them. What was wrong with her?

"If anyone should be terrified, it's me," he whispered. "I'm trusting you, something I swore I'd never do again. And I busted more than a few rules to get this dog here. And I don't want to spend one minute without you today or maybe tomorrow or maybe for the whole three weeks until Stella can see again."

She bit her lip. "How did this happen?"

"Quickly." He leaned forward and punctuated that with a light kiss. "Let's just go with the flow."

"Until one of us drowns."

He broke into a slow, endearing smile. "But what a way to go."

"Josh."

"Shhh. Nothing is happening, Darcy. It's…for the dogs. *We* didn't spoon in a cradle last night, did we?"

"But we thought about it."

"All night." His admission did nothing to cool down the inside of the truck, which was getting warmer by the second. "And I'll think about it tonight."

"Me, too," she admitted. "What are we going to do about that?"

He lifted one shoulder and half his mouth in a sly smile. But before he could answer, Stella raised her head and barked, done with being a doggie sandwich between two sex-starved humans.

"Let's go," he whispered. "We'll figure it out."

Darcy doubted that, but climbed out of the truck anyway. A few minutes later, they entered Farrow Hall, where Vestal Valley College's Department of Veterinary Medicine was located, then headed upstairs to the labs to see Dr. Walker and her team.

Inside the cool, clean room, the comfortingly familiar sound of barking dogs in a pen soothed Darcy, but had the opposite effect on Stella. She immediately started barking, wrestling to get out of Josh's strong hold, then finally giving up and smashing her face against his chest to shake in fear.

"I feel ya, sister," Darcy murmured as she stroked her head.

A moment later, Dr. Walker greeted them, introduced them to some fellow vets and student techs, and put her capable hands around Stella to take her away for a few minutes. Someone else whisked Josh away to sign some additional papers before the procedure, and suddenly Darcy was all alone in the middle of the lab.

She wandered over to a penned-off area where four other dogs, all similar mid-sized as Stella, but different breeds, were being held for the same study. One Maltese turned in circles, hit the plastic wall, barked, and backed away in surprise. Another brown mix lay on the floor, madly licking his front paw to the point that Darcy knew it could bleed before long. A terrier in a nervous stance barked without ceasing. And the last one, a little dachshund with a milk chocolate coat and giant brown eyes, was pressed into a corner, quivering.

"Oh." She could literally feel her heart breaking as she looked at each little victim of SARDS and realized how many dogs could be saved if this worked.

"We're doing the right thing." Josh's voice and large hand on her back was like a thick layer of balm on her wounded heart.

"I was just thinking that," she said, looking up at him, knowing there were tears in her eyes. "I want to help them all."

He nodded. "I do, too. So much so that I signed a piece of paper that says I will not remove Stella from this study until it's complete. If Savannah comes back and wants to take her out of it—"

"Why would she?"

"I don't know, Darcy. I don't know where she is or why she did all the things she's accused of or what's going through her mind. I don't know, and honestly, I don't care. Except where Stella's concerned."

"Well, she can't have her back." Darcy straightened as she made the statement. "We won't allow it. She'll have to fight me for her."

"Us," he corrected. "She'll have to fight *us*."

They stared at each other for a long time, and with each passing second, Darcy could actually feel herself getting closer, needing more, wanting him. Not physically—she hadn't moved an inch, and neither had he. But emotionally, which was so much scarier.

Us.

"You can say goodbye to her now." One of the vet techs broke the moment, coming closer with Stella in her arms.

"Oh, baby." Darcy reached for her little head, kissing her right on the snout and getting her nose licked. "Good luck, you little love bunny."

Her tail wagged wildly as Josh stroked her head and murmured into her ear. "Hang in there, kid. And we'll see you soon." He kissed her head and added, "And you'll see us, because this is going to work."

After a second, the tech backed away. "She'll do great, I promise. Let's put her with her fellow patients."

The woman walked to the enclosed pen and reached over, but Stella clung and clawed, her back legs kicking wildly in fear.

"Oh, Josh." Darcy grabbed him to keep herself from running over and smothering Stella with reassuring hugs.

"It's okay," he said, but his voice sounded as shaky as Stella's legs.

"She's fine," the tech assured them, easing Stella to the floor.

But she didn't look fine. She turned in circles, barked frantically, and panted when she finally found a spot not far from the dachshund. That dog looked up and around, slowly inching closer to the scent of a newcomer.

"That's right, Riley. You say hi to Stella."

Riley nudged Stella, making her bark once, then they sniffed each other, and finally both settled to the floor, side by side, shaking in perfect, terrified unison.

"If that wasn't so cute, I'd be crying right now," Darcy admitted.

"Come on," Josh said, putting his arm around her, something in his voice and touch telling her he knew exactly what she was feeling. "They'll call us when we can come and get her. Let's go pick up Kookie and spend the day designing your salon." He guided her toward the door, but she took one more look over her shoulder at the two new buddies.

"Come on, Darce," he said again, adding a little pressure on her shoulder. "Let's get our minds off this for a while." But she didn't move. "Kookie's waiting for you. She needs you, too."

That almost worked, but her feet were like lead, immovable, keeping her where she could see Stella and all the dogs who were scared, hurting, and in their dark, dark worlds.

"I need you, too," he whispered, pulling her very close. "I don't think I could handle this alone."

Of course, he knew exactly what to say to get her out of there.

By the time they got back to Ambrose Acres, Darcy and Josh had talked and teased each other out of their funk. They agreed to not worry about Stella, but to spend all their time and energy on the grooming salon project that Josh couldn't wait to start.

"What did you say it was called?" he asked her as they crossed the street to the apartment. "The Dog's Paw or Spa?"

"Spaw—s-p-a-w. It's a play on words. Get it?"

He threw her a quizzical look. "Yeah. Kind of."

"You think it's dumb?"

"No, it's clever, but aren't you worried about people typing it properly into a search engine or maps program?"

"Ohhh." She drew the sound out. "I hadn't thought about that."

"Maybe we can come up with a new name."

Next to him, her step slowed a bit.

"Or *you* can," he added with a laugh.

"No, no, it's fine. Ella and I have been brainstorming for a while, and it was The Dog Spaw or Bitter Bark Bow WOW, with the wow in all caps."

He really tried not to react. "Okay."

"You hate it."

He draped his arm around her as they headed up the stairs. "I think you can do better."

"Or we can." She jammed her shoulder into his body playfully.

They were still laughing as they climbed the stairs to the second floor of the building, but it was drowned out by the sound of a saw, a clunk of a sledgehammer, some tinny rap music, and the desperate, repeated bark of a dog.

"Is Kookie in there?" Darcy shot forward with panic in her voice, reaching the top of the stairs seconds before Josh did. The door to Unit 3 was wide open, propped by a toolbox. The remnants of the bathroom that was being removed today were strewn in the hall and visible living room, including a sink and busted-up cabinet.

But the barking was coming from behind the door to Darcy's apartment, thank God.

"Oh, that scared me," Darcy said, rooting through her bag for keys. "Why is she still so worked up?"

"The construction noise," he suggested. "Let me go check on those guys. They should be finished with the demo soon, or at least can the music."

"It's okay," she said, unlocking the door. "We'll take her with us today." She disappeared inside, cooing reassurances to Kookie before he could answer.

Climbing over the toolbox, he glanced around the unit, bypassed the now missing linoleum floor in the kitchen, and headed to the master bath where Carlos Juarez, the subcontractor who'd been here almost every day for the other two renovations, was on his knees in the bathtub, popping out the old yellow tile.

"Greetings, Mr. R." Carlos gave a warm smile. "Wanna carry a bathtub downstairs?"

Not particularly. Josh glanced around, certain he'd paid for two men to demolish this bathroom in one day. "You alone, Carlos?"

"No, I actually have a new guy with me who just started, but he ran down to the truck to get some plumbing tools." He tipped his head to the exposed pipes from behind the sink. "That em-effer's been on since the seventies, I swear. And we can do the heavy lifting when I get this tub out. But I know you like to get your hands dirty."

Not today. "I'm actually going to run over to another job site."

Carlos lowered the chisel and raised a brow. "You buying another building, Mr. R?"

"Not yet, but doing a favor for a friend. It's the lady who lives next door, actually."

Carlos frowned. "The one with the dog?"

"Guilty." Josh leaned against the doorjamb and crossed his arms. "She usually takes the dog to work, if the barking's been bothering you."

"Not at all." He wiped the palm of his hand on his unshaven face, looking a little unsure. "She was fine until your lady friend showed up and wanted to get in."

His lady friend? "Who was here?"

"I don't know her name, but some woman was here and said you were supposed to be here to let her in to that apartment."

Who could that have been? "Did you get her name?"

"Sorry, no. Bill talked to her more than I did. He should be back any second."

Josh pushed off the wall, hoping Darcy would know who it might have been. "Thanks, Carlos."

"Sure thing. And don't worry about the tub. Billy's a beast, and he could carry it himself if he had to."

"Call me if you need anything." He started out, then turned. "Call me if that woman comes back, too."

Josh headed through the apartment and rounded a corner, damn near slamming into a wall of man and muscle, both of them jerking back.

"Whoa!"

"Sorry, I..." Josh blinked up at the face of the other man, who was not much taller than he was, but who was wide and tanned and familiar. "Bill

Bainbridge?" The name of the tradesman he'd used on many jobs for Bucking easily popped into his head.

"Hey, Mr. Ranier." He extended a meaty hand, glanced at it, then wiped it on his workpants before offering it again. "Good to see you, sir."

Stunned to see someone from his old job, Josh shook his hand. "What brings you up here?"

His chunky cheeks reddened. "You, sir."

"Me?"

"Gotta be real, Mr. R. Lot of subs can't stand working on Bucking jobs anymore. Pay's fine, and the bennies are good, but..." He shook his head. "I don't like cuttin' corners, sir. You know how that company builds now."

To squeeze every drop from a dollar. But Josh was too smart to say that, giving the other man a confused frown.

"I talked to a couple of guys who said your subs were hiring, and I figured you were a known quantity. Hope that's okay, sir."

"Of course," Josh said, zipping through what he knew about the guy. Punctual, strong, and enough of a perfectionist that he was happy to have him here. "I'm glad you found me."

Lifting a wrench, Bill stepped by. "I'll get back to work, then."

"Sure. But before you do, Carlos said a woman was up here trying to get in the other unit. Did you get her name?"

He huffed out a breath. "The queen of England? I mean, she acted like she owned the place and you promised her you'd let her in that apartment." He lifted his brows. "She wanted me to get her in.

Wanted it bad. Like…she mighta paid good for the favor."

Holy hell. Savannah? Did she hear Kookie bark, and assume it was Stella? She'd never been inside the building and didn't know which unit was his. A slow, cold fear snaked through him. Could that lawyer have reached her and told her what he'd signed with her power of attorney? Would she be that selfish to take the dog and deny her a chance to see again?

He had to admit, he had no idea.

"What did she look like?" he asked.

"Long, dark hair. Maybe twentysomething. Pretty, but I couldn't help her, not that I would have," he added quickly.

That sounded an awful lot like Savannah.

Which meant he had to protect Stella. Even if he had to hide her somewhere for the duration of her treatment, he had to keep that dog long enough for this procedure to succeed. He didn't care how many rules he had to break.

Chapter Eighteen

Darcy curled in the corner on a beanbag chair, one of the few things Cilla Forsythe had left behind when she moved out of her travel agency office. Midafternoon sun poured in from the wide front window that looked out down a side street, with a corner of Bushrod Square visible. On her lap, Kookie snored contentedly, and on the floor, Josh had about fifteen pages of rudimentary sketches spread out.

He worked—hard—when he didn't want to deal with a problem, Darcy decided. It was his escape mechanism. Since they'd left the apartment building and set up camp here, he talked very little about the fact that Savannah must have come looking for her dog. He merely dove headfirst into the idea of building out a grooming salon in this space without taking a break except for lunch.

And as much as Darcy wanted to concentrate on his great ideas, she couldn't help playing various Savannah scenarios in her head.

"So, here's the reception area," Josh said, flipping a page for her to view. "And if you want, we can put a glass panel there so your customers can see their dogs in the blow-dry area, or whatever you call it."

"Styling and finishing." Darcy gnawed her lower lip. "What if she comes back in the middle of the night?"

Josh's shoulders moved with another sigh as he looked up. "I'll handle her."

"She does have a right to her dog. And we don't know how 'legal' that paper was, since your mother said that lawyer will do anything they pay him to do."

"It's legal enough."

"But would Savannah actually deny Stella a chance to get her sight back? Is she that awful?"

Back to the paper and pencil, he didn't answer. Maybe he didn't know. Maybe he did.

"We have to figure out how to keep her from getting Stella for a few weeks," Darcy said. "Dr. Walker said this could be over in a month, even less."

He nodded slowly. "Are you sure you only want one sink?"

She pushed off the beanbag chair to land on the floor next to him. "Joshua Ranier." She screwed up her face. "What's your middle name?"

"Caleb."

"Joshua Caleb? Someone liked the Old Testament."

"My dad."

"Joshua Caleb Ranier," she finished her original thought, getting his attention. "You can't ignore the problem of Savannah. We have to figure this out."

His dark eyes grew pained. "Every time I realize how little I knew about her, it's like I'm gut-punched again. I thought I loved her."

"But did you know it?" she asked.

"I…" He considered the question. "How do you know if you really love someone?"

"Beats me, but my mother always said she knew. Big believer in love at first sight, if not first few sights, and obviously my dad believes that, too."

"Was theirs love at first sight?"

She couldn't tell if the question was another deflection technique, but she humored him and answered. "So they say, although I'm sure that since almost forty years have passed, the meeting has been romanticized. Dad was dating another woman, and she and he decided to set up two friends on a double date."

"The setting-up thing started early, I see."

She laughed. "I never thought about that, but yes. Only, that time, it was the Dogfather himself who got hit by Cupid's arrow. He says he walked into the bar where Annie Harper was waiting to meet Dad's friend and was thunderstruck from the moment he laid eyes on her."

"He didn't know her before?"

She shook her head. "She was a friend of Katie, his girlfriend at the time. By the end of the night, he decided he was in love, and to hear my mom tell the story, the same happened to her." She smiled. "They retold it on their anniversary every year, which was always celebrated *with* the kids."

"How'd your mom's friend take the news?" he asked. "Must have been a kick in the heart."

She gave him a sympathetic smile, appreciating that he saw the romance from the jilted woman's point of view. "Dad says he told her right away and they broke up. Whoever the guy was didn't care, since Dad and Mom obviously hit it off. By week's end, he and Mom were 'an item'—their words, not mine. They got married young, too." She raised a brow. "Well *under* nine months from the day Liam was born."

He chuckled, shaking his head, scanning her face. "Your family is a freaking thing of beauty, you know that? Does anyone ever go off the deep end or argue or make unforgivable mistakes or try to ruin one of the others?"

"No," she said. "And I know Gideon has been awful to you, and you have bad blood. But is it possible you're painting the whole family with a broad brushstroke? Even your mother? Malcolm and Brea didn't seem so terrible. People mellow with age, Josh, and change."

He shot her a look. "You're determined to make me like them."

"Or try to see them in a positive light." Suddenly, her eyes widened as an idea hit. "Why don't we stay at Waterford Farm? We can move in with the dogs, and Savannah will never find us there. My dad would…" Her voice trailed off.

"Not do anything to aid and abet dognappers," he finished.

She made a face. "You're probably right about that. In fact, if he knew Savannah was here and wanted Stella, he'd say we'd have to tell her where she is. Are you sure?"

"That she'd stop the procedure? I have no idea. I don't know her at all."

"No, no. I mean are you sure it was her? Maybe the lady who lives in the downstairs came up or the Realtor?"

"Mrs. Crane is a nice older woman, but no one Bill would describe as 'pretty,' and she wouldn't try to get into your apartment. On the off chance it was the real estate agent, I texted her and she said she hasn't been near the building since she toured it with you, and she hasn't sent anyone there since there are no units ready to rent."

And Darcy had checked with Molly and Ella, not offering explanations, but confirming they hadn't been over to see her. No one else knew her new address yet. "If Savannah wanted Stella back, why wouldn't she call you? Or return your ten messages?" she asked.

He eased back, thinking. "From the first, her phone clicked into voice mail without ringing. I don't know if she got them. She doesn't have read receipts on her phone, so I don't know if she read the texts I've sent. She might have cut herself off or lost her phone for all I know."

"It could have been anyone, though," Darcy said. "Someone one of the workers accidentally let in who lives across the courtyard. Kookie can be annoying as hell when she goes on a barking rant."

He nodded, looking at the papers but, she suspected, not seeing his rudimentary drawings.

"The fact is we don't know it was Savannah, Josh, and we need to find out."

"Which is why we're going to stay and see if she comes back, but we won't let her get Stella."

"How?" she asked.

"Stella can stay at your place. If she knocks and the dogs bark, you hide Stella and tell her that was your dog she heard and that I am out of town and took Stella with me."

She played it out in her mind, then held up her knuckles for a tap. "Good plan, HL."

"Except, what if she comes to my apartment first, and I'm there?" he asked.

She couldn't resist a saucy smile. "Then stay with me."

He grinned right back. "Good plan, Miss K. But what if she stakes out the building and sees us leaving with the dogs?"

"Uh, hide them in bags? Oldest dog trick in the book."

He started to smile, then chuckle, then threw his head back and let out a laugh that came from deep inside his impressive chest.

"What?" she asked.

"I never..." It took him a few seconds to stop laughing. "I never break rules, Darcy Kilcannon." He stopped for a second. "Wait. What's *your* middle name?"

"Colleen, after my aunt we talked to when we got here, the one who's next door running Bone Appetit."

"Darcy Colleen Kilcannon."

The way he said her whole, full name did something wild to her body, making nerves ping and adrenaline splash and blood rush to her heart to make it pound. "Yes?"

"You make me break rules."

"Nope. Stella does."

He shook his head. "You make me trust you," he said. "And that is a cardinal rule I swore I'd never break."

She attempted to swallow, but her mouth was dry and her throat tight with emotion. "We're even, then."

"You trust me?"

"I'm..." She glanced at the paper on the floor. "Not doing a damn thing alone like I wanted to."

"Alone..." He put his hand on her cheek, angling her head, preparing for a kiss. "Is highly overrated."

"It is when together feels this good," she whispered.

He closed the space and kissed her, softly and sweetly and with so much promise she could have cried. His fingers coasted over her cheek, while his tongue coaxed her mouth open so she could taste more of him.

Heat curled through her, settling low in her belly, plucking at her, torturing her, making her want—

A tap at the window made Darcy jump, fast and hard. She whipped around, half expecting the evil glare of a "young brunette," so it was nothing but relief to see a *familiar* young brunette with her face pressed against the glass, unabashedly staring at them. Then howling in laughter.

"Oh Lord. That's my cousin," she said, pushing up to unlock the door that she shouldn't have locked but had because...Savannah. As she opened the latch, she realized Ella had never met—

"Hot Landlord?" she guessed, pointing at him.

Josh chuckled and stood up to greet her. "Crazy cousin?"

And like that, the ice was broken as the real introductions were done and Ella seized the sketches with her usual infectious enthusiasm and boundless drama.

"This is astounding!" She practically whirled around, waving papers, pointing at this imaginary station and that soon-to-be kennel bank. "You are a godsend!"

"I don't know about that," Josh said. "But I'm happy to help. I love projects like this, and I can do it all myself."

Ella raised her eyebrows in Darcy's direction. "Hot *and* handy."

Darcy gave a smug look. "I can pick 'em."

"Well, I'm thrilled you can help, Josh, because the sooner she opens this business, the sooner we'll be sharing customers." Ella set the page down and slid an arm around Darcy. "What's going on? Your text was cryptic."

No surprise that even without words, Ella could read through her lines. "Well, we're in the middle of this..." The words trailed off, sounding silly even as she said them, but Josh put his hand on her shoulder.

"You can tell her, Darce. I know you tell her everything."

She looked up at him, touched that he understood and even more touched that he trusted Ella simply because he knew she did. "We've got a problem," she admitted. "And it might require us to commit dognapping."

Ella's eyes widened.

Josh let Darcy tell the whole story, including why Savannah might be in hiding, but left out the fact that she'd slept with Josh's stepbrother. Of course she'd share that later, but not with him here. Anyway, leaving the dog with no way to get in touch with her told Ella all she needed to know about Savannah.

"There's no question you're doing the right thing," Ella announced when Darcy finished. "The dog needs a chance, and you're not hurting her, or doing

244

anything but the kindest, most humane thing. What are you worried about?"

"That she'd take her away and end the procedure," Darcy said. "And who knows? Maybe she'd try and sue us or wreck this business or Josh's. She's kind of a loose cannon."

Josh snorted. "Darcy loves a good understatement."

"I know, right?" Ella laughed, obviously delighted that he knew Darcy that well. "Well, if I can help you, I will. Leave the dog with me at the store if you need to, or at my house. I'm fully behind dognapping for the blind." She gave Darcy a quick hug and reached for Josh, but he held up a hand and snagged his phone to read a text.

"We can pick up Stella," he said with a breath of relief. "She's doing great."

They all hugged, then, a group thing with Josh's big arms around both women and a couple of kisses on cheeks. Darcy leaned back and looked from one to the other, a sudden, unexpected, and shocking wave of emotion rolling over her. Longing, joy, wonder, hope, and…something that felt an awful lot like surrender.

She wanted both of them to be in her life. To care for each other. To matter.

Oh God. If she fell in love with Joshua Caleb Ranier, would she be giving up her independence? She didn't know, but right then, she longed to find out.

Josh didn't want to leave. He'd settled on the sofa in Darcy's living room with one dog on each side of him after they'd finished dinner, cleaned up, and split the last of a bottle of wine. It was getting late, and all he needed to do was push up, say good night, and leave her alone.

But he couldn't move.

Darcy knelt in front of the coffee table, a tablet open to pages of grooming salon ideas, her long hair pulled up in a messy ponytail, any bits of makeup she'd had on earlier in the day smudged off by now.

He guessed it was natural that comparisons to Savannah would rise up in his head and heart. One woman painted her face as if it were an art form; the other probably never wore false eyelashes in her life. One preferred high-end restaurants and late-night clubbing; the other threw some chicken in a pan, popped open a mediocre bottle of wine, and made no apologies for changing into flannel shorts and an oversized T-shirt that said Jurassic Bark with a cartoon dinosaur dog. One had lied, cheated, stolen, and God knew what else. And this one?

She was a flipping angel.

So, yeah, comparisons were rising up, and all they did was make him want even more to not move.

Darcy turned the tablet from one side to the other, cocking her head to consider whatever she was looking at. "I swore I wasn't going to do this."

"Work on the salon ideas all night?" Because he really could use a little more than dog company on this couch.

"Fall into the pit of pink." She lowered the tablet and looked at him. "I want to outgrow it, you know? The grooming studio at Waterford is pink."

"There is a lot of pink in your life." He tapped the sofa, which was probably not "pure" pink, but he didn't know what else to call it. Peach? Raspberry? Something fruity.

"But I get to start fresh at the salon. And what am I drawn to?" She turned the tablet, and he squinted at something that looked, well, pink. "Could you die?"

He laughed and fought a yawn. "Die," he repeated.

"Too late. You're already dead on your feet."

"Technically, I'm on your pink sofa."

"That's mauve and I really wanted to do the salon in blues. But I love pink. I can't deny who I am."

He chuckled. "Why mess with perfection?"

She beamed up at him. And he fought another unwanted yawn, making her laugh. "Look, you're wiped out. We both are. You go. I'll get the girls into bed."

He chuckled at the statement, which sounded so familiar and parental. "They're happy where they are," he said, patting both furry white bodies. "And so am I."

"Then stay." The words popped out fast, simple, eager. "Didn't we decide that was the right thing to do in case Savannah comes a-knockin'?"

"We did, but..."

Getting up on her knees, she semicrawled across the space between them, then settled down in front of him. "It would be fun."

"Fun?" He grinned, and she laughed. "Yes, Your Majesty, Queen of the Understatement. It would be fun." He leaned closer. "It would also be..." Dangerous. Intimate. A massive step away from friends with or without dogs.

As each second ticked by and he didn't finish the sentence, she inched closer, little by little.

"Nice," he finally said.

She smiled. "Speaking of understatements."

"Really nice."

"Mmm." She propped her elbow on his knee. "That's all you got?"

He leaned all the way over, getting his face right in front of hers. "What do you want me to say, Darcy? That I want to spend the night with you more than I know how to express? That once I get in bed with you, I won't want to stop or leave or sleep anywhere else? That I know that making love is going to change everything, and when I kiss you I don't care?"

He saw tiny goose bumps lift the little blond hairs on her arms and her throat move as she tried to swallow, silent.

"If you can handle all of that, and you want it as much as I do, then I'll stay. And fun's going to take on a whole new meaning."

Her mouth opened to a sweet little o, but nothing came out.

"Too much?" he asked.

"Could you just…" She breathed the words.

"Wait?"

"Just…" She pressed her hand on his knee, the muscles in her arms straining as if she was fighting the need to slide her hand up his thigh. He watched her knuckles turn white, felt her pulse hammer against him, heard the hitch in her next breath. "Hold me?"

He looked at her, not trusting his response, because his first answer was, *No*. He couldn't *just* hold her. What did she think he was made of?

"I'm scared she'll show up again tonight, and I…" She bit her lip until it turned white under her teeth. "I don't want to be alone."

His heart nearly collapsed. Damn it. He'd never thought of that. He was thinking with one part of his body only. Of course she was scared. Of course she wanted him there. Of course it didn't have to be about sex.

Not tonight. Not yet.

Slowly, he stood, and both dogs startled at the disruption of their sleep. "Come on."

"Where are we going?"

He brought her up with one hand. "We'll walk the dogs in the courtyard, make sure the entire building is locked tight, and then we'll come back up, and you'll go to bed."

"And you?"

Looking down at her, he tapped her nose. "I will sleep right here on the not-really-pink sofa."

"You don't have to do that."

"I want to."

"I want you to," she admitted. "I mean, I wanted you to say you'd sleep in my bed, but...the man's got rules."

"And the woman's got to have her space."

That made her sigh. "Think those walls will ever come down? For either of us?"

"Yes." Why lie? It was only a matter of time. "Maybe when Stella can see, we'll have some clarity, too."

She slid against him, wrapping her arms around him and laying her cheek against his chest. "All the more reason to root for her."

Chapter Nineteen

By Saturday afternoon, life had taken on a rhythm that felt entirely right to Josh, with the only cloud on the horizon the fact that they were always waiting for that visit from Savannah, but it never came. Nothing changed when he tried calling or texting, either. Except, now her "voice mail was full" so he mustn't be the only person trying to track her down.

He slept on Darcy's couch, which was both wretchedly uncomfortable and utterly good. Especially those mornings when she slipped onto the couch after he woke up to cuddle with him, sharing quiet talks and long, hungry kisses. Each kiss, each touch, each deeply intimate morning together took them closer to the inevitable. But by silent agreement, they waited. They both knew that once they made love, neither one would be "alone" again, and that changed everything. And that made every bit of physical contact even more electric and meaningful.

But they'd agreed to wait for Stella to see, and the anticipation was sweet and, somehow, even sexier than giving in to what they wanted.

But now, Josh worked out a now-familiar crick in his neck and looked around at the amazing progress they were making in the salon. Primarily because, as much as he'd thought he would, Josh wasn't tackling the job alone.

Liam, Aidan, and Trace had all jumped at the chance to help move the project to completion when they'd talked about it over dinner at Waterford Farm on Wednesday. For one second, he'd seen Darcy hesitate, probably because she still clung to the idea that taking too much help from the family made her "dependent," but Josh welcomed the assist and the company of these men. And credit to Darcy, she accepted their offer happily with nothing more than one of those silent looks of agreement she so frequently shared with Josh.

Garrett had a rescue dog to deliver today, so he couldn't help, and Shane had training all morning, but planned to come over after lunch. Their father was working with Molly on a vet emergency in the town office, but he'd be over after that as well. Darcy had taken the dogs to Waterford Farm so they'd be safe from the construction dangers, but she would return later.

That left Josh working with two former military men and one former convict, all tied by blood or love to Darcy and committed to making her salon as perfect as she was. While Josh measured and cut two-by-fours for the reception wall, Liam assembled a row of various size crates and cages they'd brought from Waterford to hold the furry clientele. Trace was setting tile, and Aidan worked on the sink plumbing. They moved like a well-oiled machine, despite the fact that they were hardly trained subs. They listened to each other and respected the work.

Josh blew out a breath, feeling the quicksand of the Kilcannon family pulling him in deeper. The only thing as dangerous as falling for a woman again was falling for her family, too. As he knew, he'd have to trust them as much as he'd have to trust her if this thing continued.

This thing. He didn't know what it was, exactly, but being with Darcy had added a dimension to his life he hadn't expected and didn't want to lose. It didn't need to be defined, did it? No one was asking for it to have an official name, least of all Darcy, who in true free-spirit style couldn't care less what people thought of their budding romance.

A few feet away, Liam adjusted the top of an oversized cage. "This one will be for the big boys and has to be the most secure."

His every move was carefully watched by Zelda, a black and tan dog who looked a lot like a German shepherd, but was actually a Belgian Malinois. Liam had assured him Zelda was perfectly well-behaved and safe at a construction site, a fact Josh wouldn't argue. Looking at that dog, he wouldn't argue anything.

"Help me level this, Trace," Liam said.

"On it." Trace pushed up from where he was setting tile around the bathing sink and pulled back the short sleeves of his T-shirt, revealing heavily inked, but impressive biceps.

Aidan tossed a level to Trace, who caught the tool with one hand. "Don't you have to leave soon, Trace?" he asked.

"Half an hour. Maybe more. I wanted to wait until Shane got here to finish this tile."

"Don't want to be late to interview the wedding planner," Liam said with a wry chuckle. "As if you're going to get an opinion."

"Seriously," Trace said. "Between Pru, Gramma Finnie, and my wife-to-be, I don't have a whole lot to say about the wedding, other than 'I do.'"

Liam laughed as he attached the final set of bars to the top of the cage and held it in place while Trace laid the level along the top beam. "You should have been at mine," Liam said. "People went to a double engagement party, and a wedding broke out."

Josh recalled the story Darcy had told him of how Liam and Andi had had a "surprise" wedding right in the house at Waterford Farm to stave off a custody battle for her young son.

"It worked, though," Josh said. "Your son was safe."

"And we still haven't gotten around to that pesky annulment that was supposed to be part of the deal." Liam grinned over his shoulder. "Truth be told, I didn't know what hit me. And that was before I had a newborn."

"The Dogfather hit you," Trace teased. "Once he picks the match, that ship has sailed into the sunset."

"True that." Liam gave the dog cage a good shake. "Think that'll hold a big beast?" he asked Trace.

"I've seen jail cells that were less secure. Hell, I've been in one," he added, making them laugh.

They didn't even judge him for that, Josh thought. The man had been imprisoned for fourteen years and he still was accepted and loved by this clan. Of course, he'd gone to prison unfairly after he'd accidentally killed a guy who'd attempted to rape a woman, and, in the process, missed the first thirteen years of Pru's life, since he didn't even know he had a daughter.

But, thanks to Daniel Kilcannon, the family was now reunited…and meeting with wedding planners.

"I better test the strength of this one," Liam said, shaking the cage, then glancing at the dog. "Zelda. In."

Instantly, the dog rose, trotted to the open crate, and walked in with plenty of room even for a huge dog. She turned to look at Liam as if she wouldn't breathe without being instructed to do so. Liam closed the crate and locked it by sliding a dead bolt, the way all the smaller crates they'd installed that morning closed.

"Zelda. Out."

The big dog took a breath, looked from one side to the other, then put a massive paw on the lock, worked her one paw pad through, and slid it open.

"Holy…wow." Josh took a few steps closer, while the other men reacted with hoots and little surprise. "How'd she learn to do that?"

"Training," Liam said. "And if she can, another dog can." He opened the door and fluttered his fingers over the dog's head, silent, staring at the crate and thinking.

The affection was all Zelda needed, returning to her spot to bask in the tiny bit of praise.

"I don't think I've seen this dog around Waterford," Josh said, still astounded.

"Zelda's an obedience-school dropout who prefers to stay at home." Liam grinned at the dog. "But we love her anyway. And so does Jag."

At the word *Jag*, Zelda's ears popped up and her big tail thumped once, cracking Josh up.

"If that's what drops out of your obedience school, I'd hate to meet the valedictorian."

"We get ten to twelve grand for those," Liam told Josh. "And send them to compounds so the trillionaire types can be safe."

Like the ones that prowled Buckingsham Palace grounds. "I have a combination lock," Josh said. "Unless she can crack those, too."

Liam laughed. "Not yet. And that's perfect. We can resize the hole, and this large crate can be escape-proof."

After getting the lock for them and Liam filed a new hole, Josh asked more about the K-9 training program, a topic that made even the usually quiet Liam talkative.

"Zelda didn't quite make the cut," Liam explained after he told Josh what was involved. "And she's not people-oriented enough for Trace's therapy training. But I kept her because..." Liam grinned at the dog before taking the screwdriver Trace handed him. "Every once in a while, there's one you can't let go."

"Kinda like a woman," Trace mused as he angled the drill into the new locking system.

"God knows we've all been there," Aidan said on a laugh.

"Maybe not all," Liam added with a quick look at Josh, the words almost drowned out by the high-pitched whine of the saw. "Yet."

Josh let the two-by-four remnant clunk to the floor, making the others laugh at his reaction. He looked from one to the next, snorting softly at how pathetic they were at hiding what they wanted to know.

So maybe *this thing* needed a name after all. He didn't think *we're waiting until Stella can see so we can rip each other's clothes off and never come up for air* would cut it with this crew. So he'd better get the topic off him and on them.

"Just to set the record straight," he finally said, "Dr. K assured me that he had no hand in matchmaking this time."

Their expressions shifted to something more like *that's hilarious* and *only an idiot would believe that*.

Josh picked up the next two-by-four and laid it precisely on the measuring line. "I believe him when he says he wasn't setting us up," he said. "Of all the things I've learned about Daniel Kilcannon, one is that he's a man of integrity."

"He doesn't lie," Liam agreed.

"Well, then, he told me straight up to my face that he didn't have any 'intentions' when he suggested Darcy look at the unit in my building. Maybe this time, it's...organic." Whatever *it* was.

"Maybe," Aidan said.

"Always that chance," Trace muttered.

Liam's grunt was thick with skepticism.

"I believe him," Josh insisted. "And I think one of the reasons is because he doesn't want you guys messing with his personal life and setting him up with every woman over fifty and under seventy-five who doesn't have a wedding ring on her finger."

This time, the looks they shared were guilty, and

for a moment at least, Josh and Darcy were forgotten.

"Mostly we're kidding," Trace said.

"It's more of a family joke," Aidan added.

But Liam was quiet, looking down at his next nail. "You might be right," he finally said. "We should probably back off and can the mob mentality."

Josh suspected the oldest Kilcannon sibling could rightly call a shot like that and his siblings would fall in line. But Liam had to call it, not Josh. Dr. K was their father, not his. "All I'm saying is you might not have the same magic touch your dad has."

"But you do admit it's magic," Aidan said.

Josh considered that. Magic? "Maybe there's a little psychology involved," he suggested. "Like you know he's behind it, so it has to work."

"Doesn't matter," Liam said, low enough that it might have been for no one's benefit but his own. "Because every damn one of us is happy."

"Single people can be happy," Josh challenged, keeping the edge out of his voice.

Aidan looked amused. "Man, you are drinking Darcy's Kool-Aid."

"Speaking of…" Trace pointed a subway tile to the window. There, side by side with the big red setter between them, Darcy walked with her father, deep in conversation punctuated by laughter so loud and sincere, Josh could hear it through the glass. "God only knows what they're cooking up."

"World domination," Aidan joked.

"The next match," Trace suggested.

Liam snapped the big combination lock into place, closing it with a noisy click. "Magic. Because, like it or not, my friend, that's what it is."

Josh couldn't argue with a man who made that much sense.

Darcy leaned her head back against the headrest in Josh's truck, closing her eyes to think about the week that had passed in a flash. So many great moments smashed into every day, she could hardly find the time to unpack each one and relive it. Like today, at Sunday dinner, when they'd ridden four-wheelers all over Waterford and she shared her best memories, and her worst. Later, a bunch of them took a pack of dogs for a walk to the lake, and when a few fish jumped, Garrett saw Josh's reaction and suggested that next Sunday they come early and fish.

Next Sunday. That would be, what? Three in a row? Josh never *didn't* want to go to Waterford Farm, in fact. He connected with her brothers, laughed with her grandmother, was patient with Christian, comfortable with her father, and fit in like...like...

Like he *belonged* there.

Josh reached for her hand in the dark cab of the truck, interlacing their fingers. "Thinking about Stella's treatment tomorrow?" he guessed.

"Mmmm." She gave the noncommittal answer because she didn't want to lie. Not once in the time they'd known each other and gotten closer and closer had Darcy lied to him.

"You heard what your dad said, Darcy. They didn't expect any change this week. So don't worry. I think we'll see a turnaround between the second and third treatment, like he said."

"I guess."

She felt his gaze on her. "That was what you were thinking about, right?"

Sometimes it felt like he knew her a little too well. "I'm thinking about my family...and you."

Even in the dim light, she caught his somewhat surprised look. "Did I blow it today somehow? I meant to let Christian win that last game, but—"

"Josh, stop." She squeezed his hand and brought it to her mouth for a quick kiss. "They love you."

"It's mutual."

He *loved* them. Did he...*mean* that? "So, have I made a convert out of you? You on board the families-rock train?"

"Yours does," he said. "I mean, you are all so devoted to each other."

She felt her brow pull as she considered that. "We love each other, if that's what you mean. I think most families do, Josh."

"It goes deeper than that." He stared at the dark road that led into Bitter Bark, narrowing his eyes. "You'd do anything for each other. Drop whatever. Look what your brothers and Trace are doing with your salon and how they all want to help each other with parts of Waterford Farm that don't fall under their control."

"You mean how they were all brainstorming the vet tech replacement or making suggestions for how to get those two rescue dogs to two different places in the country on the same day?" She recalled the dinner conversation, which had been nothing but normal. "That's how we run the business."

His sigh sounded pained. "I think that's the part

that blows me away the most. You all run a business together. You don't co-exist as relatives. There's no jealousy, no in-fighting, no backstabbing."

"God, no." She dropped her head back again. "I'm grateful that there's not."

"I'm jealous," he admitted. "And the more time I spend with them, the more time I want to spend with them."

Speaking of jealous, a twinge of something that felt an awful lot like that emotion crawled up her back, settling in her chest, making her uncomfortable. "I'm glad you like them so much."

After all, wasn't he the one who'd said you marry a family, not a person? Was he falling in love with the Kilcannons...or—

The sharp trill of Josh's cell phone broke into her thoughts.

"Oh, that can't be good," he said, reaching to the console where he kept his wallet and phone when he drove. "Sub probably canceling for tomorrow." He flipped the phone over and glanced at it, grunting.

"Carlos?" she asked. "He's so reliable."

"Malcolm." His voice turned to ice. "The last person I want to talk to right now."

"Not counting Gideon and Savannah."

He threw her a dry smile. "True. I'll let it go to voice mail."

"Why? It might be important."

"Or it might be a guilt trip. He probably lost another candidate for the job he wants me to take and is juicing up the deal." He shook his head and dropped the phone. "No, thanks."

"It wouldn't hurt to talk to him."

"It'd hurt me."

She studied him for a long time. "Why, Josh? Because he sides with Gideon on most things? Because he married your mother? Because he needles you now and again? Or because…"

"He's not Pops," he finished, swallowing hard at the confession.

Pops. She'd heard him refer to his father with the cute nickname that always made her—and him—smile. But there was no smile tonight.

"That's his greatest sin?" she asked. "Did he try to take your father's place?"

He choked. "Guy never picked up a rod and reel in his life. Wouldn't know what to do with a model car if it bit him. And he sure as hell doesn't know his way around a brisket smoker."

She reached over and took his hand, tenderly rubbing his knuckles, knowing the pain that digging deep and thinking about those memories caused. She got hit when she smelled a powdery perfume, or walked by a store in town where she and her mother had shopped, or made the mistake of looking into her parents' room and realizing Mom wouldn't be curled up on the settee in front of the fireplace, reading a novel.

"But, Josh, it's not his fault that he's not Pops. He's who he is, and he really does love your mother. And, in his way, you. Isn't that really all you can ask of him?"

He stayed silent, but threaded his fingers with hers.

"Have you ever asked him to go fishing?" she whispered.

He opened his mouth like he was going to laugh or argue, but then he closed it.

"So, no," she guessed.

"He prefers a good cigar on the veranda with Gideon."

"Does he invite you to join them?"

"Yeah, but I—"

The phone rang again. Josh's hand tensed, the tautness running up his arm and making his jaw clench. Darcy didn't say a word, but loosened her grip so that he could answer the phone if he wanted to.

It rang a second and third time, making Darcy bite her lip to keep from suggesting he answer. He knew what was right. He knew what he should do. He knew—

He jerked his hand away on the fourth ring and tapped the phone screen, and suddenly the dashboard lit up with the call on speaker. So he wasn't just answering, he was sharing the conversation with her.

"Hey, Mal," Josh said, his voice tense.

"Oh, Joshua. I'm so glad you picked up." His stepfather's voice filled the cab, making both dogs, who'd been sleeping in the back, sit up at attention. Stella barked once, but Kookie's quick lick quieted her.

"I'm driving," Josh said, probably to explain why he flat-out ignored the first call and didn't return it. "What's up?"

"It's Gran."

Josh sucked in a quick breath. "What happened?"

"Nothing…yet. But she's fading and asking to see you."

Darcy blinked in surprise. He'd talked about his stepfather's mother, who was deep into her nineties and "forgetful"—which was probably the Bucking way of avoiding the word *dementia*. He seemed to lump her in with the rest of the family, not meriting any real discussion.

"Me?" he asked, confirming her suspicions. "She probably means Savannah."

Now, that surprised her, making Darcy turn in her seat a little. Savannah?

"No, she specifically said you. She wants to see you. Has something to tell you before…" His voice grew thick. "She isn't long for this world, Joshua."

He blew out a breath, turning onto the street in Ambrose Acres where the brownstone was located. He also didn't spare a look at Darcy, who he must have known would tell him he had to go. The woman was dying. And she was family.

But he'd make up some excuse, of course. He wouldn't go back there unless Stella's well-being was at stake. Which was stubborn and stupid and deeply disappointing. How could she fall for a guy who—

"I can be there tomorrow morning," he said. "I'll leave here at daybreak."

Oh. Darcy felt her heart tumble around helplessly.

"She can't see anyone until late afternoon," Malcolm said. "It takes her the better part of the morning to be dressed and up."

"Okay. I'll be at her place around three." He finally looked at her, his eyes filled with warmth and hope and something she didn't dare name because it might be that four-letter word that started with L and ended with forever.

"Good, good," Malcolm said. "We have dinner with the Hermans tomorrow night. Would you like to join us?"

"We'll take a rain check."

We. Darcy's heart took another ride down a rollercoaster. Was he asking her to go with him? Or simply assuming she would because…*we*?

"You're welcome to stay here," Malcolm added.

"No, thanks," he said. "Will you be at Gran's tomorrow?"

"I'm tied up all day and it's you she's asking for, Joshua."

He pulled into his spot and parked the car. "Then someone should let her know I'll be there."

"Thank you," Malcolm said stiffly. "I admit I thought you'd say no."

Josh held Darcy's gaze and lifted his hand to her cheek as he responded, "No problem, Mal. It's…what families do."

She closed her eyes as the words hit. As sweet as anything he could have said right then. Maybe he *was* falling for her family, but if that softened his heart toward his own, then it was a good thing.

After he said goodbye to his stepfather, he leaned across the console and kissed Darcy for a long, long time. When he finally broke the contact, his eyes were still closed.

"Am I invited?" she whispered.

"You don't need to ask. But Stella's next treatment is tomorrow."

"My dad will get her there and back," she said. "Remember, we're friends with dogs *and* families."

Which, as he loved to remind her, was infinitely more complicated. And wonderful.

Chapter Twenty

"We're not far from where I grew up," Josh said as he exited the highway into the tony Myers Park section of Charlotte where Bernice Bucking lived, a good hour south of the mansion in Cornelius, but close to the hospitals and medical practices she needed.

"Really?" Darcy inched forward, glancing around at the tall pines and hills, instantly interested. "You lived around here?"

"Until I was twelve, we lived about half an hour east. Way east. On the proverbial other side of the tracks."

"Can you take me there and show me the house?"

He swallowed, quiet for a moment. If he didn't want to do that, why had he even mentioned the fact to her? Because he *did* want to take Darcy there. He wanted to let her deeper and deeper into his life. "Sure, if you want."

"Do you visit often?"

"Malcolm's mother or my old house on Doverdell Drive?"

"Both."

He gave a shrug. "When I got my driver's license, my house was the first place I went," he admitted. "We'd been living at Buckings..." He stopped, shaking off the nickname, which was so tied up with his distaste for the family. "At Bucking Manor for four years, and I was itching to get back. I remember it being so small, I almost laughed."

"Anything would be in comparison to that place."

"Yeah, I guess. And I went once on the ten-year anniversary of Pops's death. Not since, though."

"Surprising, since you must be here to see your grandmother frequently."

He threw her a look, not sure she quite understood his relationship with his grandmother. "I don't come here frequently," he said. "Gran is cut from Bucking cloth. Cold, distant, far above the masses. Savannah had a better relationship with her than I do, frequently helping her dress for events."

"And maybe helping herself to Gran's jewelry," Darcy added.

He angled his head, not responding right away. "I'm not going to say I fully understood what Savannah might have been up to, but I'm having a hard time wrapping my head around that. She has— had—a good job and didn't seem to need money. If she did, she never asked me."

"Will your grandmother recognize you?" she asked.

"She's not..." He stopped himself once again. "Yes," he finished, knowing that reminding the world that Buckings were *step* family was wearing thin, at least with Darcy. "She's not *that* forgetful, but she knows what's going on. She's sick, though. She has battled COPD for years, which is no surprise considering she was a heavy smoker most of her life. She's got bad arthritis, impaired vision in one eye from macular degeneration, and she had some heart issues about ten years ago. She's almost ninety-five, so she spends a good part of her day in bed."

"That's less than ten years older than Gramma Finnie, and she practically runs up two flights of stairs."

"They couldn't be more different, as little old ladies go. For one thing, Bernice Bucking never met a person, place, or thing she couldn't pass judgment on. Few mere mortals reach the bar she sets for perfection, although she has a surprisingly close relationship with my mother."

"Then why doesn't she live closer to Christine and Malcolm? Wouldn't they take care of her?"

"She refuses to embrace the fact that she's in her nineties and infirm. She insists on living alone, although I'm not sure the amount of nurses on staff qualifies as 'on her own.' She likes to give the impression she is strong and independent."

"I like her already," Darcy said with a laugh.

"You like my whole family," he teased. "A hell of a lot more than I do."

"I like families in general," she said, peering at the elaborate gated entrance with the word *Rosebay* engraved in marble. "Holy cow, this is another wealthy area."

"Her husband started Bucking Properties and built a sizable fortune. Malcolm inherited the company and took it to the next level, or six. Gideon will run it into the ground." He shrugged. "Sorry. You'll never make me like him."

After being cleared by the guard, he drove through the wide, perfectly manicured roads of an exclusive neighborhood that catered to the elderly with big dough. The houses were almost all one story, mostly brick or columned stucco. Behind the perfect facades lived that handful of older folks who could afford the best health care, the nicest homes, and a way to go gently to the finish line.

Gran's home was at the end of a cul-de-sac, a rambling red-brick ranch. Just cruising down the quarter-mile-long driveway lined with birch trees tightened Josh's stomach a bit.

"You're already tense, and we're not even at the front door," Darcy mused.

"How can you tell?" He hadn't said a word about the churning inside him.

She reached over and tapped right under his jaw. "This little vein pulses whenever you have to talk to someone in your family. It's your Bucking Artery."

He laughed, reaching up to grab her hand and kiss it. "It bleeds green for money."

"She's ninety-four and dying. Why are you so uptight?"

"I don't know," he admitted. "I've seen her maybe twice in the last year, and both times she was pleasant enough. Pleasant being relative, of course, but the bite seemed to be gone from her."

"She asked for you to come. Maybe she's making amends for mistakes in her life. Give her a chance. She might slip you a million dollars with her granny kisses."

He squeezed her hand. "Do you always see the best in people? Even when it isn't really there?"

"I try to," she said. "No one is all bad or all good. People have facets, and I try to see the bright parts. That's something my mother taught me."

He stopped the truck, killed the engine, and turned to her. "You would have liked my dad," he said, always reminded of Pops when she talked about her mother. "He was the same way. Saw the good in people, made the best of bad situations, never quit trying."

"Make me a promise," she said softly.

"I'll be nice to her," he replied.

"Of course you will, because you're a gentleman, *like your father*." She inched closer. "Promise me that when we leave today, you'll take me to where you grew up and tell me every single thing you can remember about him."

"That would..." Take a lot of trust. "Not be very interesting for you."

"I'll be the judge of what's interesting. Promise?"

He answered with a kiss that he intended to be quick and light, but she wrapped her fingers around his neck, tunneling into his hair. She flicked her tongue over his and made the softest whimper against his lips.

"Okay," he said on a helpless laugh. "I promise. Anything else?" He kissed her again. "'Cause the answer will be yes."

"*And* be nice to her."

He was still smiling about that when a housekeeper let them in, offered them refreshments in a sitting room, and disappeared.

"Does no one in your life answer their own door?" Darcy cracked as she wandered to a fireplace mantel to look at pictures. "So which one is the evil stepbrother?" she asked.

He joined her and scanned the pictures of Bernice, George, Malcolm and his first wife, Amy, and several of Josh's mother. There were a few of Brea and Gideon, and Josh's high school graduation picture that, for some reason, made Darcy let out a little moan.

"She'll see you now." The housekeeper returned and gestured for them to follow, taking them through the main floor to a spacious wing where sunshine poured in, highlighting the finest workmanship on the floors, chair rails, wainscoting, and finishes of a Bucking-built house. A *Malcolm* Bucking-built house, not the corner-cutting son inheriting the business.

A white-clad nurse with dark hair and stern features stepped out to greet them as they reached a large solarium, introducing herself as Delia and speaking in hushed tones.

"Mrs. Bucking is awake, and lucid, but won't tolerate company for very long," she said. "But she's happy to see you and Savannah now."

Josh inched back at the mistake. "This is Darcy, not Savannah."

The woman's dark brows drew together. "She said…I'm sorry. She told me you'd be with someone named Savannah."

"Understandable mistake," Darcy said quickly. "It's fine. And if you think it's more appropriate…" She looked from Josh to the nurse. "I can wait out here so a new arrival doesn't upset her."

Before the nurse could answer, Josh put a firm arm around Darcy. "I want you to meet her," he said. If anyone was going to help him see the good in this crusty old woman, it would be Darcy.

"I'm sure it's fine," the nurse said. "But remember, she's drifting in and out of clarity. Whatever she says, humor her."

"Will do," Josh promised.

They passed through the final door into the queen's chamber, where a massive wood four-poster bed took up a good portion of the room. On one side, barely big enough to make a lump under the covers, his white-haired grandmother lay still with her eyes closed.

"Bernice," the nurse said. "Your grandson is here."

"Stepgrandson," she replied without opening her eyes. "The other one wouldn't bother to grace my doorstep unless he thought it would change the will."

Josh threw a quick glance at Darcy as if to confirm all he'd said, and her eyes widened in a silent response.

"Hey, Gran." He stepped closer to the bed, still holding Darcy's hand.

Her eyes opened quickly at the sound of his voice, the once blue faded to gray now, foggy, moist, and surrounded by parchment skin. "Where's Savannah?"

"I really don't know, Gran. This is Darcy."

Toothpick arms pulled out from the covers, trying to push herself up to see. Just that much movement made her cough a few times, then sigh and lie back on her pillows. "I need to speak to Savannah."

Could she seriously be that rude? "I'm not with Savannah anymore, Gran. We split up, and I don't know where she is. I'd like you to meet Darcy Kilcannon, who—"

"I don't want to meet Darcy Kilcannon," she managed to bark. "I want Savannah Mayfield."

He puffed out a breath and turned to Darcy, who had her bottom lip captured under her teeth as she backed away.

"I'll just..." She pointed her thumb to the door. "Wait outside."

"You'll wait right here," Gran ordered, the insistence in her voice making her cough again.

"Gran, please." Josh came closer. "I'm sorry I didn't bring Savannah today." A lie, but whatever. "But I'm here. And I'm happy to see you." Another lie. "And Darcy means a lot to me." Finally, the truth. "I heard you asked to see me."

"Not true," she said. "Or maybe I did and forgot. But when I heard it was you, I assumed Savannah was here to return the jewelry she, uh...borrowed." She lifted thin white brows as if to say they both knew nothing had been *borrowed.*

"I can't help you, Gran. I'm sorry that happened, though."

"Not as sorry as your mother, who was supposed to get all that when they put me in the ground." She pointed a crooked finger. "Which won't be soon, and she knows it."

"Maybe Savannah will come back," he said. "In the meantime, please say hello to Darcy."

Her crinkly old lips pursed, but she shifted her gaze to Darcy, scrutinizing her, or maybe trying to see through the fog of her age. "Hello. I'm sure you're very nice. But I'd rather not get invested again, if you don't mind. I don't misjudge people often, but apparently I did in the case of your other girlfriend, Joshua."

"You're not the only one, Gran," he said softly, earning a squeeze of his hand from Darcy.

"I liked her," she admitted, sounding as ashamed of the fact as he sometimes was. "She showed up here every Monday at eleven o'clock to set up my clothes for the following week. Shoes, accessories, and jewelry, like a good lady-in-waiting, although I think they call them *stylists* now."

Now that sounded more like the woman he knew, although Savannah had never told him this. Why not? Probably because he hated the Buckings so much, it would have ticked him off for her to be so nice to one of them.

A little more shame curled through him, making him let go of Darcy's hand and step closer to the bed.

"Of course, I didn't always get out of bed on bad days, but the fact that she came…" She turned her head, her wispy white hair brushing against the pillow. "Oh, I really judged her wrong. If she wanted money, she should have asked. I'd have given it to her."

"If I talk to her again, I'll try and get your things back. What's missing, exactly?"

"Diamonds, for one thing. And that includes the yellow diamond double-B earrings that George had made for me on our fiftieth anniversary. A sapphire bracelet, a Van Cleef emerald brooch, and at least a ring for every finger. Things that don't matter much to anyone but me," she added sadly. "Things I wanted to share with people I love when I'm gone."

His heart hitched a little, not ever remembering her admitting to loving anyone, with the possible exception of George Bucking, who died more than twenty years ago.

"I'm sorry," he said again. "If it's any consolation, she fooled a lot of people."

"Nobody fools me." Her gravelly voice was rich with disdain. "And I think that's what bothers me the most."

"Don't let it," he said. "You have to move on."

Her foggy gaze moved toward Darcy, who'd politely backed away from the bed. "I see you have."

He gave a soft laugh. "Darcy and I are friends."

She sucked in a breath, too long and too deep, and it made her hack long enough that the nurse came in, shooting Josh a warning look. While she tended to his grandmother, he walked to the other side of the room, where Darcy perched on a settee.

"I hate to say this, but she's kind of sweet," she whispered.

"Yeah. I never saw it that way, but…"

"Maybe too sweet, letting non-family members have access to all that jewelry."

He nodded. "I feel responsible. My mother may have brought Savannah here as a stylist, but I—"

"It was Brea." Gran's voice floated over the room, between coughs, proving her judgment skills might be fading, but her hearing sure wasn't. "She brought Savannah here. Don't beat yourself up, Joshua."

Darcy and Josh shared a look as the nurse refilled Gran's water and nodded to them. "A few more minutes," the woman said as she walked out. "Bernice needs her sleep."

Josh ventured back over as Gran settled back on her pillows, her spotted, knotty hands crossed on top of the spread. "Tell me something about her," she said. "About this new girl of yours. Tell me what you love about her."

He stood stone-still at the word *love*, not wanting to correct the old woman, but not exactly sure how to answer the blunt and awkward question. With the truth, as always.

"She has a good heart," he said. "And she puts family above everything else."

Behind him, he heard Darcy sigh softly.

"You deserve that," Gran said as her eyes closed. "I'm tired now. Goodbye, Joshua. Thank you for coming. Thank your friend, too." She smiled, but didn't open her eyes. "Goodbye," she whispered.

He repeated the word and backed away, turning to Darcy.

"Come on." She slipped her arm through his and gently nudged him to the door. "It's time to go."

To her credit, Darcy didn't once say *I told you so* or remind Josh that deep inside his mess of an extended family lived a few decent people. Instead, she held his hand and talked very little as they drove to a much-lower-rent district almost a half hour away.

Nor did she bring up the ugly subject of Savannah and how she'd fooled a lot of people. Instead, she studied the tract homes that all looked essentially the same as when he'd lived here, though the trees were twice as tall. Turning onto his street, he braced for the impact and slowed as they reached 543 Doverdell Drive.

"That's the house," he said, yanking her attention back to follow his gaze to a tiny white house with a car port. The shingled roof was torn in places, and some of the siding was lifted. The front porch hadn't seen a coat of paint in a decade or two, and no one really loved the lawn. The lawn with a red and white For Sale sign stuck in the front.

"Looks pretty much the same, I have to say."

"It's…sweet. Like a little kid drew a house with two windows and a blue door."

He laughed. "It's a dump, Darcy, but I always loved that house. There are two bedrooms, a living room, and a kitchen. One bathroom and, if it's still there, a decent-sized deck on the back that my dad built that overlooks a pond that was always stocked with fish."

"You can buy it, Josh. Remodel it and keep it as a memory of your young, happy childhood."

He started to laugh as they continued to drive right by the house. "You can't go back, you know. Haven't you ever heard that?"

"But you know what a For Sale sign means?" She put her hand on his. "You could probably get in there to see it. Would you like to?"

"What would that accomplish?"

"Closure?" she suggested.

He didn't answer, but turned the corner, then the next, and then they were back on the street where he grew up, cruising one more time toward the house, this time much slower.

"I memorized the number on the For Sale sign if you change your mind," she said.

For some reason, the offer got to him. He blinked at her, seeing her profile in stark contrast to the humble house behind her, seeing a woman who knew him, who got him, and who cared deeply for him. A woman he somehow knew he could trust.

"What's wrong?" she asked, dropping her head back and turning her face to him, giving him yet another view of the present and the past in one glance.

Maybe even the *future* and the past.

"Nothing's wrong." As a matter of fact, everything was unbelievably right. "Why?"

"You're looking at me like…like it's the first time you've ever seen me."

"I wish he could have met you," he admitted. "I never knew how much until this minute."

She took his hand and brought it to her lips. "I want to see this house. Let's knock on the door."

He searched her face, considering the idea, almost discarding it, then… "Okay. What do we have to lose?"

"Oh, maybe a couple of those overstuffed bags of old hurts and disappointments you cart around."

The answer made him smile while he parked on the street, and they went together, hand in hand.

"We'll say we're looking for a house?" she asked. "Or is that against your rules?"

"It's a lie, so, yes, but…it's moot. There's a lockbox, so I doubt anyone is here."

A few minutes later, that was confirmed when no one answered the door. He started to turn back to the truck, but Darcy tugged on his hand and took one step down to the grass. "Let's look at the back. I want to see that pond."

"Darcy, I don't…" *Not the pond.*

She narrowed her eyes. "I can't know him, but I want to know about him."

He took the step and put an arm around her, swallowing hard and realizing he was choked up. "If we get shot for trespassing, it's your fault."

"Live dangerously." She pulled him to the side of the house.

They walked past a hedge and a trash can, reaching the back in less than twenty steps. The back deck was screened in now and completely empty. In fact, when he squinted through the kitchen window, it looked like the whole house was empty.

"Think they've moved out?" Darcy asked with a little too much suggestion in her voice.

"We're not breaking and entering," he shot back.

"Fun-killer."

"Anyway, it isn't the inside of the house that holds memories." He turned her from the porch to the pond, almost obscured by trees but visible enough to transport him back more than two decades. "They're right back there."

"Oh." She breathed the word and moved toward the trees. "That's so pretty. That's North Carolina, right there." She crossed the grass, and he followed, slipping between two mighty pines that his father had planted for a full view of the water. "It reminds me of Waterford," she said.

"Yeah, one-half of one percent of Waterford."

"It's the vibe." She turned and looked up at him. "No wonder you loved it."

"I loved him," he said simply. "The place is only as good as the people."

Holding hands, they walked the rest of the way to the water's edge. "This isn't our property, obviously, but the guy who owned it lived way back there, through those woods. He never cared if we fished here. And man, did we fish."

He reached the spot of grass where he and Pops used to set up camp, spreading their tackle box and rods. "Can't be, what? Two hundred feet from one side to the other? But it was like living on a great lake to five- and six- and seven-year-old me."

He stood still, looking out over the water toward the trees, the splash of a catfish transporting him back. He could hear Pops giving fishing instructions and life advice while he tied a red wiggler on his favorite fine-wire hook.

"He used to say a bad day fishing is better than a good day working." He grinned, remembering Pops's voice. "And then he'd sigh so loud I swear the fish could hear him. Called it the 'contented sigh of a fisherman.'"

She wrapped her arm around his waist and let her head fall on his shoulder. "He sounds wonderful."

"He was."

He stayed quiet for a long time, letting go of everything but the rush of memories. The time Pops brought a canoe home from one of his trips and they took Roscoe out in it and tipped the whole thing over, discovering that the dog could swim. When they'd come back here at night, Josh was as interested in catching fireflies in a jar as that elusive bass Pops swore was waiting for them.

"I couldn't come out here after he died," he admitted. "Not for a long, long time. I had this...this thing in my head that Mom was wrong, that he was on a long driving trip, and any day that rig would pull up to the front, and he'd climb out with his arms loaded with gifts. He always brought me something, usually marbles or baseball cards."

She tightened her grip, listening.

"When that didn't happen, I got really mad."

"Understandable," Darcy said. "You were what, eight or nine?"

"I took it personally. He left me. He abandoned me. I trusted him not to, but he did anyway. I couldn't comprehend death at that age." An old anger welled up, familiar and bitter. "Just as I got used to life without him, I ended up in Bucking hell. God, he would have hated those people."

"But your mother doesn't, and she loved him and missed him."

He nodded, turning from one beautiful view to another—the woman next to him. "I never stopped resenting the Buckings for taking me away from this." As he said the words, he realized even more. "And I've never forgiven my father for leaving and not coming back."

"You have to," she said simply. "You'll never really trust anyone until you forgive him, and her, and them. My mother used to say that without forgiveness, you're hollow inside."

He took a slow, deep breath, wrapping his arms around her and pressing her into his chest.

"Like I said, I wish he'd met you. We never once talked about girls, you know, since I was so young. But I know he'd have adored you."

She looked up. "Because I have a good heart and put family first?" she asked, echoing his answer to Gran.

"Because *I* adore you," he said. "And that would have been enough for him." He lowered his face and kissed her, feeling light for the first time in years, but still weighed down by need.

"I'm buzzing," she murmured, leaning back.

"I do that to you."

"And more." She reached into the pocket of her dress, pulling out her phone to glance at it. "Text from...oh my God, Josh."

"What?"

"Stella saw light." She turned the phone so he could read the text from her father.

Stella blinked twice into light. Not again, but we'll take it. JW says it's a great sign.

"You know what that means?" she asked.

Oh, yes. He knew exactly what it meant.

"She'll get her sight back," Darcy continued, tapping the phone to reply with happy emojis. "She'll be able to see, Josh. Light is the first step. If she sees light—"

He cut her off with a kiss, sure and deep and long. "Let's go to my house."

She broke contact and searched his face, silent.

"It's about forty-five minutes from here on the Catawba River, and I'd love to take you there."

She sighed. "I don't know."

What? Had she changed her mind? "You still want to wait?" Because he *couldn't*.

"Your house, huh?" She bit her lip and narrowed her eyes. "It depends on the landlord. Is he hot?"

Lowering his head, he slid his hand deeper into her silky hair. "Some say so."

She moaned into the kiss. "Will he break rules?"

"He's trespassing this very minute."

"Does he like dogs?"

"What he likes is you."

She tipped her head back and closed her eyes. "Take me home, Hot Landlord. Please."

Chapter Twenty-One

Darcy didn't know what to expect from Josh's house, which he'd mentioned in passing, but had never described. Something small and unassuming, of course, simple, masculine, and comforting. It was all those things and so much more.

"Why didn't you tell me how amazing this place is?"

"I wanted to bring you here instead. Words don't do it justice."

No kidding. The A-frame-style wooden home sat nestled among pine trees, a good twenty-minute drive from the closest small town, so deep in the hilly woods, you couldn't see the house from the winding road that led up to it. He parked in the driveway and led her up at least twenty stairs to a wide deck that surrounded the whole structure.

Inside, one wall was a stone fireplace, and the other three were glass, looking out over a whitewater-tipped river lined with thick green pines and massive birch, oak, and maple trees that probably flamed with color in the fall.

"Oh, Josh." She sucked in a breath as her gaze drifted from one glorious view to the next. "It's gorgeous. It might not have the memories of Doverdell Drive, but I can see why you picked this spot."

"Exactly. I built it myself."

"Really?" She took a few steps closer to the glass, checking out the spacious deck, grill, and comfy couches under a pergola. "How could you ever leave?"

Behind her, he wrapped his arms around her waist, pulling her against his hard chest and big body. "Bitter Bark has some beautiful things to see, too." He dipped his head and lifted her hair to kiss her neck, sending a million chills over her skin. "Anyway, I'm not leaving it forever. I'll always come here to chill and fish and escape the world." He slowly turned her to face him, taking her from one breathtaking view to another. "Which is what we're about to do."

"Fish?" she teased.

"You already caught me, Darcy Kilcannon." He lowered his face so their mouths could meet. "Hook, line, and sinker."

She reached up to wrap her arms around his neck, taking a minute to graze the solid biceps and shoulders built for a woman to cling to. As his hands coasted down her back and sides, she sank deeper into him, starving for this time when they were utterly alone, hidden in his secret, private treehouse.

"It's magical," she whispered as he trailed kisses along her jaw.

"It gets better."

She leaned back, knowing they should probably talk, tour, and take their time, but her whole body was vibrating with need, and his seemed to get tauter and harder by the second.

"So will you show me your bedroom?"

He angled his head. "There is a room with a bed, dresser, closet, and bathroom," he said. "And another for guests, which you are not. But..." Still holding her, he guided them both to the sliding glass door, unlatched it, and dragged it open, filling the room with the heady scent of pine and earth.

"I sleep out here as often as in there," he said, drawing her past the sitting area to another section of the deck where a bed-sized chaise perched one level up, offering a commanding, panoramic view. "Let's watch the sun set over the trees."

"I'd love that."

"I'll be right back," he said, adding a kiss and easing her to the chaise.

Sighing, giving over to his every suggestion, she settled in. The sunset was in its early stages, starting to kiss the tree line, but low enough for the summer temperatures to have dropped to an inviting level.

Sparks of anticipation flickered over her whole body as she kicked off her shoes and smoothed the cotton maxi dress she'd worn to meet his grandmother. She turned at the sound of Josh's footsteps to find him crossing the deck carrying a bottle of red wine and two glasses, a throw blanket over his arm.

"Room service," he teased as he set the bottle and glasses on the table next to her. "Except, I have nothing to eat in this house except stale crackers."

"I'm not hungry." Not for food, anyway.

"And you're probably not cold, either." He tossed

the light blanket to the foot of the chaise and sat on the side, scooting her over. "But you might be both by the time the sun sets."

He poured two glasses of wine, handing her one, staying seated with his back to the view, facing her. "Here's to Stella," he said, raising his glass. "The blind dog who helped me see."

She tapped his glass and took a deep drink, leaning back to enjoy the gorgeous view of Josh and the trees and…well, mostly Josh. "Speaking of Stella, my dad's last text was reassuring, don't you think?"

"Yep. I love that she's sound asleep in her cradle at Waterford."

"That we almost forgot to take." She leaned closer to him. "But you made us go back and get it when we were halfway to Waterford this morning."

"She can't sleep anywhere else," he said with a shrug. "Gotta pamper my girl."

Her heart dropped a little. "How are you ever going to give her back?"

"We'll cross that bridge," he said. "Right now, I won't give her back. If Savannah showed up and wanted her, I would literally dognap Stella to finish these treatments."

"And to think I thought you were a dog hater when I first met you."

"I told you it was because I care about them that I didn't want them in the building." He dipped down and stole a kiss. "You were predisposed not to like me."

"No, I was predisposed to kiss your face off and then not like you."

"That was your first thought when you saw me?"

286

She let her gaze drop down his body, then reached out her hand to flatten her fingers over his T-shirt, pressing hard enough to feel the shape of his shoulder, pec, and then one outstanding ab after another. Down to the button of his jeans. "Maybe not only your face."

"Yeah." His voice was thick and gruff, and he covered it with a drink of wine. "Same."

"First thought?" she asked. "Sex?"

He started to answer, then angled his head. "No. First thought was, 'Run, Josh Ranier. Run fast and hard and away from this creature.'"

Her jaw dropped. "Really?"

"Really. I knew from the moment I looked into your eyes that I could get lost there. I knew that all my determination not to get involved again would go right out the window. I knew you were every rule I shouldn't break but wanted to."

Each sweet compliment fluttered over her skin, as effective as if the words fell from his fingers and found secret places to make her weak with need. She didn't answer but closed her eyes and leaned back to enjoy each sensation, feeling him take the wine glass out of her hand before she dropped it.

"But I didn't run," he whispered.

"Thanks to Stella."

"I'd have found another reason to be near you," he said, easing his body onto the chaise next to her. "I'd have made up an excuse to see you. Dreamed up a rationale to touch you."

He grazed his finger over her arm, featherlight and perfect.

"Like that?" she asked.

"Like this." He trailed his touch up to her shoulder,

sliding under the strap of the dress, then down, over the rise of her chest.

Darcy finally opened her eyes to find him inches away and shivered at the intensity in his expression. "Out here?"

"Right here." Kissing her again, he reached up to the top of the chaise and freed the latch, lowering them flat. "Right now." He eased the strap of her dress to the side, sliding it lower to reveal more skin to kiss and touch. "I'm not waiting another minute for you."

"I'm the one who's been waiting for you."

"We both waited, and that's officially over."

She breathed in, filling her lungs with the musky scent of him, of the forest, of the clean Carolina air that tickled her skin. She heard him moan, or maybe that was her, their sounds and skin already connected, their bodies moving in a natural, timeless rhythm, their breathing growing heavier each second.

"You're so beautiful," he murmured, easing the dress all the way down to press more kisses on her breasts and over her bra.

She answered by tugging on his shirt, wanting him to stay with her, lost clothes for lost clothes. He sat up, grabbed the collar of his T-shirt, and yanked it over his head in one easy move, giving a sly smile that said he knew exactly what mattered to her.

"Oh, Hot Landlord," she said on a satisfied sigh as she pressed her hands on his chest. "So perfectly named."

Still kneeling over her, he laughed. "How did this happen?"

"Um, you brought me out here, gave me wine, and started taking my dress off?"

"I mean you. Us. This." He shook his head and moved his gaze over her nearly naked body. "You." He barely whispered the last word. "You…" He reached under her, unhooked the bra, and very slowly eased it off, staring at her breasts. "You."

She had to laugh at the genuine awe and the sheer delight his admiration sent through her. She arched her back in invitation, and he lowered his head to suckle and taste her, the heat of his tongue making her cry out softly, then bite her lip to be quiet.

"No one for miles, sweetheart," he muttered as he drifted south to kiss her belly. "Make all the noise you want."

But she couldn't make any, because every move rendered her speechless. Hot, searing kisses and long, lazy licks and strong, capable hands that easily removed her dress, his jeans, and the rest of what came between them.

When he produced a condom, all she could do was dig her fingers into his hair and bring him in for a grateful kiss. "My rule follower."

He took that kiss and leaned up, searching her face, his gaze still dizzyingly intense. "I thought it was just Stella, you know?"

She frowned. "Stella…nope." She stroked his face. "Sorry, not following."

"Who makes me break rules."

"All for a good cause," she assured him. "You're not thinking about that document or convincing Terry to let us into an apartment? Not now?"

"No, now I'm thinking about you." He positioned himself over her, the weight and size and power of him enough to make her lose it.

"As you should." She rocked into him, wrapping her legs around his hips, ready and weak for more of him.

He hesitated just a second. "I don't want to regret this."

She opened her mouth to tell him her low regard for regrets and maybe to beg a little bit. But all she could tell him was the truth. "You won't regret this, Josh Ranier. You won't regret me. I promise."

He closed his eyes and rocked into her, filling her, holding her, transporting her to a place where there was nothing but the sensation of sweet, strong, sexy Josh. Every time he said her name or kissed her mouth or groaned in complete pleasure, she felt closer to him.

So close they became one. So close all the lines were blurred. So close she didn't care about her stupid independence. She wanted only him, like this, all the time. All the time. *All the time.* It was the polar opposite of independence. It was...completion.

When her mind finally surrendered to that, so did her body. And as she lost the last shred of control to total satisfaction, all she could do was kiss his mouth. Kiss his cheeks. And kiss her independence goodbye.

"How does he know?"

In his arms, Darcy groaned away some sleep, her body limp with contentment and draped over Josh. It was well past midnight with the moon high outside his bedroom window, and they were both spent from that bottle of wine, a pizza they'd shared, and another long, sweaty, ridiculously amazing hour of making love. Only this time, they'd started in the shower and finished in his bed.

"How does who know?" she muttered.

"Your dad."

She popped up, suddenly alert. "He knows? What? What does he know?"

He laughed, curling his fingers into her hair and easing her head back down to his shoulder. "I meant how does he know who to match his kids with? What's the secret to his success? Has he ever failed?"

"No, but there's always a first time."

Not this time. But Josh kept that thought to himself, not wanting to get too deep into an intimate conversation when they were both on the verge of sleep. But the fact remained that, barring something Josh couldn't even imagine, the Dogfather had another W on his scoreboard.

At least it felt that way right now.

"Seriously, he's never done a setup in which the two people didn't click?" he asked.

On a long sigh, she turned, rustling the sheets with her bare skin. She settled on her back, right next to him. "You know, what my dad does is not really a 'setup' in the classic sense. Not a blind date, per se. It's not like the empty seat next to the single person sitting at the table suddenly gets filled. He's more subtle than that. He puts his victims into the same situation and sees if anyone comes out alive."

He snorted. "Victims?"

Laughing softly, she turned. "Well, they don't know what's about to hit them."

Yeah, he got that. Eyeing her, he asked, "You're not wallowing in second thoughts over there, are you?"

"Me? You were the one talking about regrets at the most inopportune moment."

"I don't have any. Do you?"

"Not a single one," she promised, tiptoeing her fingers over his bare hip to splay them on his stomach. "Didn't you feel me brand you with a nice, bright pink DK?"

"Mmm." He covered her fingers with his hand. "Marked by my woman. I like that."

"Your woman," she whispered.

"Was that your pulse I felt jump fifteen beats a second?"

She laughed. "Only five. I'm okay."

"Are you?" He turned on his side, wrapping his arm around her waist to pull her into him. "Because I want you to be okay with this. With us."

She nuzzled his neck, kissing his skin. "We sailed past okay outside on the deck."

"And where did we end up?"

Inching back, she looked up at him, her eyes glinting in a stream of moonlight. "I don't know, HL. But I'm hanging on for a long ride."

He let the promise hit his heart, waiting for the doubt and fear and urge to run. None came.

Stroking her cheek, he brushed back a strand of hair, studying the angles of her cheekbones and her creamy, flawless complexion. "So, he did it again. Back to my original question: How does he know?"

She considered that for a long time, never looking away. "I guess he knows our hearts," she finally said.

"He knows where the holes are, and then he meets someone who seems like they could fill them."

"Where are the holes in your heart, Darcy?" He wanted to know. He wanted to fill anything and everything of hers.

"I don't want to be coddled, like the baby of the family. I don't want to be taken care of or for people to have lower expectations of me because I'm the youngest. I don't want to need anyone. But that can be a lonely existence." She ran her finger over his lower lip, thinking. "When my dad was slyly suggesting I live in your building, he said something very telling. He said, 'There's a big difference between independence and loneliness.' See? He knew the hole in my heart."

"You're lonely."

She exhaled softly. "I guess I was. I didn't know it, really, until..." Her eyes filled a little, and she blinked as if the moisture surprised her. "Until now."

Something inside his chest shifted, like his heart lifted, repositioned itself, and found a new place to pump. "I feel exactly the same way."

She smiled and leaned in to kiss him, but he inched back to make a very important point.

"I have a different theory about your dad," he said.

She choked a soft laugh at being denied the kiss. "Okay, what is it?"

"It's luck. Timing. And maybe he didn't do anything at all, but is enjoying taking the credit for it."

"No, he's got the magic touch. And I say..." She leaned in for that kiss she was determined to get. When they parted, she smiled. "More power to the old guy. And he will get his comeuppance in the form of some very lively dates we are all lining up for him."

He shook his head. "You might regret that."

"Or we might dance at his..." She closed her eyes. "Yeah, maybe we're not ready for that."

He laughed softly. "However, your family can probably handle anything. There's never been one quite like them."

"You know." She poked his chest playfully. "I think you like them more than you like me."

"I like them a lot," he agreed. "But..."

"But what?" she asked after his hesitation lasted a few seconds.

"You know how you 'sailed past okay' out on the deck?" He stroked her shoulder and ran his hand down her side, lingering at the dip of her waist and resting on her hip.

"Yeah?"

"I did, too. But not then, before that. I don't know when. I haven't known you very long, Darcy, but I'm falling hard. Fast. For real." He felt his throat tighten at the admission, and from the look on her face, he knew she heard the fear and longing and honesty that gripped him. And happiness.

She closed her eyes and pressed against him, holding him in the dark, silent and still for a long time. So long that he thought she might have fallen asleep, until she sighed and whispered, "Does that scare you?"

"To death," he admitted.

She answered with a slow, wet, dreamlike kiss and a whisper in his ear. "Same."

Chapter Twenty-Two

J osh and Darcy went straight to Waterford Farm the next day, anxious to see Stella. She hadn't reacted to light again, despite many tests, but she was happy to hear their familiar voices.

"Come on, Stella baby," Darcy cooed, holding her little face toward the sun that streamed into Josh's truck as they drove to Ambrose Acres. "Don't you see that brightness, sweet girl?"

But Stella didn't blink the way any seeing creature would at the bright summer skies over Bitter Bark. She stared the same way she did in a dark room or if the light of a flashlight passed over her eyes.

Darcy huffed out a breath and hugged her closer, turning to check on Kookie, who lay on the backseat, staring at both of them.

"You're a good girl, too, Kooks. You take such good care of Stella."

Her tail swished a tick-tock, acknowledging the compliment.

"Are you sure you can keep her all day?" Josh asked as he pulled into his parking spot behind the apartment building. "Because I can check on both of them during the day. I'll be up in Unit 3 working on the kitchen all day. All the cabinets are coming out and floors are being ripped out."

"No, too much noise for Stella," she said. "That's no place for dogs." She added a saucy grin. "What kind of landlord would let dogs in that building, anyway?"

He tapped her on the chin. "One with a weakness for a certain tenant and…" He ruffled Stella's fur. "A certain dog." Then he turned to Kookie. "And you, kid number two."

She lifted her head, and responded with one bark.

"Uh, number one," he corrected. Turning back to Darcy, he gave her that same smile he'd been wearing since they woke up this morning. A little goofy, a little lost, a little perfect. "I wish we could have stayed there."

"We can go back," she said. "It's an amazing place for a weekend escape." She lifted Stella a little. "And we can bring our friends."

He studied the dog's face closely, inching back and forth from eye to eye. "Come on, kid. You can do this. This is your week. You're going to see something soon."

Darcy moved Stella to the side to kiss him lightly. "Give her a little time. She's got this."

After a few more minutes of lingering with the dogs and each other, they gathered up their things and leashed the dogs to head in, able to hear the construction noise the minute they got inside the building. Stella, most sensitive to loud noises, barked and backed up, pulling at her leash.

"Let's keep her down here in your place while I run upstairs and change for work," Darcy suggested.

"Good call." He pulled out his keys and unlocked the door marked with a gold 2, frowning as he did. "What the hell?"

"What's wrong?"

"The door wasn't locked. I would never leave the door unlocked."

He opened it slowly, and Darcy noted that he blocked her body and view as he did. But she heard him mutter a dark curse and instantly got up on her tiptoes to see over his shoulder. At first, it looked normal, but when he stepped inside and she could see more, there was nothing normal about it.

"Stay back there," he whispered, holding up one hand to underscore the order. Darcy didn't walk any closer, but leaned in as far as she could, sucking in a soft breath at the sight.

Ransacked. It was the only word possible for this mess. Sofas opened, drawers gaping, things pulled out of the entryway closet and strewn all over the floor.

Josh disappeared out of sight for a moment, probably looking in the bedrooms and kitchen, but Darcy could see enough in the living room to know there was only one thing to do: call the police.

"Okay," she heard Josh call. "You can come in. There's no one here."

Swallowing hard, she took tentative steps in, being careful not to touch anything. But instantly, Stella and Kookie pranced right over a jacket lying, inside out, on the floor.

"No, no," Darcy said, scooping up Kookie with one hand and Stella with the other as he walked back in. "What did they take?"

"Nothing." He stepped over some boots that must

have been in the front closet, taking Kookie from Darcy's loose grip. "That's what's so weird. My laptop, tablet, some valuables on my desk, all right out in plain sight. I wasn't robbed. I was…"

"Searched?"

"I don't know." He looked around again. "Whoever did this was desperate and in a hurry."

"And able to get in without picking the lock," Darcy noted, glancing at the doorknob that looked untouched by any kind of tool. "You didn't, um, happen to give Savannah a key?"

"No, of course not." He frowned and looked around. "Savannah? This doesn't look like anything she'd do. She's actually too methodical to leave a mess like this."

"But someone must be looking for something. What would you have that Savannah would want?"

"I have no idea." He shook his head, as perplexed as she. "The only thing I have of hers is…Stella."

They both looked down at the dog in Darcy's arms, quivering at the noise from upstairs, and probably the tone of their voices. Still, she stared straight ahead in her own little cone of darkness.

"Oh, Stell." Darcy dropped her head and kissed the dog. "This is hard on you, baby."

In Josh's arms, Kookie looked up and licked his chin, which would have been cute and adorable, except they were standing in chaos, with trouble all around.

"Think, Josh. What could Savannah want that you have? Something she left with you when you were dating?"

He gave a blank look and shook his head again. "Nothing."

"Did she give you anything when she gave you Stella?" Darcy persisted, certain they were closer to another puzzle piece, but no matter how she turned it, nothing fit.

"Some treats, toys, and...the bed." He said the last two words slowly and with the light of an idea in his brain. "She said she couldn't ever be apart from it. She had to sleep in it, all day, all night."

"Yeah? So...do you think something is in the bed? Something she wants?"

"But why would she give it to me?"

"Because..."

"She's hiding something in it," he said.

"Gran's jewelry?" She spun around to the door. "Let's go."

"Whoa, wait." He managed to get her arm. "Let me go."

She angled her head and narrowed her eyes.

"Let's go together," he amended with a nudge on her back. "I want you to be safe, not stupid."

"I get that." She didn't particularly want to go alone anyway, with the possibility of a crazed Savannah waiting to jump out of the closet and attack. Or even the possibility that Savannah had been in her apartment, rooting around. Although, payback was fair; Darcy had rooted through Savannah's apartment.

Upstairs, they stopped at her door, and she handed him the keys, taking the dogs' leashes and stepping back to let him go first.

The door was locked, which gave her some hope, and when his shoulders sank with a quick breath of relief, she knew they were in the clear.

"It looks fine," he said, stepping aside to show her. "I was worried because she was pounding on this door last week demanding to get in."

"Probably because she heard dogs barking and assumed this was where Stella was." Darcy followed him in, and they both went straight to the fluffy pillow that Stella had long ago forgotten about once she'd discovered the cradle. "In fact," she mused, "Stella never actually seemed to prefer that dog bed at all."

Josh lifted the fluffy, puffy, round bed, turning it over slowly, looking for a zipper. "Maybe she wanted to make sure it was in a safe place and—"

"You'd always have Stella in a safe place," she finished.

He found the zipper for the fleece covering, drawing it along the side slowly as if something might fall out. Darcy watched, her heart hammering, her throat actually dry.

But nothing fell out.

"Here," she said, setting the dogs' leashes down to help him pull out the foam rubber cushion that formed the round "mattress" of the bed.

She tugged at the foam, and he pulled at the fleece until a satin bag rolled like a fat burrito popped out and fell to the floor.

"Whoa." Darcy jumped back in surprise, and Kookie headed right in the direction of the noise, but Josh beat her to it.

They both knew what it was before he unwrapped the covering to reveal a blinding display that belonged in a museum. There was the sapphire bracelet and emerald brooch, ridiculous yellow diamond earrings with silver twin Bs dangling from each, a solid diamond choker, and at least a half-dozen rings with rocks the size of almonds.

Josh's shoulders dropped as he let out a breath of pure disgust. "I didn't believe it," he said. "I didn't want to believe it, I know, but deep inside I didn't think she was capable of this."

"But why tear up your apartment if she told you not to separate the dog from the bed? Stella wasn't there, and neither was the bed. Why not leave the place alone?"

He shook his head. "She must be desperate. Maybe she knew I'd been to Cornelius and heard what she'd done. Of course I'd look for the jewels in the stuff she left me, and maybe she thought I hid them in my apartment."

"Wow." She gingerly lifted one of the earrings. "Hideous but worth a fortune."

He closed his eyes. "I can't believe I trusted her."

"What do we do? Report it?"

"That would send my mother into a tizzy."

Darcy recalled the woman's horror at the idea of bringing the police in on family dirty laundry. "Return it all, then."

"Yeah, I will. But for the moment…" He raised his brows. "It's a way to get Savannah back here."

"Why do you want that?"

He searched her face for a moment. "Bargaining power."

"For?"

His gaze shifted to Stella, who'd curled into a ball on the floor. "I can't let her go," he said quietly. "Blind or with vision, we can't let that dog go. I want

Savannah to sign whatever she has to so that dog is mine forever, with no legal question in the air."

"No argument from me." She plucked a ring from his hand. "I wonder why she didn't take the jewelry and sell it."

"Maybe she's waiting for Gran to die."

Darcy made a face. "In the meantime, there's a safe in my grooming salon office where we can keep this. She could show up anytime."

"And you, Stella, and Kookie will never be in this building alone." He inched closer. "Don't give me any grief, Miss Independent. You have to be as safe as these jewels." He added a kiss on her forehead. "Because you *are* the real jewels."

She smiled up at him, getting up on her tiptoes to kiss him. "Call the police or not?"

"I think I'll take a page out of the Bucking handbook and wait on this one."

"Are you going to tell your family?"

He looked at her like she was out of her mind. "They'll want it all back right away, and then I lose my bargaining power."

"At least tell Gran," she said. "She should know the jewelry's safe, and I bet she'll understand enough to let you keep it until Savannah comes back."

"I will, but not quite yet."

Darcy rolled her eyes. "Suit yourself, but communication is at the heart of a family that works. Try it."

"Soon."

And Darcy knew how huge that concession was for him.

Chapter Twenty-Three

Two weeks later, and they still hadn't heard from Savannah.

But Darcy was constantly aware of people around her, like right now, perched on a stone wall in the shade of the main library at Vestal Valley College, studying her surroundings. But the campus was nearly empty in the dead of summer, except for Kookie, sunbathing a few feet away on the grass.

Her gaze shifted across the quad, where she spotted her father coming out of Farrow Hall, too far to read his expression. He spotted her almost immediately, holding up his hand to tell her to stay comfortable where she waited for the clearance to go get Stella, who'd completed her fourth—and final—treatment.

Stella no longer had to be held for observation after the treatments, so Darcy was planning to bring her, along with Kookie, to the salon for the afternoon. Stella did like to sleep after the stress of a morning with Dr. Walker and her shots, so Josh had carried the cradle into the salon, which was now almost ready to open for business. Except she still didn't have a name she loved, something she was determined to finalize today.

She'd planned a quiet but productive day with the dogs in the new salon, contacting clients to arrange first appointments and finishing some of the last decorating touches. She had to order the sign, too, but kept putting that off while she brainstormed names that she—and Josh—loved.

"How'd it go?" Darcy asked as Dad got closer, unable to stand the suspense any longer. Judy Walker had invited him to observe this last round, a fact that would have been more than mildly interesting a few weeks ago. But now that it had been four weeks since they'd started, Darcy's only concern with the veterinarian ophthalmologist was not her availability for Dad, but her capability where Stella was concerned.

"It went well," Dad said as he reached her. Instantly, Kookie jumped up from the grass and tippy-tapped over, looking past Dad and around the quad for her best pal. "She's doing fine." Dad reached down and gave Kookie a pat, as if she needed to know the news, too.

Darcy pushed off the low wall to meet him. "Did she see light again?" Sadly, they'd never been able to get her to respond again after that one time, and, based on what Dr. Walker said that morning, her retinas didn't seem to be reacting to the antibodies coursing through her system, trying to heal her. But that didn't stop Darcy from praying for a miracle.

"No, but Riley has full vision."

She sucked in a breath, a burst of joy for the sweet little doxie she'd come to love when they brought Stella in early for treatments, along with a pang of deep envy. "That's awesome. That means it can work."

"Judy's over the moon. And Ziggy is repeatedly responding to light. He's bound to regain his sight, which is another huge victory. The test needs three of the five subjects to see in order for the research to be quantifiable and approval for the procedure to go through the next level of testing."

"And the others? Penny and Angel?"

"They're about where Stella is. Now, in one case, a dog Judy worked with regained her sight fully and suddenly. But all the rest responded to light first."

"So that could still happen?" she asked hopefully.

He took her face in his hands and held it the way he often did when delivering news she wasn't going to like. "Honey, you might have to accept defeat this time. If she were going to see, Judy thinks she'd be responding to light more than that one time. And since it was me testing her at home, they can't even document it. The researchers aren't seeing it."

She bit her lip and fought the burn of disappointment behind her lids. "I wanted this so much."

He drew her closer, offering the strength of a comforting hug she'd leaned into all her life. It helped, but didn't take the ache away. "You are loving her so well, and Kookie is changing her every day. She's a fighter, Darce. She'll have a good and happy life without her vision."

She swallowed the lump in her throat. "It's not fair."

"Think of it this way," he said. "Since she's disabled, maybe her owner will let you and Josh keep her."

Dad knew everything about Savannah, and though

305

he wasn't thrilled with the decision not to alert the authorities about the break-in at Josh's, he understood their position.

Now, with almost two weeks since the break-in, there was nothing they could do but wait, although they planned to take the satin bag and its contents to Gran this weekend. The Buckings might not prosecute, but Savannah had too much to lose by coming back.

"Speaking of Josh," Dad said, looking around. "I'm surprised he's not here. I'm pretty used to seeing him whenever I see you now."

She laughed. "Yeah, me too. But it's a huge day at the renovation," she said. "They've removed a whole outside wall, and they're installing the French doors. He wanted all hands on deck to get the place secured before the storms they're forecasting roll in." It had rained every day this week, and that had been a challenge for Josh. And this news was going to hit him hard.

"And you might be right about Savannah letting us keep her," Darcy added. "She's in too much trouble to come begging for her dog. What's the statute of limitations on dogsitting in your opinion? When can we safely claim her as ours?"

"Ah, so you *are* a 'we' and 'ours' now."

"And you..." She poked his shoulder with her finger. "Are freakishly gifted for matching people who belong together."

He denied that with a solid shake of his head. "I wish I could take credit for this one, but I honestly can't. I had no intention of sending you off into the arms of another man, Darcy. You may never believe me, but it's true."

"Josh believes you."

He put an arm around her and gave a squeeze. "I *would* have picked him for you, though. He's a good guy who has your best interests at heart. And Stella's, which, as you know, tells me all I need to know about a person."

"You really like him, Dad?" She felt a little silly asking, a little like a child who needed Daddy's approval, but his opinion mattered so much.

"I really do. I think he's steady, strong, and stable."

She sighed at that, in complete agreement, needing to ask one more question about one more important opinion. "Do you think Mom would like him?"

He stayed very still for a moment, staring straight ahead before answering. "One time, when you were, oh, maybe twelve or thirteen, your mother and I were discussing you." He stopped for a moment and closed his eyes. "In the morning," he added, "before we'd get up to take care of any kids or dogs, I'd sneak down and get coffee and bring it up so we could talk in bed."

Darcy's heart softened at the memory of tiptoeing past her parents' room—a sanctuary children never entered when the door was closed—and hearing their voices. The sound of her mother and father quietly planning their day or discussing their kids or laughing in the predawn light reminded her of all things good in her world. And it reminded her of something else…mornings with Josh, planning, discussing, and laughing.

"You'd been going head-to-head with Aidan that week," Dad said. "Arguing over everything and creating a constant level of stress that we both abhorred."

"Oh, I'm sorry."

He chuckled, like the issue was so far in the distance that he couldn't give her apology any credence. "I was furious with you and wanted to rein you in, discipline you, take something away or give you extra chores. But your mother had a whole different approach."

"Which was?"

"She gave you and Aidan a dog to care for together. Do you remember Dagwood?"

"Oh my gosh, yes. That big black Lab mix? He was deaf."

Dad lifted his brows.

"I forgot about that foster. No one wanted him because he couldn't follow commands until Aidan and I figured out how to teach him hand signals."

"And I don't think you two have ever had an argument since then."

Maybe a few, but nothing serious. "She forced us to work for a common good. But also, Aidan and I had so much fun that summer."

"And that's what Stella has done for you and Josh. So if anyone deserves the credit, it's Stella. And maybe your mom, who I swear does my backup work from the great beyond."

"It's like she's still conferring with you during your mornings in bed with coffee."

Dad let out a sad sigh, barely able to hide the sudden punch of pain.

"I'm sorry," Darcy whispered. "I didn't mean to make you grieve."

"Don't be silly." He slipped his arm around her and headed them back to Farrow Hall, waiting long enough for Kookie to catch up. "It's just that remembering those talks sort of makes me…"

"Lonely?" she suggested.

He started to answer, then closed his eyes in resignation. "Maybe. Maybe I am lonely, sweet Darcy," he sighed. "Maybe I am."

A month ago, she'd have launched into a speech about the power of independence and how wonderful it could be, but now, those words would sound hollow. Dad was right…there was a fine line between lonely and independence. And now that she was on the other side of it, she wanted to drag him over, too.

But not until he was ready, and not a minute before.

Josh was up to his eyeballs in subcontractors, problems, and setbacks all afternoon and into the early evening as the clouds rolled into Bitter Bark. Except to let Darcy know he'd be working late, he ignored everyone and everything but the construction. They'd finished reinforcing the balcony, but the metal screws weren't up to his standards, so they'd bagged the railing for today.

And the next blow to his construction plans was delivered at nearly seven o'clock by a clueless truck driver who showed up two and a half hours late with a replacement window, not the French doors.

Josh could practically feel the steam coming out of his ears.

"We cut space for doors," he explained to the man, pointing to the gaping opening that took up much of the eat-in kitchen wall.

The other man shrugged. "I can have the doors here tomorrow, but it's almost seven and the distribution center is closed."

Josh looked away to dig for composure, but his gaze landed on the fat, dark, and ominous late afternoon clouds gathering beyond the courtyard.

"Come back first thing in the morning," he instructed the man. He turned and damn near slammed into the wall of man that was Bill Bainbridge, who'd turned into one of Carlos's most reliable assistants.

"I can get the poly sheeting from my truck," Bill said. "We can close up that hole real good, sir."

Josh considered that, and the amount of damage the storm could do. "That sheeting is for floors and probably wouldn't keep us dry." He headed to the opening to check the clouds. "The cabinets are out, the floors are gone, and all that's left is one counter that could get wet, but it's coming out."

"Okay." Bill reached for his toolbox, lingering long enough that Josh turned to look at him and catch the color rise in the other man's face.

"Something wrong, Bill?"

He cleared his throat. "I don't know if this is my business, sir, but I feel like I gotta say something."

At the serious tone in the question, Bill had Josh's full attention. "About what?"

"I mean, I don't want to step into private family business, but…"

"Family business?" For a second, he wondered if he meant the Kilcannon family, since that was the only family around him for the last month.

"But when I saw your brother in town, I—"

"*What?*" Josh backed up in disbelief. "Gideon? He's not here."

"Uh, yeah he is." Bill stabbed thick fingers in his hair and pulled back, clearly uncomfortable. "I saw him going into the Bitter Bark B&B this afternoon with that same queen of England woman who was knocking on the other apartment door a while back."

A slow, cold sweat tingled the back of Josh's neck. Gideon and Savannah were here. Why?

All of the day's irritation disappeared under the weight of this new travesty.

"Like I said, sir, I don't want to poke my nose where it doesn't belong."

"No, no, it's fine. I'm glad you told me." With a quick look at the gaping hole in the kitchen, he made a decision. "The B&B, you say?"

He nodded. "With a suitcase, so I guess they're checking in."

His stomach roiled. "Okay. Good to know. Uh, why don't you pack up for the night, Bill?"

"You sure? I can hang the cheap stuff now, if you want. It'd be something before this rain hits."

"Not necessary," Josh said. "I have to go to town. Let's close up shop."

"Sure thing, Mr. R."

Josh didn't even bother to say goodbye. With an old familiar anger ricocheting through him, he strode out the door without even closing it, powered down the staircase and out the front, barely noticing the first fat drop of rain that hit his face. Was it possible Gideon was here for an innocent reason? Family support? Was Josh's hatred the thing that blinded him, like Darcy said?

He'd talk to Gideon, he decided as he pushed the gate open. He'd *communicate* with him, since she—

"Josh."

He whipped around at the sound of his name and a familiar voice. "Savannah."

"Can I talk to you?" She took a step forward, pushing up sunglasses that weren't needed on this cloudy evening to reveal red-rimmed eyes without a speck of makeup. Deep, dark shadows and bloodless skin exacerbated the look of someone in a lot of pain. Or trouble. "It's really important."

Chapter Twenty-Four

The rain started slapping the front window steady and strong while Darcy puttered around the salon as twilight descended.

Josh had texted earlier that he'd be working late at the job site, so Darcy was in no rush to go out in this weather. No rush to deliver the bad news about Stella's sight. Instead, she soaked in the atmosphere of her little salon, imagining it bustling with freshly clipped and bathed pooches, all wearing brightly colored bandannas as they waited in their crates for pickup.

And she showered both Stella and Kookie with extra love, even though they didn't feel the weight of the disappointment that the study hadn't been Stella's ticket to restored vision.

Both of them were currently in the cradle on the other side of the reception desk—no crate for those two. Kookie, worn out from her guard-dog duties, snored contentedly, but Stella was up, quivering a little because of the rain and the occasional roll of distant thunder.

"Don't worry, love," Darcy crooned to her. "We'll let the storm pass before we venture out."

Another rumble made her bark, and Darcy turned sharply at the sound, too. That wasn't thunder, but someone pounding on the glass outside. She pushed back to round the reception desk and get a better look at a man in a suit jacket and tie. He pointed to the door with eyebrows raised in question. She didn't recognize him from around Bitter Bark, that was for sure.

"Can I talk to you?" he yelled.

A little uncertain of that, Darcy shook her head. "We're not open for business yet." She raised her voice so he could hear her through the glass and over the noise of the rain.

"It's about Joshua," he said loudly. "It's urgent."

Joshua? The only people who called him that were…his family. She made a face of confusion and tried to get a better look at the guy through watery glass and waning light. Did she know him? He did look vaguely familiar. Had she met him at that anniversary party in Cornelius? Was he—

"I'm Gideon Bucking," he yelled.

Holy moly. He was the evil stepbrother.

"I need to talk to you about Joshua. Very important."

She backed away from the window and considered grabbing her phone to call Josh before she did anything. He wouldn't like her welcoming his archenemy into the salon, but she could hardly let him stand out there in the rain.

What if Gideon came with Savannah to take Stella? But then, what if he was able to officially let Josh take ownership of the dog? That would be good news.

Or maybe he wanted to threaten her to get back the jewelry Savannah had stolen and hidden in the dog bed. Could he know about that?

Uncertain and tentative, she unlocked the door and opened it a crack to keep out the rain and the man.

"You're Darcy, right?" He came closer, and she immediately remembered the picture she'd seen of him on his grandmother's mantel. Yes, this was Gideon, a handsome, chiseled man with intense green eyes and thick, dark hair. Much smaller and thinner than Josh, but he didn't exactly look like the devil incarnate. "Can we talk?" he asked, shaking off some water.

"Josh isn't here," she said.

He let out a frustrated exhale. "I wanted to talk to him in person, and I have no idea where he lives."

"What do you want?"

He closed his eyes with a grunt. "Bad news, I'm afraid. Our Gran has passed."

"Oh." She pressed her hands to her mouth, the news hitting hard. "I'm so sorry."

He shook his head slowly. "We couldn't tell him by phone. I've been enlisted as the family emissary to deliver the news. Can you help?"

The family emissary? Gideon?

"You look stunned, but believe me, it was expected."

"That's not why…" She gathered some composure. "I can call him for you."

"No, no." He looked past her as if waiting for an invitation, but something self-protective kept her from issuing one.

Josh didn't trust this guy, so should she?

"I really don't want to break the news over the phone," he said. "I've heard you've been a wonderful influence on him. Brea couldn't stop talking about you, and Christine raved. I thought you'd be able to help me."

She searched his face, taking in his narrow lips, clear eyes, and clean-cut bones, all the while clinging to the fact that this man betrayed Josh in the worst imaginable way. No way she would throw open the door and welcome him with open arms.

"Can I come in?" he asked after a long, awkward beat.

"I'm sorry, but I can't." Behind her, both dogs were barking now, aware of the new arrival, and that made her remember Savannah and the possibility that she'd blow in here and take her dog. She peered past him into the rain. "Are you with Savannah?"

"No," he said simply. "That was a grave mistake, and if I can be completely candid, it's one of the reasons I'm here and not, say, Brea or Joshua's mother. This death has rocked our family a little. A lot," he added with a dry laugh. "Life's short and…" He made an effort to swallow. "Sometimes a man has to fall on his sword."

She blinked at him, gauging every word and finding each one…genuine. She certainly agreed with what he was saying. Would Josh? *Could* Josh? It would be so good for him to have that closure and peace regarding Gideon and his family.

"I thought you might facilitate that," he said. "I heard you have a very close family and maybe have some skills the Buckings—and Raniers—are lacking."

Was this possible? A thrill of victory danced up her spine. Of course, weeks of being with Josh and hearing little but disregard for his family—especially Gideon—made her skeptical, despite how much she wanted to believe the man in front of her. "I'm not sure he's ready to take that apology, Gideon, but I'll give him the message when I see him. And maybe—"

"Is that Stella?" he asked, peering over her shoulder and almost muscling his way in. "Has she regained her sight? Brea said there was a slim chance."

There it was again...the note of something *real*. Like he honestly cared about Stella's eyes. Could Josh have been that wrong about this man? He'd admitted his perspective had been off where the Buckings were concerned, but could it have been *that* off?

"Not yet," she said, unwilling to go into the day's disappointing news regarding Stella's eyes. "But I'll be sure and tell Josh how much it matters to you."

But did it matter? Wasn't he supposed to be uncaring, arrogant, and resentful about anything where Josh was concerned?

He wiped some rain from his face, leaning closer. "I'd really like to tell Joshua myself. Face to face. Man to man. Brother to brother." He grimaced. "I know I owe him so much more than an apology, but I want to start somewhere, and I want to do it now. Can you take me to him?"

Could she? She could at least tell him the address of the brownstone in Ambrose Acres, then call Josh and warn him that Gideon was coming. Maybe persuade him to give his brother a chance.

"Is he far from here?" Gideon asked.

"He's on the other side of the square and down a few streets," she said. "A section called Ambrose Acres. Do you know it?"

He put his hand on his ear. "I can't hear you with

the dogs and the rain. Right there, did you say? Across from the playground area?"

"No, much farther." She glanced over her shoulder and checked the dogs, then pushed the door open a bit more. Taking one careful step onto the sidewalk, she pointed the way. "Straight up there to the end of the square."

He walked farther away, toward the street, to get a better view. "I'm sorry, I'm not sure where I should go."

"That way." She gestured south. "I'll give you the address, and you can put it in your GPS."

He held out both hands in a plea. "Come with me, Darcy. Please. He listens to you. I don't have any hope for this if you're not there."

She let out a breath, knowing he was right. She had to be the peacemaker in these talks, or they'd never happen. Sometimes she had to take matters into her own hands.

"Let me get an umbrella. Hang on." She stepped inside and hesitated, feeling like she should invite him in out of the rain.

He caught her uncertain look and smiled. "It's fine," he said. "You don't have to trust me. I'll stand right here in the doorway, I promise you."

She nodded at the reassurance, letting the door partially open to him. He stayed under the overhang and made no move to come in. She grabbed her phone and texted Josh.

I'm on my way home. Bringing Gideon. Have an open mind.

She added a heart emoji, stuffed the phone in her back pocket, snagged an umbrella from under the front counter, and kissed the dogs. "Be right back."

Then she headed into the evening rain with high hopes that she could sprinkle a little Kilcannon magic on the Buckings since, deep in her heart, she knew she wanted both families connected by love. Was that possible? Or was she living in a fantasy world where all families could be like hers?

There was only one way to find out.

"I've been trying to reach you for almost a month, and *now* you want to talk?" Josh looked past Savannah, bracing for the sight of his stepbrother. "Where the hell is he?"

"Who?"

He cocked his head and sliced her with a look. "I don't have time or interest in this today, Savannah. Where is Gideon?"

"Is Gideon here?" Her voice rose with near panic as she wiped away a raindrop that hit her face.

"You tell me, but I won't believe a word you say. Oh, and my grandmother's jewelry? I found it and put it in a safe. Thanks for the hot mess you left in my apartment."

Tears filled her eyes as she stared at him, then a sob broke. "Oh God. You believe them."

"Well, let's see, Savannah. Shortly after you had sex with my stepbrother, you hid a hundred grand worth of my grandmother's jewelry in a dog bed, handed over your blind dog, skipped town, and ignored about fifty calls and texts telling you I had an emergency with her. My entire family has accused you of stealing, and my apartment's been ransacked by someone looking for loot. So, yeah, I believe them."

She searched his face, silent. "I guess you do, since I've never heard you call them 'my' family or refer to Bernice as 'my' grandmother."

He hadn't even realized he'd said that. "I've changed. What do you want? And don't say that jewelry, because you aren't getting it. And don't even think about Stella. You and your boyfriend can get the hell out of town *now*."

Her face crumpled as she fought a sob. "I haven't seen Gideon since he left me in a New York hotel room weeks ago." She took a shuddering breath and touched the side of her face, grimacing a little. "And none of that, not a single word of what you're accusing me of, is true."

"You didn't sleep with him?" he challenged.

She ran her fingers through messy hair. "That's when everything changed."

"You don't say."

"He seduced me, and I fell for it, Josh. I wasn't happy in our relationship, and I had a moment of weakness, but that's not what it was for him. He was planning and scheming, and I didn't know it."

"To mess up my life."

Her eyes flashed. "To get those jewels."

"What? Why the hell would he do that? The jewels would be his when Gran dies."

"Oh, no," she corrected. "They'd be your mother's, and that's something Gideon can't stand. He hates her, Josh. He hates you and her, and he used me to be sure those family heirlooms stayed in the right family."

"So you hid them in a dog bed with instructions that the bed never leave Stella's side, knowing that meant I would essentially be babysitting your contraband, not just your dog."

"Josh, I've been framed," she insisted, pushing wet hair back as the rain picked up to a steady drizzle. "Gideon stole them and blamed me to make sure I take the fall."

"Gideon went into Gran's closet and stole her jewels? You expect me to believe that?"

"I guess it was Gideon, but I didn't know who it was then." She swallowed. "I wasn't supposed to find them in my apartment. They were planted there some time after people started accusing me of stealing."

"Then why didn't you give them back to Gran when you found them and clear your name?"

"Because of my mother," she admitted softly.

"Your *mother*? The one you hate and don't talk to?" This was getting more preposterous by the minute.

"She was really sick, and I knew I might be facing huge medical bills. So I kept them as an insurance policy, but I had to hide them, so I made up the story of Stella being dead and sent them off with her to you. I figured you were far away enough that no one would know you had her, and I never dreamed you'd go to Cornelius to see your family."

He closed his eyes, disgusted by the web of deceit, buying none of it. "So you think it was Gideon who stole his own family's jewelry to frame you and now he wants it all back?"

"I didn't think so then," she said again. "At first, he was sweet and offered to go with me to take care of my mother. That was the off-the-grid trip I told you about."

He choked a laugh. "Gideon was going with you to see your mother in Buffalo? Savannah, you *are* a pathological liar. And I—"

"I'm *not* lying," she insisted, grabbing his arm. "Gideon dumped me in New York, because it was a way for him to get me out of town so he could send someone into my apartment to 'find' one or two of the pieces of jewelry to be sure I took the blame for all of them being gone."

"So who wrecked your apartment if Gideon hid the jewels and he was the one who sent someone to get them?"

Her eyes flashed. "It wasn't wrecked. I took everything apart to start packing and I found the jewelry. Then I kept looking for more but how do you know that?"

"I went there. Terry let me use the key. I needed to find out who you used for a vet, because all I cared about was Stella."

She closed her eyes and let out a guilty sigh. "She's been forgotten in all of this."

"Not by me."

"Listen to me. I trusted Gideon, then we got to New York, and he found out the jewelry wasn't in my apartment. I guess he sent someone to look. He was…" She touched her cheekbone and flinched. "He was furious, actually."

His stomach clenched, along with his fists. "What happened?"

She shook her head, silent for a moment. "I got away from him, went to stay with my mother, and threw away my phone so no one could possibly track me. I helped her through...to the end."

He huffed out a breath, but before he could muster sympathy, she stepped closer.

"You have to believe me, Josh."

No, he didn't have to believe anything. It didn't make enough sense. "You want me to think Gideon stole jewelry that belongs to his grandmother to keep it from my mother and framed you for it?" It was preposterous...except they were Buckings. And this was Gideon. "He'd have to give them back to Gran, and then they'd go to my mother anyway. What's the purpose?"

"Not if Gran dies without giving the jewelry to your mother. She hadn't yet, but I know she was going to. It's not in her will, but she was going to give it to her before she died."

Now that, he believed. Gran liked his mother, and possession was nine-tenths of the law. Gideon couldn't fight it in court if Malcolm's wife had the jewelry on, and Malcolm wouldn't abide that anyway. But why would jewelry matter to Gideon?

Everything mattered to him. So maybe she was telling the truth, or some version of it. "Then what's Gideon doing here?"

"He must be looking for that dog bed."

"You *told* him that's where you hid the jewelry?"

"I told Gran. A few days ago, after my mom's funeral, I was in so much pain. I screwed up my life, my relationship, everything. Bernice Bucking was always so good to me, like my own grandmother. I wanted her to know the truth, so I called her and told her that you had the jewelry in a dog bed." She looked at him, her dark eyes awash in agony. "My guess is she told Gideon."

"But my apartment was broken into weeks ago, not a few days ago," he said, seizing on the hole in her story.

"Did he get the dog bed?"

"No, it wasn't in my apartment."

She shrugged. "Then he's back, and I guarantee you he's looking for that dog bed."

He glanced at the building, blinking into the rain as he looked at Darcy's apartment, where what was left of the bed they'd strip-searched could be found on the living room floor.

"No one's getting in there," he said. Not that it mattered. The bag of jewelry was in the safe in Darcy's salon. "I'll get Gran's jewelry back to her."

"But I need to clear my name. That's why I came here. To get the jewelry and return it and publicly vindicate myself before she dies, but that could happen anytime. If Gideon's here…" She followed his gaze to the building. "He'll go where Stella is, because I told Gran that's how I was making sure the dog bed, with the jewelry inside, was safe. Somehow he found out. Expect him any minute."

He stood there, feeling his T-shirt start to stick from the rain, and a slow cold sweat that started with her words. *He'd go where Stella is.* Stella was with Darcy.

Gideon could find Darcy. Josh wouldn't put anything past him. Or maybe this was all Savannah's latest lie, and she planned to search his apartment the minute Josh left. He wasn't about to take that chance.

"Can I see her, Josh?" She gestured toward the building. "Can I see my dog?"

And she'd use that tactic. "Let's get something straight, Savannah. Stella is *my* dog. You can lie, cheat, and steal your way wherever you want to go in life, but you are not taking her from me. Is that clear?"

She opened her mouth to argue, then the wind went out of that sail. "Okay," she said quietly. "But can I go inside? It's pouring."

"Do you think I'm that stupid?"

Her shoulders collapsed. "You'll never trust me, will you?"

Probably not. But there was a woman he trusted who might be fooled—or worse—by a man she'd never recognize. And she mattered more. A lot more. More than jewels, family, or whether or not these were lies.

"I have to go."

"Josh, please."

"What? What do you want from me? I'm not giving you the jewelry, no matter what you tell me. I'm not giving you Stella. And I'm not giving you access to my home."

"Then give me…" She struggled to swallow. "Forgiveness. I'm not lying about any of this, but even if you don't believe me, forgive me."

He stared at her.

"It's all I need. It's all I want. I messed up my life, and I'm going to move on and start over, but I need to know you forgive me."

He waited for the anger, the resentment, and the betrayal that had become a companion for a long time to bubble up and strangle him. But nothing came. Not a single bit of hatred for this woman who had made so many mistakes. His eyes were open, and all they could see was…Darcy. And who had taught him more about giving people a chance than Darcy?

"I forgive you," he said softly.

She let out a half sigh, half sob.

"You can wait out the rain under the overhang." He pushed open the gate for her, but she shook her head.

"No, I'm going back to Buffalo. My mother left a mess, and I'm going to clean it up and start over up there. Thanks, Josh. You always were one of the good guys."

He nodded, not sure what to say.

"Give Stella a kiss for me."

He watched her walk a few steps, then turned and took off. He reached into his pocket to get his phone, realizing with a thud that he'd left in such a hurry that it was still upstairs. But there was no time to go get it.

He had to get to Darcy before Gideon did.

Chapter Twenty-Five

Gideon moved slowly for a man determined to make peace with his brother. He was quieter now that they could hear each other, barely bothering to stay under the umbrella Darcy held, answering her questions with one-syllable responses.

In fact, he was so curt, she grew uncomfortable as they walked through Bushrod Square. "So, was your grandmother in the hospital or at home?" she asked.

"Home."

"Was she alone or with family?"

He threw her a look. "Is it much farther?"

"A little ways." Maybe it was the stress of relaying this news to Josh that had him so uptight. She tried a different tact. "I met Bernice briefly and thought she was..." She laughed softly. "A character. Not exactly a sweet old lady, but so colorful."

"Didn't take you too long to worm your way into the family, did it?"

The question made her slow her step. "Excuse me?"

He stayed silent, as if he regretted the outburst.

"It was you who asked me to facilitate this meeting," she reminded him. "So no actual 'worming' involved."

"Right." He closed his eyes as if digging for patience, and when he opened them, he looked over her shoulder in the direction they'd come, then let out a frustrated sigh.

"If you're unhappy with our progress, you could walk a little faster, you know."

"I know, but..." He turned back and continued on at the same maddeningly slow pace.

"I'm sure it isn't going to be easy," she said, trying again. "But I've been talking to Josh a lot about his relationship with you. I do think that deep inside he wants a family connection and to put all the past behind him. He wants to communicate."

He responded with a shudder that could have been fear...or disgust. A betting woman would have said the latter. An insane optimist who saw the best in people hoped that betting woman was wrong.

"After spending time with my family, which, as you said, is very close, I think he—"

"I get it," he cut her off. "Just take me to the apartment building."

Wait. Had she told him Josh was at an apartment building? How did he know that? The first coil of true concern wrapped around her chest, bringing her to a complete stop.

"Like I said, you can use your GPS, and I'll go back to..." She started to turn in the direction of the salon, but he instantly put a hand on her shoulder, nudging her forward.

"No, no. You're right. I'm tense. Dreading the

confrontation. Let's keep going. I still think it's important that you're with me."

"Why?" she asked, even though he'd already explained. Something in the way he was acting made her feel he wanted more than peacemaking from her.

"Because..." He rooted around for an answer. "He cares about you. His mother and Brea both said you're a very good influence on him, so he's going to listen to you."

She was quiet for a moment, hearing a dog bark in the distance, loud enough to be heard over the rain, but her mind was on Christine and Brea Bucking. How did those women get that much out of the brief time she was there?

"The decision to accept your apology is Josh's, not mine," she finally said.

"He'll do the right thing."

"He always does." Maybe it was the elephant in the room that needed to be addressed. After all, no one had mentioned that Gideon had slept with Savannah. "But what you did was pretty rough."

He slid her a sideways glance, and this time, there was no doubt. It was disgust. And this time, his touch was more of a prod than a nudge. "Keep going. It was rougher for me than him."

"To have sex with his girlfriend?" she choked.

He stared straight ahead, silent. "Things are not always what they seem," he said, softly enough that she almost didn't hear it over the rain hitting the umbrella and the dog bark that grew louder.

No kidding. Like how going with him to see Josh seemed to be a good idea ten minutes ago when this guy was normal and not a complete jerk.

Darcy stopped again, decision made. "You can find it from here. I'm going to go back—" She turned, but he grabbed her arm, forcefully not letting her turn. "Hey!" She tried to wrest away, but his green gaze turned icy and direct.

"You're coming with me."

"Like hell I am." She yanked away, but failed to get loose.

He moved in with a menacing look. "You will if you want to see that dog again."

The threat made her sway, nearly dropping the umbrella. "What?"

"If what we want is in that baby bed with dogs in it, then you'll be free to go. If not, you know what the ransom for Stella will be."

The baby bed with... She blinked at him, her heart rising up in her throat. "*Ransom?*"

"Just keep moving." He ground out the words and squeezed her arm.

Indignation shot through her, along with a healthy dose of fear. She managed to jump back and smash the umbrella in his face, whipping around in time to hear an insane bark and see a flash of something white. Wet and white, running and barking and frantic.

"Kookie!" She dropped the umbrella, launching toward the dog.

"Get up." Gideon got a hold of her arm and wrenched so hard she cried out as she came to her feet.

Kookie practically stood on her hind legs, wildly barking in a way that could mean only one thing: Something had happened to Stella. Her long fur was drenched, smashed to her tiny body so she looked like a drowned rat, howling the way Darcy wanted to.

"You bastard," she growled at Gideon, fighting him off with every ounce of strength she had. "What did you do? What did you *do*?"

"My guess is the jewelry isn't where we were told it was." He ground out the words, fighting to get control of her.

"We?" Was it Savannah? Then she wouldn't hurt Stella. But someone else might.

"You want that dog, you know what you have to do."

White-hot fury and spitting rain blinded her as she thrashed, managing to free one arm. What should she do? She had to find Stella. She had to save her.

Rounding up every ounce of strength she had, Darcy pulled back her right hand, balled it up in a fist, and let it fly so hard she kept spinning after it smashed his chin with a satisfying thud. He was stunned long enough for her to swoop down, grab Kookie, and haul butt across the square, nearly face-planting as she rounded the very bench where Josh had taken off her shoes.

But no one was there tonight. The square was deserted, without a soul to beg for help. She didn't dare slow down to get out her phone. Someone took Stella, and she couldn't let them get away.

She squeezed the terrified dog in her arms, rocked by anger at Gideon and at herself. Why had she trusted him? Why had she tried to take Josh's family matters into her independent hands? He was right about Gideon!

With the street in sight, she ran across the grass, slipping and sliding so frequently she had to fight to hold on to Kookie. Her knees hit the ground with a painful thud, but she managed to get right back up again. As she did, she stole a glance over her shoulder, a flash of lightning illuminating Gideon, maybe fifty feet behind her. He wasn't going to get her. He *wasn't.*

But in seconds, she could hear his feet pounding, his breath panting.

She tore into the street, running straight to the salon where the front door hung gaping open. But she'd locked it!

No, she'd closed it, and it had automatically locked. But as she reached the sidewalk opposite the salon, she could see the door ajar. Someone had placed a small block to prevent the door from closing and locking. Not someone—Gideon. He must have done it while she'd texted Josh.

Just as she stepped into the street, a car whipped out from a side street, bringing Darcy to a standstill and splashing her with a rooster tail of water. Damn it!

It was enough time for Gideon to catch up with her. He grabbed her arm, and she let out a wail that would have brought out anyone in any nearby store if it hadn't gotten lost in a clap of thunder. He smacked his hand over her mouth, cursing mightily in her ear and pushing her across the street. She kicked, tripped, and swung her body so hard, they both went tumbling as a pickup came barreling toward them.

For a moment, everything froze—time and space and Darcy's heartbeat. She opened her mouth to scream and opened her arms to push Kookie out of the way as the truck fishtailed to a screeching halt and the driver's door opened.

Through the rain and dark, a powerful figure emerged, stealing what breath Darcy had.

Josh.

"Get off her, you son of a bitch!" Josh tore at them, driving a knee into Gideon's chest while he gave Darcy a solid push to safety and freedom. "Get the dogs," he ordered her as he seized Gideon's collar and dragged him to his feet.

Kookie had already torn to the store, barking maniacally. Darcy leaped up to follow her, running in and whipping the door open to gasp in shock at what she saw.

The cradle was in bits, cracked and chopped and annihilated. The cushions the dogs slept on were sliced to ribbons. And the pink anxiety jacket that Stella had been wearing lay on the floor in tatters.

"Oh my God. Oh my God." Sobbing, she fell to her knees and picked up the jacket, pressing it to her mouth to keep from screaming.

A second later, Josh dragged his much smaller stepbrother into the salon and thrust him up against the wall. "Where is she? Where is Stella?"

Gideon's jaw locked as he stared back. "You're not getting them," he spat out. "Your gold-digger mother isn't getting them."

"I don't give a rat's ass about jewelry. *Where is my dog?*"

Gideon closed his mouth and eyes and stayed quiet while Josh added more pressure. "Tell me!"

Dead silent, he didn't move.

With a grunt of disgust, Josh spun him around and

threw him against the oversized dog crate. "Who took her?" he demanded. "Where did they go?"

"Wait for a text, little brother. You'll get your instructions."

Josh straightened as if a lifetime of anger and hate shot up his spine, making him squeeze Gideon's shoulders and push him again. This time, Gideon stumbled backward, tripping on the edge of the crate. Before he took his next breath, Josh grabbed the door of the crate and dealt a thud of a blow to Gideon's solar plexus.

As he doubled over with a grunt, Josh shoved his whole body into a space big enough to hold one of Liam's *Schutzhunds* and strong enough to keep him there. Gideon was still balled up as Josh slammed the door and smashed a combination lock through the latch.

"Hey!" Gideon shouted as he looked up and realized what had happened. "Let me out."

"Where is Stella?" Josh demanded.

Gideon rattled the cage like the trapped animal he was, while Josh backed up to check on Darcy. He didn't say a word, but wiped a finger over the tears that streamed down her face as she squeezed a shocked and bedraggled Kookie.

"Savannah came to the apartment," he told her, catching his breath while he scooped up Kookie to comfort them both. "She must have done this. I don't know how, but I know that she did."

Darcy looked down at the broken cradle and crumbled with a sob. "That's been in my family for years."

"I'm sorry, Darcy." He bent over to pick up a piece of the wood.

"Give me a second," Darcy said, heading to the back office. Bending down to the safe under the desk, she turned the dial, entirely certain Josh would agree with this decision. Stella was worth it.

Pulling out the green satin satchel not much bigger than a cosmetic bag, she closed the safe and returned to the reception area to dangle the loot in front of the jerk in the cage. "Is this what y'all are looking for?"

His eyes flashed with horror. "How'd she miss that?"

She. So it was Savannah. "You know what, Gideon Bucking?" Darcy asked. "You don't deserve a family." She put her arm around Josh, who was still holding Kookie. "But you do, Josh. Let's go get our dog."

He guided her to the door. "Leave him, or call the sheriff?"

"Oh, no. Leave him in there." She yanked the door behind her and heard it lock. "He's not getting out until Stella is in our hands."

Kookie barked once, in total agreement.

Chapter Twenty-six

"I can't believe I damn near bought some sob story about her mother." Josh gave in to the regret along with the adrenaline dump that coursed through him after the fight.

"And I can't believe I stuck my nose in your family business and tried to smooth things out that were never made to be smooth." Darcy reached over the console as he drove them to Ambrose Acres. "I'm so sorry, Josh. I should have never given him one moment of consideration." Then she gasped. "Oh my God, I forgot to tell you something."

"What?" He glanced at her, hearing true concern in her voice.

"I mean, it might not be true, but he said your grandmother passed away."

He closed his eyes as the news hit. "Damn," he muttered.

"Wouldn't your mother have called?"

"I haven't looked at my phone since I texted you this afternoon," he admitted, still processing the loss. "But it does make sense that Gideon and Savannah would move into high gear to retrieve this stuff now that she's dead. My mother probably would have gotten the lion's share since Gran actually liked her."

"I'm sorry," she said. "I know you weren't close, but still."

He turned to her. "Thanks. It's the perfect end to a perfect day, which could actually get worse."

"Yeah, it could."

He glanced at her, hearing the depth of pain in her voice. "I can handle Savannah, Darcy. My only concern is Stella, and honestly, you don't have to worry there. She might be crazy and unpredictable, but she loves that dog and would never hurt her. Say what you will about Savannah, but Stella loved her."

"Then why'd she rip off her anxiety jacket?"

"Maybe she thought we hid the jewelry in it?" He shook his head, another thread of the conversation with Savannah coming back. "And just to make things confusing, she *gave* Stella to me this afternoon, and then she kidnapped her back. It doesn't make any sense."

Darcy looked stunned, then her jaw opened wide. "Maybe it's not Savannah who has Stella."

They stayed silent for a second as that hit home.

"Brea?" They said her name at the same moment.

"Although I would never have taken her for quite that evil," Darcy added.

Josh returned his attention to the road, turning over all he knew about his stepsister. "She's a conniver," he said. "But always sugar-coated and sweet."

"She does have a lot to lose where the jewelry is concerned. Brea Bucking could actually wear those BB earrings."

He threw her a look. "Told you my stepfamily sucks."

"I'm starting to believe you, but it still makes more sense that we're up against Savannah."

"You better hope we are," he said.

"Why?"

He swallowed and turned onto the street. *Because Brea really doesn't like dogs.* But he didn't have the heart to tell her that now. "Because Brea's smarter than Savannah," he said instead, and it was true.

He couldn't argue. He pulled up to the apartment, staying far enough away that they couldn't be seen, but able to watch the entrance and see at least one window of each of the four units, but all of them were dark.

"Doesn't look like anyone's here," he said, mentally thanking God the downstairs tenant was on vacation.

"There's no guarantee she'd come back here," Darcy said. "Though if she saw you leave, it's a safe bet."

"Gideon mentioned a text, so I better go up and get my phone. You want to wait here and watch for her, or come with me?"

"I'll come," she said. "Let's go, Kooks."

The little dog scrambled up from Darcy's lap, planting her paws on the door, barking in a way that they both knew meant she wanted one thing and one thing only: Stella.

Josh put his hand on Darcy's arm. "Let's leave her."

"In the car?" She sounded appalled. "Not on your life."

"I can't risk another dog because my ex is a lunatic."

She thought about it, but shook her head. "We'll lock her in my apartment, and she'll be safe there. Or

I'll keep her in my bag and hide her, and we'll have come full circle."

"Have we?" he asked. "Or are we running around in circles?"

"Hey." She put her hand on his face. "We're in this together, remember? For the dogs. You and me and Kookie and Stella."

"We're our own little family," he said, the word catching in his throat.

"It's a good start, Josh."

He leaned forward and kissed her. "A great start. Let's go. Bring the dog and the bag of priceless jewelry."

"Words you never thought you'd say," she joked.

He managed a smile, grateful for a woman who could find humor in this.

With Kookie tucked in Darcy's shoulder bag and a sack of gems in his hand, they headed toward the building, grateful that the rain had slowed to a drizzle.

As they reached the gate, Josh looked up at the window of Unit 4 and could have sworn he saw a flash. "Whoa." He inched Darcy close to the shrubs and peeked up again. "I think someone's in the construction site."

Which was the last place on earth he wanted Stella.

"Oh no, Josh. That's so dangerous," Darcy said, echoing his thoughts.

He stood for a moment, thinking through every possible scenario, none of them good. "If she puts Stella down, one clap of thunder and Stella could run." To the open balcony. His stomach clenched. "She cannot get near that balcony, Darcy. She'll…"

"Then I'll catch her." She dismissed his look of

horror with a confident wave of her hand. "Won't be the first time I've saved her in that courtyard."

"You can't."

She arched a brow in sheer defiance. "You go up, I'll stay down here, and I will catch her if she falls. Your job is to make sure she doesn't. But remember, Josh, a loud noise, a scary word, anything and she'll run with no idea where she's going. And I can tell by the way you're looking at me, you're going to argue, but—"

"No argument." He took her face in his free hand. "You're brave and beautiful and I...I..." *I love you.* "I wouldn't want anyone else with me on this." *Or in life.*

She held his gaze, her expression mirroring what he felt in his heart. "That's what friends with dogs are for." She gasped as she said the words. "That's it, Josh. The name of the salon."

He almost laughed. "Now?"

"No, not now. But it's great, isn't it? It's...us."

He gave a quick kiss. "Yes, it is. You ready to do this?"

"Yep."

He led her toward the gate, unlocked it, then they headed into the building without making a sound on that lock, either. In the echo chamber of the main entrance, they stood still, listening but hearing nothing.

"I'll be in the courtyard," she mouthed, blowing him a kiss. "Trust me, Hot Landlord."

"Oh, I do, Miss Kilcannon." And he'd never meant anything more. Secure with her as backup, he headed for the stairs, moving stealthily.

He stopped at the top and pressed against the wall to listen again. With another step, he could see both apartment doors were closed, and no light escaped. He had a key to both, but he didn't bother with Darcy's apartment. The light he'd seen was in the one under construction. And, if she'd moved to Darcy's apartment and got away, so be it. At least no one would fall off the balcony.

But he had to be quiet, so as not to scare Stella, who didn't bark when she was this freaked out. She wouldn't run to him but to the farthest possible corner...or balcony. Even if Savannah screamed or yelled, it could be dangerous. He'd have to silence her, then get Stella.

And if push came to shove, he had a bag of jewelry stuffed in his pocket for negotiating power.

Careful not to make a noise, he turned the key in the lock, then the knob. It clicked, but not with a loud echo. He eased the door open to see nothing but blackness. And a wave of hot air.

He inched toward the kitchen, suspecting that poly either hadn't gone up or hadn't held, because that much outside air shouldn't be coming in. Then he heard another sound. The softest whimper, a moan from inside a tiny chest, the sound Stella made when she was shaking and he held her against him.

Light wouldn't scare Stella; sound would.

Knowing that, he took another step and reached his arm out for the main kitchen switch, flicking it and bathing the room in enough light to see...

"Brea." He barely whispered her name, wishing he was more stunned at this revelation.

She stood inches from the wide-open wall, the darkness of the courtyard behind her, Stella in her arms. "How the hell did you get in here?"

"The door was open and I walked in. It sounded like someone was in the kitchen, and it was that big lug who wouldn't let me in a few weeks ago when I tried, so I knew he couldn't be persuaded by my charm." She nodded to the front. "I went in that bedroom and waited him out." She lifted Stella an inch. "This creature cooperated by shaking too hard to bark. When I heard him leave, I came right over here and made some fresh air."

Behind her, a sheet of thin plastic tarp hung partially over the window, barely attached with some tape. Bill had stayed behind after all, trying to help.

"I sent a text to you, and then I heard your phone ring." She nodded to the cell phone on the counter. "So I waited for you to come and get it. And her."

"*You* took her?"

"When Gideon finally got Darcy out of that place. I wouldn't have, Josh, but the bed that *supposedly* contained what I want was quite empty. Savannah must have lied to Gran, but we'll never know now. She's dead."

His stomach clenched. "Savannah?"

"Gran," she said with a laugh. "I didn't stick around for the actual last breath, since I knew time was running out. Gid helped me, of course, because he can always be counted on for one thing and one thing only: to make your life hell."

Josh snorted, because truer words had never been spoken. "But you haven't."

"Sometimes I do, but my misdeeds are always

behind the scenes and done with so much more grace than my brother has." She took a half step closer. "Now that Gran is dead, I'll take her jewelry or make it very obvious that you and Savannah schemed to steal it. Or we can blame Savannah and call it a day. You hate conflict, so that could work, too."

"Is old jewelry that valuable to you?" he asked, mentally scoping the room, the opening where the balcony was, the remaining countertop near her to consider all the possibilities for safely getting Stella. "It doesn't even look like something you'd be caught dead wearing."

Her eyes narrowed. "It belongs to a *Bucking*." She spit the words at him. "The earrings say BB—Brea Bucking. Not Christine. Not some truck driver's wife who screwed her way into wealth." She shuddered. "God, I can't stand that woman."

"You've hidden it well," he said, holding her gaze but planning how he could lunge and get that dog.

"And Gran?" she continued. "Her inexplicable fondness for your mother has been worrisome, but then she got very serious about her jewels. I had to get them out of the house, so setting up Savannah was easy. Again, my brother was happy to lend a hand and ruin your relationship."

So Savannah *had* been telling the truth.

"Until Sav went off the rails, too, but no matter. You'll give me the goods, which I will cherry-pick for myself or sell the rest on principle, and Savannah will take the blame."

No, she wouldn't. He took a few steps closer, painfully aware how close the woman and dog were to the opening, and that the balcony behind her was exactly twenty-two inches wide. One good footstep, maybe two.

"Give me the dog, Brea, and you can have whatever you want."

"Give me the jewelry, Joshua, or little Miss Stella is going to have a nasty accident." She turned to the window.

"You wouldn't."

She hooted softly. "I have never liked this dog. I have never liked this dog's owner. And, to be honest, I've never liked you." Then she added a coy tip of her head. "I know what you're thinking. I'm a phony."

"That's the least of the things I'm thinking about you right now."

"You never met my mother, Joshua. I assure you the apple doesn't fall far. Just ask my father, which is why he's so blindly and madly in love with yours, who is the polar opposite of Amy Bucking. Now there was a world-class, manipulative, disingenuous, cutthroat bitch disguised as a damn angel. Gideon tries, but he can't pull it off like I can. It's an artform being this fake."

"I'm sure she'd be proud of you." He took a few more steps, sick of this and her. "Give me the dog, Brea."

She lifted her brows and took a step backward, turning slightly. "Say goodbye, Stellie."

He yanked the satin bag from his pocket. "You're contemptible."

"Thank you." She added a dazzling smile and pointed to the counter on the wall within reach of her hand. "Set it there. *After* you open it up and show me what's in there."

"Fine." He yanked on the tie and eased the sack open, widening the top to show her.

"The earrings," she said. "I want to see the BB earrings."

Muttering a curse, he stuck his hand in and pulled out a necklace, a bracelet, then found one yellow diamond earring, showing it to her. "Okay? Now give me the damned dog." He set the bag on the counter but held his hand close.

She reached for the jewelry, and he slapped it away.

"The *dog*, Brea."

She bent over, not taking her eyes from him, lowering Stella to the ground with one hand, and reaching for the jewelry with the other.

"No!" he said, hating himself the minute the sound came out of his mouth. Instantly, Stella backed up, right onto the balcony. "You idiot," he ground out at Brea under his breath. "She's blind."

"She is? I thought she—"

From the balcony, Stella let out a low, slow growl, the most aggressive sound he'd ever heard her make. She got low, her ears flat, her eyes...pinned on Brea. Focused, clear, and full of genuine contempt. Stella certainly saw through this phony.

Wait. Could she...*see*?

Josh took one step forward, but Stella lunged at Brea's hand, clamping her mouth on the bag, and snapping her head and landing squarely on the kitchen floor. Brea screamed and swung her hand at the dog, sending a shower of diamonds and emeralds and bracelets and earrings all over the balcony and into the courtyard below.

"You little—" She thrust herself toward the dog,

but Josh vaulted forward and grabbed Brea's arms, stopping her before she got Stella.

"Go, Stella." He tried to modulate his voice and not scare her, but Stella was uncharacteristically not scared, staring at Brea like she'd enjoy taking another pass at her.

Yes, she was...*staring at Brea.*

Still forced back by Josh, Brea thrust a leg at Stella, missing her by inches. "Jump, you stupid—"

Josh whipped Brea to the side, leaning her toward the balcony. "Don't tempt me, Brea."

She tried but couldn't get free. He *had* to hold her. Had to keep her away from that dog and keep Stella away from the balcony. But Stella was scared now, with a familiar fear back in her eyes after the near kick, backing up, inches from the balcony's edge, her body vibrating with every move.

"Darcy," he called. "Get ready. She's going to—"

"Shhh." The sound came from behind him. "I'm right here. Don't scare her. I'm gonna get her right now." Darcy's words were soft, sweet, and monotone, spoken in a voice that wouldn't frighten Stella.

Brea pushed again. "Get...out..."

Josh squeezed his stepsister's arms and looked down at the BB earring on the floor in front of him. "One kick and this will be lost in that courtyard forever."

She snarled like Stella just had.

"Okay, Stella," Darcy whispered, coming closer. "I've got sweet treats," she sang gently. "Cookies for my girl."

Stella stopped moving, looking behind Josh, staring at Darcy. Yes, she was definitely staring! "She can see you, Darcy. But she doesn't know your face."

Darcy let out a little moan of happiness, crouched low on the ground as she reached the opening to the balcony. "But she knows my voice."

Stella took one step closer.

"And she knows my treats."

And another.

"She knows how much I love her."

Stella closed the space, took the treat, climbed up into Darcy's arms to lick her face.

"And she loves me."

"So do I," Josh whispered, finally letting go of Brea, who whipped into action, snapping up jewelry from the floor and balcony. But Josh reached for Darcy and Stella, guiding them both inside to safety and wrapping them in his arms. From Darcy's bag on the floor, Kookie barked and managed to scramble out and run to them.

"Josh, I didn't think I could catch her," Darcy explained breathlessly. "One look up at the balcony and I knew I couldn't do it. I couldn't risk it. I hope you don't—"

"Shhh." He kissed her words away, pulling her closer. "You did everything right."

"She can see, Josh!" She lifted Stella, who studied one, then the other, then dog-kissed their faces in unabashed joy. "She's not blind anymore."

"And neither am I." He inched back to gaze into Darcy's eyes. "And I'm looking right at the woman I love."

"That's funny," she said with a typically sly Darcy Kilcannon smile. "I'm looking at the man I love."

And best of all, Stella was looking at both of them.

Chapter Twenty-seven

"You like it?" Daniel, as Josh thought of the man after nearly four months in and around the Kilcannons, raised his brows in question.

Josh cast into the deepest blue of the water, hearing the smooth whir of the line as his bait and hook arced and splashed into the lake at Waterford Farm.

Turning the reel with an easy, familiar twist of his wrist, Josh couldn't wipe the grin off his face. "Are you kidding? Never had anything so smooth. I love it. It's a great birthday present, sir. Thank you." He hadn't expected any gifts, since a Kilcannon Sunday dinner birthday celebration was gift enough. But Darcy's father had surprised him with the fishing rod when they came home from church that morning, and they'd also left the table before dessert was served so Josh could test out the new equipment.

"None of my boys have the patience for fishing," Daniel said. "Oh, I've had them out here on many occasions, and Liam probably lasted the longest, but the rest of them don't have whatever it takes to make a good fisherman."

"My dad used to say the most important thing about fishing is to respect the fish." He laughed, remembering Pops making such a big deal about the fish. "He said they have souls, too."

"Sounds like a man after my own heart." Daniel reeled in an empty hook, settling down on a bench so weathered it must have been out here for decades. As he selected some bait, he said, "In my sons' defense, fish don't have as much personality as some animals..." He gestured toward Rusty, sleeping at his feet, and Stella, curled on the grass under a maple bursting with autumn colors. She wasn't quite asleep, but deep in her favorite pastime—watching Josh's every move. "But souls nonetheless."

The two men shared a look over Stella's resting body. "I really don't know how to thank you for what you did," Josh said.

"Don't thank me. Judy Walker did the work, and it looks like Vestal Valley will be the first DVM to claim immunoglobulin success for SARDS. Stella, Riley, and Ziggy are the stars." He frowned for a moment. "That is what you're thanking me for, right? Not a match made in heaven?"

Josh laughed at the inside joke the two of them shared. The Dogfather still refused credit for the latest romance in the family, although no one but Josh really believed him.

"Yes, it is, although, since you bring up the subject of matches made in heaven..."

"Judy Walker is dating someone," he said. "And that someone isn't me. And I'm okay with that," he added before Josh could say anything.

"You know I've never joined the family fun in that

regard." Although, in the months that had passed since he and Darcy had been together, she and her siblings had certainly tried to rope him into the Dad Dating Game.

Bait on, Daniel stood again, raised his rod and cast with an easy flair that reminded Josh so much of Pops. "But you've joined them in so many other ways." The older man slid a sideways look with enough question that Josh knew exactly what he was angling for...and it wasn't a fish.

"You have a great family," Josh said simply.

"I certainly do."

"And I don't."

The other man didn't answer that, reeling in a bit to get his line right. "Is that what's stopping you?" he finally asked.

As much as Josh wanted to deny the truth, he'd never bother with anything but complete candor with this man. "I always tell Darcy you marry a family, not a person. And I'm afraid that goes both ways."

Daniel tipped his head and gave him a questioning look.

"Your family is nearly—no, it *is* perfect," Josh said. "So I'm clearly the winner. But I bring my own baggage, sir. I have stepsiblings who've made some very, very bad decisions." Not that anyone got arrested for their misdeeds, but Malcolm Bucking had demoted Gideon to a line manager's job in the company, and Josh had agreed to help Bucking Properties as a consultant in its new house-flipping division, which was probably worse punishment.

Josh had no desire to leave Bitter Bark, where he'd almost finished the reno on one building, had purchased another, and basked in the glow of the newfound success of Friends With Dogs, Darcy's grooming salon. But he'd been traveling to and from Cornelius, giving advice and mending fences.

Brea had been ostracized by the society that mattered to her and was currently on an extended vacation in Europe that could last into the next millennium for all Josh cared. His mother did end up with the jewelry Gran wanted her to have, including a beautiful antique engagement ring that Josh found a few weeks later in the courtyard. When he'd taken it to his mother on his next trip there, she'd suggested he keep the ring as a thank-you for all he'd done. Apparently, it had belonged to Gran's sister, who had impeccable—and expensive—taste. He often carried that around with him, in case he suddenly wanted to give it to someone.

But something stopped him.

"So, it's your family that's stopping you?" Daniel asked, startling Josh with how he'd read his mind. "Because you think it's not fair to join Darcy to a family you don't really love and respect?"

He laughed softly. "Man, you're good."

"I'm old. And I know young men, four in particular, a lot like you." He came a few steps closer, adjusting the rod. "Son, I understand your whole 'you marry a family not a person' principle."

"I hope so, because it's the only thing keeping your kids from lining up a blind date every night for you," Josh teased. "I tell them all the time to be careful what you wish for."

He laughed, but his expression grew serious. "There's a flip side to that concept, you know."

"A flip side?"

"You are more than the people you grew up with in a house, or names on a family tree, or who happens to sit around a table at the holidays. Yes, that group might be loving and supportive. But if they aren't, that doesn't make you less of a person. In fact, it's an opportunity."

He smiled. "I see where Darcy gets her optimism."

"I'm a realist," he said. "Annie was an optimist. But, son, you have the chance to change the branches of that tree and grow in a different direction. And not only that, I'd venture to say your family, with all its issues, could benefit from Darcy Kilcannon."

"They already have."

He shrugged as if he didn't even have to speak to make his point.

Josh looked at him. "I want to be worthy of her in every way."

He put a hand on Josh's shoulder. "I believe you are."

The compliment, the advice, the man fishing in the sun...it all blended together to give Josh a feeling of certainty and contentment that he hadn't felt since Pops died.

"Then I guess there's only one last thing to do," Josh said.

Daniel lifted his brows in expectation.

He cleared his throat, pinned his gaze on Daniel, and took a breath. "Sir, I love your daughter. I swear I'm going to make her safe and happy and secure." He waited a beat, as much to enjoy the look on his future father-in-law's face as to gather steam for what he wanted to ask. "May I have your blessing to ask Darcy to marry me?"

The blue eyes looking at him filled instantly, and the corners creased with a smile. "I never thought I'd want to say those words, but yes, you have my blessing to ask Darcy to marry you." He blinked back some tears.

As the two men hugged, Stella came strolling over, rubbing her head on Josh's jeans as if any affection had to go to her. He bent over and gave her some love. "You hear that, kid? Now if she says yes, we'll—"

"Whoa!" Daniel turned as a fish tugged on his line, hard and insistent, making Stella jump up and bark. "Wasn't expecting that." Laughing, he reeled in a little sunfish that whipped wildly on the line.

"He's a baby," Josh said, helping by taking the fish with one hand and easing the hook out of its mouth with a skill he could tell Daniel appreciated. "Back you go, young man. Your time hasn't come yet." He tossed the sunfish, and it disappeared into the lake, sending ripples over the water.

"But yours has," Daniel said, beaming at Josh. "We'll clean this up later, but if we don't get up there and have your cake soon, my mother will come down here to howl at me."

He put a hand on Josh's shoulder and led him toward the house, with Stella and Rusty hot on their heels. As they walked, Josh took one more look over his shoulder at the tackle box, fishing gear, and the lake. And he could have sworn he heard Pops let out the contented sigh of a fisherman.

Darcy snuggled up next to Josh when he came in with her father, anxious to sneak him away to give him two presents she was so excited about.

"I have something for you," she said. "Can you come with me?"

"I was told there'd be cake." He bent down to kiss her. "And candles and such."

"They're setting it up, but I have something to give you." She tugged him toward the porch, where she'd left the wrapped box.

Out there, they could hear the family laughing and joking as they gathered around the table, but Darcy couldn't wait another minute.

"Did you have fun with my dad?" she asked as she brought him around to the side of the porch where they could see the entire south vista of Waterford, the whole property on fire with late autumn crimson and gold.

"We fished," he said. "And talked."

"So that was fun."

He smiled at her and pulled her in for a kiss. "For me, yes. What have you been doing?"

"Wrapping." She pointed to the box. "Go ahead."

"Darcy. You gave me about six gifts this morning, one of which isn't polite to talk about in company."

She bit her lip and laughed, sliding her arms around him and looking up. "More where that came from, HL. This is actually from your mother."

"My…" He let out a little laugh. "I forget you spend time with her when we're in Cornelius."

"She wanted you to have…well, open it."

He dropped onto the edge of a rattan sofa, and she got next to him.

"Okay, a present from my mom. Can't say I've had...never mind." He corrected himself. "She does give presents frequently but I've never liked them very much."

"You're going to like this since it's yours already."

He frowned as if that wasn't clear, but her heart kicked up a beat, as she knew how much this was going to mean to him. "How can she give me a present that's already mine?" he asked.

"You did for me when you reconstructed Stella's cradle."

He smiled at her, and she got a shiver of joy remembering the moment he unveiled his "secret project."

"Quit looking at me and open the present," she insisted.

"I can't quit looking at you," he admitted. "I love you."

"Same, but..." She pointed at the box, itching for his reaction.

He lifted the lid and spread the tissue, staring in, slowly sucking in a breath. "Oh my God."

"Did you know that Buckingsham has an attic?" she asked.

He looked up then, a mix of wonder and disbelief in his eyes.

"I think a house that has an attic isn't a sham at all, don't you?" Her eyes filled with tears just seeing the emotions roll over his handsome face. Shock. Sadness. And joy.

"She kept them?" He could barely say the words. "I thought...I thought they were lost forever."

Darcy shook her head. "Every one. Your entire collection. And that's not all. Keep looking."

He scooped up a handful of marbles, the glass tapping together in his big, callused hands. "This is a cobalt vortex." He plucked out one blue marble and held it between his fingers. "It's the color of the sky in the summer and your eyes when you're incredibly happy. Like right now."

"Keep looking," she urged.

He felt around, and then he froze, and she knew he'd reached the model car in the bottom.

"A 1967 GTO," she said.

He closed his eyes and slowly pulled out the meticulously detailed model car, holding it as reverently as he sometimes touched her. "Pops made this."

"She saved it for you, Josh. She knew it was important."

He tried to swallow, but looked like he was having a rough time. "Darcy. I love you so much. Thank you. For everything."

She reached up and put her hands on his face. "I love you, too. And so does your mother, who has been waiting for years to give these to you."

"Let's go, you two!" Pru clapped twice, stepping out to the patio. "We're going to need every one of the firefighters who are here to put out the flames if you don't head to the table and blow out the candles."

Darcy and Josh separated slowly. "General Pru has spoken," she told him. "Let's go make a wish." She sure knew what hers would be if she were blowing out those candles today.

They cruised into the dining room, arm in arm.

Darcy took a moment to look around at the house packed with family who made this and every Sunday dinner a celebration of more than the day of rest, but a way of life. She so belonged in this room, with these people, with this man next to her. Yes, she loved her business, her apartment, and her life. But her heart would always be right here…and with him.

"Here we go, laddie." Gramma Finnie came out with a tray ablaze with candles. "If ye don't like this chocolate, I made your favorite bread pudding, of course." She grinned up at Josh as she passed. "Best you ever had, right?"

"Ever," he assured her. "Do I have to blow all those out?" he asked on a laugh, getting a hoot and holler in response.

"You can always enlist help," Shane said. "Darcy's full of hot air."

"You're hilarious, bro," she said.

"I can do it, Josh." Christian sidled up next to him. "I'm real good, but you have to make the wish."

"You got it, buddy." Josh put his hand on the little boy's shoulder and guided him to the cake.

"And they have to sing," Christian told him. "It's not a birthday unless everyone sings."

"I've been to enough birthday parties here that I know that."

The singing started, loud, off-key, and precious to Darcy's ears. She didn't take her eyes off Josh, the man she'd had no idea she needed but couldn't live without. As the last note was belted out, Christian inhaled noisily and blew his heart out. But suddenly Josh stepped back and crouched down and…got on one knee.

All of the cheers and clapping and noise slowly faded into the background as Darcy's thumping pulse nearly deafened her.

Everyone grew silent and still, and nearly twenty people Darcy adored and one she loved with every cell in her body looked at her.

"Darcy," Josh whispered, holding a small black box. "You are wild, funny, unpredictable, beautiful, hopeful, and have more heart and soul than any person I've ever known. I don't want to change any of that. I want to soak it up for the rest of my life. I love you. I love everything about you. I love your laugh. I love your passion. I love your dog. And I love your whole family."

No one, not even Shane, whispered a joke at this sacred, special moment.

"Darcy Colleen Kilcannon, will you marry me?"

She put her hands over her mouth, not bothering to blink back the tears. "Yes, Joshua Caleb Ranier, I will." She gave him her hand and felt the ring slip onto her finger, and then he rose to wrap her in his arms, twirling her around with a kiss that brought the house down.

"Nice work, Dad," Garrett said over the racket.

"It wasn't me." Dad looked down at baby Fiona in his arms. "Someday you'll tell them, Fi."

"The man is six for six," Molly announced.

"And then there were none," Liam added.

"It *wasn't*—"

"It's okay, Uncle Daniel," Ella said. "You can start on the Mahoneys next."

"Not until he goes on at least six dates," Shane called out. "We each get to set him up."

"That means twelve," Chloe corrected. "In-laws get a say, too."

While everyone laughed and Kookie barked and Stella found her way to Josh's shoe, Darcy closed her eyes, pressed her head against Josh's chest, and let the family fade away. Then, all she could hear was the steady heartbeat of the man who'd helped her grow into exactly the woman she was meant to be.

The Dogfather

Looking for more of the Dogfather? Because Daniel himself must find love. (And it might not be through the handiwork of his kids!) And there are four Mahoney cousins who need some Kilcannon magic. But first…there will be another Kilcannon Christmas novella!

If you want to stay up-to-date on every release, sign up for my newsletter.

www.roxannestclaire.com/newsletter-2/

And join the private Facebook group of Dogfather fans for inside scoop, secret tidbits, and fun giveaways!

www.facebook.com/groups/roxannestclairereaders/

I answer all messages and emails personally, so don't hesitate to write to roxanne@roxannestclaire.com!

Fall In Love With
The Dogfather Series...

Sign up for the newsletter for the next release date!

www.roxannestclaire.com/newsletter/

Available Now

SIT...STAY...BEG (Book 1)

NEW LEASH ON LIFE (Book 2)

LEADER OF THE PACK (Book 3)

SANTA PAWS IS COMING TO TOWN (Book 4)
(A Holiday Novella)

BAD TO THE BONE (Book 5)

RUFF AROUND THE EDGES (Book 6)

DOUBLE DOG DARE (Book 7)

Coming Next

BARK! THE HERALD ANGELS SING (Book 8)
(A Holiday Novella)

OLD DOG NEW TRICKS (Book 9)

The Barefoot Bay Series

Have you kicked off your shoes in Barefoot Bay? Roxanne St. Claire writes the popular Barefoot Bay series, several connected mini-series all set on one gorgeous island off the Gulf coast of Florida. Every book stands alone, but why stop at one trip to paradise?

THE BAREFOOT BAY BILLIONAIRES
(Fantasy men who fall for unlikely women)
Secrets on the Sand
Scandal on the Sand
Seduction on the Sand

THE BAREFOOT BAY BRIDES
(Destination wedding planners who find love)
Barefoot in White
Barefoot in Lace
Barefoot in Pearls

BAREFOOT BAY UNDERCOVER
(Sizzling romantic suspense)
Barefoot Bound (prequel)
Barefoot With a Bodyguard
Barefoot With a Stranger
Barefoot With a Bad Boy
Barefoot Dreams

BAREFOOT BAY TIMELESS
(Second chance romance with silver fox heroes)
Barefoot at Sunset
Barefoot at Moonrise
Barefoot at Midnight

About The Author

Published since 2003, Roxanne St. Claire is a *New York Times* and *USA Today* bestselling author of more than fifty romance and suspense novels. She has written several popular series, including The Dogfather, Barefoot Bay, the Guardian Angelinos, and the Bullet Catchers.

In addition to being a ten-time nominee and one-time winner of the prestigious RITA™ Award for the best in romance writing, Roxanne's novels have won the National Readers' Choice Award for best romantic suspense three times, as well as the Maggie, the Daphne du Maurier Award, the HOLT Medallion, Booksellers Best, Book Buyers Best, the Award of Excellence, and many others.

She lives in Florida with her husband, and still attempts to run the lives of her young adult children. She loves dogs, books, chocolate, and wine, especially all at the same time.

www.roxannestclaire.com
www.twitter.com/roxannestclaire
www.facebook.com/roxannestclaire
www.roxannestclaire.com/newsletter/

85330365R00222

Made in the USA
Middletown, DE
23 August 2018